"Bad news," he said briefly.

Zavac's smile faded and his eyes n ... "What's gone wrong? Couldn't you g ... I'll skin that factory foreman. He swore blind on three different gods that he'd have it ready!"

Vargas shook his head at the second question and made a negative gesture with his hand.

"No, no," he said. "The rope's all here. It's in the skiff and the men are busy loading it onto *Raven*."

Zavac frowned. "Then what's gone wrong?"

"It's that Skandian ship," Vargas told him.

"What about it?" Zavac snapped. "That ship has become the bane of my life. Don't tell me you saw it again."

"I saw it, all right. It's only a few days behind us—although by now that may be a little more."

"What?" Zavac exploded with rage. "How did they catch up to us so soon?"

Vargas shrugged and shook his head. "It doesn't matter how they did it. The fact is, they're on our trail. I've arranged things so they'll probably be delayed in Krall, but they'll soon be on the river again."

"How did they find us?" Zavac raged. "How did they know we turned into the Dan?" He let out a string of curses and slammed his open hand on the table in fury.

Vargas waited patiently until Zavac's outburst was done.

"We were betrayed," he said calmly.

Read all the adventures of

RANGER'S APPRENTICE

And the companion series

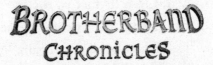
BROTHERBAND CHRONICLES

BROTHERBAND
CHRONICLES

BOOK 3: THE HUNTERS

BROTHERBAND
CHRONICLES

BOOK 3: THE HUNTERS

JOHN FLANAGAN

PUFFIN BOOKS
An Imprint of Penguin Group (USA)

PUFFIN BOOKS
Published by the Penguin Group
Penguin Group (USA) LLC
375 Hudson Street
New York, New York 10014

USA * Canada * UK * Ireland * Australia
New Zealand * India * South Africa * China

penguin.com
A Penguin Random House Company

Published in Australia by Random House Australia Children's Books in 2012
First published in the United States of America by Philomel Books,
a division of Penguin Young Readers Group, 2012
Published by Puffin Books, an imprint of Penguin Young Readers Group, 2014

THE LIBRARY OF CONGRESS HAS CATALOGED THE PHILOMEL EDITION AS FOLLOWS:
Flanagan, John (John Anthony). The hunters / John Flanagan. p. cm.—
(Brotherband chronicles ; bk. 3) Summary: Determined to recover the Andomal and to prevent the pirate
Zavac from doing more damage, Hal and his brotherband crew pursue Zavac to the lawless fortress of
Ragusa, where, if Hal is to succeed, he will have to go beyond his brotherband training and face the pirate
one-on-one in a fight to the finish.
ISBN: 978-0-399-25621-9 (hardcover)
[1. Seafaring life—Fiction. 2. Adventure and adventurers—Fiction. 3. Pirates—Fiction.
4. Friendship—Fiction. 5. Courage—Fiction. 6. Fantasy.]
I. Title. PZ7.F598284Hun 2012 [Fic]—dc23 2012020986

Puffin Books ISBN 978-0-14-242664-7

Printed in the United States of America

1 3 5 7 9 10 8 6 4 2

In memory of my mum, Kathleen Frances Flanagan.
I wish she'd been around to see all this.

BOOK 3: THE HUNTERS

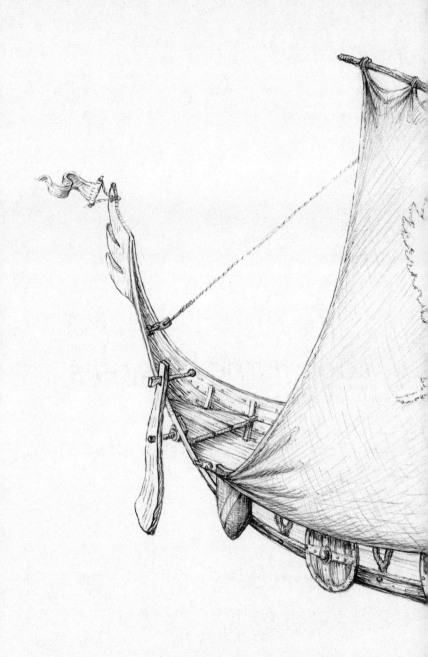

BOOK 3: THE HUNTERS

A Few Sailing Terms Explained

Because this book involves sailing ships, I thought it might be useful to explain a few of the nautical terms found in the story.

Be reassured that I haven't gone overboard (to keep up the nautical allusion) with technical details in the book, and even if you're not familiar with sailing, I'm sure you'll understand what's going on. But a certain amount of sailing terminology is necessary for the story to feel realistic.

So, here we go, in no particular order:

Bow: The front of the ship, also called the prow.

Stern: The rear of the ship.

Port and starboard: The left and the right side of the ship, as you're facing the bow. In fact, I'm probably incorrect in using the term *port*. The early term for port was *larboard*, but I thought we'd all get confused if I used that.

Starboard is a corruption of "steering board" (or steering side). The steering oar was always placed on the right-hand side of the ship at the stern.

Consequently, when a ship came into port it would moor with the left side against the jetty, to avoid damage to the steering oar.

One theory says the word derived from the ship's being in port—left side to the jetty. I suspect, however, that it might have come from the fact that the entry port, by which crew and passengers boarded, was also always on the left side.

How do you remember which side is which? Easy. *Port* and *left* both have four letters.

Forward: Toward the bow.

Aft: Toward the stern.

Fore-and-aft rig: A sail plan in which the sail is in line with the hull of the ship.

Hull: The body of the ship.

Keel: The spine of the ship.

Steering oar: The blade used to control the ship's direction, mounted on the starboard side of the ship, at the stern.

Tiller: The handle for the steering oar.

Yardarm, or yard: A spar (wooden pole) that is hoisted up the mast, carrying the sail.

Masthead: The top of the mast.

Bulwark: The part of the ship's side above the deck.

Belaying pins: Wooden pins used to fasten rope.

Oarlock, or rowlock: Pegs set on either side of an oar to keep it in place while rowing.

Telltale: A pennant that indicates the wind's direction.

Tacking: To tack is to change direction from one side to the other, passing through the eye of the wind.

If the wind is from the north and you want to sail northeast, you would perform one tack so that you are heading northeast, and you would continue to sail on that tack for as long as you need.

However, if the wind is from the north and you want to sail due north, you would have to do so in a series of short tacks, going back and forth on a zigzag course, crossing through the wind each time, and slowly making ground to the north. This is a process known as **beating** into the wind.

Wearing: When a ship tacks, it turns *into* the wind to change direction. When it wears, it turns *away* from the wind, traveling in a much larger arc, with the wind in the sail, driving the ship around throughout the maneuver. Wearing was a safer way of changing direction for wolfships than beating into the wind.

Reach, or reaching: When the wind is from the side of the ship, the ship is sailing on a reach, or reaching.

Running: When the wind is from the stern, the ship is running. (So would you if the wind was strong enough at your back.)

Reef: To gather in part of the sail and bundle it against the yardarm to reduce the sail area. This is done in high winds to protect the sail and the mast.

Trim: To adjust the sail to the most efficient angle.

Halyard: A rope used to haul the yard up the mast. (Haul-yard, get it?)

Stay: A heavy rope that supports the mast. The **backstay** and the **forestay** are heavy ropes running from the top of the mast to the stern and the bow (it's pretty obvious which is which).

Sheets and shrouds: Many people think these are sails, which is a logical assumption. But in fact, they're ropes. Shrouds are thick ropes that run from the top of the mast to the side of the ship, supporting the mast. Sheets are the ropes used to control, or trim, the sail—to haul it in and out according to the wind strength and direction. In an emergency, the order might be given to "let fly the sheets!" The sheets would be released, letting the sail loose and bringing the ship to a halt. (If *you* were to let fly the sheets, you'd probably fall out of bed.)

Way: The motion of the ship. If a ship is under way, it is moving according to its course. If it is making leeway, the ship is moving downwind so it loses ground or goes off course.

Back water: To row a reverse stroke.

So, now that you know all you need to know about sailing terms, welcome aboard the world of the Brotherband Chronicles!

John Flanagan

PART 1

THE HUNT

Land! I can see land!"

It was Stefan, calling from the lookout position in the bow of the *Heron*.

There was a buzz of interest from the crew as they surged forward to get a sight of the coast—at this stage, no more than a distant, hazy line on the horizon.

Hal heaved a silent sigh of relief. They had been out of sight of land for four days, cutting diagonally across from the eastern coast of the Stormwhite Sea to head for the southern coastline. After days without any reference points or landmarks, with nothing but the waves to see, niggling fears had begun to gnaw at his confidence. What if he had misread his sun compass? What if Stig had let the ship stray off course while Hal was sleeping? What if Hal himself had made some simple, fundamental error that had led them off on the wrong path?

When you sailed out of sight of land, he thought, there was always the worry that you might never sail back into sight of it.

He shook his head, realizing how groundless his fears had been. Four days, after all, was a relatively short ocean trip. He knew of Skandian seafarers who had sailed for weeks with no sight of land. He had done so himself, on ships commanded by other people. But this was his first time in command.

Thorn came aft from his favored spot by the keel box. His rolling gait easily matched the movement of the ship and he smiled at his young friend. He'd spent many years at sea but he knew all too well what must have been going through Hal's mind.

"Well done," he said quietly.

Hal gave him a quick smile. "Thanks," he said, trying to look nonchalant. Then he couldn't keep up the pretense any longer. "Must admit, I had a few sleepless moments."

Thorn raised an eyebrow. "Only a few?"

"Two, actually. One lasted for the first two days. The other for the next two. Apart from that, I was fine."

The fact that the young skirl could admit to his concerns was a sign of his growing maturity and confidence in his own ability. He was growing up fast, Thorn thought. But then, command of a ship had that effect on a person. He either grew into the responsibility or it crushed him.

In the bow, Stig had climbed onto the bulwark alongside Stefan, but on the other side of the bow post. He shaded his eyes, then turned and called back down the length of the ship.

"I can see three hills," he shouted. "Two big, one small. The small one is in the middle. They're a little off to port."

Thorn saw the look of pleasure that came over Hal's face. He nodded his admiration.

"Sounds like Dwarf Hill Cape," he said. "Wasn't that where you were aiming?" It was a near-perfect landfall—an impressive achievement for a neophyte skirl. Thorn was an expert sailor, but the intricacies of navigation had always proved too much for him.

Hal rearranged his features, trying to hide his pleasure.

"Should have been dead ahead," he muttered, but then the smile broke through again. "But that's pretty good, isn't it?"

Thorn clapped him on the shoulder. "It's very good. For an old coast crawler like me, it's beyond comprehension."

Hal nodded forward. "Looks as if our prisoner is finally taking an interest in things."

Rikard, the Magyaran pirate Thorn had broken out of the Limmat jail, was standing up to peer toward the land. For the past few days he had remained huddled by the mast, restrained by a heavy chain that secured him to the thick spar.

"He knows he's near home," Thorn said. "The entrance to the Schuyt River is only a few kilometers up the coast, and that leads to the Magyaran capital."

"Are we planning on setting him free?" Hal asked.

Thorn shook his head. "Not until we know he's telling us the truth about Zavac's destination. If he is, we should be able to find someone who's seen the *Raven* when we head down the Dan River. He's just going to have to wait till then."

After they had left the port of Limmat behind, Rikard made

good on his promise to tell them where Zavac was heading. Zavac was the pirate captain who had earlier stolen the Andomal, Skandia's most prized artifact. He stole it while Hal and his crew were charged with its protection, so they had a personal interest in regaining it from him.

With that in mind, they had pursued Zavac down the length of the Stormwhite, always one step behind the elusive Magyaran ship, a large black craft named the *Raven*. They caught up with Zavac and the *Raven* at Limmat, a harbor town on the east coast. Zavac, in company with two other ships, had led an attack on the town and occupied it. The crew of the *Heron* had been instrumental in defeating the invaders and driving them out. Many of the pirates had been either killed or captured in the ensuing battle, but Zavac and his crew had escaped in the closing stages, ramming and nearly sinking the Skandian ship *Wolfwind* in the process.

According to Rikard, Zavac and his crew were heading for the Dan River, a mighty waterway that ran all the way from the north of the continental mass, on the Stormwhite's coast, to the south, close by the Constant Sea. At the southern end of the Dan was a fortified citadel called Raguza, a pirate haven governed by a council of pirates and thieves. Raiders from the Stormwhite and the Constant Sea sought refuge there, knowing they would be protected from pursuit and revenge. Ships harboring in Raguza paid a tribute to the city's governing body. Usually, this was a tenth share of any booty they had on board. It was expensive, but it was worth it to enjoy the security and freedom from pursuit that Raguza offered.

Zavac, of course, was carrying a large supply of emeralds plundered from the secret mine at Limmat. Some of those emeralds should have gone to the men who had assisted in the invasion and occupation of the town. But they had been defeated and killed or imprisoned, and he had absconded with their share. With such a rich haul, he had no further need to raid during the current season and had obviously decided to relax and regroup in the citadel.

Now, as the *Heron* moved closer to the coastline, Rikard seemed to sense their attention on him. He turned to look at them, then beckoned to Thorn, who walked forward to speak to him.

"What is it?" he asked, knowing the answer before Rikard gave it.

"Are you going to set me free?" he said, pointing at the approaching coastline.

Thorn shook his head. "I think we need the distinct pleasure of your company a little longer."

"I've kept my part of the bargain! You promised you'd set me free," Rikard protested.

"No. I promised I'd set you free once we're sure you've kept your part of the bargain. I also promised that if you haven't I'll throw you overboard."

"Well, is there any need to keep me chained up like this?" Rikard angrily rattled the chain that secured him to the mast. "After all, there's nowhere I can escape to."

Thorn smiled at him. "That's in case you decide to do me out of the pleasure of throwing you overboard. Wouldn't want you taking matters into your own hands."

Rikard scowled at him and slumped down to the deck once more. He could see there was no point in arguing any further. In the few days he had been on board, he had learned that Thorn was not a man to change his mind easily.

"I know you can't wait to get back to Magyara and join another pirate crew," Thorn said. "But you'll just have to put up with us for a while yet." He turned and walked back to the steering position, where Lydia and Stig had joined Hal.

"Are you planning on putting ashore?" Lydia asked as Thorn came within earshot. Hal pursed his lips, then shook his head.

"We'll run along the coast for another day. That'll bring us to the mouth of the Dan. We can go ashore there. We need to find out if anyone's sighted the *Raven*."

He had a constant, nagging worry that Zavac may have headed off in another direction entirely and they had spent the past four days on a wild-goose chase.

"The boys could use a good night's sleep," she said. "So could I."

The *Heron* wasn't the most comfortable place for sleeping. The crew could bed down on the planks between the rowing benches. But the constant need to adjust to the ship's pitching and rolling, and the frequent showers of spray that broke over her, made it difficult to get deep, uninterrupted rest.

"Another day or so won't hurt them," he said.

She smiled ruefully. "Or me?"

"Or you. Sorry. We'll all have to wait. The sooner we find out we're on the right track, the happier I'll be."

Lydia nodded. Hal's point was a valid one and she realized that he had probably had the least sleep of anyone on board. He and Stig shared the responsibility of steering the ship and Hal tended to take on the lion's share of that.

"Not worth checking in any of the coastal towns here?" Stig asked, but Hal shook his head.

"If she's been sighted here, that doesn't tell us she's gone down the river. She could have continued heading west along the coast."

Stig sighed good-naturedly. "Oh well, I guess that means another night of sleeping on those hard planks. Why did you design this ship with so many ribs? There always seems to be one digging into *my* ribs."

Hal grinned at his friend. "I'll bear it in mind next time I build a ship," he said. Then, as so often happens when someone raises the matter of sleep, he found he couldn't suppress a huge yawn.

Thorn eyed him thoughtfully. "You look as if you could use a good night's rest yourself."

Hal shrugged, blinking his eyes rapidly to clear them. Now that Thorn mentioned it, he was aware how dry and scratchy they were.

"I'll be fine," he said, but Thorn wasn't to be put off.

"I've been thinking. You should have someone else trained to take over the tiller," he said.

Stig made a big show of clearing his throat. "Um . . . have we noticed that I am here? Or am I just a piece of chopped halibut?" he asked. "I seem to recall taking over the helm several times in the past few days."

"I'm aware of that," Thorn said patiently. "I mean you should have a third person ready to take over."

"Couldn't you do that?" Lydia asked.

Thorn looked at her. "I could. But if we get into a sea battle, Stig and I are the logical choices to lead a boarding party. We're the two best fighting men on the ship. And Hal has to be free to operate the Mangler."

The Mangler was the name they had given to the giant crossbow mounted in the bow of the ship.

"Did you have anyone specific in mind?" Hal asked. Thorn's reasoning made sense, and a third helmsman would lessen the strain on him and Stig in what looked to be a long and hard journey ahead.

"I was thinking Edvin," Thorn said. "Stefan and Jesper are working well together raising and lowering the sails, and Ulf and Wulf have a natural affinity for sail trimming. Edvin is a bit of a loose end at the moment."

Hal smiled. "It might be more tactful to say he's an unrealized potential asset," he said. "But, yes, that's a good idea. Plus he's smart and he listens. He'll get the hang of it quickly enough. Let's go talk to him." He nodded to Stig, who took over the helm. Then he and Thorn made their way forward, to where Edvin was sitting beside the supine form of Ingvar, who had been wounded in the attack on the watchtowers at Limmat.

Edvin was concentrating on something, his head bent over as he worked two long, thin sticks back and forth, setting up a rapid click-clicking sound. A ball of thick yarn lay on the deck between his feet.

"Edvin?" Hal said. "What are you doing?"

Edvin looked up at them and smiled. "I'm knitting," he said. "I'm knitting myself a warm, woolly watch cap."

Hal and Thorn exchanged a glance.

"I wonder if we might have made a mistake?" Thorn said.

Knitting, you say?" Jesper frowned at the thought of it, but Stefan nodded in confirmation.

"Knitting. He had a big ball of yarn and two needles and he was . . . knitting."

They looked aft to where Hal was introducing Edvin to the finer points of steering the ship. Stig and Thorn stood to one side, watching. While Edvin had begun his instruction, Lydia had taken his place tending Ingvar. The *Heron* was on a long reach, with the wind from the starboard side, and there was little for the sail crew to do. Jesper and Stefan, whose task was to raise and lower the yardarms, had moved aft to sit and talk with the twins, Ulf and Wulf, at the sail-trimming sheets.

"I'm not sure that I want someone steering the ship if he spends his spare time knitting," Stefan said.

It was a ridiculous non sequitur, but the others seemed to agree with the sentiment. They all looked at Edvin once more.

"How do you knit, anyway?" Jesper wondered.

Ulf shrugged dismissively. "It's quite easy, actually."

They all looked at him. Predictably, it was Wulf who responded. "Is that so? Perhaps you'd tell us how it's done then."

Ulf hesitated. He'd seen his mother, aunt and grandmother doing it and it seemed easy enough. They could knit without looking at what they were doing—and they could carry on a conversation about the weather or the price of salt cod while they did it. So it stood to reason that it was easy. Particularly if his aunt could do it.

He realized that the other three were all looking at him, waiting for him to answer. He waved a vague hand in the air.

"Well . . . you get some needles . . ."

"Knitting needles?" Stefan asked, and Ulf frowned at him, not appreciating the interruption.

"Of course knitting needles!" he said with some heat. "Did you think you'd use darning needles for knitting?"

"Why do they call it darning?" Jesper put in.

Ulf gave him an annoyed look. It seemed that everyone was bent on interrupting him this morning.

"'Cause that's what you say when you stick the needle in your finger," Wulf suggested, and the three of them laughed. Ulf maintained his dignity, and directed a pained look at his brother.

"That's quite good, Ulf," Jesper said to Wulf. Ulf rolled his eyes to heaven. This was getting to be too much, he thought.

"*I'm* Ulf," he said shortly. "He's Wulf."

"Are you sure?" Stefan asked, a ghost of a smile hovering at the corner of his mouth. "He looks like Ulf to me."

"You know," said Wulf thoughtfully, seeing a way to annoy his brother, "I *could* be Ulf. When I woke up this morning, I wasn't completely sure who I was. I thought, maybe they've woken the wrong person."

"That's what our mother said the day you were born," Ulf countered. "She looked at you and said, *Oh no! That's the wrong one. That ugly baby couldn't be mine!*"

Wulf drew himself up a little straighter and faced his brother, his body language confronting. "And you'd know that, would you?"

"Yes. I would. Because I was born before you. I remember waiting around for ages for you to arrive. And what a big disappointment that was for everyone," he added triumphantly. He was on a roll. The fact that he was the firstborn gave him a certain moral ascendancy over his brother in these arguments.

Wulf's face was beginning to redden. "Do you seriously expect us to believe that . . . ?" he began, but Lydia, a few meters away, interrupted in a low, warning tone.

"Let it drop, boys. We are at sea, after all."

They looked at her and she jerked her head toward the stern of the boat, and the small group clustered round the tiller. Wulf's mouth twisted into an uncertain line. Hal had banned any bickering between the twins while the ship was at sea. Up until now they had managed to control their natural inclination, but the previous four days had been uneventful and they were becoming bored.

"I don't think he heard us," he said quietly and was disconcerted when Thorn answered, without looking at them:

"Oh yes, he did."

Ulf and Wulf exchanged a startled look. In actual fact, Hal had been too busy instructing Edvin to pay any attention to them. But they weren't to know that.

"In any event, tell us all about knitting," Wulf said.

His brother glared at him. He'd assumed that they'd moved on from the discussion about knitting. But Wulf wasn't letting him off the hook as easily as that. Ulf took a deep breath.

"Well . . . you need needles—knitting needles," he added quickly. "And you need a ball of yar—"

"How many?" Jesper interrupted.

Ulf frowned. "Just one. One ball of yarn."

But Jesper was shaking his head. "No. How many knitting needles?"

"Two," Ulf said, a warning tone in his voice. "Two knitting needles, one ball of yarn."

"If you used four needles, couldn't you knit twice as fast?" Stefan asked, with an air of innocence that was all too obviously faked. Ulf turned a withering look on him, then resumed his discourse.

"Then you wrap the yarn around the needles and sort of push them in and out and you . . . well, you knit." He made an expansive gesture in the air as if that explained it completely. The others eyed him skeptically.

A few meters away, Ingvar's eyes flicked open as Lydia placed a damp cloth on his forehead.

"What are they blathering on about?" he said. His voice was weak, which worried her. He should have been recovering a lot more quickly. She smiled at him now. It wouldn't do to show him that she was concerned.

"They're talking about knitting," she said. "They're idiots."

He tried to nod but it was a feeble movement. He muttered something she didn't catch and she bent closer.

"What was that?"

"Knitwits," he said more clearly. "They're knitwits." He laughed at his own joke, but the movement seemed to cause him pain and he stopped. She took his hand and squeezed it gently, wishing there were more she could do for him.

Jesper was unsatisfied with Ulf's explanation. Now that the subject of knitting had come up, his curiosity was piqued and he wanted to know more about it. Truth be told, he was bored, and any subject could have claimed his interest at the moment. He turned to Lydia, who had begun sponging Ingvar's neck and face with a wet cloth once more.

"Lydia, how difficult is knitting?" he asked. She paused in what she was doing, then looked up at him.

"How would I know?" she said in a level tone.

He shrugged. "Well, you're a girl, and it's kind of a girly thing, so I thought . . ."

His voice trailed off as he realized that Lydia was holding his gaze very steadily. She let the silence between them drag on for some time, watching him grow more and more uncomfortable. Finally, she answered him.

"I don't know, Jesper. I don't knit."

"Oh," he said, relieved that the awkward moment seemed to have passed. You never knew with Lydia, he thought. She wasn't like most girls and that long dirk she wore was very sharp.

"But I can sew," she said, and he looked at her quickly. Something in her tone told him she had more to say on the matter. He swallowed nervously as her eyes bored into his, daring him to look away. Some response seemed to be indicated.

"You can?" he asked.

"I can. And if you ever ask me a stupid male question like that again, I'll sew your bottom lip to your ear."

He nodded several times. "Right. Right. Lip to ear. Point taken. Understood. Let's talk about something else, shall we?" he suggested to the group in general.

"What else do you want to talk about?" Wulf asked. Jesper darted a nervous glance at Lydia, who seemed to have lost interest in him and had gone back to tending Ingvar.

"Anything. Anything but knitting."

On the steering platform, Edvin was beginning to get the hang of things. He glanced quickly astern at the ship's wake. It was a respectable straight line—not arrow straight the way Hal could keep it, but not too bad at all.

"We'll make a helmsman of you yet, young Edvin," said Thorn, and the boy's face flushed with pleasure. He took the ship off course by a few degrees, then practiced bringing her back on course, easing the tiller just before she got there.

"That's good," Hal told him. "Did you want me, Lydia?"

The slim girl had come aft to the steering platform and seemed to be waiting to catch his attention. She nodded at Edvin.

"Edvin, actually, if you can spare him. Edvin, can you come and look at Ingvar? I don't think he's doing so well."

I thought he was getting better," Hal said as he followed Edvin and Lydia to where Ingvar was lying on his improvised bed in the waist of the ship. The huge boy had been wounded by an arrow during the attack on Limmat. Edvin pursed his lips. He looked worried.

"I thought so too. But he took a turn for the worse yesterday and he seemed to deteriorate during the night. I was hoping it was only temporary. But now . . ." He didn't finish the sentence.

Ingvar was asleep—if you could call it sleep. It was more accurate to say that he was unconscious. His eyes were screwed tight shut and his head tossed back and forth on the pillow. His cheeks were sunken and his skin looked waxy and pale. There were dark circles under his eyes. Edvin knelt beside the huge form and gently placed his hand on Ingvar's forehead. His worried expression deepened and he gestured for Hal to feel Ingvar's forehead.

Hal did so. He turned an alarmed look to Edvin.

"He's burning!" he said. Ingvar's skin was fiercely hot and dry to the touch.

Edvin nodded unhappily. "I know," he said. "I actually thought he'd be better off to be at sea. That infirmary in Limmat was a dark, stuffy place, full of fevers and sickness. Orlog knows what you could catch in an unhealthy atmosphere like that. I thought the fresh sea air would be better for him, and the surgeon agreed. As I say, he seemed to be recovering."

"What's caused it?" Hal asked.

"He's very weak and he hasn't slept well. That means he can't build up strength to fight the sickness. I think there's an infection started up in the wound again. That's what's making him so feverish."

"What can you do?" Hal asked Edvin. The soft-spoken boy had been trained during the brotherband period as the *Heron's* medical orderly, but it had been a perfunctory training only.

He shrugged. "I honestly don't know, Hal. All I can suggest is that I clean the wound again, then do what I can to keep him cool and hope the fever breaks. If we can get him through the fever, and let him rest properly, he should begin to recover again. At least, I think so."

Hal considered Edvin's words. He looked up to the nearby coastline.

"Can you do all that while we're at sea?" he asked.

Edvin hesitated, then shook his head. "Not really. We're pitching and rolling too much."

Hal nodded. It was a reasonable assessment. He had a brief, horrified vision of what could happen if the ship lurched suddenly while Edvin was probing the wound.

"But once you've done that, we can put to sea again?" he asked. Edvin's unhappy expression told him the answer before he spoke.

"He can't rest properly with the deck pitching and heaving like this. You know how it is, Hal. Your body tenses and prepares for the movement. You brace yourself against the roll when you sense it's coming. Ingvar needs solid sleep. That's the best healer for him. And he can't get it while we're at sea. In fact, that constant tensing and bracing might well have aggravated the wound in the first place."

"How long then?" Hal asked.

Edvin shrugged. "I don't know. Maybe one night. Maybe two. If he can rest properly and I can keep him cooled down, he should improve. We'll need to keep bathing him with damp cloths to bring his temperature down."

"And if we don't?" Hal asked.

"If the fever doesn't break, he could die," Edvin said. Lydia looked at him in alarm.

"It's that bad?" she said, and he nodded.

Hal looked away, cursing silently. Each time he got close to Zavac, something intervened. Outside Limmat, he had had to choose between going after the pirates and leaving Svengal and the crew of *Wolfwind* to drown. Now he was faced with another choice, with Ingvar's life in the balance.

And there was another, practical consideration, in addition to his concern for his friend. Lydia voiced it.

"You need Ingvar if you're going to use the Mangler," she said quietly.

"I know that."

The huge crossbow would be their main weapon in the event of a fight with the *Raven*. Only Ingvar had the strength necessary to cock and load it. Ulf and Wulf could do it together, of course. But in a sea fight, they would be kept busy adjusting the trim of the sails as the ship maneuvered. That was the problem. Everyone on the ship had an assigned role and everyone was needed in that role. Particularly Ingvar.

Once Hal had that thought, it was easier to come to a decision. He rose and looked at the coastline running past them, shading his eyes with his hand.

"We'd better find a place to go ashore," he said.

They ran on for several kilometers before he found a suitable landing place. The coastline was, for the most part, open beach. And it was swept by the northeast wind that was blowing. If the wind got up any further, they could find themselves in trouble in such an exposed position.

Eventually, he spotted what he was looking for. The land rose and the long, unbroken beach gave way to rocky, low cliffs. There was a narrow opening that led to a cove. He lowered the sail and proceeded farther inshore under oars to inspect it. It turned out to be exactly what they needed. There was a sandy beach on the eastern side of the cove, and the headland would provide shelter from the wind.

The crew lay resting on the oars for several minutes while he inspected it, looking for broken, swirling water that might indicate rocks hidden just below the surface, studying the action of the waves to make sure there was no concealed reef across the mouth of the cove. Finally, he nodded to himself.

"Stig," he called, and his first mate gave the order for the rowers to begin pulling once more.

Hal steered the little ship into the cove. Stefan had resumed his position by the bow post, searching the water's surface for any signs of danger. But there were none, and the *Heron* cruised smoothly to a small strip of sand Hal had marked out.

"In oars," he called when they were less than twenty meters from the sand. The oars clattered in the rowlocks as the crew brought them inboard, then clattered once more as they were stowed along the line of the ship.

"Bring the fin up, Thorn," Hal ordered, and Thorn heaved the heavy fin up from its lowered position in the keel box. As he did so, Hal felt the now-familiar drift as the ship lost the steadying lateral force of the keel. Then there was a gentle grating sound as the bow ran up onto the coarse sand, finally canting over slightly to one side. Without needing to be told, Stefan dropped over the bow onto dry land, carrying the beach anchor inland and driving it deep into the sand.

As ever, Hal felt the strange silence that came with the lack of movement from the ship. The constant background chorus of small noises—the slap of ripples along the hull, the muted groaning of the rigging and masts—had ceased and his voice seemed unnaturally loud as he spoke.

"Let's get a camp set up."

The Herons moved to the task quickly. They were well practiced now in making camp. They used a large tarpaulin draped over a central ridgepole to create a long A-shaped tent. Edvin and Stefan busied themselves building a smaller shelter for Ingvar.

When the camp was ready, Stig approached Hal and jerked a thumb toward Rikard.

"Will we leave him on board?"

Hal considered the question, then shook his head. Rikard was securely chained to the mast and there was little chance he could escape. But Hal was reluctant to leave him unattended on board the ship. He knew Rikard was bitter at not being released and he feared he might damage the *Heron* in some way.

"Bring him ashore. Chain him to a tree and throw a blanket over him," he said. He glanced up. There were a few clouds sliding gently across the blue sky, but no dark masses that might indicate rain. A blanket should be sufficient cover.

Ulf and Wulf unchained Rikard and led him to a stout pine tree at the edge of the beach, some twenty meters from the main tent. They fastened the chain round the bole of the tree, tested that it was still firmly attached to the hard leather cuffs padlocked around Rikard's wrists, then handed him a blanket.

"Make yourself comfortable," Ulf said. Rikard grunted at them and scowled as they smiled back. Then they turned and headed back to the campsite.

"Let's get something to eat. I'm starved," Ulf said.

"You're always starved," Wulf replied.

"That's because I'm older than you. I've been waiting longer for my dinner."

Rikard waited as their voices faded away, then looked down to study his bonds. The leather cuffs were stiff and inflexible. They were padlocked in place and would be impossible to loosen with his bare hands.

But Rikard had more than his bare hands. He pulled the blanket over himself and reached down inside his knee-high boot. A long, razor-sharp blade was concealed in a specially fashioned sheath, running down the inside of the boot and hidden by a flap of soft leather. On board, under constant scrutiny and with crew members always close by, he'd had no opportunity to access it.

He smiled to himself. Now things were different.

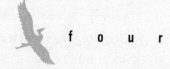

al stooped to enter the small tent where Edvin was caring for Ingvar. The wounded boy was lying on his back, on a soft bed of pine boughs overlaid with a thick blanket. Another blanket covered him but, as Hal watched, the big boy muttered and tried to toss it to one side.

Edvin was kneeling beside the prone figure, with a basin of cool water and several wet towels. He took hold of Ingvar's arm and stopped him from tossing the blanket aside. He was worried by the fact that he could do this so easily. Ingvar's strength had become legendary among them, but now . . .

Sensing Hal's presence, Edvin looked up. "He's as weak as a kitten," he said.

Hal nodded and knelt on the opposite side of the bed. He

reached out and laid his palm on Ingvar's forehead. The heat coming from the big boy's skin was frightening.

"He seems to be worse," he said sadly. "Am I imagining it, or has the fever grown stronger?"

Edvin shrugged. Then he dipped one of the towels in the water basin and began sponging Ingvar's forehead, face and neck.

"I've no real way of measuring it," he said, "but I think you're right. He definitely seems to be reaching a crisis point."

Hal looked at the new bandage on Ingvar's side, above the hip. "You've redressed the wound?"

Edvin glanced at it and nodded. "Cleaned it and rebandaged it. That's all I can do."

Ingvar's skin had dried again. The fleeting comfort of the water was gone and he tried to move restlessly on the bed. Gently, Edvin restrained him.

"Settle down, Ingvar," he said softly. "Take it easy."

He took a fresh towel from the basin. Once again, the relief was almost instantaneous and Ingvar quieted under the cooling touch.

Hal studied Edvin as he tended to Ingvar. He was small in stature and, like all of the Herons, he'd been something of a social outcast as he grew up in Hallasholm. But he was studious and highly intelligent, Hal knew, and when he took on a task, he stuck to it.

As he had that thought, he realized that Edvin was close to exhaustion, with the emotional strain of his concern for Ingvar and the physical effort of his nonstop ministering to his shipmate. He reached out and took the damp towel from Edvin's hand.

"I'll take a turn for a while," he said, and when Edvin looked up to remonstrate with him, he added firmly, "There's nothing here that I can't do. You need to rest. You need a break. Go and get something to eat. The others have had dinner, but I told them to save some for you."

Edvin looked at him suspiciously. "They've had dinner? Who cooked?"

"Stig," Hal told him.

Edvin pulled a face. "Stig cooked?" Among his various tasks, Edvin was the official crew cook and he had misgivings about the other boys' abilities. When they'd first set out from Hallasholm, each of them had cooked in a roster, and the efforts of most of the others had been decidedly unpalatable. Edvin had finally taken on the role of cook, declaring that he had no wish to be poisoned.

"He's improved a great deal." Hal grinned. "Either that or he was foxing in the first place and didn't want the job. In any event, he caught some nice snapper in the bay and he made a fish stew. Lydia found some wild onions in the forest, and he rummaged through your stock of spices and flavorings."

Edvin continued to look doubtful, so Hal played his trump card.

"Thorn had a second helping," he said.

Edvin raised his eyebrows in surprise. Thorn was a notoriously picky eater.

"In that case, I'd better try it." He rose from his kneeling position beside Ingvar, watching as Hal continued to bathe the wounded boy with cold water.

"Call me if there's any problem," Edvin said.

Hal nodded. "I will. Tell Lydia to come and take over from me in two hours. And get some sleep yourself."

He wet the towel in the basin, wrung it out again and continued to bathe Ingvar. It was frightening to see how quickly the thin film of water seemed to dry on his overheated skin. Satisfied that Ingvar was in good hands, Edvin turned and left. Hal heard his soft groan of relief as he straightened up once he was outside.

It was just before dawn. Hal became aware of the birdsong in the trees lining the beach as the birds sensed the coming sunrise and began their daily chorus. He'd resumed caring for Ingvar, taking over for Lydia sometime after midnight.

He'd nodded off several times as he watched over the big boy. Each time, he had been roused by Ingvar's muttering as the waves of fever ran over him. He continued the seemingly hopeless task of cooling his friend's body with the towels. The water bucket was almost empty, he realized. He'd have to refill it.

Ingvar seemed to improve at one stage. His calm periods lasted longer between the bouts of muttering and tossing. For a while, Hal felt a ray of hope, thinking that he might have turned the corner and begun to recover. Then he deteriorated once more, so that the water barely eased his discomfort. The fever was bad enough in itself, Hal thought. But it was also draining Ingvar's strength. His body couldn't relax as it fought off the floods of burning heat that raced through it. And as his strength became further and further depleted, he had fewer reserves to fight the sickness and it took a firmer hold on him. It was a vicious cycle.

He heard a soft footfall outside the tent and looked up as Thorn entered.

The old sea wolf studied his young friend, seeing his red-rimmed eyes and haggard expression.

"How long have you been here?" he asked.

Hal shook his head uncertainly. The daylight outside the tent was growing stronger.

"I don't know," he said. His voice was thick with fatigue. "A few hours, I guess."

Thorn knelt and took the damp towel he was holding from his unresisting grasp.

"You're not going to do him any good if you end up collapsing yourself," he said.

Hal turned an unhappy look on him. "I'm not doing him any good anyway," he said. "It's hopeless, Thorn. We're losing him."

Ingvar stirred, muttering and moaning softly. Thorn wet the towel and applied it to his forehead.

"Nothing's ever hopeless," he said firmly. "And he's not lost yet. We keep going and we keep trying as long as we can. That's what being in a brotherband is about. We don't give up on our brothers. We give them every possible chance."

Hal's shoulders sagged and he sighed deeply.

"You're right," he said. "It just seems so futile."

"And it'll seem that way right up to the point where the fever breaks," Thorn told him. "But we've got to stay positive. We've got to give Ingvar all the time and care he needs to recover."

"And if he doesn't?" Hal asked.

It tore Thorn's heart to see his young friend so despondent. He knew Hal was feeling responsible for Ingvar's condition and he knew he was too young to cope with that sort of guilt.

"If he doesn't," he said firmly, "then at least we'll know we did everything we could. Everything," he repeated. He watched carefully, seeing the boy's shoulders begin to rise again as he took a deep breath and regained control of himself.

"You're right," Hal said. "Thanks, Thorn."

He reached out to take the towel again but Thorn shrugged him away.

"I'll look after him for a while," he said. "You go get some sleep. You look worse than he does."

Hal gave him a tired smile and rose from his kneeling position beside Ingvar. He walked in a crouch to the doorway, stood upright in the open air outside, and rubbed the stiffness out of the small of his back with both hands. He yawned and stretched. Then he glanced across the campsite and was instantly awake. There was a crumpled blanket lying beside the pine tree.

Rikard was gone.

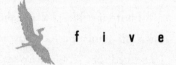

All thoughts of fatigue left Hal as he pounded across the clearing, shouting to alert the others. Thorn was the first to react, erupting from the small tent and following the young skirl to where the blanket and chain lay discarded beside the pine tree.

Ulf was on sentry duty and he was the next to arrive. His ax was thrust through a loop on his belt and it banged awkwardly against his hip as he ran from the beach to join them. Lydia wasn't far behind him.

"He must have had a knife hidden somewhere," he said bitterly. He looked up at Thorn, who was scanning the trees, looking for some sign of the missing prisoner. "Did anyone bother to search him?"

Thorn met his gaze and shook his head. "I took him out of the town jail, remember? It didn't occur to me that he might be armed. I assumed they would have searched him."

There was no note of apology in his voice. Perhaps he had made a mistake, but it was an understandable one. And there was no sense in beating his breast about it now. Rikard had been carrying a knife. He had cut through his bonds. And now he was gone. Instead of bemoaning the fact, Thorn was determined to get him back.

"Where do you think he's got to?" Ulf said. He started toward the tree line but a curt order from Lydia stopped him before he had gone two paces.

"Don't go there!" she snapped. When he looked at her, eyebrows raised, she continued in a more conciliatory tone. "Sorry, Ulf. I had to stop you before you went blundering in there. I don't want you covering up any tracks he may have left."

"I don't blunder, I'll have you know," Ulf said, with some dignity. "I'm a very light treader."

"I stand corrected," Lydia said. "In that case, don't go treading lightly in there, if you don't mind."

Honor satisfied, Ulf nodded agreement. "Well, if you put it that way . . ."

Stig, Jesper, and Edvin had joined them by this stage.

"What's happened?" Jesper asked. The answer was obvious. But it was a perfectly natural reaction, Hal thought.

"Rikard escaped during the night," Lydia told him. Jesper drew breath for another question but Thorn forestalled him.

"He had a knife. He cut through the leather cuffs."

"That would have taken a while," Stig said. "Those cuffs were boiled, toughened leather—they were nearly as hard as wood."

"He had all night to do it," Hal told him. He knelt down and picked up the cuffs, examining them. One had been severed in a series of short, jagged cuts. The other was cut in a much cleaner, straighter line.

"He must have done this one first," he said, pointing to the ragged edge. "It would have been more awkward with his hands fastened. He wouldn't have been able to get a comfortable position or much purchase." He mimed the awkward movements of a man with his hands bound together, trying to work on an imaginary cuff. "He must have been at it for hours."

"He was still here when you relieved me, Hal," Lydia said thoughtfully. "I remember noticing him just before I waved to Jesper." She turned to the former thief. "Do you remember seeing him when you went off watch?" she asked.

Jesper frowned, thinking. "I'm pretty sure I did," he said. "Yes. He was here then, I'm sure of it."

Then he hesitated. "At least, I think so. Maybe he was still here then." He frowned. "I'm not sure. I wasn't really looking for him."

"Does it matter?" Ulf put in, and Lydia looked quickly at him.

"If we know when he got away, it'll give us an idea of how far he might have gone," she said, and he nodded, appreciating the point.

Stig was about to say something when they were distracted by a feeble cry from the small tent. Edvin looked around the group gathered by the discarded chains. Only Stefan and Wulf were absent and they were notoriously heavy sleepers.

"Is anyone with Ingvar?" he asked, and they all exchanged guilty looks. In the confusion following the discovery that Rikard had escaped, they had all forgotten their wounded friend.

"Sorry, Edvin . . . ," Hal began, but Edvin was already running toward the tent.

"It's all right. It's my job, after all," he called back to them. There was an awkward pause, then Thorn called their attention back to the matter at hand.

"All right, so we can assume he was here until at least an hour after midnight. Then Stig took over for Jesper. My guess is that he would wait another hour for Stig to get tired and bored."

Stig drew himself upright. "I don't get tired and bored when I'm on sentry-go," he protested.

Thorn met his gaze unwaveringly. "*Everybody* gets tired and bored on sentry-go."

Stig subsided. "Yeah. I guess so. Maybe I got a little tired—and even a little bored."

Thorn glanced at the eastern horizon, gauging the time. There was a gray light flooding the sky but the sun was yet to appear.

"So let's say he has a four-hour start on us," he said.

"On us?" Hal said.

Thorn shrugged. "On me, then," he said, correcting himself. "I'm going after him."

"And just where are you planning to look?" Lydia asked him. He paused, then raised an eyebrow at her.

"Well, I rather thought I'd start in the forest," he said.

She looked at the trees, then back at him. "It's a big forest. Which direction were you planning on looking? Bear in mind, he could have gone any way but north."

The sea lay to the north. It was the one direction Rikard could not have taken.

"Do you know how to track?" she continued. "How to look for signs and follow them?"

Thorn hesitated. He had spoken in the heat of the moment. He was quietly furious with Rikard. He didn't like to be bested by anyone and he counted the pirate as a very low-life specimen indeed. He realized now that Lydia was right. But, being Thorn, he didn't want to admit it straightaway.

"I figure he'll be heading for Pragha. That's east of here. That's where I was planning on heading."

"That's if he's silly enough to head there straightaway," Lydia countered. "After all, he knows you know he wants to go there. He'd be a fool if he just went straight in that direction."

"He is a fool," Thorn said angrily, then wished he hadn't.

"He was smart enough to keep his knife hidden. And smart enough to get away."

"What are you getting at, Lydia?" Hal put in. "We're wasting time here."

She looked at him and nodded. "Exactly. We're wasting time. And we'll waste more if we go tramping aimlessly about the forest looking for him. I'm suggesting that I go after him. I can track him. That's what I do, after all. You can come with me, Thorn," she added, and he performed an exaggerated bow in her direction.

"Oh, well, thank you very much. Tell me, why didn't you just come out and say that in the first place?"

"Because I know what you would have said. *No. I work better alone. This is no job for a girl. I'll be looking for Rikard with one eye and looking after you with the other one.* That sort of claptrap. Am I right?"

Thorn instinctively went to deny it, but then stopped and grinned, a little sheepishly.

"Pretty much," he admitted. "All right. You've made your point. Let's get our things together and go after him."

"Is it really necessary, Thorn?" Hal said. "He's told us where Zavac is headed."

The old sea wolf nodded fiercely. "Yes, it is. He may have lied to us. Once we know the *Raven* is really heading down the Dan, I'll happily let him go. I'll help him over the side with my boot, in fact. But until we're sure, we may still need him."

Hal nodded, satisfied. "That makes sense. You'd better get going then."

"I'm coming too," Stig said, but Lydia shook her head.

"No," she said. "Three of us will make more noise. It'll be bad enough having Thorn blundering along with me . . ."

"You know, any more of these compliments and my head won't fit in my helmet," Thorn said mildly.

She glanced at him, unsmiling. In truth, she knew Thorn could move in almost total silence. She'd seen him do so on more than one occasion. But Stig didn't have the same skill and she'd said it to spare his feelings.

Stig opened his mouth to object, but Hal forestalled him. "She's right. Lydia and Thorn will be more than a match for Rikard. You'll stay here, Stig."

Stig flushed, about to make an angry rejoinder. Then he took several deep breaths and forced his anger down.

"All right," he said. "If you say so."

Interesting, Thorn thought to himself. There was a time, not too long ago, when Stig would have argued and bickered about Hal's order. They're all growing up, Thorn thought, and faster than I can keep up with.

Lydia nodded her gratitude to Hal. As the group broke up and headed back across the clearing to the campsite, she contrived to get beside Stig. She touched his arm and he turned to her, so that they fell behind the others.

"I didn't want to say it in front of him," she said softly. "But Hal's going to need you here—in case things don't go so well with Ingvar."

She saw understanding dawn in his eyes. "I hadn't thought of that," he said. He patted her on the shoulder. "Good luck. Make sure you bring that snake in the grass back with you."

She smiled. "Don't worry. I'll find him. Thorn will bring him back."

It took less than five minutes for Thorn and Lydia to make themselves ready. They took a blanket each. Thorn rolled his in a small tarpaulin that would serve as a tent if the weather turned, then filled a water skin and slung it over his shoulder. Lydia strapped on her heavy leather belt, with the dirk and atlatl hanging from it, quickly checked the darts in her quiver, then passed the strap over her head. The atlatl was a throwing stick with a hooked end that she used to impart extra power to the darts when she threw them.

While they were making their preparations, Stig went to the provisions sack by the cook fire and put together a package of dried meat and fruit and two small loaves of bread that had been baked the day before. He passed it to Thorn.

"Ready?" the old sea wolf said to Lydia, who nodded. "Then let's get going."

"Aren't you taking your club-hand?" Hal asked. He'd noticed that the heavy studded club was lying with the small pile of Thorn's possessions inside the tent.

"For Rikard?" Thorn said. "I don't need it. I've got my saxe." He patted the leather hilt of the heavy knife that hung from his belt.

Hal nodded. Now that he thought about it, Thorn wouldn't need the heavy war club to deal with Rikard and it would simply have been more weight to carry.

"Are we going to stand here talking all day?" Lydia asked. "It'll be noon before we get away at this rate."

Which was hardly fair, as the sun had only just slipped above the eastern horizon. Thorn raised his eyebrows to Hal in an exaggerated manner, then bowed and, with a sweeping movement of his arm, gestured for her to precede him.

"Your pardon, lady. Please lead the way and I will follow."

She sniffed disdainfully as she strode across the clearing to the tree line, Thorn on her heels. "Try not to put your big sailor's feet all over the tracks."

Thorn grinned at Hal. "It's going to be a long couple of days."

Lydia ignored him. Hal signaled for the others to stop before they reached the spot where Rikard had been bound. They chorused their good-byes and wishes of good luck. Lydia glanced back at Hal.

"Take care of Ingvar," she said. Then she turned away. She

stopped at the pine tree, casting around the ground close by. At this point, the sand of the beach was interspersed with a scrappy cover of coarse grass. But there was still enough soft sand to hold a heel print from Rikard's boot. A few meters farther on, she found another, then a third. They led directly into the tree cover.

"So far so good," she said to herself. Then she added over her shoulder, "Stay behind me, Thorn."

Thorn was tempted to make a pithy reply, but realized her instruction made sense. He said nothing and moved quietly in her footsteps. Inside the trees, the low-lying early sun created a confusing pattern of bright glare and dark shade. The contrast between the dazzling light and the shadows made it difficult for the eye to focus. But Lydia moved confidently. Before long, a patch of damp soil showed another heel print.

"He would have done better to get rid of those boots," she said. Rikard had been wearing high leather sea boots, with hard soles and heels. They looked quite dashing, and they were sensible enough on board ship, where waves would wash over the deck. But they were far less practical when the wearer was running through the tangled undergrowth, vines and roots that littered a forest floor. She pointed to a small indentation in the thick leaf mold that covered the ground.

"He fell over here," she said.

Thorn bent to peer at the mark. "How can you tell?" he asked. He was amazed that she had noticed the small indentation.

"That was made by the palm of his hand when he threw it out to save himself," she told him in a matter-of-fact tone. She glanced round to where several tree roots protruded from the ground a couple of meters before the hand mark.

"Probably tripped on one of them. You might even see the scuff mark from his boot if you look."

Curious, Thorn stooped and inspected the tree roots. Sure enough, there was a small mark where the bark had been bruised, exposing the lighter inner wood of the root.

"Remarkable," he said, looking at Lydia with new respect. "How do you know all this? How did you spot that handprint, for example? I would have walked straight past."

She smiled at him. "Which means you'd probably starve if you had to hunt for your food," she said. "I've been doing this for years. You train yourself to concentrate, to study every small mark and sign on the ground. If you'd noticed that dent, for example, what would you have thought?"

Thorn shrugged. "I would have thought it was a dent."

She nodded. "That's right. I try to see every small mark like that and ask what caused it. There's a reason for everything, after all."

"But it could have been caused by a pinecone falling from the trees and hitting the ground," Thorn pointed out.

"It'd need to be a pretty heavy pinecone to make that dent," she said. "And besides, if that were the case, there'd be a pinecone lying beside it."

Thorn smiled. "That's true," he said. "Well, I must say, I'm impressed. Very impressed."

"It's nothing much," she said. "If you practice anything long enough, you get good at it."

Despite her offhand reply, she was secretly gratified by Thorn's admiration of her tracking skills. He had a way of getting under her skin with his teasing and his remarks to Hal about her being "a keeper." He might appear to be a shabby old one-armed sailor, but she had seen him in action during the attack on Limmat and was in awe of his lightning speed and agility and hand-eye coordination. He was a master warrior, she knew, and such people were difficult to impress.

She had continued pacing slowly through the forest, bent over, her eyes questing from side to side, then up and down and side to side again, as she followed the signs that Rikard had left. She stopped and straightened.

"Hullo," she said. "He finally got smart." She turned back to Thorn, a few paces behind her. "Which way is Pragha?"

He pointed to his left. "East."

"Well, he's gone west. Must have decided he'd throw us off the track if he did that."

It was so obvious that she wasn't saying *I told you so* that Thorn felt obliged to say it for her.

"You told me so," he said.

She smiled, and a very satisfied smile it was. "Yes. I did, didn't I?"

"So how do you know?" Thorn asked. He'd moved forward and was searching the ground to the right for more telltale indentations. He could see nothing. She touched his arm.

"Look up," she said, pointing. He raised his eyes to the level she was indicating—about shoulder height. Two thin branches had been pushed back and were half broken.

"He headed west down this small side trail," she said, indicating a narrow path between the trees. "You can see where he pushed past this bush and broke the branches."

"An animal could have done that," Thorn said, but she shook her head.

"It would have to be a big animal. Besides, animals usually move more carefully than sailors. You can see it was done in the last few hours. The sap is still damp where the twigs are broken. I think if we check the trail a little farther along . . ." She moved into the side trail, turning sideways to avoid breaking any twigs herself. Not that they were expecting to be followed. It was an instinctive action, borne of years moving through forests like this one. She went a few meters, then called softly.

"Aha! Yes, here's our old friend the sea boot again. Bless him for wearing them."

She gestured for Thorn to follow her and moved farther away from the first trail, eyes seeking, searching and finding more signs of Rikard's passage.

"You sailors like leaving a wake wherever you go, don't you?" she commented. She plucked a small white thread from a sharp branch and held it up for him to see.

"Of course," she continued in a conversational tone, even though her eyes continued to search nonstop, "he was staggering through here in the dark, so he was bound to bump into things." She pointed to a thin, thorn-festooned creeper that was tangled around a larger branch. Thorn looked for some sign that it had snagged another piece of cloth but could see nothing. He shook his head and she explained.

"There are other creepers like that around here. See? But they all hang vertically. That one's at about sixty degrees. It got caught up on our friend's clothes—probably the leather vest he was wearing, because there's no sign of any cloth or thread on it. He kept moving and pulled it from its normal position until he broke free and left it snagged around the branch."

"Remarkable," Thorn said softly.

She shrugged. "You simply have to look for things that are not in the normal pattern." She suddenly laughed, stopping to indicate the ground at a point where the trail turned to the right. Thorn stepped up beside her. He could see a scuff of footprints around the base of a thick tree, which was obviously the reason why the path changed direction.

"He was probably running," Lydia explained. "Or at least, moving as quickly as he could. And it would have been pitch-dark under the trees, so he didn't see the path changing direction. He ran straight into this tree. You can see his footprints leading up to it, then these others when he staggered back. See how the heels are more deeply indented as his weight was thrown back on them?"

"Yes. I'd noticed that," Thorn said loftily. She turned a disbelieving look on him.

"You did?"

He nodded. "I did. I'm a quick learner. Now that you've shown me how it's done, I reckon I could get the hang of this tracking business—if I practice for fifteen or twenty years."

"Perhaps you'd like to lead the way now?" she offered, gesturing for him to go ahead of her.

"No, no. You seem to be doing quite well for the moment,"

Thorn told her. "If you get into any trouble, just give me a shout and I'll take over."

She shook her head at him. "Are you aware just how insufferable you can be?" she said, and he cocked his head to one side, considering.

"Yes. But, like anything else, it's a matter of practice. And I practice constantly."

"I'd noticed," she muttered, and led off again. After another ten meters or so, she remarked, "Looked like he hit that tree pretty hard. He'll have a sore head when we find him."

"He'll have more than that if he puts up a fight," Thorn said darkly. And this time, there was no underlying humor in his voice.

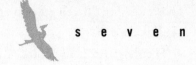

s the day slowly passed, the members of the crew took turns looking after Ingvar.

A sense of gloom hung over them as Ingvar showed no signs of improvement. He hovered on the very fringes of consciousness all day.

As one person's shift ended and another took his place, the question was always the same.

"Any change?"

And the answer was always a sad shake of the head.

In fact, there was a progressive change. Ingvar was growing weaker by the hour, but nobody wanted to draw attention to the fact. The Herons moved about their chores—cutting firewood, airing blankets and tightening the ropes that fastened their tent in place—in an unhappy silence. If anyone did speak, it was usually no more than a few words, spoken in an undertone, as if loud voices would disturb their stricken friend.

Hal had excused Edvin from the task of looking after Ingvar. At first, Edvin had resisted.

"I'm the healer in the crew," he said. "It's my job."

Hal shook his head gently. "There's nothing you can do that the rest of us can't handle," he said. "You've said yourself, all we can do is try to keep him cooled down and wait to see if the fever breaks. And we all know how to do that. I'd rather you went back to your job as cook. It'll take your mind off things and the quality of food will improve."

In fact, Stig had been doing a creditable job preparing the meals for the crew. But everybody knew Edvin would do it better. Edvin reluctantly agreed and Hal made a further point.

"I want you to get some decent sleep, as well," he said. "You've been wearing yourself out looking after Ingvar and I don't want to have two sick crew members."

"I slept last night," Edvin protested. Hal looked at him for a long moment. Edvin finally dropped his eyes. "Well, I rested. I couldn't really sleep. I was racking my brains, trying to think of something I could do for him." He paused and said hopelessly, "But there wasn't anything. I went through the healer's manual they gave me when I trained, to see if there was anything in there about how to treat a fever."

"What did you find?" Hal asked.

Edvin shrugged unhappily. "Nothing much. Just: *Keep the patient cool and wait for the fever to break.* If only there was something I could give him, I'd feel I was doing more. There was a note in there about willow bark. Apparently some of the primitive tribes from the east use it to treat fevers. But do you see any willows around here?"

Hal dropped a hand on his shoulder. "So we're doing all that can be done. And any one of us can handle that as well as you can. Get some sleep for when we really need you."

Edvin's shoulders drooped. "I'll try, Hal. It's just I feel . . . responsible."

"Responsible? For this? You can't help it."

Edvin nodded. "That's what I mean. I *can't* help it. I can't do anything to help Ingvar. And that's my job. It's the one thing I really trained for and now I can't do anything. The rest of you trained as warriors, and you trained as the skirl. You've all done your jobs. But the first time there's been a real task for me, I've failed."

"That's crazy, Edvin, and you know it. The healer's manual says there's nothing more you could do—unless you count some crazy notion about willow bark. Now go and rest. We're going to need you."

Edvin sighed deeply. "If you say. Although what you'll need me for is beyond me."

He walked slowly to the main tent. Hal watched him enter, then sat down on a log by the fire. The coffeepot was keeping warm in the edge of the embers and he reached out and poured himself half a tin cup. It had been made several hours previously but he lacked the energy to make a fresh pot. He drank the bitter, grainy liquid in a couple of mouthfuls, then tossed the dregs into the fire. They hissed on the hot coals.

"You look about as cheerful as I feel."

It was Stig. He sat on the log beside Hal and, together, they stared morosely at the gray and red embers of the fire. Eventually, Stig spoke again.

"What were you discussing with Edvin?"

Hal picked up a stick of firewood and stirred the coals with it, watching the flames rekindle.

"He feels responsible for Ingvar's condition."

"That's ridiculous. He did a great job getting the arrow out and treating the wound. I couldn't have done that."

"He just feels there should be something more he can do— other than sit and wait," Hal told him.

Stig pursed his lips thoughtfully for a second or two. "Well . . . there isn't, is there?"

"Of course not. He did say something about the eastern tribes using willow bark."

"Willow bark?" Stig frowned. "What do they use willow bark for?"

"Apparently, they use it to treat fevers. I don't know how." He poked the embers again and, when the fire flared once more, tossed the stick onto it and watched the flames begin to lick their way along the stick.

"There's a creek at the far end of the beach," Stig said, and Hal looked up at him, puzzled by the apparent change of subject.

"So?" he said.

Stig shrugged. "So where there's a creek, you sometimes find willow trees. Maybe we should go and see?"

They looked at each other for several seconds. "Can't hurt, can it?" said Hal.

Stig spread his hands out. "We've got nothing better to do."

They made their way to the creek, several hundred meters away. Where it issued into the cove, it was narrow and fast running. But as they followed it inland, it gradually widened and the flow became more sedate. Half a kilometer from the beach, on the inside edge of a sweeping bend in the stream, stood a small grove of willows.

"How do we give it to him?" Stig asked.

Edvin surveyed the generous pile of willow bark Stig and Hal had brought back to the camp. He scratched his head thoughtfully.

"I guess I could pound it up, soak it in hot water and smear it on him—like a poultice," he said.

"Let's try that, then," Hal said.

Edvin looked up at him and nodded. There was a sense of purpose about him now that he had something specific to do. He cut some of the bark, then pounded it with his pestle and mortar, adding hot water from a kettle standing in the fire coals. He scraped the resultant stringy paste into a bowl and rose to his feet.

"Let's see what happens," he said, and led the way to the small tent. The crew, sensing that something was afoot, followed. Stig and Hal crammed into the tent with Edvin. The others jammed the doorway, peering in. Stefan was forced to move back against the canvas wall. He looked suspiciously at the bowl.

"What's that muck?"

"Mashed-up willow bark," Hal said.

Ulf, peering round the edge of the doorway, assumed a knowing look. "I thought it was."

His brother snorted. "Be the first time you ever thought anything," he said scornfully.

Ulf turned to face him. "I'll have you know——"

"Shut up, you two," Hal said, without looking up from Ingvar. He spoke quietly, but there was an unmistakable note of command in his voice. Ulf opened his mouth to say something further, then thought better of it. There was a soft *clop* as he shut it.

Edvin opened Ingvar's shirt and smeared the gray-green sticky mess of bark and water and sap onto the boy's chest. At least, he thought, the water has cooled a little by now, so it might help. Ingvar stirred once, muttered, then let his head fall to one side. Edvin waited a minute or so, then placed his hand on Ingvar's forehead.

"Any change?" Hal asked.

The healer shook his head despondently. He sat back on his heels, defeated.

"Maybe it'll take a while to have any effect?" Stig suggested.

Edvin turned his gaze on the tall first mate. "And maybe it won't."

"Edvin . . ." Stefan's voice was tentative.

The healer turned to look at him. Edvin was tired and defeated. The brief moment where he thought he might be able to do something positive for Ingvar had passed.

"Yes?" he said.

Stefan made an apologetic gesture. "Well, I know you're the healer . . . I mean, you did the healer training after all . . . ," he began.

Edvin interrupted him. "Not that it's done much good."

Stefan made a gesture, dismissing the statement.

"But I was thinking, if my mam wanted me to take any herbs

or such, like this . . ." He indicated the smeary mess on Ingvar's chest. "She'd usually make it into a tea and get me to drink it."

Stig pointed at the willow bark goo. "Would you want to drink that?"

Stefan shrugged. "No. But then, I didn't want to drink most of the stuff Mam made me."

Edvin considered the idea. Hal noted that his face had lost its earlier animation, when Edvin had felt he had something tangible to do for Ingvar. The healer had been disappointed by the lack of success in smearing the willow bark paste onto Ingvar's chest. He needed to get that enthusiasm back, Hal thought.

"Why not try it, Edvin?" he said. "It can't hurt."

The slightly built boy came to a decision. He rose from his position by the bed and brushed past the group at the doorway.

"Why not?" he said.

He returned to the campfire, the crew straggling behind him. He took more of the bark, mashed it with the pestle and mortar, then infused it in boiling water. Once the water had taken on a pale green tinge, he strained the larger bits of bark from it, pouring it through a piece of clean linen into a cup. He dipped his finger in it and tasted.

"Bitter," he said.

"That's a good sign," Jesper said knowingly. They all looked at him. "Medicine is supposed to taste bad," he explained. "The worse it tastes, the better it is for you. Everyone knows that."

Hal considered the point for a moment. "You know, that's quite true. I've never come across a pleasant-tasting medicine." There was a general murmur of agreement from the others.

Once again, they followed on Edvin's heels as he returned to the tent. Stig and Hal entered with him, the others clustered at the entrance as before.

Stig knelt beside Ingvar and raised his head and shoulders so that Edvin could pour the liquid into his mouth. Ingvar spluttered, coughed some of the liquid out; then, as Edvin tilted back his head, he swallowed several mouthfuls before coughing again and spraying more of the bitter liquid down his chest. Edvin put the cup back to his lips and waited while he drained the last few drops. Then Stig lowered the big boy back onto his pillow.

They watched expectantly. One minute grew into two. Then three.

"Should I keep sponging?" Stefan asked. Edvin nodded, his eyes fixed on Ingvar. After five minutes had passed, he shook his head sadly.

"Well, it was worth trying," he said. "Chalk it up as another failure."

He rose and left the tent without another word. The others drew aside to let him pass. An uncomfortable silence settled over the group. Finally, Hal broke it.

"Stefan, you've been on duty long enough. Who's your relief?"

"That'll be me, Hal," Jesper said, holding up his hand. Hal nodded to him and he moved inside the tent to take Stefan's place. Stefan breathed a sigh of relief when he could finally straighten up from his crouched position beside Ingvar.

They left Ingvar in Jesper's care and walked in a loose group back to the fireplace. Edvin was standing at the edge of the beach, staring at the sea.

"You know," Stig said unhappily, "I really thought that was going to work."

He began to prepare a simple meal of bread and salted meat, setting aside a portion for Edvin and Jesper. Hal put the coffeepot on to boil again and the five of them sat in miserable silence, eating. None of them had much appetite. None of them believed now that Ingvar could survive another day. The fever was too fierce and his strength was so depleted.

Their fears seemed to be confirmed less than an hour later. Jesper burst out of the little tent, looking wildly around him.

"Hal! Edvin! Come quickly! Ingvar's in a really bad way!"

They all pounded across the sandy grass, fearing the worst. Jesper, totally distraught, ushered Hal and Edvin into the tent.

"He's taken a turn for the worse!" Jesper babbled. "He looks terrible! It just happened all of a sudden!"

The others clustered round the entry, jostling to look inside, fearful of what they would see.

Ingvar was on his back, moaning quietly. The pillow under his head, his jacket and the blanket across him, and the mattress under him were all totally sodden as perspiration poured out of his body in a flood. Jesper looked at them wildly.

"He's going to die, isn't he?"

It was Edvin who slapped him on the back, almost sending him sprawling across the sweat-soaked figure on the mattress.

"No, you idiot!" he said happily. "He's going to live. The fever's broken!"

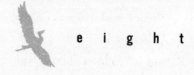

The light's fading. We'll have to stop soon," Lydia said. She had been down on one knee in the leaf mold that covered the ground, studying the latest sign of Rikard's passing. She stood up, brushed the damp bark and leaf fragments from the knee of her tights and looked up into the tree canopy. Thorn followed her gaze. The light that filtered down through the leaves and branches was much dimmer now.

"Not much point going on if you can't see his tracks," he agreed.

She nodded. "We've got maybe another half hour. Then I'll have to stop. Can't risk missing his trail in the bad light. We'd have to backtrack tomorrow and that'd cost us more time than we'd save by going on."

"Fine," said Thorn. This was her area of expertise, after all. She'd done a masterful job so far, spotting the small signs that Rikard left behind. Thorn had found himself enjoying watching her at her task. He had a deep respect for people who possessed skills that he didn't, like Hal's unerring accuracy as a navigator and his ability to sense wind and tide changes.

The small signs that she indicated and explained to him were obvious—once they had been pointed out. That was always the case, he knew. It was easy to notice something once somebody else had noticed it for you and drawn your attention to it. He knew that without Lydia he would have stumbled blindly through the forest, while Rikard moved farther and farther away from him. That thought prompted a question.

"Are we getting any closer to him, do you think?"

Lydia paused and looked over her shoulder at him. "How would I know?"

He shrugged. "I don't know. I thought you trackers could work out stuff like that. Like when you're following an animal, you poke around in its droppings to see if they're still moist. That sort of thing."

She turned fully now to face him and frowned at him, hands on her hips.

"I don't know if you've been paying attention," she said, "but, up until now, we haven't found any of Rikard's so-called droppings. And if we do, I'm certainly not going to go poking around in them. You feel free to do so if you want to," she added.

Thorn looked a little aggrieved. "That was just an example."

"It was a pretty bad one."

She turned away and began following the faint signs in the soft forest floor once more. After some twenty meters, her eyes intent on the ground ahead of her, she remarked casually, "Have you noticed he's slowly veering back to the east?"

Thorn hadn't. On the deck of a ship at sea, with a clear sight of the sun's position in the sky, he was able to orient himself instinctively. Here, in the gloom of the forest, with the sun an invisible and indistinct presence, it was a different matter—particularly as the light deteriorated.

He glanced now at the nearest trees, looking for the moss that grew on their trunks. Here in the north, it grew thickest on the south side. He realized that she was right. Rikard had been heading due west for some time. Now he had changed direction. The path they were following headed southeast. And as Lydia continued to track him, it was veering farther to the left.

"You were right," she said. "He's heading for Pragha."

Thorn grunted. "I may have been right," he admitted. "But I never would have found him. This will take him in a wide loop to get there."

She glanced at him with interest. In her experience, dominant males—and Thorn was certainly one of those—never admitted that they had made a mistake. Usually they would bluster and rationalize to prove they had really been right. Her regard for the shabby old warrior grew accordingly. He was obviously confident enough in his own abilities to admit to the occasional failing, and to give due regard to others when it was due. Knowing Thorn's penchant for teasing her, however, she decided it would be wiser not to let him know that her respect and affection for him were growing.

There was a small rivulet in their path and she stepped carefully through it. The water was barely eight centimeters deep. As Thorn went to follow her, she held up a hand to stop him, then pointed to a heel print in the soft mud of the far side.

"I think we are getting closer," she told him. "There's water still pooled in this heel print. We can't be more than two hours behind him. Any more than that and it would have dried out."

He stopped in midstream, peering at the wet footprint.

"Is that as reliable as droppings?" he asked. He couldn't help the trace of a grin that twitched the left corner of his mouth. She regarded him steadily.

"Maybe not. But it's a good deal more pleasant to contemplate," she said, then gestured for him to complete his crossing of the stream. She looked around. The ground rose for a few meters, then there was a small clearing to one side of the track.

"We might as well camp there," she said, indicating the spot. Thorn nodded. They made their way to the space among the trees. There were ferns and long grass covering the ground, which they quickly trampled down to provide a flat area for their camp.

Although *camp* was perhaps a misleading term. This close to their quarry, they both knew, without any need to discuss it, that there would be no fire. Thorn unslung the small tarpaulin that he carried bundled in a tight roll. He raised his head, sniffing the air experimentally.

"Think it's going to rain?" he asked.

Lydia followed his example. "Unlikely."

He nodded. "I agree. The ground is pretty wet, so we'll use the tarpaulin under us as a ground sheet. If it does rain through the night, I guess we can just wrap it over us."

He spread the waterproof canvas out and they placed their blanket rolls on it. Then he unwrapped the ration pack that Stig had put together for them. As night crept through the forest, they had a frugal dinner of dried meat and fruit and one of the loaves of hard bread. Lydia took a long swig from the water skin, then passed it to Thorn. As he drank, she raised her head and turned to the east. Thorn noticed the movement and lowered the water skin.

"I smell wood smoke," she said. He sniffed the air and nodded. Incredible how far the smell of burning wood could reach, he thought.

"He's obviously confident that he's not being followed," she said.

"Why wouldn't he be?" he replied. "Remember, he doesn't know you're a tracker. He thinks the rest of us are just sailors and that's not a skill we have. He's gone in a long loop to throw any possible pursuit off the trail. Probably thinks that if anyone is trying to follow him, they're miles away. I imagine he's pretty pleased with himself."

"I imagine he's pretty annoyed that he left that blanket behind," Lydia replied. "It's cold and damp in the forest. That's probably why he lit a fire."

"More fool him," Thorn said, spreading his blanket out and

rolling it round him as he lay down, his head pillowed on his folded sheepskin vest. He sighed contentedly and shut his eyes. Lydia regarded him for a few moments.

"Isn't one of us going to keep watch?" she asked.

He replied without opening his eyes. "Good of you to volunteer. Wake me in two hours."

"So, there's no consideration of the fact that I'm a delicate female?" she asked.

"None at all. Welcome to equality. Besides, I'm old and I need my rest."

She grinned at him as he lay there, eyes shut, rolled in the blanket. As his breathing grew deep and even, she took her own blanket and moved to the side of the clearing. No sense in keeping watch out in the open where she could be easily seen, she thought. It was unlikely that Rikard or anyone else would come looking for them. It was unlikely that he was even aware of their presence. But it never hurt to take precautions and both she and Thorn knew it. She found a fallen tree among the tall ferns and settled down with her back to it, seated on her folded blanket.

Gradually, the sounds of the forest became more apparent to her. The click of crickets and the thrum of frogs, along with the occasional airy swish of a night-flying bird's wings.

Ten minutes passed before she heard a voice from the blanket-wrapped figure on the tarpaulin.

"Delicate female, my backside!"

They changed places four times through the night. Thorn was on watch when the birds in the forest began to give voice to the fact that dawn was imminent. He watched the sleeping girl, curious to know if that unmistakable portent of the coming day would penetrate her consciousness. Knowing what he now knew of her, and her field craft and stalking skills, he was willing to bet that it would. And he wasn't disappointed. After a few seconds of the tentative birdsong, Lydia stirred and sat up. Her eyes darted round the clearing and came to rest on Thorn's shadowy figure, sitting by the fallen tree.

"It's nearly dawn," she said and, when he nodded silently, continued in an accusing tone. "Then you've been on watch for over three hours. You should have woken me."

He shrugged. "No sense in it. I wasn't sleepy and I thought you could use the extra rest. After all, you are a delicate female."

As soon as the light was stronger, they were on the move again. Rikard had settled on a due east direction now and they could follow him more easily. The smell of wood smoke, which they had noticed the previous evening, was still strong in the air. Although now it was more the smell of dead ashes and embers.

"I wouldn't be surprised if we come up with him soon," Lydia said, keeping her voice low.

"You think he's a late sleeper?" Thorn asked, in a similar muted tone.

She nodded. "He wasn't the fittest specimen I've ever seen. He's overweight and in poor condition. He traveled pretty hard yesterday. And those sea boots of his are heavy and clumsy—a poor choice for hiking through the forest."

"Sailors don't go in for hiking," Thorn replied. "And he was first mate on his ship, so he'd do little of the hard work."

"What do first mates do?" she asked.

"They watch other people do the hard work," Thorn replied, and she turned to look at him, the barest trace of a smile on her lips.

"Sounds like your job description," she said.

He raised his eyebrows haughtily. "I can do any of the tasks aboard ship," he told her with dignity. "I can row. I can tend sails. I can steer. I simply choose not to."

"I'd noticed," she said, and now the smile widened. But he didn't reply immediately. When he did, he pointed ahead of them, down the track.

"Well, well, who do we have here?" he said.

She looked around quickly, and immediately made out the huddled form in a small glade off the left side of the track. It was Rikard, still fast asleep, curled up beside the smoldering remains of a fire.

"Shall we awaken Griselda with the kiss of true love?" he asked.

She frowned, uncomprehending. "Who's Griselda?"

"She's the sleeping maiden in a very popular Skandian children's tale," he told her. "She needed the kiss of true love to awaken her." He gestured toward the snoring figure, inviting her to approach him. She grunted disdainfully.

"You go ahead and kiss him if you like," she said. "He's no true love of mine."

They had stopped at the sight of him. Now Lydia slid a dart from her quiver and clipped it to the atlatl as she moved stealthily forward. A part of her mind registered the fact that Thorn was keeping pace with her. But he made no sound.

He's good at this, she thought. I'm glad he's on my side.

In spite of their stealth, however, something alerted the sleeping Rikard. It may have been some sixth sense, some primal awareness of approaching danger, because Lydia was certain they had made no sound. Suddenly, he sat bolt upright, looked down the track and saw them, barely ten meters away.

Then, with a cry of terror, he leapt to his feet and ran.

Lydia's action was instinctive. Her right arm went back, the dart and atlatl already in position.

"Don't kill h—," Thorn began.

But her arm whipped forward and the long dart hissed away through the morning air. It flashed at knee level between Rikard's legs, tangling between them. The shaft snapped with a loud crack, but it had already done its work, throwing him off balance. He lurched and stumbled, then fell flat on his face. Before he could recover, Thorn was upon him. His wooden hook snagged the front of Rikard's leather vest. He hauled the pirate to his feet, then hit him with a thundering left, sending him crashing back to the ground once more.

This time, he stayed down.

Thorn looked at the two halves of the shattered atlatl dart. Then he shook his head in admiration at the tall, slim girl.

"That was outstanding! Absolutely outstanding!" he said. "Throwing it between his legs to trip him. That was the most amazing cast I've ever seen!"

She hesitated, tempted to accept his unstinting praise. But then honesty got the better of her and she dropped her eyes in embarrassment.

"Not so great," she said. "I actually missed. I was aiming to hit him in the left leg."

He looked at her in silence for some seconds, then asked slowly, "You were planning to put that great, sharp, iron warhead through his leg?"

She nodded, and he continued.

"And did you consider how we might get him back to the ship with a huge hole in his leg?"

She shrugged. "I thought you could carry him. After all, I've done all the work so far."

The sun had dropped below the level of the treetops in the west when Thorn, Lydia and Rikard emerged from the forest and onto the beach once more. Rikard was unshackled. Thorn had decided there was no need to tie him or restrict him in any way. Before they set out, he had taken the pirate to one side and spoken quietly to him.

"You saw how good the girl is with that dart thrower of hers," he said. "If you try to run, she'll skewer you. And this time, she won't aim for your legs. Understand?"

Rikard looked nervously at Lydia, licking his dry lips. He nodded several times. They made their way back through the forest, with Lydia in the lead, Rikard following her, and Thorn bringing up the rear.

As they left the shadows of the forest behind them, Lydia suddenly let out a glad cry and broke into a run. She had seen a large figure moving slowly toward the campfire.

"Ingvar!" she shouted, and as he turned to face her, she arrived in a rush and threw her arms around him, nearly knocking him over.

"You're all right!" she said.

He grinned at her. He had lost a lot of weight and there were dark circles of exhaustion under his eyes, but he was definitely in better shape than when she had last seen him.

"Edvin cured me," he said. "He made me drink some foul potion and next thing I was sweating like a pig, and then I was better."

She continued hugging him. She had developed a deep affection for the big, slow-speaking boy.

"I thought we were going to lose you," she said. "I am so glad to see you've recovered!"

Stig was watching with some interest. He noticed how Lydia kept her arms wrapped around Ingvar as she spoke. Suddenly, Stig threw up his hands with a loud cry and fell to the ground, moaning.

"Oh! Now I've caught the fever too!" he said. "I'm burning up! Absolutely burning up!" He rolled on the ground for a few seconds, then stopped and leapt to his feet. "Praise be! I'm cured!"

He held out his arms expectantly to Lydia, waiting for a hug in his turn. She raised a sardonic eyebrow at him.

"Get over yourself," she said, and he shrugged, grinning.

"Well, it was worth a try. I see you found our prisoner."

At the edge of the forest, Rikard watched keenly as Lydia's attention was distracted by the sight of Ingvar. He looked surreptitiously toward the trees behind him, then realized Thorn's attention was riveted on him. The old sea wolf smiled. It was not a pretty sight.

"Not a good idea," Thorn told him. "Just keep walking." He gestured toward the campsite and they made their way across the beach to where the crew were gathered around Lydia, eagerly plying her with questions about her pursuit of Rikard. She replied diffidently, not wanting to appear boastful. But as Thorn arrived, he took over the answering for her.

"She was amazing!" he said. "Simply amazing. She could tell exactly where Rikard had been. 'Look,' she'd say, 'that dirty patch of air is where he was breathing yesterday.' Or, 'Look at that, the imprint of his little toe on a piece of rock.' And once, she could even tell me what he'd eaten for lunch."

"How did she know that?" Wulf asked. Thorn had known it would be one of the twins who would take the bait. He smiled disingenuously.

"We found a pile of his droppings and she poked around in it. Told me what he'd had for lunch, his birthday and his mother's name."

The crew all looked at Lydia, then, unconsciously, withdrew half a pace from her. Her cheeks flamed scarlet with embarrassment and rage.

"I did NOT!" she shouted, glaring at Thorn.

He grinned innocently at her. "Well, maybe not his mother's name. I thought you were guessing there."

She stepped a pace closer to him. Her hand dropped to the atlatl attached to her belt.

"You keep this up and I'll put a dart through you, old man," she threatened.

His grin widened. "Aim for my legs. That way I know you'll miss."

She shook her head in defeat. It was impossible to have the last word with Thorn. He was incorrigible. She turned to the rest of the crew.

"I promise you I did not poke through a pile of Rikard's droppings," she said. One or two of them still looked doubtful, so she shouted, "I DIDN'T!" That seemed to convince them. But Wulf still had a puzzled look on his face. She looked at him, challenging him to speak.

"Could you *really* see where he had been breathing?" he asked. She sighed, then decided the best course was to go along with it.

"Yes," she said, and turned away for the main tent. Hal fell into step with her.

"Good work," he said, dropping a hand on her shoulder. "And welcome back."

"Thanks." She allowed him a brief smile, then it faded. "How do you put up with Thorn?" she asked. "He can be so annoying! But then, he's so incredible! Rikard made a run for it and I brought him down with a dart. But he'd barely hit the ground when Thorn was on him. He picked him up off the ground, then knocked him cold with one punch. I've never seen anyone move so fast!"

Hal nodded. "He can be pretty surprising, all right."

She shook her head in frustration. "But then he can be so annoying! I swear to you, I did *not* poke through Rikard's droppings. Why does he say things like that?"

"Because he likes you." Hal smiled. "He admires you. So he teases you. Haven't you heard how he talks to me?"

She hadn't thought of that. Now that she did, she said doubtfully, "I suppose so. Still . . ." She threw her hands in the air, dismissing the subject. "Tell me, what did Edvin do to cure Ingvar?"

Briefly, he told her about the willow bark and how Edvin had administered it to Ingvar.

"So which one did the trick?" she asked when he'd finished. "The poultice or the tea?"

He frowned. "I'm not sure. We all assumed it was the tea. But maybe the poultice took a while to have an effect. Or maybe it was the combination of both. Whatever it was, he's better."

"He's still very weak," she said, and he agreed with her.

"I'm giving him another night's rest on dry land," he said. "We'll put to sea tomorrow morning."

The mouth of the Dan River yawned before them. It was at least one-and-a-half kilometers wide where it emptied into the Stormwhite. The tide was running out and the river brought a steady supply of detritus from the land with it—logs, tree branches, leaves, even the occasional dead animal—and a layer of brown mud scoured from the banks and mudflats farther upriver. The brown water stained the surface of the Stormwhite for several hundred meters before it dissipated and blended in with the seawater.

The land on either side of the river was low-lying and thickly forested. There was a steady breeze blowing from the sea that would drive *Heron* upriver at a good pace. As the ship rocked gently on the water, Hal climbed onto the bulwark by the steering position, steadying himself with one hand on the backstay. He shaded his eyes with the other hand and peered at the surface of the river, looking for telltale swirls and eddies that might indicate sandbanks, shoals or rocks. But the broad surface appeared calm and unruffled.

Thorn stood on the deck below him. "It's a major trade route," he said. "It's cleared regularly so that it's navigable for hundreds of miles through the continent."

"So the navigation notes tell me," Hal replied. "But it never hurts to be sure." He dropped lightly to the deck and rubbed his hands in anticipation. "Well, let's go up the river and see what we can find."

He took the tiller and called to the twins to sheet home the sail. As he swung the ship into the river, he brought the wind over their port quarter. Ulf and Wulf let the sail out accordingly, then adjusted it so that it formed a smooth, bellying curve. The *Heron* began to knife through the small ripples, throwing up a bow wave against the force of the out-flowing tide. Hal glanced at the shoreline to gauge their progress and nodded to himself. They were making good headway.

"Be quicker when it turns," Thorn said.

"We're doing all right as we are."

They sailed on, the river bubbling and chuckling against the hull as they moved farther and farther from the sea. It was a strange, almost eerie feeling to see the green, low-lying banks on either side, instead of the empty, wave-tossed sea stretching out to the horizon. They were headed toward the western bank, and after fifteen minutes or so, Hal decided they were close enough to it. He uttered a warning to the twins and swung the bow to port. They hauled in on the sail until the ship was sailing on a reach, angling across the broad river, the wind now well on their beam. The river surface was much calmer than the Stormwhite's. The ship still rolled, but it was a gentle, pleasant motion, and there was none of the violent pitching they had experienced on the open sea.

The crew, with little to do, sat back on the rowing benches and relaxed. Ulf and Wulf made occasional small corrections to the trim of the sail as the wind veered slightly.

As they neared the end of that long reach to port, they saw the first bend in the river approaching to starboard. There was an air of expectation on the ship as they waited to see what was around the next bend.

That was the difference, Hal thought, between sailing on a river, even a massive one like this, and on the open sea. Every bend in the river brought the prospect of something new and exciting—even dangerous.

"Stand by to wear ship," he called. Here on the river he didn't need to bellow his orders. The crew moved to their stations. Stefan and Jesper manned the halyards, ready to run the new sail up while the other came down. Hal kept his eyes on the headland to starboard. He nudged the tiller, beginning a turn to port, then called the order.

"Wear ship. Up starboard sail."

The bow swung as the port sail came down, flapping loudly, and the starboard sail rose in its place. Ulf and Wulf shifted from one side to the other and trimmed the new sail to the wind. The *Heron* slipped round the bend, and the new stretch of river opened before their expectant eyes.

More trees. More low-lying banks. Nothing out of the ordinary. The tension, the expectation of something new and different, went out of the crew like air escaping a punctured ball. Hal felt his hands relax on the tiller as he studied the long, empty stretch of river that lay before them. In the waist of the ship, Ingvar was resting on the special bed Hal had made for him. Hal had constructed two stout X-shaped frames, and Ingvar's stretcher was suspended on ropes from them. As the ship rolled, the bed swung gently and remained level.

Not that the *Heron* was rolling too much on the river, Hal thought. Although he realized that in a strong wind or a storm, this placid stretch of water could be whipped up into short, dangerous waves. Edvin sat close by the bed, looking studiously down at something in his hands. Hal peered more closely. The healer was knitting again.

"Picture of a bloodthirsty raider, isn't he?" Stig said. He had gone forward in case he was needed when the ship turned. Now he had returned to his normal position, close by the steering platform. Hal grinned.

"It's a new age, Stig," he said. "And Edvin is the new age sea wolf. Perhaps you could get him to knit you a nice battleax cover."

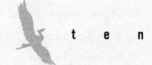

The *Heron* continued to glide down the wide river on a smooth zigzag course, changing tack every ten minutes or so to angle back and forth between the two banks. The water was calm and the wind was moderate, so there was little to occupy the crew, other than the occasional sail raising or lowering. They lolled back on the rowing benches, enjoying the warm sunshine. Some of them even dozed off.

Thorn regarded them with a scowl on his face. He made his way back to the steering platform, where Stig was coaching Edvin in steering technique. Not that there was much to teach on this placid river. Hal was hunkered down in the very stern, his back against the stern post, watching them. He glanced up as Thorn approached, smiling at the frown on his old friend's face.

"You look happy," he said.

Thorn snorted angrily. "This is getting too much like a boat trip with my old aunt Hortense," he said disgustedly.

Hal thought to himself that Thorn had been spending too much time around Svengal. The skirl of *Wolfwind* was always inventing imaginary aunts to illustrate his point. He looked along the length of the little ship, taking in the recumbent figures sprawled on the benches or on the deck, noticing how the shadow of the mast and sail moved across the deck and back again, in time to the gentle rolling motion.

"It is rather pleasant, isn't it?" he agreed.

Thorn's scowl grew fiercer. "It's too pleasant! They need work and they need discipline. They're getting soft again. Edvin is actually knitting, for Gorlog's sake!"

Hal stood up, studying the crew in more detail. Thorn was right, he thought. One of the problems with a long voyage like this was that the crew had too much time to relax. Before the attack on Limmat, Thorn had drilled them until they were hardened and ready for battle. Now, if the *Raven* suddenly appeared round the next bend, his wisest course would be to turn tail and run. He chewed his lip thoughtfully.

"What do you suggest?"

Thorn jerked a thumb at the eastern shore. They were currently on a port tack and angling toward the low, wooded bank.

"Put ashore an hour early. They need some drilling and some hard work. I need to whip them back into shape—both physically and mentally. They have to be ready for a battle at any time. At the moment, they're not."

Hal nodded. At the end of each day's sailing, they would put ashore and camp on the riverbank. It was more comfortable than sleeping on board, and Edvin could have a proper cook fire to prepare hot meals and drinks for them. He scanned the eastern bank, looking for a good campsite. Half a kilometer ahead of them, he could see a spot where the bank ran down to the water's edge in a grassy slope. There was a section of open ground between the ever-present trees. He indicated the location to Thorn.

"How's that?"

The old sea wolf shaded his eyes, studied the spot and nodded. "Looks perfect."

The crew were a little surprised when Hal gave the order to put ashore. They were expecting to continue upriver for at least another hour. The sun hadn't sunk to the level of the treetops on the western bank, which was usually the signal for them to put ashore.

As usual, Hal judged the beaching perfectly. The sail came sliding down with a rush of canvas and rope, and Stefan and Jesper gathered it into tidy bundles as the bow ran gently onto the sand and grass of the shore with a soft, grinding sound, the upward curve of the keel and bow post letting it ride up onto the land for several meters.

There was the usual clatter and rattle of gear being stowed. Hal tied off the tiller and gestured for Stefan to take the beach anchor ashore and moor the ship securely. The others looked at him curiously.

"Get the camp ready," he said.

Within ten minutes, the big sleeping tent had been pitched,

with a screened-off area to provide Lydia with some privacy. A fireplace had been prepared and a supply of firewood gathered from the deadfalls that littered the forest floor. Edvin's cooking supplies had been stacked neatly by the fireplace. Rikard, bound now by the chain padlocked around his waist, was unshackled from the mast and secured to a tree once more.

Jesper had found a freshwater spring, where he filled two buckets. He placed them down beside the fireplace and looked around curiously. There was still plenty of daylight and he wondered why they had stopped so early.

"What now?" he asked, of no one in particular. His heart sank when it was Thorn who answered.

"Now," he said, savoring the words, "you're mine. All mine."

Several of the others felt that same sinking feeling as they realized that he had his old hickory baton in his hand. They wondered where that had come from. They hadn't seen it since their time at Shelter Bay. He swished it idly through the air, then drew a line on the ground in front of him.

"All right. One line. Along here. MOVE IT!"

They jostled one another as they hurried to form up, galvanized by the last two words, delivered in Thorn's best drill master bellow. Ingvar limped into place at the end of the line but Thorn shook his head.

"Not you, Ingvar. Not yet," he said gently.

Ingvar peered at him, leaning slightly forward to see the shabby figure more clearly.

"I'm fine, Thorn," he said. "I can handle it."

Thorn stepped closer to him. "Let me see that wound," he said, and Ingvar hitched his shirt up, exposing the arrow wound in his side. Thorn gestured with the baton for him to turn round.

"And the other side," he said. He studied the entry and exit wounds. The flesh around them was still reddened and the lips of the wounds hadn't closed properly yet. Nor had they scabbed over completely. There was a hint of moist flesh visible in each.

"You're not ready," Thorn told him. "You could tear those wounds open again. And I doubt you've got your full strength back. You're skin and bone."

Ingvar shook his head stubbornly. "I don't want people thinking I'm a shirker."

Thorn couldn't help smiling at him. "You? A shirker? Never. But don't try to overdo things. You can start laying a fire for Edvin if you want to do something."

Reluctantly, Ingvar moved out of the line and limped toward the fireplace. Jesper watched him go, then held up a hand.

"Thorn? I don't feel I've got my full strength back either."

Thorn smiled at him. It was a terrible sight. "Then what you need is exercise, my boy. Lots of it. That'll build you up. Now let's see how high you can jump. All of you!"

It was an old and familiar routine. They leapt high in the air, clapping their hands over their head as they did so. Thorn moved behind them, pacing down the line, the hickory baton swishing threateningly. The urge to look for him was irresistible.

"Don't turn around!" he warned them. "Pretend I'm not here."

Then, as they faced the front again, the hickory baton would *crack* against an offender's backside, sending him leaping a little higher, usually with a shrill squeal of pain and anger.

"Good jump, Jesper!" Thorn said happily as the baton encouraged Jesper to a leap that was much higher than normal. "Looks like your strength is just *flooding* back!"

He kept them at it for half an hour, varying the exercise between jumping and clapping, then running short wind sprints, then crouching on their haunches and walking like ducks. He even had them make quacking noises, which brought a cheerful smile to his face. He glanced up and saw Lydia watching them, also smiling at the incongruous sight of a line of boys waddling, backsides low to the ground, and quacking like ducks. He gestured to her with the baton.

"Care to join us, Duchess? Show these clumsy boys how it's done?" he invited.

But she shook her head. "I'm fine as I am, thanks."

He grinned at her. He hadn't expected her to fall for his challenge, but it was worth a try.

At the end of the half hour, he called a break, then sent Stefan and Edvin to the ship to bring the wooden practice weapons. He paired the boys off and set them to practice combats, one on one. Lydia watched with greater interest as he moved among them, adjusting a shield angle here, demonstrating a more efficient cut or stroke there.

"Remember," he called. "Don't overswing. Balance is important. Stay in balance or I'll have you all up on the rolling poles again!"

Lydia was impressed by the way he could sense a fault in a boy's action with sword or battleax, and correct it, demonstrating the correct technique, having the student repeat it over and over until he had perfected it. She could never pick the initial fault, but once the corrected method had been explained and demonstrated, she could see the improved smoothness, power and balance in each stroke.

She shook her head in admiration. Where did he learn all this stuff? she thought.

She repeated the question to Hal and Stig that evening, as they sat around the campfire after dinner. Thorn had moved a little away from the main camp, as was his practice. The other boys were chatting or, in Edvin's case, knitting. Stig looked to check that Thorn was out of earshot. He knew the old sea wolf didn't like people talking about his past. But Lydia was part of the crew now, he thought.

"In Skandia, we have an annual competition to determine who's the Maktig for the year," he began.

Lydia frowned at the word. Usually, they spoke the common tongue, but Maktig was obviously a Skandian word.

"Maktig?" she repeated. "What's that?"

"It means the Mighty One," Hal put in. "The champion warrior of the entire country. Young men come to Hallasholm from all over for it. They have to compete in wrestling, running, survival contests and mock battles, where they have to show expertise with all weapons—spear, ax and sword. It's a knockout competition."

"Sometimes literally," Stig said, grinning. Hal looked at him and nodded, grinning as well.

"So I take it that Thorn won this . . . Maktig . . . contest when he was younger?" she said.

"It was before our time," Hal said. "He would have been in his twenties, I guess. He competed against both our fathers."

"And beat them both," Stig added. Lydia formed her lips into a small moue of appreciation.

"Well, that's pretty impressive," she said. "That explains a lot."

"It's more than that," Stig told her. There was a distinct note of pride in his voice. He paused for dramatic effect, then went on, "He won it three years in a row."

Lydia's eyebrows went up at that. "I take it that was not exactly normal?"

"Nobody else has ever won it more than once. Before or since," Hal said quietly. "If Thorn hadn't lost that hand in an accident on board ship, he would have been the greatest warrior in the history of Skandia."

Stig looked at him. "He is the greatest warrior in the history of Skandia," he said firmly. "Hand or no hand."

Hal paused, looking off to the dark figure some ten meters away, looking out at the river and the stars.

"You know," he said, "you may just be right."

The weather changed during the night.

The wind veered from the north into the east, bringing with it low-lying clouds and a persistent rain, which it drove before it until it was almost horizontal. The surface of the river, so blue and placid the day before, was now sullen and gray, with uncomfortable-looking choppy waves whipped up by the wind.

The crew stood in the shelter of the sleeping tent as they ate their breakfast. Accustomed to sudden weather changes, Edvin had kept a supply of firewood dry. He and Stig had used the small tent to shelter the cook fire and he had managed to put together a hot meal for them—bacon and toasted flat bread. There had been some boiled potatoes left over from the previous evening and he had fried these. Ingvar wolfed down his helping, then went back for more.

Lydia smiled at him. "I'd say you've recovered. Your appetite certainly has."

He peered at her, smiling diffidently. "I've got a lot of missed meals to make up."

It was amazing what a couple of days of rest and good food had done for him, Lydia thought. His face had lost the gaunt, sunken look that had marked it and the dark shadows under his eyes were gone. He had more energy as well, moving a lot more confidently than he had previously. The only thing holding him back was the wound in his side. It was still tender and he was careful to avoid putting any undue strain on it.

Hal, Thorn and Stig stood a little away from the others, sheltering under a tree.

"Going to be a cold, wet day," Thorn said.

Hal smiled. "Just like home." He crammed the last of his bread and bacon into his mouth, washed it down with a gulp of the mint tea Edvin had brewed and made a face. It was hot and warming, but he didn't like the taste.

Stig noticed the expression. "We need to get some more coffee," he said. They had exhausted their small supply some days previously.

"Might be lucky to find it in these parts. It's not a popular drink here. Still, we're lucky to have a hot drink at all," Thorn told him. He glanced around, tossing the dregs of his tea onto the ground.

Hal took the hint. "Time to get going," he said. He called to the crew to break camp and load the ship.

Heron lurched and bumped uncomfortably in the short, steep waves whipped up by the wind. The crew huddled miserably against the thin, driving rain. The *Heron*'s decks were open, without any shelter from the weather. They had donned sheepskins and leather jackets, but none of them had adequate headgear and the rain had their hair hanging in wet strings down their faces. Most of them knew that in cold weather, the greater part of the body's heat was lost through the head. But, being boys, they had taken no heed of the fact and had not bothered to provide themselves with any form of headwear. Of course, while they had nothing to do, they could drape pieces of toweling or canvas over their heads. But when they were raising the sails or trimming them or attending to other tasks about the ship, the canvas and towels would tend to slip off or blow free, and their head and hair would be saturated.

All except Edvin, who sat smiling quietly, with his splendid new watch cap firmly in place on his head. Normally, he wore it rolled up, so that it came down only as far as his eyebrows and the tops of his ears. But now he rolled the sides and back down so that his ears and neck were sheltered. The wool still retained its natural greasiness, so that the thin rain beaded on it, then rolled off without soaking in. He tucked a towel around his neck to stop the water from running down inside his collar and sat contentedly beside Ingvar. The big boy was covered by a length of tarpaulin, with two sticks arranged to hold it free of his face.

Jesper eyed the healer enviously, his eyes fixed on the thick woolen cap.

"That looks really warm," Jesper said to Edvin, moving to sit beside him. Edvin looked up at his crewmate and smiled.

"It is," he said. There was perhaps a hint of smugness in his voice. He had taken a lot of teasing and implied insults over the fact that he knew how to knit. The phrase *it's kind of a girly thing* rang in his memory.

Jesper put out a tentative hand. "I wonder . . . could I try it?" he asked.

Edvin considered the request, then shook his head. "Your hair's soaking. You'd get it all wet. And it's lovely and warm as it is."

Jesper nodded. He was conscious of the fact that the others in the crew were watching, and listening to the conversation.

"I guess so." He paused. "I don't suppose you'd knit one for me?"

Edvin cocked his head to one side, considering. "You don't think that might be a bit . . . *girly*?"

Jesper hurriedly shook his head. "'Girly'? What's girly about knitting?" Then, sensing a hostile glance from Lydia, he hurriedly amended that statement. "And what's wrong with being girly in any case? I'll pay for the wool," he offered.

Edvin smiled at him, a calculating smile. "You'll pay for more than the wool," he said. "You'll pay for my time."

"Well, of course I will," Jesper said, although he was less than delighted with the idea. He had assumed that Edvin would be only too pleased to show the true value of his skill. However, the sight of that warm, thick cap was irresistible.

"Would you knit me one too?" Wulf called out, a fraction of a second before Ulf said:

"I want one too."

They glared at each other.

"I'll pay you," Wulf said quickly.

Ulf glared at his brother. "I'll pay you more."

And now Stefan realized he was being left out of this cap-buying frenzy. "I want one too," he said.

Edvin was thoroughly enjoying himself now. He smiled at his shipmates as they began to bid noisily for his services, each one offering more than the other. Not that their offers meant a great deal, he realized, since none of them had any money in the first place.

"So how will we decide who gets the first one?" he asked.

Stig's voice cut across the squabbling boys, silencing them.

"We'll do it by rank," he said. "I'm first mate, so I'll get it."

The others fell silent. They looked decidedly unhappy about that. But as well as outranking them all, Stig was bigger and stronger than any of them. Once the question of rank came up, however, Edvin looked to Hal, who outranked all of them.

"What about you, Hal? Do you want one?"

Hal, alone among the boys, had a hat—a battered old shapeless felt hat with a narrow brim. Thorn, of course, knew the value of warm headgear and had a raggedy old fur cap. And Lydia, being a girl and far more sensible than the boys, had a leather hood that she had donned and tied under her chin. But the idea of having a uniform style of headwear for the crew appealed to Hal. The watch caps would, in some small way, compensate for the fact that they had lost the horned helmets that had been presented to them when they won the brotherband competition. The caps would help give them a sense of belonging, and bind them together a little more.

"I think we all should have one—including Lydia," he said. "I'll pay you out of the ship's funds."

There was a chorus of agreement from the crew. Hal could tell that they liked the idea of having these smart watch caps. Edvin was taken aback for a few seconds. Then a slow smile spread across his features. In a matter of a few minutes, his knitting had gone from being a strange aberration, worthy of faint ridicule, to an essential skill that would serve the crew of the *Heron*. In addition, he would make some considerable money out of the venture. Whereas the other boys were talking pie in the sky when they offered to pay him, Hal had at his disposal a considerable amount of money, provided originally by Thorn, to buy items for the ship.

"I'll need more wool," he said.

"Shouldn't be a problem," Hal replied. "We should reach a river port soon. You can buy it there while we ask about the *Raven*."

"Who gets the first cap?" Jesper asked. "After all, it was my idea."

Hal considered the statement. "That's true," he said. "But I'm the skirl, so the first one goes to me. Next to Stig. After that, we'll draw lots to decide."

He smiled at the crestfallen look on Jesper's face. Democratic procedures were all very well, he thought. But sometimes, rank should have its privileges.

L ate that afternoon, *Heron* slipped quietly into the river port of Krall, on the western bank of the river.

Krall was a small town. Its residents earned their living from the traffic that plied its way up and down the river. There were stalls selling ship's stores—canvas, timber, iron work for deck fittings and so forth. On the outskirts of the town was a rope manufactory, where ropes of all sizes were braided, from thin painters to tie a skiff to a wharf to heavy, tarred ropes that would serve as the standing rigging on a ship.

In the center of the town was a food market that operated every second day. Along the riverfront was the usual selection of eating houses and taverns to cater for the various appetites of the crews who stayed overnight. Some were large, well lit and cheerful. Others were smaller, dingy and less reputable. Usually these were in alleys set back from the broad avenue that ran along the riverfront.

All in all, it was the standard mix of businesses that would be found in most ports, anywhere in the world.

The port itself was formed by a deep, U-shaped bite taken out of the riverbank, which formed a natural shelter. The water was deep right to the edge of the land and several large ships were moored alongside the bank, which had been reinforced with stonework. Other vessels, usually smaller and in varying states of disrepair, were moored to long, rickety timber jetties that ran out like fingers into the river.

As ever, Hal had lowered their distinctive yardarm and sail and brought the *Heron* into the port under oars. The Mangler was covered by a heavy tarpaulin. Thorn stood beside him as they made their way toward the shore. The sea wolf was casting his gaze around the harbor. After a minute or two, he saw what he was looking for and pointed.

"Over there."

He was pointing to a short jetty jutting out into the river, surmounted by a small, flat-roofed timber building on its very end. A gold circle with two diagonal black lines through it was painted on a board above the building's doorway—the universal sign for money.

"That's the toll wharf," Thorn said. "Take us alongside."

Hal slid the little ship alongside the wharf. The river was at half tide and the timber surface was a meter above their deck. Stig balanced on the gunwale, then jumped nimbly up onto the jetty, taking the mooring lines that Stefan and Jesper tossed up to him and making them fast around the timber bollards. Ulf and Wulf tossed wickerwork fenders on short lengths of rope over the side, then the others hauled the ship in close, the fenders squeaking under the pressure.

Thorn checked that he had his purse attached to his belt, and that there was a sufficient weight of coins inside it. Then he nodded to Hal.

"Come on."

They stepped up from the railing onto the wharf and made their way to the toll office.

In addition to the money spent by passing ships in the taverns, eating houses and chandleries, riverside ports like Krall derived a considerable income from tolls—charges levied on the ships that moored here for a day or two, in search of relaxation and diversion. The money went to the town council and was used, in theory, to maintain the port facilities. In practice, most of it found its way into the purses of the councilmen themselves.

Hefty taxes were also levied on those businesses that had their premises on the prime real estate of the waterfront avenue.

Thorn paused to look and see if there was a table of rates posted. Sometimes, they were assessed according to the ship's length. Here there was nothing. He grunted and turned to Hal.

"That means they'll charge us whatever they think we can afford," he said. "And then a bit more. And you thought Zavac was a pirate."

He pushed open the door and they entered. Inside, there was one large room with windows overlooking the river. A wooden counter ran across the middle, separating new arrivals from the officials seated at desks on the other side. There were currently three of these in place, with another two desks unoccupied. One of the toll collectors glanced up, then rose to walk forward to the counter. The others paid them no attention at all.

The official was a solidly built man, a little under average height and with an obvious liking for the pleasures of the table. His waist was circled by a heavy leather belt with a set of keys dangling from it. The dull scarlet jerkin he wore bulged out over the belt, all but concealing it at the front. He was clean shaven but his jowls were heavy and he had a double chin. He was sweating lightly. "What can I do for you?" he asked.

Thorn reflected that the question was an unnecessary one. There was only one reason why two strangers would enter the toll office. But he answered politely enough.

"Looking for a mooring overnight," he said. They had long ago agreed that when in port, Thorn would act as the ship's captain. A skipper as fresh faced and young as Hal could only excite interest, and they didn't wish to draw undue attention to themselves.

The toll collector heaved a sigh, as if they were interrupting his day for no good reason.

"All right, let's take a look," he said, and led the way out onto the dock. The crew glanced up at the sound of his footsteps on the planks as he paced the length of the ship, hands on his hips. His lips moved silently, no doubt making mental calculations.

The toll collector studied the crew, then looked at Thorn.

"Bit young, aren't they?"

Behind the man's back, Stig scowled at him. Hal made a small hand gesture for Stig to calm down. It would do them no good to alienate the toll collector, particularly before he'd assessed how much they were to pay.

Thorn met the man's eyes for several seconds, holding his gaze and saying nothing until the toll collector shifted uncomfortably, aware that his words might have been provocative. Finally, Thorn answered.

"They're young. So they work cheap. Is that any problem of yours?"

"No! No!" The man made a fluttering gesture with his hand. There was something unsettling about Thorn's unwavering stare. He glanced to where Rikard was huddled by the mast. The chain around his waist was obvious.

"Who's that?" he said, frowning.

"He tried to desert. And he backchatted me. I'm teaching him a lesson," Thorn said.

The man shrugged. It sounded reasonable. Then he came to a decision.

"You're staying overnight? That'll be fifteen korona."

The korona was the Magyaran unit of currency. Presumably that meant they saw a lot of Magyaran ships passing through here. But Thorn was shaking his head.

"I don't have that. I'll give you seven," he said bluntly. He tapped the purse at his belt and it made a muted jingling sound.

"Twelve," the man replied without hesitation.

"Nine," Thorn said, "and I'm paying in Limmatan nobles."

The Limmatan noble was worth slightly more than the korona. The toll keeper considered, then nodded agreement. They shook hands and Thorn transferred the money to him.

"You can tie up at mooring number eight, on the second jetty across," the toll collector said, pointing to an unoccupied mooring. The moorings were all numbered, with the numbers painted on warped and cracked boards in fading letters. So much for the up-keep of port facilities, Thorn thought.

"There's one other thing," Thorn said, and the toll collector turned back to face him, his thumbs hooked in his belt. "We're looking for a black ship called the *Raven.* Has she passed through here in the last few—"

Before he could finish, the toll collector was shaking his head.

"No! Stop right there! I don't get involved in that sort of thing. I'm not an information bureau. I don't say who's been or who's coming. It's none of my business and I don't intend to make it so."

"I could make it worth your while . . . ," Thorn suggested. But all he got in return was a hard look.

"You don't know what's worth my while," the man said. "Your mooring rental is good until noon tomorrow. If you're still here then, you'll pay for another full day. Don't make trouble in town." He glanced at Rikard once more, then turned on his heel and stamped back into the office, slamming the door behind him.

"Friendly type," Hal remarked.

Thorn shrugged. "I'd guess a great deal of his business comes from Magyaran ships passing through. He's not going to spill the beans on them. Let's shift to that mooring."

"Yep. Saw that black ship not six days ago," the one-legged man told them. "Passed through here, stayed a couple of nights, then went south."

Hal, Stig and Thorn exchanged a quick glance. The one-legged sailor noticed it and leaned forward. "Reckon that might be worth another drink, eh?" he suggested.

Thorn nodded. "That could be the case. If you could tell us the name of the ship."

They were in one of the dingier taverns in a narrow alley set back from the main thoroughfare that fronted the river. The one-legged man had attached himself to their small group, fascinated by the sight of Thorn's beautifully crafted hook. His own prosthetic was a crudely carved peg leg.

"She was the *Raven*. And her skipper's name was . . ." He paused, frowning. "Z . . . something. Zara? Zamat? No . . ." He turned and called across the crowded, noisy room to another old sailor who was seated alone at a small table, blearily regarding the contents of his tankard.

"Morgan! What was the name of that fellow from the black ship? Zara, or Zaba or something, wasn't it?"

"Keep your voice down!" Thorn told him. It didn't do to have their business shouted out across a tavern, he thought. But it was too late. He glanced around the room. A couple of drinkers had turned to look at them as the one-legged man shouted to his friend. Thorn noticed a swarthy, stockily built man at the bar who was watching them. As Thorn looked his way, he casually turned back to the bar.

Morgan looked up from his ale and frowned, trying to collect his thoughts.

"Zavac," he called thickly, and the one-legged man pounded the table in triumph.

"That's it! Zavac! Nasty piece of work he was too. Now, how about that drink?"

Thorn scattered several coins on the table in front of the man.

"Here. And get one for your friend. You've earned it."

Pegleg looked at the coins with delight. There was more money on the table than he could scrape together in a week. He gathered the coins in, then looked hopefully at Thorn's hand again.

"So where did you say you got that fancy arm piece? Somewhere round here, maybe?"

Thorn shook his head. "Up north," he said. "In Skandia."

"Hmmm. Pity." He paused, looking down at the coins on the table in front of him. He tried to count them, but they were blurring and shifting. "Nothing else you need to know, is there? I see most of the ships that come through."

"No. That's all we wanted to know," Thorn told him. He couldn't believe their luck. This was the first tavern they had entered and Pegleg was the first local they had asked about the *Raven*. And they hadn't even had to seek him out—he'd come to them. Thorn could sense the barely contained excitement in his two young companions.

"Let's get back to the ship," he said, and they rose. He glanced once more at Pegleg. "Thanks for your help."

The old sailor waved a hand in the air. "Anytime. Anytime at all. And give my love to Zabar."

As they left the tavern, Thorn glanced quickly at the swarthy drinker seated at the bar. But the man seemed to be paying no attention to them. The other drinkers who had turned to look when

Pegleg had shouted across the bar also seemed to have lost interest in them. Satisfied, Thorn followed his companions.

The man at the bar was slumped to one side so he could watch the Skandians without seeming to. He waited until the door had closed behind them, then slipped from his stool and hurried across the room after them.

As he went past Pegleg, he contrived to jostle him heavily, knocking him from his own stool. He bent to help the other man back up. As he did so, he leaned close to him and whispered, "You've got a big mouth, friend. You should keep it shut."

Nobody noticed the thin stiletto that he slid into the old man's side. Pegleg's gasp of pain was lost in the tavern's babble of shouting, drunken voices. Pegleg slumped forward over the table. The swarthy man patted him cheerfully on the back.

"Best sleep it off, old man. You'll feel better in the morning."

Then he hurried out of the tavern. The three Skandians were still in sight at the end of the alley, heading toward the riverfront. Staying in the shadows, he went after them.

There was a watchman patrolling at the foot of the jetty where *Heron* was moored. He wore a mail shirt and a shaped, hard leather helmet and carried a spear. A short sword hung from his belt. He nodded a greeting as Thorn, Hal and Stig hurried back to the ship.

The rickety jetty vibrated under their urgent footsteps. They jumped down onto the deck of the *Heron*. The others, sensing their urgency, gathered around them.

"Have they been here?" Stefan asked.

Thorn nodded. "They're a couple of days ahead of us." He looked at Jesper. "Did you get all the supplies we needed?" While Stig, Thorn and Hal had sought information in the taverns and eating houses, Jesper and Edvin had visited the market to restock their basic supplies.

"Most of it. Couldn't get coffee, unfortunately."

Thorn grunted. "Can't be helped."

He made his way forward to where Rikard crouched, watching them. He reached into his purse and searched for a key. Then he bent and unlocked the padlock fastening the chain around Rikard's waist. He unlocked the loop that went around the mast, coiled the chain and dropped it into the lowered section of the hull where the rowing benches were situated. Rikard regarded him with suspicion.

"What are you doing?" he said, not sure whether he should move or not. He'd witnessed Thorn's lightning-fast movement before and decided discretion was called for. Thorn made a shooing motion with his hand, as if Rikard were some kind of annoying insect.

"You're free. You told the truth, so go."

Rikard frowned, not sure what was going on.

"Go? Go where?" he asked. "It's the middle of the night. Where am I supposed to go?"

"Anywhere you like. That was the deal. You tell us where Zavac is headed and I'll set you free. Well, we know where he's headed, so I'm keeping my part of the bargain. Go." He repeated the shooing gesture.

"But . . . it's the middle of the night," Rikard said once more.

Thorn shook his head impatiently. "You already said that. In fact, it's relatively early for a place like this. The taverns will be open for hours yet and frankly, I want you off this ship as soon as possible."

The assembled crew gave a low murmur of assent. It wasn't a

friendly sound. Rikard realized he might be lucky to be leaving with a whole skin. But still he hesitated.

"How will I get to Pragha?" he asked. "I haven't got a penny on me."

"I suppose you could work your way," Thorn said. "But I know that would go against your nature." Reluctantly, he reached into his purse and counted out three Limmatan coins, and some smaller change he'd received in the tavern. He handed it to Rikard, who looked aggrieved.

"That's not much," he complained.

Thorn stepped closer to him. When he spoke, his voice was low but full of menace.

"It's a darn sight better than hanging," Thorn said. "Don't forget. That was your alternative. Of course, if you like, we could always carry out that sentence here and now."

Rikard looked at the coins, then at Thorn. He came a decision, putting the coins in his pocket and half running to the railing. He'd come aboard with nothing, and that was how he was leaving now. He leapt up onto the jetty, clearing the ship's rail, and hurried away without a backward glance, as if fearing Thorn might change his mind.

"Don't forget to write," Jesper called, waving a mocking hand. Several of the others laughed, then Hal called them to order.

"Right!" he said crisply. "Let's get cracking! Zavac's got several days' lead on us and I want to catch him before he makes it to Raguza."

The crew ran to their stations and began to ready their equipment. Attracted by the noise, the watchman made his way up the jetty and called to Hal.

"You there! On the ship! What are you up to?"

"We're getting under way," Hal told him. But the watchman shook his head before he had finished the statement.

"Not now, you're not. No arrivals or departures between sunset and dawn."

"Don't be absurd!" Hal replied, with some heat. "There's no reason why we shouldn't go now." But the watchman was adamant.

"There's every reason," he said. "Council likes to know that people don't leave in a hurry because they've done things they might be ashamed of. So, no night departures, understand?"

Hal sighed with exasperation. He looked up at the figure on the jetty, silhouetted against the night sky.

"D'you think you could stop us if we really decided to go?" he asked.

The watchman jerked his thumb at something over Hal's shoulder. "I mightn't. But they certainly could."

Hal spun round to look. Lying out in the open water of the harbor was a guard boat—an eight-oared craft with a dozen armed men on board. Hal's shoulders sagged.

"Oh," he said. "Yes, they could probably do the job." He looked around in frustration. "I guess we'll stay here."

"I guess you will."

On the shore, the swarthy man watched as Rikard ran along the jetty to dry land. The pirate looked back over his shoulder several times, as if expecting Thorn to change his mind. Then he reached the shore and hurried away, plunging into the first side alley he saw. Anywhere to escape from Thorn's unblinking stare.

The swarthy man's name was Vargas and he was third mate on the *Raven*. He had stayed behind when the ship left, waiting for a supply of rope Zavac had ordered from the rope factory. *Raven*'s standing rigging, the heavy ropes that supported the mast from front to back and side to side, was frayed and old. Knowing the rope manufactory was here, Zavac had taken the opportunity to buy new supplies. It was far cheaper to buy from the manufactory than to pay the profit for traders farther down the river. But the heavier cables were in short supply and he'd been unwilling to wait while they were being woven. Accordingly, he'd detailed Vargas to wait behind, hiring a fast-sailing skiff to bring them when they were ready.

They were loaded on the skiff now, coiled neatly on the decks. Vargas had intended to have one more comfortable night in Krall. But now he thought Zavac would want to know that the young crew of Skandians had discovered their whereabouts, and that they were close behind him. He knew he'd have no trouble slipping out of the port in the skiff. She was a lot harder to see than a full-size ship, after all. And she could easily be taken for one of the squid fishing boats that plied the river at night.

But, before he left, there was something he had to take care of. He'd recognized Rikard as the former mate of the *Stingray*. He had obviously betrayed the fact that the *Raven* was heading down the Dan River. Now that his information had been shown to be true, they had set him free. It was just bad luck for Rikard that Vargas had witnessed his betrayal.

Vargas hated traitors.

Rikard, still casting anxious glances over his shoulder, as if expecting to be called back at any minute, hurried round the corner into a dark alley.

And stopped short as he found himself confronted by Vargas.

"Hullo, mate," the swarthy man said, smiling. "Recognize you, don't I? Weren't you with Nagy on the old *Stingray*?"

Rikard hesitated. Alexander Nagy had been the skipper of the *Stingray*. The man did look familiar, he thought. And he seemed friendly. It could be good luck to run into an old shipmate. Maybe he could help him get to Pragha.

"That's right," he replied. "Can't quite place you, though. What ship were you with?"

Vargas continued to smile easily, and stepped closer. "I was on the *Raven*," he said. And he saw the quick flash of fear light the other man's eyes—confirming his treachery. "The ship you just betrayed."

He stepped forward and rammed his knife up and under the other man's ribs, shoving and twisting until it reached, and stopped, his heart.

Rikard shuddered briefly, then staggered back as Vargas jerked the knife free. His hands went to the blood welling from the terrible wound. He gaped at Vargas, not quite understanding.

Then fell dead on the filthy cobblestones of the alley.

Vargas checked briefly to make sure he was dead. Then he

turned and hurried through the darkened streets to where his skiff was moored.

"Stow all that bedding and loose gear," Hal ordered. "Then man the oars. Stig, get ready to cast off."

There was a sense of bustle and purpose about the *Heron* as she prepared to get under way. The sun had just risen above the eastern bank of the river, and its early morning light flooded the town. The oars rattled and clattered as the crew raised them from the bottom of the rowing well and placed them across the line of the ship, ready to run out. Stig stepped across to the jetty. The tide was full now and the ship's rail was level with the splintered old planks. He moved to the bow rope, ready to cast it off, but Hal held up a hand.

"Just a moment," he said. He'd seen a delegation approaching down the jetty, moving quickly to forestall them. For a moment, he considered casting off and getting away. But he discarded the idea. In the confines of the harbor, they'd be easily overtaken by the guard boat.

As the group of men grew closer, Thorn stepped up beside him.

"Hello," he said quietly. "What have we here?"

There were ten armed men—soldiers of the town watch, from their uniforms—and another who was obviously their officer. Accompanying them was the toll collector they'd dealt with the day before. They strode purposefully toward the *Heron*, bypassing other ships moored on the same jetty. They stopped as they reached the little ship. The officer jerked his head at Stig.

"Leave the ropes," he said curtly. "Get back on board."

Stig looked as if he was about to argue. Hal knew it would be useless.

"Do it, Stig," he said. His friend looked at him, then at the watch officer, then shrugged. He stepped across onto the deck of the *Heron*.

The officer and toll collector did likewise. Hal raised his eyebrows. It was a breach of etiquette not to ask permission to come aboard. He felt a vague sense of worry gnawing at his insides.

Thorn stepped forward. "Is there some kind of problem?"

The watch captain sized him up briefly, then drew himself up to his full height. He was several inches shorter than the old sea wolf. But he could see the ragged figure had only one good arm.

"Could be," he said. "Man was found murdered in Tinkers Alley this morning. Knifed."

Thorn pushed out his bottom lip. "How does that concern us?" he asked.

The captain scrabbled in his belt purse for a few seconds, and produced three Limmatan noble coins.

"He had these on him," he said. "When we asked around, this man"—he jerked a thumb at the toll collector—"said your ship was the only one to pay in Limmatan coins. And when he saw the body, he recognized him. Said you had him chained up to the mast when you came in."

"So you think I killed him?" Thorn said, and the captain nodded emphatically.

"That's certainly the way it looks to me," he said. "And until you can prove otherwise, you're not going anywhere."

Why would I kill him?" Thorn asked. "I'd finished with him. So I paid him off and let him go. He was a troublemaker."

The officer shrugged. "Could be for any number of reasons. But we know there was bad blood between you. Armant here"—he indicated the pudgy toll collector—"says you had him chained up on deck. You told him the man had back-chatted you and you were teaching him a lesson. Maybe you had a further fight. Maybe you paid him off, then had words with him. You say yourself he was a troublemaker. So you followed him and killed him."

Thorn nodded thoughtfully. "In which case, why did I leave those Limmatan coins on him? Why wouldn't I take them? They were sure to point back to me, weren't they? As your man here says, they're not very common in these parts."

The guard captain stopped, mouth open to reply, as he considered what Thorn had said.

"Well, who else would have done it?" he asked.

Thorn raised his eyebrows. "A thief, perhaps? Or are you going to tell me that, out of all the river ports I've ever been in, Krall is the only one totally devoid of such people?"

"In which case, why did *he* leave the coins on him? Funny kind of thief who kills a man, then leaves his purse untouched."

Thorn shrugged. "For the same reason I wouldn't have left them on him. They're uncommon. If the man was killed, then a few days later someone turned up spending Limmatan nobles, it would be a sure pointer to the fact that he was the killer."

The captain considered the answer, his mouth screwed up in a tight, crooked line. There was a certain logic in what the old Skandian said. But he wasn't willing to admit it, not yet.

"It's thin, Skandian. Too thin. At the moment I'm looking at a dead body, and a man who admits that there was bad blood between him and the victim. That's a lot more evidence than some theory about a thief who kills a man, then doesn't take his purse because the coins in it aren't seen very often. More likely a thief would kill him, snatch the purse without looking, and then run. Later, he might decide that the Limmatan coins were a giveaway and he might get rid of the evidence. But to simply leave them behind on the night? I don't think so."

Jesper stepped forward.

"Did he still have the pearl?" he asked.

The captain frowned at the question. "Pearl? What pearl?"

"Rikard wore a pearl on a silver chain round his neck." He turned to Hal and Stig. "Didn't he?" he asked, by way of confirmation. Instantly, they nodded. "Quite a reasonable size, it was, a freshwater pearl with a slightly pink coloration. I offered to buy it from him but he refused to sell. I was actually thinking of taking it myself," he added.

Thorn repressed an annoyed shake of his head. It was a good lie, he thought. But Jesper, like so many people who believed they were smarter than those around them, had made the cardinal sin of embroidering too much. In his attempt to confuse the issue with the story of the nonexistent pearl, he had opened himself to suspicion.

The captain rounded on him. "So maybe that's what you did," he said. "You followed him when he left and stuck a knife in him to get the pearl." He turned to one of the soldiers. "Was the victim wearing a pearl when you found the body, corporal?"

The man shook his head doubtfully. "I don't recall. I'm sure if he had been, I'd have noticed it." He looked at the guards grouped around him for confirmation. They all shook their heads uncertainly. None of them had noticed a pearl. But they weren't willing to swear that there hadn't been one.

"I didn't take it!" Jesper said. His voice was shrill as, too late, he realized his mistake. "I was on board all night."

The captain studied him for several seconds. This was a better theory, he thought. Now he had a real suspect, one who had admitted coveting the pearl worn by the victim.

"Can you prove that?" he asked.

Jesper cast a slightly panicked look around his companions.

"They'll tell you!" he said, but the guard captain shook his head skeptically.

"They're your friends, of course they'd cover for you," he said. "Is there anyone else who could swear you never left the ship?"

Jesper opened and closed his mouth several times. He couldn't think of anyone.

"As a matter of fact, there is," Hal said quietly.

All eyes turned to him instantly. He pointed to the sentry at the foot of the jetty.

"The sentry was there all night. He saw us come ashore, then saw Rikard leave the ship when Thorn set him free. Then he told us we couldn't leave before daylight. He can testify that none of us left the ship after Rikard did. Is that good enough for you?"

The guard captain stepped onto the jetty and hailed the sentry, beckoning for him to join them. Hal exchanged an annoyed glance with Thorn. They finally had concrete information that Zavac was only a couple of days ahead of them. Now this idiot official was wasting their time with his accusations. Hal was chafing at the delay, eager to be on their way, and aware that they needed to catch up with Zavac before he reached the sanctuary of Raguza.

The sentry jogged along the jetty. Reaching them, he saluted, grounding the haft of his spear on the jetty's planks with a hollow thud.

"Did anyone leave this ship during the night, sentry?" the captain asked him.

The man shook his head immediately. "No, sir!" he declared.

Thorn spread his hands out, palms upward. "There. What did I tell you? Now can we please be on our—"

"At least, not since I came on duty," the man added, a note of apology in his voice.

Thorn sighed audibly. The captain glared at him, then turned back to the sentry.

"And when was that?"

"Four in the morning, sir. I have the four till eight watch. Nobody left the ship after four o'clock, sir. That's definite."

"Well, who was on duty before you?" Thorn demanded in an exasperated voice. The man looked at him, then made his reply to the guard captain.

"Dellon, sir. He had the midnight to four duty. I relieved him. Anson is due to relieve me, but he's running late," he added, a little aggrieved.

"We don't care who's due to relieve you," Thorn said acidly. "Where's this Dellon character?"

The sentry shrugged. "At home, I suppose." Then, seeing the next question coming, he added, "I don't know where that is. I only see him when we're on duty together."

"Oh for Gorlog's sake," Thorn muttered. The captain made it very obvious that he was ignoring him.

"Who would know where he lives? And who would know who was on duty before him, and where he might live?"

"They'd know that at the port office, I suppose. They organize the guard."

The captain nodded his thanks and turned to one of his men.

"Soldier, get along to the port office and find out where this Dellon lives. Then go and fetch him." He pointed to another man. "You find out who was on watch before him, then go and bring him here."

The two men saluted and turned away, strolling down the jetty. It was too much for Thorn.

"AND GET A MOVE ON!" he bellowed.

The two men didn't wait to find out who had shouted at them. The tone of command was unmistakable—and irresistible. They doubled their pace, their thudding feet setting the old jetty vibrating.

Thorn glared at the captain. "And now I suppose we wait?"

The captain nodded stiffly. "That's exactly what we're going to do."

Thorn turned away to look out to the river. "Wonderful." He scowled.

It took half an hour for the second soldier to return with the sentry who had taken the eight to midnight watch. He had seen Thorn, Hal and Stig return from the tavern, and had also witnessed Rikard's departure. He confirmed that nobody from the *Heron* had gone ashore while he was on watch.

"There!" Thorn said angrily. "What more do you want? Rikard went ashore at nine. This man was here for a further three hours and saw nobody follow him. In fact, he saw us getting ready to leave harbor." He looked at the sentry, who nodded agreement.

"That's right, sir. I had to tell them they couldn't leave before daybreak."

"At this rate," Thorn said, "we'll be lucky to leave before night-fall! I'm getting well and truly sick of this. I've a good mind to leave right now."

The captain made a gesture to one of his men, who stepped forward, his spear held at the ready across his body, at an angle of forty-five degrees.

"I've got an armed squad here, ready to stop you," the captain said. "You seem to have forgotten that."

"And you seem to have forgotten that we're Skandians, not gut-less pirates or river rats. If I really wanted to leave, I'd simply do this."

And before anyone could react, he stepped toward the guard. His left hand flashed out to grip the spear at its midpoint, thumb down. Then he twisted his hand and the spear upward in a half circle and jerked backward, all in one rapid motion. Caught un-prepared, the soldier felt his weapon twisted out of his hands and snatched from his grip. A heartbeat later, Thorn had leveled the razor-sharp point at the captain's throat, holding it one-handed, as if it were no heavier than a small knife.

The rest of the squad dropped their hands to their weapons, then froze as they saw the danger to their captain. The crew of the *Heron* came to their feet as one. There was a multiple rasp of steel on leather as they drew their saxes.

For a moment, the jetty seemed about to explode with violence. Then Thorn snorted in disgust and threw the spear down on the planks. He held the captain's eyes with his own.

"That's what I'd do if I really wanted to leave," he said. "Count your lucky stars I'm a patient man. But I warn you, my patience is running out."

Fortunately, at that moment, the other guardsman returned with the delinquent Dellon. It took a few minutes for him to confirm that nobody had left the ship during his watch. With exceedingly bad grace, the captain turned to Thorn.

"Very well, it appears that you may be telling the truth," he began. But Thorn held up a hand to stop him.

"It *appears* that I *may* be telling the truth?" he said. "You've just had one narrow escape, thanks to my forbearance. Are you really sure you want to take a risk by insulting me?"

The captain looked into the cold eyes fixed on him. He recalled the feeling of the sharp spear point just touching the skin of his throat and the lightning speed with which Thorn had moved. This was no helpless, one-armed cripple, he realized. This was a very dangerous man. He swallowed nervously.

"I'm sorry," he said, his voice thick. "You are telling the truth. You're free to go."

"And about time," Thorn said, the disgust obvious in his voice. He gestured to Hal. "Take her out, Hal."

"Stig! Get those mooring ropes! The rest of you, ready on the oars!"

Stig ran lightly along the jetty, unlooping first the bow rope, then the stern rope, from their bollards and tossing them aboard. Then he stretched out to the stern post and pushed the stern away from the jetty as he leapt back on board. The port-side rowers shoved with their oars to widen the gap, then, at Hal's command, both port and starboard sides bent to their oars and sent the *Heron* surging back with three firm strokes.

Clear of the jetty, the little ship pivoted one hundred and eighty degrees with the port-side oarsmen rowing ahead and the starboard side backing water.

"Give way together," Hal ordered, and steered for the river outside the little harbor. Thorn glanced up at the wind telltale—a long streamer that was blowing virtually straight on the stern post.

"Let's get her under sail as soon as we can," he said to Hal. "We've lost enough time fooling around here."

Zavac was relaxing in a tavern in Bayrath, a large river town south of Krall, when Vargas found him.

Now that he was sailing down the calm waters of the Dan, with Raguza only a few days away, Zavac felt as if a load had been lifted from his shoulders. After several weeks with no report of the Skandian ship that had been pursuing him, he finally could believe that he'd given them the slip. Apparently, when he had turned into the Dan and headed south for Raguza, they had lost his trail.

Of course, the Skandians were open-sea sailors, he thought. The idea of confining themselves to the relatively narrow waters of a river would be unnatural to them. Presumably, the small ship with the strange sail pattern was still blundering around the Storm-white Sea, asking for news of the *Raven* in every port she entered.

And getting none.

He signaled the tavern keeper for another jug of brandy and leaned back in his chair, sighing contentedly. He heard the door open, felt the sudden gust of the draft that it let in, just as quickly shut off, and looked up. Vargas had entered the room and was looking around, obviously searching for him. He raised a hand over his head.

"Here," he called, and Vargas began to shove his way through the tightly packed crowd toward Zavac's table.

He arrived a few seconds after the brandy jug Zavac had ordered. The pirate captain smiled.

"Good timing. Have a drink."

He poured the rough spirit into a spare tumbler on the table. Vargas nodded his thanks, drank deeply, then wiped his mouth with the back of his hand.

"Bad news," he said briefly.

Zavac's smile faded and his eyes narrowed in suspicion. "What's gone wrong? Couldn't you get the rope I ordered? I'll skin that factory foreman. He swore blind on three different gods that he'd have it ready!"

Vargas shook his head at the second question and made a negative gesture with his hand.

"No, no," he said. "The rope's all here. It's in the skiff and the men are busy loading it onto *Raven*."

Zavac frowned. "Then what's gone wrong?"

"It's that Skandian ship," Vargas told him.

"What about it?" Zavac snapped. "That ship has become the bane of my life. Don't tell me you saw it again."

"I saw it, all right. It's only a few days behind us—although by now that may be a little more."

"What?" Zavac exploded with rage. "How did they catch up to us so soon?"

Vargas shrugged and shook his head. "It doesn't matter how they did it. The fact is, they're on our trail. I've arranged things so they'll probably be delayed in Krall, but they'll soon be on the river again."

"How did they find us?" Zavac raged. "How did they know we turned into the Dan?" He let out a string of curses and slammed his open hand on the table in fury. The tavern keeper looked up at the sudden sound, and Zavac made a dismissing gesture. The tavern keeper frowned. He could sense trouble brewing. He reached below the bar and made sure that his heavy, studded cudgel was easily to hand.

Vargas waited patiently until Zavac's outburst was done.

"We were betrayed," he said calmly. "I saw Rikard with them."

Zavac's eyes narrowed as he sought to place the name. "Rikard? Who in the Blue Fiend's name is Rikard?" It was vaguely familiar, he realized. Vargas took another sip of brandy before he answered. Times like these, he knew, it was best to go slowly with Zavac. The man's temper had a tendency to flare up, leading to unfortunate, unpleasant results.

"He was on the *Stingray*," he said, after a pause. "He was Nagy's first mate."

Realization dawned on Zavac's face. "That's right," he said softly, as memory came back to him. Then he frowned again. "But weren't he and the rest of *Stingray*'s crew caught by the Skandians when we burned their ship?"

"That's what we all thought. But somehow, he escaped. And somehow, he ended up with the Skandians. He was with them when they sailed into Krall harbor. They actually had him chained up. My guess is, they spared him in return for him telling them where we were heading."

"And of course," Zavac said thoughtfully, twisting one of the long ringlets that hung down his cheek around a forefinger, "we'd planned to rendezvous with Nagy and his men at Raguza."

"So he would have known we were heading down the river," Vargas concluded, and Zavac nodded slowly. He looked at his crewman from under lowered lids.

"How did you learn all this?" he asked. It was in Zavac's nature to be suspicious.

Vargas wasn't insulted. He'd known the pirate captain for several years and he knew that people who weren't suspicious didn't last long in this line of business.

"I saw the Skandians in a tavern," he said. "The big one with the wooden hook for a hand . . ."

Zavac cursed again. "I thought he was a harmless drunk!" he said. "He was always hanging round the harbor in Hallasholm when we were there. Remember?"

Vargas nodded. "Odds are he was spying on us for that buffoon they call the Oberjarl," he said. "But he's no drunk and he's certainly not harmless. There were two others with him. The big blond boy and the smaller one—the half Araluen."

While the *Raven* had lingered in Hallasholm, pretending to be in need of repair, Zavac and his men had learned as much as they could about the crews of the two brotherbands that would compete in the final race. They had planned to steal the Andomal, a priceless ball of amber, while the triumphant brotherband was guarding it, and Zavac always believed it paid to know your enemy—or your prospective victim.

"He's the one to watch," he said bitterly as Vargas mentioned Hal. "He's as cunning as a bilge rat, that one."

Vargas twisted his lip in a sneer. "Not so cunning," he said. "After all, he left his men asleep when they were supposed to be guarding that treasure-ball."

"Maybe. But he learns fast. Look at what he did in Limmat. Then after we rammed that wolfship, he nearly caught us. Would probably have done so if he hadn't turned back to help them."

His crewman was still unimpressed. "Lucky for him he did," he said, but Zavac was shaking his head at him.

"Don't underestimate them, Vargas. That would be a big mistake. So how did they find out about us?"

"Well, obviously Rikard told them we'd be heading down the Dan, but they probably didn't trust him. When I saw them, they were asking if anyone had seen the *Raven* passing. One drunken old fool told them he'd seen us. Actually shouted about it in the tavern. They left pretty smartly after that and I followed them back to their ship."

Zavac swore quietly. "Stupid old fool. Everyone on this river knows you don't give out information to strangers. I'd like to get my hands on him."

"Too late." Vargas smiled mirthlessly. "I already have. I slipped a knife into him on the way out. Left him looking as if he was sleeping it off at the table."

"Good!" Zavac said viciously. "What happened next?"

"I followed them back to their ship, and watched as they set Rikard free. He'd been chained to the mast. The one-handed one gave him some money and they let him go. I went down a few alleys and got ahead of him." He paused for dramatic effect. "And let me say, his betraying days are over. After I dealt with him, I slipped out of the harbor and headed down here to let you know the news."

"So they're only a day or two behind us," Zavac said.

"A little more than that. They wouldn't have been allowed to leave harbor until sunrise. And even then I think they might have been detained." He saw the questioning look on the other man's face and explained. "I left Rikard where his body would be easily found. The authorities knew he was from the Skandian ship. And I left some other evidence. He had three Limmatan coins that they paid him off with. I left them in his purse. Odds were they're the only ship in harbor paying their way with Limmatan nobles."

"So the authorities would have held them for questioning," Zavac said slowly.

Vargas nodded. "Almost certainly. If only to get a nice big bribe for themselves. So we have a little time. But I thought maybe we could arrange to have them detained more permanently here in Bayrath. After all, the Gatmeister's a friend of yours, isn't he?"

The Gatmeister was the elected official who ruled the large river port. His position was the equivalent of a town mayor.

"He's a friend of anyone with a deep enough purse," Zavac said cynically. "Fortunately, mine is pretty deep."

"And nobody goes up or down the river without his permission," Vargas said.

Which was the crux of the matter. The citizens of Bayrath had chosen to build their city at a point where the river narrowed. The banks were only two hundred meters apart at the narrowest spot. The Bayrath town council had narrowed this gap farther by building jetties out from either side. Then they closed the gap between the jetties with a boom made from three massive logs.

No ship could proceed up or down the Dan River unless they paid a hefty toll to the town—or, more correctly, to the Gatmeister himself.

Doutro, the Gatmeister of Bayrath, looked at the pile of five heavy gold coins on the table before him. He was an impressive sight, tall and well built, with a hawk nose, prominent cheekbones and dark brown, deep-set eyes. His dark hair was graying at the edge, which gave him a distinguished look. This was accentuated by the gold-trimmed purple robe he wore and the thin gold circlet set on his head.

"So you're saying you'd like this ship delayed?" he said. His manner was noncommittal.

Zavac nodded. "The ship and its crew. There are nine of them. An old Skandian with one arm, and eight boys."

"And how long should I detain them?"

Zavac carefully added another five gold coins to the stack on the table, placing each one with exaggerated care.

"Permanently would be good," he said.

The Gatmeister pursed his lips. Another gold coin was placed beside the ten already stacked.

"Of course, I'd need some pretext to arrest them," he said.

"They killed Rikard," Zavac told him, then added by way of explanation, "Nagy's first mate on the *Stingray*."

Most of the pirates who frequented Raguza and traveled up and down the Dan were well-known to the Gatmeister. They and the town enjoyed a long-established and profitable business relationship. The pirates paid the toll to the Gatmeister whenever they passed through the boom—which was quite often. In return, he allowed them a generous discount. The two groups, pirates and town council, did well off each other. And when a ship's captain needed the occasional favor—as Zavac did now—the Gatmeister was always willing to consider granting it.

For a price.

Apparently, that price was eleven large gold coins. Doutro nodded slowly. He didn't care whether they had killed Rikard or not. In truth, he didn't care if Rikard were dead or not. But the first mate's murder provided him with the thin excuse that was all he would need to arrest the *Heron*'s crew.

"So I could hold them on suspicion of murder. Then I can try them, find them guilty and hang them," he said.

Zavac nodded. "And confiscate their property, and their ship."

Doutro said nothing for a few seconds. Then he reached out and divided the tall stack of ten coins into three smaller stacks. He opened a drawer on his side of the table and swept the coins into it. They clinked together in a most pleasant way, he thought.

"I can't see any problem with that," he said.

*H*eron came round a bend in the river with the wind from her port side. Her prow split the water, throwing up a white bow wave. Behind her, the wake of disturbed water was arrow straight.

"There's a town up ahead!" Stefan called from the bow. It was an unnecessary warning. Nobody could miss the sprawling town, almost a city, that lay on the eastern bank of the river.

Hal had taken the opportunity to buy a map of the river before they left Krall. It was rough and a little shy on detail, but better than nothing.

"That'll be Bayrath," he said. "The map shows it's where the river narrows. Ease the sail, boys, while we take a look."

He called this last instruction to the twins. Obediently, they let the sail out a little, easing the driving force of the wind against it.

Heron slowed, the loud hiss of her bow wave dying down to a quiet murmur.

"What's that in the river?" Lydia asked, pointing ahead to the narrow gap between the jetties that were built out from either bank. There was a dark line across the surface of the water. Hal shook his head, frowning.

"Don't know," he said. "The map doesn't show anything."

"It's a boom," Thorn said quietly. He pointed to the two craft moored at the ends of the two jetties. Each had a derrick—a kind of crane—set amidships, in place of a mast. As they drew closer, they could see heavy cables running at an angle from the derricks, down into the river. "Those two boats control it, letting it open or shut to let traffic through."

"Why would they want to shut it?" Stig asked.

Thorn looked at him. "So they can make people pay them to open it. It's called a toll," he added patiently.

Stig shook his head in disgust. "That's outrageous!" he said. "Do they think they own the whole river? They have no right to restrict traffic."

"They don't have to own the whole river," Thorn replied. "Just this part of it. As far as they're concerned, we can travel the rest of it without charge."

"Let go the sheets and lower the sail," Hal called quietly. As the sail came down, the way slowly fell off the ship and she drifted, rocking gently. The wavelets made their usual *pok-pok-pok* sound against the timber hull.

The boom was downriver from the town and its harbor. As

Hal studied it, Stig was still voicing his disgust with the people who inhabited the riverside towns.

"They're nothing but parasites, these people!" he said. "They constantly have their hands out, demanding money from honest travelers. First Krall, now this. Somebody should bring a fleet of wolfships down here and burn them out."

Thorn grinned at him. "Spoken like a true sea wolf, Stig. There's hope for you yet."

"Well, maybe when I'm older, I might do just that," Stig threatened.

Hal had been studying the eastern jetty and he finally made out what he was looking for—a timber building with the circle and twin bars symbol outside it. There were mooring facilities close to it.

"Looks like that's the toll office," he said. "Run out the oars and we'll go and pay whatever they're asking."

They rowed steadily across the river. Hal took the *Heron* in on a curving course, bringing her round to run at a shallow angle to the jetty. When he judged the moment was right, he ordered the rowers to ship their oars, and hauled on the tiller in the last few meters to bring the ship alongside, almost parallel. Stig, ready on the bulwark, jumped up onto the jetty and hurried to secure her bow and stern. Jesper and Stefan tossed the wicker fenders overside to protect the hull from the rough timbers of the jetty.

"Well," said Thorn, "here we go again. This is getting to be all too familiar."

But this time, things turned out to be quite different. As he stepped up, poised with one foot on the bulwark and the other on the timber decking of the jetty, there was a rush of feet and a party of armed men emerged from the toll office and from behind the building. They fanned out quickly into a semicircle, weapons drawn, surrounding Stig and Thorn, who were the only members of the crew ashore.

Thorn's left hand dropped to the hilt of his saxe as he quickly assessed the situation. Then he withdrew it. There were at least twenty of them, he realized. And they were all fully armed, carrying shields and wearing chain mail armor and helmets. Half a dozen of them had short, thick-limbed recurve bows, arrows on the string and half drawn. The odds were simply too great.

One of their number, an officer, judging by the superior quality of his armor, stepped forward as he saw Thorn's hand fall away from the heavy knife.

"Good thinking, northman," he said. "But I think I'd like to see you get rid of that knife altogether."

He gestured with his sword point at the saxe hanging by Thorn's waist. Realizing he had no alternative, Thorn unbuckled his belt with his left hand, coiled it around the sheathed saxe, and tossed it into the ship. Out of the corner of his eye, he saw Stig measuring the distance to the nearest of the soldiers. His hand was hovering close to the hilt of his own saxe. Thorn wasn't sure if the officer had noticed or not. But he was reasonably confident that at least two of the bowmen had.

"Forget it, Stig," he said quietly. The youth looked at him quickly, then realized that Thorn was making good sense. He relaxed, his tensed shoulders falling slightly. Then he too unbuckled his knife belt and tossed it on board the ship.

"Now the rest of you," the officer ordered, gesturing with his sword at the crew of the *Heron*, crouched warily on the ship. They turned to Hal, who shrugged and nodded.

"Do it," he said, and there was a series of dull thuds as the heavy knives fell to the decking. Before anyone could tell him not to, Edvin gathered the weapons and stowed them in a locker beside the rowing benches.

"Leave them," the officer ordered belatedly. Then, seeing that Edvin had already stowed the knives, he shrugged. "Never mind. Let's have you all up here on the jetty. One at a time."

"I suppose there's no point in my asking you what's going on?" Thorn said.

The officer raised his eyebrows. "Why not?" he said. "I'm arresting you. For murder."

"Murder?" Hal said, unable to contain himself. "Who did we murder? We only just got here!"

The officer eyed him dispassionately. "Then you're obviously very dangerous people to have worked so fast," he said. "My orders are to take you to the Gatmeister for interrogation."

"That's ridiculous!" Hal replied. But Thorn laid a calming hand on his arm.

"You're wasting your breath. I think I see Zavac's hand behind all this." He was watching the captain as he said the words and saw the man's involuntary eye movement, flicking up to look at him, then away again. It confirmed his suspicion.

"Captain!" one of the soldiers called, and the officer turned. The soldier in question was holding Lydia by the arm. "There's a girl here!"

Ingvar rumbled angrily, but Hal spoke quickly to him.

"Be quiet, Ingvar," he said in an undertone. Reluctantly, the giant boy fell silent. The captain was studying a sheet of paper he had taken from inside his tunic. The arrest warrant, Hal realized. He frowned over the page.

"Nothing here about a girl," he said. "I'm to arrest a one-armed Skandian and eight boys."

"I'm not one of them, Captain!" Lydia said quickly. She moved forward, her hands clasped together in supplication. "You can see I'm not a Skandian!"

The captain studied her, then looked at the rest of the crew. They were mostly fair skinned and blue eyed. She was dark haired, with olive skin. She definitely didn't look like a Skandian.

"Treacherous cow!" Jesper muttered. Then he grunted in pain as Stig shot an elbow into his ribs to silence him.

"Shut up, you fool!" Stig said, out of the corner of his mouth.

"I'm just a passenger! I paid them for passage down the river!" Lydia was saying, wringing her hands before her. "I'm from Krall. My parents are dead and I'm going to live with my uncle in Raguza." She glared at Thorn. "And they took advantage of me. They charged me double the going rate for my fare!" she added angrily.

Not bad, Thorn thought. Then, in a loud voice, he snarled at her.

"You were happy enough to pay when you came to us, girl! You pleaded with us to take you on board! You couldn't thank us enough then, could you? I'll wager you were in trouble in Krall and had to get away in a hurry. I told the boys you'd be nothing but bad luck, but you won them over with your big brown eyes!"

"Quiet," the captain said distractedly. He studied the warrant again. There was definitely no mention of a girl. There was no order for her arrest and her story was logical. He knew from his briefing that the Skandians were pursuing a ship that was headed for Raguza. He came to a decision.

"All right," he said to her. "You'll come with us. I'll let the Gatmeister decide what to do with you. The rest of you form up in pairs."

The Herons shuffled into two lines, and the armed men formed up around them, weapons drawn and ready. Lydia, before the captain could say otherwise, took her place beside him, subtly distancing herself from the crew.

"Sergeant," the captain said. But before the sergeant could call the order to move, Thorn turned to the captain.

"One thing," he said. "Just to satisfy my curiosity, who is it we're supposed to have murdered?"

The captain turned a superior gaze on him, his chin raised slightly to indicate his contempt for Skandians in general, and this ragged, one-armed beggar of a man in particular.

"He was a Magyaran," he said loftily. "An honest, hard-working sailor."

Thorn snorted in wry amusement. "No such person ever came out of Magyara," he said. "The place is a den of pirates and thieves. Does this paragon of a man happen to have a name? It's only fair if you're going to arrest me that you tell me who I've killed."

The captain fumbled in his breast pocket again for the warrant. He checked the name on it, then folded it again and put it away.

"His name was Rikard," he said.

The name was greeted with a chorus of groans from the *Heron*'s crew. He arched his eyebrows as he looked at them.

"I see you've heard of him," he said. "That does nothing to help your case."

"Oh yes, we've heard of him," Thorn said. "It's amazing how a dead man like him can keep popping up to cause us trouble."

Doutro looked up as the prisoners filed into his office and were herded into line in front of the large table that served as his desk. Always a cautious man, he had ordered that their hands be bound in front of them before they were brought in.

They were all surprisingly young, he noted, except for the one he took to be their leader. He was old, his hair, beard and mustache were gray and shaggy and untrimmed and his clothes were patched and ragged. The rest of the crew were dressed in rough seaman's clothing—a mixture of leather or sheepskin vests and woolen shirts and pants. They all wore sealskin sea boots and he noted with mild curiosity that four of them were wearing rather smart-looking knitted watch caps.

He waited for at least a minute without saying anything, simply running his eyes up and down the line as if measuring them. Usually, he found this technique to be effective in making prisoners start to talk—babbling and protesting and often inadvertently revealing facts that they would rather have kept to themselves. But this group didn't take the bait. They stood silently, eyeing him. One of them, a giant of a boy, was peering round the room, squinting as he tried to make out details. The others all returned his gaze evenly. Finally, a little annoyed, he had to break the silence himself.

"So, what do you have to say for yourselves?"

He addressed the older man, assuming he would be their spokesman. The Skandian shrugged, twisted his lips and answered.

"Aside from the fact that this is a load of nonsense? Nothing really."

Doutro raised his eyebrows. "You're accused of murder and you call it a load of nonsense?" he said. "I'd say it's a pretty serious matter."

"We were questioned by the authorities in Krall. They cleared us of any suspicion of Rikard's murder," Thorn told him. As he said the Magyaran's name, Doutro's eyebrows shot up in mock surprise.

"So you admit you know the victim's name?" he said. "That's suspicious."

"I don't see why," Thorn replied. The ghost of a smile touched the corners of his mouth. "After all, your captain told us his name."

Doutro shot an angry glance at the captain, who flushed red. "Yes, sir. I did. But they already knew him. That was clear."

"Of course we did," Thorn went on. "He was traveling on our

ship. We admitted that. But he left the ship and we were found to have no involvement in his death."

Doutro glanced down at some papers on the table in front of him. He shuffled them, bringing one sheet to the top and pretending to study it. In fact, it was a report on the need for repairing one of the boom cables, but there was no way the prisoners could know that.

"So you say," he said smoothly. "But apparently, fresh evidence has come to light. Quite damning evidence, in fact. I'm going to have to hold you here for trial."

"What might that fresh evidence be?" Hal spoke up and Doutro looked at him with some surprise. He hadn't expected any of the youths to speak. This one seemed confident, he thought, and there was an air of authority about him.

"You'll find out at your trial," he said. He saw the look of cynicism on the young man's face.

"Sounds to me as if this fresh evidence came in the form of a bribe from Zavac," Hal replied. He was watching Doutro's eyes closely, but the Gatmeister showed no sign of recognition at the mention of Zavac's name. Neither, however, did he show any sense of surprise or curiosity. And that was just as telling, Hal thought.

"Are you suggesting that justice can be bought and sold here in Bayrath?" Doutro asked.

This time, the older man answered. "Assuming that it can be," he said, "we'd certainly like to have a chance to buy some. We'll offer you double the amount Zavac gave you."

For a moment, Doutro was tempted.

"And how do you know how much that was?" he asked.

The younger man answered quickly. "So he *did* pay you to arrest us?"

Doutro allowed a momentary flash of anger to show on his face. He hadn't meant to fall into that trap. He'd underestimated these unkempt northmen, thinking of them as little more than savages, with no idea of subtlety. He pointed an angry finger at Hal.

"You speak when you're spoken to!" he ordered.

Hal allowed a small smile to play on his lips.

"What about our offer?" Thorn continued. "We'll pay for our freedom."

But Doutro had come to a decision. These Skandians were cleverer than he had thought and it would be best to be rid of them. They might pay him a large bribe now, but it would be a once-only payment. While Zavac was by no means a friend of his, he was a regular visitor and a source of continuing income.

"You'll pay for your crime," he told them coldly. "Your trial will be set for the first day of next week."

He was about to dismiss them but the captain of the guard raised a tentative hand and Doutro glared at him. The encounter with the Skandians had put him in a bad mood.

"What is it?" he snapped.

"There was the girl, sir. What should we do about her?"

Doutro drummed his fingers on the table's surface. He had forgotten about the girl. He made a peremptory gesture.

"Bring her in. Let's see what she has to say."

The captain moved to the door, opened it and beckoned Lydia

into the room. She approached the table hesitantly, casting fearful glances at Thorn and the crew as she came.

"What's your name, girl?" Doutro demanded. She replied in a small, nervous voice.

"Lydia Demarek, Your Honor. I have nothing to do with these men. I paid for passage down the river with them, that was all."

"If you want my opinion," Thorn said scornfully, "she's a sneak thief and a cutpurse. She couldn't get out of Krall fast enough. Offered to pay us double, in fact."

"You charged me double!" Lydia replied angrily. "You knew I'd have to pay!" Then she stopped as if she'd given too much away. Interesting, thought Doutro. It was clear that she was no friend of the Skandians. But she obviously had a few skeletons in her closet. That could prove useful.

"You saw the murdered man, Rikard, on board their ship?" he asked.

She tore her eyes away from Thorn, becoming meek and submissive once more.

"Yes, sir. This one . . ." She pointed to Thorn, unable to hide the spitefulness in her eyes. "Argued with him constantly. I heard him threaten to—"

"That's a lie!" It was Jesper who interrupted her, his face hot with anger. Ingvar, standing beside him, jabbed an elbow into his ribs, shutting him up. Doutro nodded encouragingly at the girl, who had turned toward Jesper, fear in her eyes.

"And you'd be willing to testify to that in court?" Doutro asked in a silky voice. He always liked to go through the motions, to make it seem as if justice had been done. Show trials like this one could be used to encourage others to pay their way out of trouble.

The girl nodded several times. "Yes, Your Honor. I'll say anything you want me to," she said in a low voice.

Thorn snorted in disgust. "And that's the measure of your justice, is it?"

Doutro looked angrily at him. "Keep your mouth shut," he ordered. He looked at the girl again. She was young and might well be quite attractive if she were properly groomed. Best of all, she was meek and submissive. He could use her as a serving girl in his house, or sell her on to someone else as a slave, he thought.

He jerked a thumb toward the door. "Take them away," he ordered.

"The girl too?" the captain asked uncertainly. "Should I put her in with them?"

"Of course not, you fool!" Doutro told him. He wondered why he had to be surrounded by idiots. "If you put her in with them, they'll probably kill her!" He paused, thinking. "Take her to my house and put her in a room there. With a guard."

The captain and three of his men started to herd the *Heron*'s crew out of the room. Thorn stopped at the door and turned back to Doutro.

"I can't help wondering . . . You said there was fresh evidence about the murder in Krall," he said. "But since we left immediately after we were cleared, and no other ship passed us on the way upriver, I'm wondering how that evidence got here before we did?"

Doutro locked gazes with him for several seconds. Then the Gatmeister dropped his eyes to the papers on his desk.

"Get them out of here," he ordered.

The Herons were conducted to a large cellar beneath the building where the Gatmeister's office was situated. It was set below ground level. A low, barred window was set into one wall, about two meters from the cellar floor, allowing light and air in from above. Stig chinned himself up to look out the window and found that it was set at ground level outside, looking into a dim alley. The floors and walls were hard stone and there were shackles set in the walls at intervals. None of these were in use at the moment. By the walls, dirty straw lay in piles, presumably for their bedding. In some places, water oozed through the stone walls and dripped to the floor below. The air was damp and stale. The cellar door was an iron grille, with heavy bars running vertically and horizontally. It looked out onto a dimly lit corridor, where a single torch burned.

"Welcome to our new home," Hal said as the door clanged shut behind them. The captain signaled to the turnkey to lock them in. They heard the heavy lock squeal as the key rattled in it. Then the guards and the turnkey walked away, their boots echoing on the stone floor.

"If I'd known company was coming, I would have tidied up," said a voice from the far corner.

They all turned in surprise. Somehow, they had expected to be the only occupants of the cellar. The speaker rose and emerged from the shadows. He was a slim man, about thirty years old. His clothing was obviously expensive, although it was overlaid with grime and damp from the cellar. He was a nondescript-looking fellow, with dark hair and a thin mustache that had been waxed at one point, but now was sagging and losing its trim shape.

"I'm Pedr," he said, and they mumbled their introductions. When they had finished, he continued. "And what are you lot in for?"

"We're accused of murder," Hal told him. Pedr stepped back, his hands raised in a theatrical gesture of shock. "We didn't do it," Hal added.

Pedr raised an eyebrow. "Nobody ever does. Everyone's always innocent. Except me."

"What's your crime?" Ingvar asked him.

Pedr eyed him for a second. "My, but you're a big one, aren't you? My crime is cheating at dice. And it does me no good to deny it, nor proclaim my innocence."

"Why's that?" Stig asked, and Pedr favored him with a smile.

"Because my victim was none other than Doutro himself," he said, sighing deeply. "So here I will languish until my wife rakes up the cash to pay my fine. Or, rather, my bribe."

"Well, we don't have that luxury," Hal told him. "Our trial is set for first day next week. And I'm guessing we've already been found guilty."

"So we're just going to have to find a way to get out of here," Thorn said. "I'm hoping Lydia can come up with something."

"Lydia?" Jesper said angrily. "Why would we depend on her? You heard how she turned on us. She's nothing but a traitor, out to save her own skin."

He realized they were all staring at him. He looked around their reproving faces.

"What?" he asked belligerently. It was Ingvar who answered.

"You just don't get it, do you? She's on the outside. She's not locked up in here with us. She made sure of that."

Realization dawned slowly on Jesper's face. Then he flushed with embarrassment as he realized all his shipmates had understood what Lydia was doing when she claimed not to be one of them.

"Oh . . . ," he said. "I suppose you're right."

Hal searched around for a dry spot on the stone floor by the wall and kicked some of the straw into a pile. He sat down, arms wrapped round his knees, his face thoughtful.

"Even if she does get us out of here," he said, "we've still got a huge problem. How do we get the ship past that boom? I checked the map when we left Krall and there's no other way south."

"That's not exactly true," Pedr said. "There's always Wildwater Rift."

Doutro's residence was several streets away from his offices. It was an impressive, three-story structure, built on a small rise with a view of the river. It was freshly painted and well kept, as were the houses around it.

"Rich Man's Hill," Lydia muttered to herself as the captain led her along the wide, cobble-paved street. It was definitely an upper-class area, unlike the mean, cramped, narrow streets they had been led through when they made their way to Doutro's office.

To circumvent any possibility of her escaping, the captain had bound her hands in front of her and attached a two-meter leather thong to the bindings. He kept a firm grip on the tether as they made their way to the gleaming white house. The doors and window frames, she noted, were painted a fresh cornflower blue. It was an attractive color scheme.

There was a short flight of wide stairs leading up to the front door of the house, but the captain bypassed these and led her to a more discreet, and less ornate, side entrance. He knocked loudly, and after a short wait, the door was opened by a huge bald man dressed in a gray woolen robe that came down to his feet. He studied the captain, then Lydia, with mounting distaste.

"What is it?" he asked.

"Doutro sent us," the captain said brusquely. Obviously, there was little love lost between the two men. "This girl is to be put in a room—and guarded. Get the household women to clean her up and put some fresh clothes on her." He saw the angry frown beginning on the bald man's face and added firmly, "They're the Gatmeister's orders."

The bald man hesitated, then nodded reluctant agreement. He might resent being ordered around by the captain, but he couldn't risk disobeying an instruction from the Gatmeister.

"Give her here," he said, holding his hand out for the leather rope the captain was using to lead her. But the captain didn't hand it over. Instead, he untied the bindings around Lydia's wrist and rolled them up, along with the leash, placing them inside his jerkin. He pushed Lydia toward the bald man, who grabbed her upper arm in an iron grip. He jerked her forward, into the house, and slammed the door without another word to the captain.

Lydia looked around. She was in the kitchen—a large, low-ceilinged room. It was dominated by a huge fireplace and cooking area at one end, and a long timber workbench that ran down the middle of the room. Pots and ladles, well used and scrupulously cleaned, hung in gleaming rows from hooks over the bench. There were three women, wearing aprons and cooks' hats, working at the far end of the room. They all stopped what they were doing to look at the newcomer. The bald man turned to them. He was still smarting over the captain's peremptory manner.

"Get back to your work!" he snarled at them. "This has nothing to do with you, so stop gawking and start working."

"You don't give orders here, Milo!" the oldest woman snapped back immediately. "This is my kitchen!"

The bald man took a pace toward her, his body language threatening. "Keep a civil tongue in your head, Dana! I'm the senior servant in this household and if I complain to the master about you, I can have you whipped!"

While this exchange was going on, Milo had lost interest in Lydia. She noticed a small paring knife in a rack on the workbench, a few meters away. She stepped toward it, scooped it up, and hid it in her sleeve.

Dana laughed scornfully. "Master won't have *me* whipped, bald-pate! He's too fond of his apple strudel for that and I'm the only one who can make the pastry light and flaky the way he likes it."

Milo scowled at her. He knew she was speaking the truth. Angrily, he turned his back on her and grabbed Lydia by the upper arm once more, dragging her across the kitchen and into a large hallway. Judging by the utilitarian nature of the furnishings and lack of decoration, they were still in the service area of the house. A narrow stairway led upward at one end of the hall. Milo paused, still holding her arm in that painful grip, and bellowed, "Erlic! Where are you? Get yourself out here!"

"Coming, master Milo!" a high-pitched voice replied. Then a side door banged open and a young man of about twenty emerged into the hall. He was wearing rough clothing, stained and discolored. He was thin and had a mean and suspicious face, which was partially covered by a red rash. He rubbed at it now.

"Leave your face alone!" Milo shouted, and the young man dropped his hand to his side. Even so, it continued to twitch convulsively, as if he wanted to scratch the offending rash once more.

"Take this girl to the third floor—the detention room. Then stay on guard outside."

Erlic turned side on, and edged away slightly, as if he were fearful of Milo's anger and was planning to escape.

"But I have Master's boots to clean," he protested.

"Then take her to the third floor, lock her in and come back for the boots. You can clean them while you stand guard."

Erlic nodded several times, not meeting Milo's angry gaze. "Yes. Yes. I can do that," he said, half to himself.

"THEN DO IT!" Milo thundered, and Erlic actually jumped backward, before recovering and bowing to the head steward.

"Yes, Milo. Come with me, girl!" Erlic ordered. He reached out to grab Lydia's arm but she brushed his hand away. Shrugging, he beckoned for her to follow. As they reached the staircase, Milo's voice stopped her.

"All the doors and windows in this house are locked, girl. And I have the keys. So don't bother trying to escape. You don't leave unless I say so. Understood?"

She nodded, trying to assume a suitably browbeaten demeanor.

"Yes, sir," she said. Then, at Milo's imperious gesture, she turned and followed Erlic up the stairs. As they moved from the second floor to the third, the stairs became progressively narrower. On the third floor, the ceiling levels were noticeably lower. These were the servants' quarters, she assumed. Erlic led her along another narrow hall to the rear of the house. Solid timber doors led off the hallway at regular intervals. She reached out and tried the latch on one. It opened easily and the door swung inward, giving her a quick glimpse into a sparsely furnished room. Erlic, hearing the click of the door handle, turned to look at her.

"What are you doing?" His voice was shrill. She shrugged, hoping to calm him down.

"Just looking," she said, pulling the door closed.

He shook his head at her. "Well, don't!" he ordered. Then he ushered her past him so he could keep his eye on her, shoving her in the back to keep her moving. He stopped at the end of the corridor, at the very back of the house. There was one door, set at right angles to the line of the corridor. It was fastened by a simple lift-latch, she saw. There was no sign of a lock or key.

Erlic raised the latch and, when the door swung open, pushed her roughly inside, slamming the door behind her. Unlike the door she had tried a few minutes earlier, it opened outward. She turned angrily at the rough treatment, then saw the reason why there was no need for a lock or key on the door. There was no handle on the inside—no way of raising the latch.

She took stock of the room. It was small—three meters by three meters. There was a wood-framed bed with a thin straw mattress and a threadbare brown blanket against one wall, a small pine table with a straight-backed chair in the same material and that was it. No closet or armoire. Not even a hanging rail covered by a curtain. Just bare walls. A jug of water with a chipped beaker stood on the table.

There was a small window, and she moved to it and studied it. The window space itself was approximately one meter square. The window was in two halves, each one hinged to swing outward. Heavy wood frames filled the window space, with small glass panes set into them. The frames were thick hardwood and, in the absence of a saw or an ax, they formed effective bars. The windows were latched on the outside, with a simple bar dropping into two metal brackets. At some stage, there must have been provision to raise the bar from the inside. She noticed a hole drilled in the top of one window frame. A cord must have run through there to the latch bar, she realized. But it had been removed after the window had been latched shut. Like the door, there was no way now to open it.

She moved to the bed, raised one corner of the mattress and hid the small knife under it. She had just finished doing this when she heard the door rattle. She stepped quickly away from the bed and turned in time to see one of the women from the kitchen enter. Erlic hovered nervously in the background, peering round the door frame. If she could get out of that door, Lydia thought, she'd be able to deal with him easily enough.

The woman set a large bucket of water on the floor and tossed a cloth bundle onto the bed.

"Milo says to clean yourself up," she said. "And put on the dress."

She left as abruptly as she had arrived. Lydia stepped to the bucket. It was full of water—hot water, she realized, seeing the vague wisps of steam coming from it. The cloth bundle consisted of a gray woolen dress—old and patched, but clean—a washcloth and a bar of soap, wrapped in a towel.

"Might as well get clean," she muttered. She went to undress, then had second thoughts. She lifted the chair onto the table and studied it for a several seconds. She saw that the legs were connected by thin dowel rods twenty centimeters from the bottom, designed to stop them flexing or twisting. She raised her hand and brought its edge smartly down on one of the dowels, breaking it loose from the chair. Then, armed with the wooden rod, she went to the door.

There had been an interior latch at one time. The hole that used to accommodate it was still in the door. She bent and peered through. Peering up on an angle, she could see the top of the iron latch outside. She worked the rod into the latch hole, angling it up until it sat over the latch, forcing it into the narrow space until it was a firm fit. Then, satisfied that the latch was blocked and the door couldn't be opened in a hurry, she stripped and washed herself all over, luxuriating in the feel of the hot water.

She worked carelessly, sloshing water in large amounts on the bare boards of the floor. She was almost finished when she heard the latch begin to move, then stop. She smiled at the pine rod protruding from the latch hole. It was moving up and down, a few millimeters at a time, as Erlic tried unsuccessfully to raise the latch. For a few minutes, he failed to notice the splintered end of the broken rod protruding through the latch hole. Then she heard him calling in that annoying, high-pitched voice.

"What have you done? You've broken the lock!"

She pulled on her clothes—the long dress would restrict her movements if she had to leave in a hurry—and moved to the door.

"Get away from there, you sneak," she called. "Try and spy on me and I'll scratch your eyes out."

She heard his footsteps as he moved away from the door, heard the creak of a chair as he sat in it, mumbling to himself. Then the sound of a brush moving backward and forward on leather. Obviously, he was polishing the Gatmeister's boots. Smiling grimly, she seized the rod and pulled it free. It might come in handy in the future, she thought.

She went to the bed. There was no pillow, so she rolled the gray dress up and used that. She stretched out on the hard, scratchy mattress and made herself comfortable. The light coming through the uncurtained window told her that it was mid to late afternoon. No point in trying to escape in daylight, she thought. She'd wait till night fell. She assumed at some stage they would bring her food. Once that was done, she'd work on getting out of here. She already had two ideas in mind.

Until then, she thought, I might as well rest and conserve my energy.

The Wildwater Rift?" Hal asked Pedr. "What's that?"

The other members of the crew moved closer to listen. Pedr smiled grimly at them.

"It's not the sort of place you'd choose to go," he said. "Not if you had any other choice."

Hal made an impatient gesture at the theatrical reply. Pedr was obviously a person who enjoyed the sound of his own voice. He wasn't the type to answer a simple question with a simple answer.

"Let's assume we don't have any other choice," he said. As he did, it occurred to him that they probably didn't.

Pedr glanced round the circle of interested faces, making sure he had their full attention.

"It's a small channel that leads off the main river, about four kilometers north of here. You would have passed it on the way."

Hal shrugged. "Can't remember it particularly," he said. "We saw quite a few narrow streams leading off the river. I assumed they were dead ends, because they weren't marked on the map."

"This one's a dead end, all right," Pedr said, with a smirk. "You could come to a really dead end if you tried to go down it."

"Can we cut the dramatics and just get a clear answer?" Hal asked impatiently.

Pedr drew back, his eyebrows arching. "Well, if you're going to be ill-mannered about it, perhaps I'll keep my information to myself," he said, a supercilious smile twitching at the corners of his mouth. He enjoyed being the center of attention, as Hal had surmised. And he planned to tell his story in his own time.

At least, that was his plan until Ingvar leaned forward and seized his wrist.

"I think that would be a bad idea," he said quietly, and began to squeeze Pedr's wrist.

The gambler went pale as he felt the amazing force of Ingvar's grip. The bones in his wrist twisted and ground together as Ingvar flexed his fingers. The pain was intense. Pedr gasped and reached forward with his other hand, trying to open Ingvar's fingers. It was like trying to open a rock.

"Yes," he said, "bad idea. I agree. Please . . . let me go?"

Ingvar held his gaze for a few seconds, then abruptly released his grip. Pedr fell back slightly. Without realizing it, he had been leaning toward Ingvar in an instinctive, and ineffective, effort to lessen the pain.

"So tell us about this rift," Hal said.

Pedr rubbed his wrist, glaring spitefully at Ingvar. But he decided it was a better idea to answer the question without excessive embroidery.

"As I said, it's a narrow channel that leads off the main river. About four kilometers back. There's a small fisherman's hut just this side of the entrance. If you know what to look for, you'll find it easily."

"And what will we find?" Stig asked.

Pedr glanced briefly at him, then back at Hal, who seemed to be the spokesman for the group.

"Well, you should know that once the river passes Bayrath, it swings out to the east in a huge winding sequence of bends that go for almost ten kilometers." He saw the impatience rising in Hal's eyes and hurriedly added, "You need to know this. It's relevant, I swear."

Hal nodded and Pedr continued. "As you're probably aware, we're on high ground here and the river splits into two streams— the North and South Dan. The northern fork, the one you've been traveling on, runs north to the Stormwhite Sea. But the other fork drops away to the south, heading for Raguza. In the next ten kilometers, the South Dan winds around and drops about fifty meters. The rift falls the same height, but it goes down a gorge and does it in about three hundred meters."

"So it's a waterfall," Hal said.

Pedr frowned, shaking his head. "Not so much a waterfall. It doesn't actually drop vertically. But it angles down in a series of steep chutes. And because of the downhill run and the narrowness of the channel, the water builds up tremendous speed."

"Rapids, then," Hal said, and when Pedr nodded, he continued, "But they are navigable? You can get a ship down them?"

Pedr shrugged. "They say that people have managed it. But I've never met anyone who did. From what I've heard, it would be difficult to get a large ship down the rift. A small boat might have a chance."

"*Heron*'s not very big," Edvin said.

Ulf shook his head. "She's no small boat."

Wulf couldn't help it, he had to speak up. "He didn't say she was. He said she's—"

"Shut up," Hal said quietly. Wulf instantly fell silent. "So where does the rift come out?" Hal asked.

Pedr nodded several times, indicating that he considered this a good question. "That's the thing. After you've gone down the rapids, the rift continues pretty well straight for another two kilometers. Then the Dan curves back from that long detour to the east and the rift rejoins it."

"So we'd end up back on the main river, and we'd save about eight kilometers of twists and turns by going down the rift," Hal said thoughtfully. Pedr looked at him as if he were crazy and shook his head.

"The only thing that's likely to make it back to the main river is a handful of splinters and the odd dead body," he said. "Your ship will be smashed on the rocks and you'll all drown."

"Are you a sailor?" Hal asked him suddenly.

Taken aback by the question, Pedr hesitated. "No."

"And you've never actually seen this rift, have you?"

"Well, not exactly. But—"

"Just answer the question. Have you seen the Wildwater Rift?"

"If you put it that way, no. I haven't."

"That is the way I put it. Basically, all you can tell us is that there is a rift and that it's a pretty frightening ride."

Pedr said nothing. It was a fairly brutal summing up of his information. Hal glanced around at his companions' faces. They were concerned, he could see. But there was no sign of fear there.

"And after all," he said to them, "do we have any choice?"

Thorn was watching them all carefully but he said nothing. He realized it was their decision to make and he had no right to influence it with his opinion. Hal was their leader and they were answerable to him.

It was Stig who replied. "No. We don't."

The others murmured agreement. Edvin offered a voice of reason in the argument.

"At least," he said, "we ought to take a look at this rift."

"Then that's what we'll do," Hal said.

Ulf raised a hand in question. "Umm . . . aren't you forgetting something? We have to get out of here first."

Wulf turned a scornful look on his twin. "Do you think Hal hasn't figured a way out by now?"

Ulf shrugged and turned to Hal. "So, Hal, how *are* we going to get out of here?" he asked. Hal spread his hands in a defeated gesture and grinned.

"I really have no idea," he said. "But I'm hoping Lydia will come up with something."

There was a sound of footsteps in the passageway, and they all turned as the jailer appeared in the dimness by the door. Behind him, they could see the shadowy forms of several armed guards.

"Stay where you are!" he ordered. They were some distance from the door and he wanted them to keep it that way. He rattled the key in the lock and opened the steel grille, peering through the dim light at the group of prisoners seated by the wall. Finally, he made out Hal and pointed to him.

"You! On your feet! The Gatmeister wants to talk to you."

Hal began to rise, but Ingvar laid a warning hand on his arm.

"Don't go, Hal," he said urgently. Hal smiled at him and gently disengaged himself.

"It's all right, Ingvar. Talking can't hurt."

He had no idea how wrong he was.

Doutro looked up at Hal as he was ushered into the office. As before, the Gatmeister was seated behind his large table, with pages scattered haphazardly on its surface. He pointed to a spot in front of him and Hal moved to it. There was no chair, so he stood and waited. He became conscious of other people in the room. He turned and saw two of Doutro's soldiers standing, backs to the wall. They had discarded their helmets and armored breastplates and were wearing short-sleeved, padded linen undershirts. They had retained their sword belts, cinched around thick canvas trousers. Their boots were felt, with leather soles, held in place by crisscross bindings.

"Face me," Doutro said coldly.

Hal turned back to meet his gaze. The Gatmeister eyed him thoughtfully, his eyes steady and unblinking.

"I've been considering your offer," he said. "It may have merit."

"My offer?" Hal asked, not understanding.

"Your friend suggested that you might pay me more than this . . . Zavac character you mentioned."

Hal smiled, but without any real humor. "Why continue this pretense that you don't know Zavac?" he said. "It serves no purpose now."

"Very well. Let's say I do know him. And let's say you offer to pay me more than he did. I might well set you free."

Hal studied the man for some moments. Doutro's face gave nothing away. His voice was calm and unemotional.

"Let's say we did make that offer," Hal said carefully. "What then?"

"I'd need to know that you had the money to back it up," Doutro said. His manner was matter-of-fact and he glanced away, seemingly disinterested. Too matter-of-fact, Hal thought. And too disinterested. And then he knew what Doutro was angling for.

"You've searched my ship," he said. Doutro looked back at him, neither confirming nor denying the accusation. But suddenly, Hal knew he was right. Doutro wasn't interested in extracting a bribe from them. He didn't need to. They were his prisoners and he could take all that they had. But first, he had to find it. To that end, he had ordered his men to search the *Heron*, looking for valuables and money. But they had come up empty-handed.

Which wasn't surprising. The *Heron*'s strongbox, which contained all their valuables—consisting of Thorn's canvas sack of coins and jewelry, a few personal possessions belonging to the crew and a small parcel Lydia had entrusted to Hal when they had left

Limmat—was hidden under an indistinguishable false panel in the central decking. The hiding place had been constructed by Hal when he built the *Heron.* The joinery was perfect and the seams were virtually invisible to the uninformed eye. The removable lid to the strongbox consisted of several deck planks of different lengths, so there was no even square set into the decking, which would have been an instant giveaway.

Hal was aware that most people built such hiding places in fairly obvious locations—either in the stern or the bow, and usually centrally located. Accordingly, he had selected a random position for his strongbox. It was positioned almost a third of the length of the ship from the stern, and offset to the starboard side. There was no logic or symmetry to its positioning. To find it, a searcher would have to rip up the entire deck. Doutro's next words confirmed his suspicion.

"Where's your money?" he demanded coldly.

Hal smiled at him. "Where you'll never find it."

Too late, he heard the sound of quick footsteps behind him, then felt one of the soldiers grip his arms, pinning them and pulling him back, off balance. The other moved in front of him, hands raised and balled into fists.

"Beat it out of him," Doutro said.

Hal tried to duck the first blow, but the man behind him held him still. The big fist exploded off his cheekbone. He grunted in pain. He saw the fist draw back again, tried to hunch down protectively, but couldn't manage it. Again, he felt the jolting power of the man's fist, smashing into his nose. Warm blood ran down over his upper lip. His vision was blurring as tears filled his eyes—a reflex reaction to the blow to his nose. Dimly, he saw the next blow coming, felt a smashing pain in the bony part of his eyebrow. It occurred to him that the man was wearing a ring. He felt it cut the eyebrow, felt more blood running down his face.

After that, he was aware of more and more blows smashing against his unprotected face. But they merged into one continual blur of pain until he was unable to distinguish one from another.

Then, mercifully, he lost consciousness.

The light through the window was fading and Lydia estimated that it must be early evening. There was no source of light in the room—no candle or lantern. She guessed that people in the detention room, as Doutro had called it, weren't trusted with a naked flame.

The door rattled again and the same woman entered the room. Lydia sat upright, swinging her legs off the bed.

"You stay where you are!" Erlic's shrill voice came from the doorway. He was watching the proceedings, as before. She shrugged and remained sitting on the bed. The woman placed a bucket by the door, then brought a tray to the table. Lydia could smell the hot food. Her stomach rumbled appreciatively. She hadn't eaten all day and whatever it was on the tray smelled remarkably good.

The woman pointed at it.

"Dinner," she said unnecessarily. She checked the level of water in the jug on the table and was satisfied that there was enough there. Then she turned back toward the door.

"Just a moment," Lydia said, and the woman turned back to her. "I need to use the bathroom."

She didn't, but she wanted to know more about the routine in the house, and how much freedom of movement she'd be allowed. The woman pointed to the bucket by the door.

"There it is," she said, then turned and left once more. The door rattled closed behind her.

Lydia rose and walked to the table. The meal was on a tin plate, with a large spoon the only implement provided. No naked flames. No sharp objects, she thought. It was a chicken and potato stew, with a chunk of rough bread beside it. As she had already noticed, it smelled delicious. She sat down at the table, taking care as she set her weight on the now-damaged chair, and made short work of it, mopping up the last traces of gravy with a piece of the bread.

She sat back unwarily, and the chair lurched underneath her. It was definitely less stable without that support rod, she thought. She belched lightly. After years spent hunting alone in the woods, Lydia's manners and social graces left something to be desired.

Well, at least they don't plan to starve me, she thought. She had a sudden flash of concern that the meal might have been drugged. But then she shrugged. Why would they bother? As far as Doutro was concerned, she was a homeless stray, possibly a petty criminal, and of little interest to him.

She rose and prowled restlessly around the room. Outside, she heard the creak of Erlic's chair as he shifted position. She went to the window and tried to peer out, but her field of vision was limited. The window was on the side of the house and she could see other houses directly across what seemed to be a relatively wide lane. The house facing her was a story lower and she estimated that it was eight meters away—too far to reach. She had already decided that her most logical escape route was out the window.

A thought struck her and she walked to the bed, pulling the straw mattress aside. As she had hoped, the bed was fashioned from a wooden frame, with a rope net to support the mattress. The net consisted of two long pieces of rough rope, strung lengthwise and crosswise. She took the knife and cut the lengthwise rope, unthreading it through the holes in the timber and pulling it loose. The result was a five-meter length of rope. She removed the crosswise rope next and gained another four meters. She replaced the mattress, balancing it precariously on the edge of the frame. It sagged in the middle but in the dim light, if anyone came, she hoped it would pass muster.

She sat and waited until she estimated that an hour had passed. It was dark outside the window now, although there was a half-moon that threw some light into the room. And she noticed now that there was an angled fanlight above the door, leaving a twenty-centimeter gap, presumably for ventilation. It admitted a dim light from the hallway.

After an hour, when nobody had returned to collect the tray, she guessed that she would be left alone for the night. She rose and tiptoed to the door, bending to listen through the latch hole. She could hear nothing for a few seconds. Then she heard the sound of Erlic's chair creaking as he shifted position. She grinned unsympathetically. Obviously, he was destined to sleep in the chair all night.

Taking the small knife, she moved silently to the window and inserted the blade in the crack between the two halves, underneath the exterior latch bar. She felt a wave of frustration as she realized the small paring knife was too short to reach all the way through. The heavy window frames were thicker than the length of the blade.

She withdrew the knife and pursed her lips thoughtfully. Using the knife to open the window had been central to her plan of escape. She hadn't considered that the blade might be too short for the task. Then an idea struck her. She padded quietly back to the bed and retrieved the dowel rod she had broken earlier. She went to work with the knife and whittled the last fifteen centimeters of the rod down to a narrow, flat shape. She tested it periodically until it was thin enough to fit through the narrow gap between the window frames. She rested it against the latch bar and began to move it upward. But the latch hadn't been raised in a long time and it was stiff. She felt the weakened rod bending ominously.

Her pulse raced and she forced herself to wait a few minutes to calm down. If she broke the rod in the window gap, she might not be able to remove the broken piece. The gap would be blocked and there would be no way she could force the latch up. Frustration built in her. The idea had seemed so simple. Slip the blade into the gap, unlock the windows. Now it might all come undone because the blade was a centimeter too short and the rod was too weak.

Suppressing a curse, she slid the knife into the gap, under the flattened rod, supporting it for most of its length. Then she lifted once more—gently at first, then with growing firmness. The rod bent at the point where it protruded past the knife blade and she stopped, heart in her mouth. Then she tried again, gradually increasing the pressure, and felt a small movement.

Again she lifted and again the latch bar moved by a half centimeter. Then it sprang free and slipped up and out of the two brackets that held it in position, falling away into the laneway. She held her breath, and heard a faint clatter as it struck the cobblestones below. She waited to see if there were any outcry from the street. But apparently nobody had noticed. She let the long-held breath go in a shuddering sigh, then moved back to the table to collect the rest of her equipment.

She dropped the knife into a pocket, coiled the rope over her shoulder and took a last look around the room. There was nothing else she could use, she thought. She walked quickly to the window, swung both frames open and stepped her left leg over the frame, ready to climb out. She boosted herself off the floor with her other leg.

The door opened.

She paused, half in and half out of the window, as light from the corridor flooded into the room. Erlic stood, his hand on the latch, watching her in shock.

"What are you doing? Get down!" he ordered. Then he made his mistake. He should have relocked the door and raised the alarm. Instead, he moved into the room and toward her, to stop her.

She stepped lightly down to meet him. As he reached out to grab her arm, she moved forward, inside his grasping hand. She slipped her right leg behind his, pivoted on her right instep and hit him on the side of the jaw with the heel of her open hand, fingers spread to increase its rigidity.

The nerve endings in Erlic's jaw sent a lightning message to his brain and he blacked out like a snuffed candle. As he reeled back from the blow, Lydia's right leg trapped his and he went down with a heavy crash on the floor. She bent over him quickly. He was breathing but he was out cold. She moved to the door and pulled it shut, hearing the latch click into place. Then she returned to the still form on the floor.

She might need the rope, so she couldn't spare any to tie him up. But she had to incapacitate him as she had no idea how long he'd remain unconscious. Probably no more than a minute or two. She glanced around the room, then grabbed the blanket from the bed, along with the rolled-up dress she'd used earlier as a pillow.

She wrapped the dress round and round his head in a tight bundle, covering him down to the neck and using the sleeves to tie it in place. If he cried out now, the sound would be well and truly muffled. Then she stripped off his belt, rolled him tightly in the blanket and fastened it in place with the belt, pulling it as tight as she could and making sure his arms were trapped firmly on either side of his body.

"That should do it," she muttered. She was about to go out the window again when a further thought struck. She walked quickly to the door and jammed the untrimmed end of the dowel into the latch hole as before, trapping the latch in place. Then she snapped off the dowel close to the door. If anyone tried to come in now, they'd first have to force the broken piece of wood out of the hole.

Satisfied that she'd done all she could to delay discovery and pursuit, she moved to the window and peered out. The roof was a steep pitch, finished in flat slate tiles. She tested one with the palm of her hand. Fortunately, there'd been no rain recently and the tile was smooth, but not slippery.

She took off her boots—bare feet would give her a better grip on the slates—and shoved them through her belt at the back. Then, with one last glance at the unfortunate Erlic, she jackknifed out the window, facing the roof, and began to climb the steep pitch to the central ridge.

She pressed her bare hands and feet hard against the slates to create the greatest amount of friction and increase her grip. Using a well-established climbing technique, she moved one hand or one foot at a time, leaving the other three to provide maximum purchase. Moving like a giant spider, she swarmed up the roof until she was straddling the ridge. There, she heaved a sigh of relief and looked around her. The moon was halfway through its nightly journey and it cast a soft light over the sea of roofs around her. Doutro's house was one of the tallest in the area and, as she had earlier noted, was placed on a high point. The view was quite spectacular. Looking toward the harbor, she could see the tips of masts belonging to ships moored there.

But she wasn't here to look at the harbor. She rose and, walking with her feet splayed on either side of the ridgepole, made her way to the rear of the house, a few meters from where she had been sitting.

As she had hoped, and as was normal in towns like this, the rear of the house was served by a narrow alley—much narrower than the side laneway. The alley gave access for service carts to haul away garbage and night soil. She looked across to the back of the house opposite. It stood several meters lower than Doutro's mansion and was barely three meters away.

An easy jump—if she ignored the twenty-meter drop to the laneway below.

She sat down on the ridgepole again and peered over the side, grunting in satisfaction when she saw what she had been hoping for. Doutro's house, like most multistory buildings, was equipped with a sturdy lifting beam and hook, so that large items of furniture could be hauled to the upper floors without the need to negotiate the narrow stairways inside. There was a similar beam on the house opposite her.

She uncoiled the rope around her shoulders and fashioned a large loop in one end. She dropped this over the hook, then fastened the other end around her waist. Then she stood and backed away from the edge of the roof, holding the loose rope out to one side. For a moment, she had a terrible picture of herself running toward the roof's edge and tangling her feet in the rope, crashing over and dropping into the gap between the two houses. She pushed it firmly aside.

She moved back eight long paces. Then she paused, staring at the line of the ridge leading toward that empty gap. Seeing the roof opposite. If she missed, the rope might break her fall and save her. Or it might send her swinging like a pendulum, to smash into the walls of Doutro's house. She pushed that thought aside too.

Then, before she could think any further, she launched herself.

She ran lightly, setting her feet on the ridge itself. As she reached the end, she hurled herself forward, releasing the rope as she went, so that it fell away in a loose curve below her.

She had her eyes fixed on the opposite roof, but she sensed the dark drop beneath her, seeming to reach up to drag her down.

Then she was across, clearing the gap by a meter and a half. The roof was lower than Doutro's and the pitch wasn't as steep. She landed on her feet on the left side of the ridge, her knees buckling with the force of the fall. They slammed into the hard slate of the roof and she grunted in pain. Then she lost her balance and began to fall, using all her strength to hurl her upper body toward the ridge. As her feet went out from under her, she scrabbled for a hold on the ridge, slipping, losing her grip, then finally holding.

She heaved herself up and straddled the ridge, giving herself a few moments for her breathing to ease and her heart to stop racing. Then she scrambled to the edge of the roof and flicked the slack rope to release it from the loading hook. It took her three attempts, sending a half loop flying across the gap, until the line jerked free of the hook and dropped away into the darkness below her.

She peered over the edge. She could see an open window four meters below her and a little to her right. That would do. She reeled in the rope, made the end fast around the cargo hook on this side, then lowered herself off the roof, her feet scrabbling for a grip on the brickwork as she descended slowly. The rope creaked ominously and she wondered how old it was. But it was too late now to worry about that. She let herself down until she was level with the open window. There was no light coming from it and she hoped that meant the room behind it was empty. She walked her way across the wall to the window, set herself, then pushed off and swung herself out, then in through the opening, releasing the rope as she went feet first into the room. She hit the floor and fell in a tangle of arms and legs, coming to her feet quickly and glancing round to get her bearings.

She was in a bedroom. A woman's bedroom, judging by the frills and flounces and lace over the bed. And sure enough, there was an elderly woman asleep in the bed.

More correctly, she *had* been asleep. She sat up in confusion now at the sudden racket of a body hitting the floor, her lacy ruffled mobcap falling over her eyes, as she peered round the darkened room. Her eyes lit on Lydia and she gasped and put her hand to her mouth in fright.

"Who are you?" she quavered.

Lydia help up a hand in a calming gesture. "I'm Lydia. How do you do?" she said, smiling. She assumed no real burglar would ever introduce herself. "I'm looking for Gerald. Is he here?"

It was the first thing that came to her mind. She thought it sounded calming and soothing—certainly much better than "I'm here to rob you blind" or "I'm here to kill you in your bed." She simply wanted to engage with the woman, to start a conversation— anything to stop her from screaming. Amazingly, the woman pointed a trembling hand at the door.

"He's across the corridor," she said. The puzzled note in her voice was all too obvious. Lydia's eyes widened in surprise and for a moment she was frozen. Then she recovered.

"Right! Sorry to bother you. Got the wrong room. Stupid of me. I'll be going along now."

She stepped quickly to the door and let herself out. Behind her, she heard a quavering voice.

"Are you a friend of Gerald's? Perhaps you should knock."

She shook her head incredulously. "Who'd believe it?" she asked herself. She glanced along the corridor until she saw a set of stairs leading down. As she descended them, moving like a wraith, she heard the elderly woman calling faintly.

"Gerald? There's someone to see you."

She encountered nobody else as she made her way through the silent, darkened house. She found the rear door, unbarred it and stepped out into the narrow alley she had just crossed, twenty meters above her present position.

"Now to get the boys out of prison," she said softly.

chapter twenty-one

The Herons heard footsteps in the corridor, then the grille door was abruptly thrown open and a limp figure shoved roughly into the room. They were startled by this sudden turn of events, and the door was slammed and locked again before they could react.

Thorn was first to move. He crossed the cellar in three long steps and knelt beside the unconscious figure who lay facedown on the hard stone. He turned him over, wincing at the bruises and cuts on Hal's face as he saw them. He cradled the boy gently on his knees as he knelt beside him.

As the others recognized their skirl, there was a chorus of angry and alarmed exclamations. Only Pedr remained where he had been sitting against the wall. He'd been in the cellar for several weeks and he was used to seeing his fellow prisoners returning this way after a session with Doutro.

"Hal? Are you all right?" Edvin asked. He knelt beside Thorn, reaching out to turn Hal's face toward the dim light from the torch in the corridor. The rest of the crew clustered around, uttering cries of anger as they saw the extent of Hal's injuries. Edvin glanced up at Stig, whose face was twisted in anger as he saw the way his friend had been treated.

"Fetch me the water jug, Stig," he said. "And someone find me a clean cloth."

They had been supplied with a large jug of drinking water. It was resting on a shelf in the stone wall, alongside a battered tin mug. Not knowing how often it would be refilled, they had been rationing the water. It wasn't a lot to share between nine of them—ten counting Pedr. Stig retrieved it now and handed it to Edvin.

The second request was easier said than done. There simply was no clean cloth anywhere in the cellar. The Herons looked round helplessly, as if hoping that one would suddenly materialize. Then Ingvar solved the problem, removing his outer jacket and tearing the sleeve out of his linen shirt. He handed it to Edvin.

"Thanks," Edvin said, without looking up. He soaked the cloth and began to bathe the rapidly congealing blood from Hal's face, squeezing the cold water out over the swellings and bruises on his cheeks and eyebrows.

He worked gently on a cut on Hal's lip. It was obviously painful, as the young skirl's eyes flickered open and he frowned up at Edvin's concerned face.

"Ow. Take it easy, will you?" The words were thick and distorted by the swollen lip, but there was a concerted sigh of relief as they saw that he was conscious and seemed to be in control of his faculties.

"What happened?" Ulf asked. His voice showed how worried he was and Hal tried to grin reassuringly at him, but the movement hurt his lip and he flinched, reaching up to touch it. That made him flinch again.

"What do you think happened?" Wulf asked angrily. "He was beaten up. That's what happened. Even a fool can see that."

"Which is why you can," Ulf replied, with some spirit. "What I mean was, who did this, and why?"

"Then why didn't you say that?" Wulf shot back. "What you said was—"

"Shut up," Ingvar said. There was a distinctly threatening tone in his voice and the twins turned quickly to look at him. He was standing right behind them. His hands were loosely curled into claws in front of him and the brothers both had the same vision— of Ingvar grabbing them by their collars and banging their heads together.

They shut up.

Hal let out a weak cackle of laughter, wincing once more as his split lip warned him against excess movement.

"Good to see things haven't changed," he said.

"Good to see you can laugh about it," Stig said. "When we get out of here, I'm going to beat the ballast stones out of Doutro."

"You'll be queuing behind me to do it," Ingvar said warningly.

Stig glanced quickly at the big boy. He had never seen such a look of fury on Ingvar's normally placid face. Stig made a placatory gesture.

"Anything you say, Ingvar. Happy to let you have first dibs," he said.

Ingvar's only reply was a rumbling growl, a primitive sound that came from deep in his massive chest. Hearing it, the twins were glad they'd stopped arguing as quickly as they had.

Edvin finished cleaning the last of the blood from Hal's face, soaked the cloth in water again and wadded it up, placing it in Hal's left hand.

"That's about all I can do," he said. "Keep that cold water against your cheek. It'll take the swelling down."

Gently, he guided Hal's hand, placing the cold compress over the purple swelling on his cheekbone. That, and the cut on his eyebrow where the ring had hit him, were the worst of his injuries. The cut was already scabbing and there was no point in trying to work on it.

"That's better," Hal said. "One good thing about being in a dungeon—it keeps the water cold."

A ripple of laughter ran round the crew. It was a pretty feeble attempt at a joke, but the laughter was more from relief that their skirl was well enough to make even a feeble joke.

"So why were you beaten?" Thorn prompted, seeing that Hal was able to talk.

Hal looked up at him. "He wanted to know the location of the *Heron*'s strongbox," he said. "I'm afraid he became a little testy when I wouldn't tell him." He took the wet cloth away from his cheekbone for a few seconds, then replaced it when it had cooled. "Mind you, if I'd known it was going to hurt this much, I probably would have."

"That probably wouldn't have stopped him," Pedr said from

his position against the wall. They all turned to look at him and he explained. "Doutro likes to see people suffer."

"Does he now?" Thorn said, his eyes narrowing dangerously. "I think before we leave Bayrath, we may have to change his attitude."

"Easy to say," Pedr replied, an edge of sarcasm in his voice. "But so far I don't see any sign that you'll be leaving. Doutro will try you on first day next week, convict you on second day and string you all up on third day."

There was a moment's silence. Then Stefan spoke.

"You know, you're sounding a little too pleased with that whole idea," he said. "I'm not sure I like that."

Ulf nodded. "I agree. I rather think it might be a good idea to kick your backside around the cellar a few times."

Wulf nodded. "For once, I agree with my brother completely."

The two of them rose and moved toward Pedr, who tried to shrink away from them against the wall. Unfortunately, the wall didn't provide a lot of shrinking room. Thorn considered telling them to stop, then shrugged. Pedr's constant, sarcastic, know-it-all attitude was wearing thin, he decided.

Ulf was leaning down over the unfortunate Pedr, reaching for his shirt collar to drag him away from the wall, when something hard bounced off his head, then rattled on the stones of the floor.

"Ouch!" he said, standing up and rubbing the sore spot, staring around the cellar. "What was that?" He looked down and saw a large pebble on the floor of the cellar. It hadn't been there a few seconds ago, he thought. Someone had thrown it at him.

"Who did that?" His voice grew louder as his anger built.

"Wulf, is that you?" It was Lydia's voice, coming from the narrow window above him.

"Lydia? Did you throw a rock at me? And anyway I'm Ulf!"

"For Gorlog's sake, does it matter?" Stig said angrily, moving quickly to a spot beneath the window. "Lydia, is that you?"

"Yes. Sorry I hit you, Wulf, I was just trying to attract your attention. I wasn't sure who was in there."

"It's Ulf," Ulf repeated, annoyed. Stig muttered something inaudible and shoved him aside. He looked up. Lydia's fingers were visible now between one of the narrow gaps in the bars above him. She fluttered them to draw his attention.

"Is Hal there?" she said.

Stig glanced around to where Hal was still lying, supported on Thorn's knees. Thorn shook his head.

"He's here. But he's been hurt," Stig said. He heard the worried note in Lydia's voice as she took in that information.

"What's happened?" she asked. "Is it bad?"

"No. He's bruised and cut up, but he'll be all right. How did you get away?" he asked.

"Oh . . . easy enough. I climbed out a window and jumped across an alley to the next roof. Made my way down from the roof and came back here to find you."

Stig raised his eyebrows. "Easy as that?"

She ignored the sarcasm and continued. "Question is, how do I get you out? What's your situation? I can't see in. This window is too narrow and it's right at ground level."

Stig glanced around. It was a reflex action. By now, he was totally familiar with the large room.

"We're in a big cellar," he said. "Stone walls and floor and just this window and a barred gate. It's locked, of course," he told her. There was a pause while she considered this.

"Where's the key?" she said. "Could I get to it?"

He shook his head, instantly aware that the movement was a useless one as she couldn't see him.

"Shouldn't think so. The turnkey keeps it on his belt and he's always got three or four guards with him."

There was a long pause while she considered this information. When she spoke again, he could sense her growing frustration. After all she'd gone through, and the risks she had taken, it was beginning to seem that there was no way she could help them.

"Maybe I could say I was a friend or something, and see if they'd let me in to visit you?" she suggested. But before she even finished the idea, it was plain that she considered that any such plan was unworkable.

"And then you could overpower all five of them and let us out?" Stig said.

She retorted angrily. "All right! I'm just putting ideas out here! Do you have any that are worthwhile?"

Stig had to admit that he didn't. But he didn't feel it was necessary to say it to her. Jesper had risen and he made his way across the cellar to stand beside Stig.

"Lydia, it's Jesper. Do you think you could find your way back to the ship?"

"Of course I can!" she said. She was obviously still angry and thought the question was a waste of time. "It's only a few blocks back to the harbor. But I can't sail it on my own, can I?"

"No. You can't," Jesper replied patiently. "But if you could get on board without being seen, you could fetch me something that might solve the problem."

Instantly, Lydia's anger dissipated. She replied now with new interest.

"What is it, Jesper? Where will I find it?"

"It's a small canvas wallet—a tool kit actually—and it's in my pigeonhole, beside my rowing bench. Port side, second from the bow."

Each crewmember had a pigeonhole, or small locker, beside his crew station. They kept personal items there. Valuables, of course, were kept in the strongbox.

"Okay. Port benches, second from the front," Lydia repeated.

"The bow," Stig corrected her automatically.

"Does it matter?" came the waspish reply. "What's in it, Jesper?"

Now Jesper hesitated. "It's my lock-picking kit," he said, with some embarrassment.

Stig looked at him, his eyebrows arching. "Your lock-picking kit? I thought you'd given all that sort of thing away?"

Jesper shrugged. "It's a souvenir," he said. "I couldn't bring myself to get rid of it."

"Just as well," Lydia said from above them. "I'll be back as soon as I can. Stay put."

They heard the soft scuff of her feet on the cobbles as she left. Stig and Jesper exchanged a look.

"What else does she expect us to do?" Jesper asked.

chapter twenty-two

L ydia ghosted through the streets leading back to the river. She stayed in the shadows by the buildings, slipping from one to another, her deer-hide boots noiseless on the cobbles. As she moved away from the official buildings and back toward the working area of the docks, the streets became narrower and darker. Houses and offices gave way to warehouses and small manufactories. Often an entire block would be illuminated by one lantern, set in a glass box at the end of the street. It was a mean, dangerous-looking part of the town. Occasionally, she saw other dark figures, slipping in and out of the side alleys.

Once, she came face-to-face with a heavyset man wearing a hooded short cloak. They came level with each other under one of the infrequent lanterns and she could make out only the lower half of his face. The upper half was shaded by the hood. She had an impression of a dark, full beard. In the shadow of his hood, his eyes were unblinking, staring at her.

He paused and for a moment looked as if he was going to move toward her. She slipped the small knife out of her pocket and held it, blade angled up in the classic knife fighter's position. The blade was short but it caught the light of the lantern, sending a reflection of light rippling across the far wall. The position of the knife, and the unconcerned, confident expression on her face, seemed to decide him. He grunted and hurried away, pulling the hood closer over his face.

She turned and watched him go. Like hers, his shoes made virtually no sound on the street and she wanted to be sure that he had gone and wasn't doubling back behind her, to take her by surprise. But he hurried on his way without looking back, eventually swallowed by the dark shadows.

By comparison, the riverfront, when she reached it, seemed to blaze with light. There were taverns and eating houses spread along the bank, each one with its illuminated sign and lighted windows. Sounds of laughter and occasional angry shouts came to her, accompanied at times by the sound of breaking glass and furniture. From time to time, laughing or shouting figures emerged onto the street, some staggering, and made their way toward the docks. The side of the street that fronted the river was bare of buildings. Ships and smaller vessels were moored directly alongside, and at intervals, jetties ran out at right angles into the semicircular basin that served as a harbor. More craft were moored alongside these finger wharves.

She moved to the river side of the street, not wanting to be

BROTHERBAND CHRONICLES

continually accosted by patrons leaving the taverns. There was less
need for secrecy here, as the riverfront street was a busy thoroughfare.

The ships and smaller craft all carried lights, set high on their
masts. She paused for a moment to get her bearings, then headed
toward the toll office, where *Heron* had been detained. She remembered a few landmarks from the previous day, when they had been
marched along the riverfront to Doutro's office, and she strode out
more confidently.

Looking through the forest of masts and halyards, she could
see the money sign that stood above the toll office, illuminated
by flaring torches set on either side. She increased her pace, then
stopped, aghast.

Heron was no longer moored alongside the jetty where the toll
office stood. She looked around frantically, in case there were two
offices and she had come to the wrong one. She quickly realized
that this was where they had been detained.

But the ship was gone.

She stopped, leaning against a waist-high pole that had several
heavy ropes looped over it. A large fishing smack bobbed gently on
the river beside her as she racked her brain, trying to figure out why
the ship had gone. And where.

Then it came to her. The jetty that served the toll office provided short-term mooring only. Ships would moor there for five or
ten minutes while their skippers paid the toll, then move on, leaving room for the next ship to pay. Doutro would hardly want the
jetty space taken up by a ship that was going nowhere and paying
no toll. He would have had it moved.

But where?

She cast around the bobbing masts and figureheads. The basin was crowded with ships and they merged together into one amorphous mass under her gaze. She knew a trained sailor, like Hal or Stig, would be able to differentiate quickly between them. But she wasn't a seafarer and ships all tended to look the same to her.

"Think," she told herself. "Think. Then look."

Logic told her that the *Heron* wouldn't have gone far. Doutro struck her as a person who would make a habit of detaining ships to squeeze extra payment out of them. Therefore, he would have a holding area somewhere close by.

She walked along the quay more slowly now, scanning the jetties that ran out into the river as she drew closer to the toll office. Tall masts, surmounted by lanterns, bobbed gently on the wavelets that slapped quietly against the bank. She blinked her eyes to clear them. The masts were beginning to blend together again. She studied them individually but could see no sign of Hal's little ship.

Then a thought struck her. She was looking for a tall mast among other tall masts. But the *Heron's* mast, without its long curved yardarm, would be much shorter than the ones she was looking at. She needed to cast her gaze lower, searching for a heavy, short mast—and the sharp-beaked *Heron* figurehead that adorned the bow post.

She moved faster now, coming level with the jetty where the toll office stood. So far, no sign of what she was looking for. She went on, past the toll office.

And on the very next jetty, across a short stretch of dark water that rippled with reflected lantern light, there it was.

There was another ship moored beyond *Heron*, tied up bow to stern. Unlike most of the others in the basin, these two showed no masthead lights. They were unoccupied, she realized.

She hesitated. The jetty was still forty meters away and she thought it would be better to study it here, rather than get closer, where she might be noticed. She knew it would be a mistake to be observed paying too much attention to the impounded ship. There was sure to be a guard somewhere and too much interest on her part might make him suspicious.

She walked a few paces closer. Where was the guard? There had to be one. Then she saw him. He had walked out to the far end of the jetty. Now he was strolling back, looking around in a disinterested way. He stopped by the ship moored behind *Heron* and, stepping to the edge of the jetty, peered down into her. Perhaps he had heard a noise, she thought. Then, seemingly satisfied, he moved on, passing the *Heron* without a second glance and pacing to the landward end of the jetty.

He was armed, she could see. A short sword hung at his side and he was carrying a spear. He wore a mail shirt but no helmet. He paused under a lantern set on a pole at the entry to the jetty and peered up and down the quay. Lydia resisted the temptation to shrink down behind the low stone wall beside her. Movement would attract his attention, she knew. She was in an area of shadow between two lamps, and he had the full light of the lantern in his eyes. If he really wanted to study the waterfront, he would have been better to do it away from the light. He was simply going through the motions.

He yawned, covering his mouth with the back of his hand, then turned and began to pace slowly along the jetty again. She could hear his hard-shod boots on the jetty planks. His back was to her, so she moved quickly, getting closer to the entrance to the jetty. There was no gate, she saw, grateful for the fact. The jetty itself was littered with gear from ships—coiled ropes, rolled sails, oars, straw fenders and half a dozen fish traps in an untidy pile.

"Must have been taken from an impounded fishing boat," she said to herself. It made sense that when Doutro detained a ship, he would strip her of her gear and put it up for sale. The value of the parts would be greater than the whole.

Moving carefully, her eyes fixed on the sentry as he paced away from her, she slipped onto the jetty itself. Crouched double, she moved away from the side where the lanterns were set, staying in the relative dimness. She was a trained hunter and it was second nature to her to move quickly but with no noise in a forest. On a bare jetty, with no deadfalls or twigs underfoot, it was child's play. She reached the pile of fish traps and slipped behind them, staying on the outer side.

The sentry had reached the end of the jetty now. He turned and began to pace back. This time, he didn't bother to look at either of the ships moored alongside. That was a good sign, she thought. He was getting bored. He'd probably been on duty for hours. He paced down to the riverfront road again. This time, he didn't pause, but turned around and began to retrace his steps. Lydia crouched, absolutely motionless, behind the wicker fish traps.

The sentry went past, barely two meters away from her. As he passed, she could see his eyes were down, staring at the planks of the jetty. Definitely bored, she thought. Once he was a few meters past her hiding place, she slipped out and began to shadow him, making sure she matched her footsteps to his, to avoid any give-away noise.

He passed the *Heron.* She let him go a few more meters, then moved quickly to the jetty's edge and lowered herself to the deck of the little ship. The ropes groaned slightly and the wicker fenders creaked as her weight made the ship move. She dropped into the space that held the rowing benches, below the center deck level, and crouched there. But the small riverside noises didn't attract the guard's attention. He continued to plod stolidly down the jetty. Staying low, she slipped over the center decking and dropped into the well where the port-side rowing benches were. Still in a crouch, she moved forward to Jesper's bench and bent to peer into the re-cessed pigeonhole under the central decking.

There was nothing there. She put her hand in and felt around, but there was no sign of the canvas wallet he had described. She checked to make sure that she was at the right bench. Then she became aware of something under her feet. She bent and peered at the deck beside the footrests for the rowers. There was a clutter of small items there. A half-carved model of a ship, a fur-lined leather vest and a walrus tusk on a leather thong.

Then she realized. The ship had been searched. That was log-ical. And the searchers had cast aside anything that wasn't of value—which meant virtually everything that wasn't in the hidden strongbox. She looked now to the spot where she knew the deck planking concealed it. It was undisturbed, so the searchers obvi-ously hadn't found it. She breathed a sigh of relief. If they'd found the parcel she had entrusted to Hal when they left Limmat, they would have been highly excited.

She hoped a canvas tool roll wouldn't count as an item of value. She looked over the rowing bench into the next space and saw it, where it had been tossed aside contemptuously by whoever had searched the ship. The roll was half undone and she checked inside. The strangely shaped, unidentifiable tools were held firmly in sewn pockets. There were no empty ones, so she assumed everything was in place. She tucked the wallet inside her jacket, then scrambled toward the foot of the mast, where she had been standing when Doutro's soldiers had arrested Hal and the crew.

Her eyes lit up with pleasure as she saw her weapons belt, with the atlatl handle clipped to it and the dirk in its long scabbard, lying beside the keel box where she had dropped it. The dirk was a plain, utilitarian weapon, devoid of any decoration or fine workmanship. A simple straight blade with a wooden handle and a brass crosspiece. Only Lydia knew how fine was the quality of the steel that formed the blade. Obviously it had attracted no attention from the searchers.

She buckled it on, setting it below the other, narrower belt she wore over her long shirt. She welcomed its familiar weight around her waist. Without it, she realized, she had felt something was missing.

The sentry's slow, dragging footsteps were coming back. She lay full length in the rowing well, in case he decided to inspect the *Heron.* She heard the footsteps pass, then continue to the landward end once more.

This time, he must have paused again. She couldn't blame him. It was a deadly boring job that he had, pacing up and down a jetty past two empty ships.

Well, empty most of the time, anyway.

He was on the move again. Peering over the top of the rowing well, she could see his head and shoulders moving away. The spear was tilted over his shoulder now. Before too long, she thought, he'd probably lean it against the wall of the small office built at the outer end of the jetty and continue without it.

He disappeared from her field of vision. She climbed out of the rowing well and slid across the central decking on her belly. At the landward side, she raised herself to peer carefully over the top of the jetty. He was two-thirds of the way along his route, giving her plenty of time to get away. She heaved herself up onto the jetty, then, in a crouch, moved to the darker side. Checking once more that he was still heading away from her, she ran lightly to the riverfront, crossing the street and merging into the shadows on the far side.

Reaching the end of his beat, the sentry yawned and spat into the black water of the river.

Another uneventful night, he thought morosely. Nothing ever happens in this town.

I think you should get up and move around," Edvin said. Hal frowned at him.

"You do realize that I'm battered and bruised all over, don't you?"

Edvin nodded. "That's exactly why you should move around. Otherwise you'll stiffen up and it'll be even harder to move when we get out of here."

"Sounds like a good idea to me," Stig said.

Hal glared at him. It was all very well for Stig to think so. He wasn't bruised and aching all over.

"Perhaps you'd like me to dance a little jig? That'll get everything loosened up and working."

Stig shrugged good-naturedly. "If that's what you want to do, go ahead."

Hal muttered something highly uncomplimentary. It had to do

with the comparative intelligence of Stig and a senile billy goat. But he allowed Edvin to help him to his feet, groaning as the movement stretched his bruised muscles and ribs.

Ingvar hovered close by. "Are you all right, Hal?" he asked.

Hal eyed him balefully. "Of course I am. I'm making these strange noises because I'm overjoyed with the waves of agony that are running through my body," he said through clenched teeth.

He took a few tentative steps, supported by Edvin. The healer was right, he thought, although he wasn't going to admit it. Moving was probably the best thing for his aches and pains. Slowly, he paced the length of the cellar, feeling the stiffness begin to work its way out of his muscles. He was young and very fit, and the injuries, although painful, were superficial. They reached the end of the cellar and he turned to retrace his steps. Edvin remained close by him, but now he was supporting less of his weight, leaving Hal to make his own way.

"Jesper! Are you there?"

It was Lydia's voice, coming from the high, barred window. All eyes turned to the narrow slit and they saw her fingers once more, fluttering in greeting. Hal stepped away from Edvin's supporting arm, forgetting his aches and pains, and hurried to stand under the window. Jesper was only half a pace behind him.

"Lydia!" he called softly. "Did you get Jesper's tool kit?"

"Hal?" He could hear the relief in her voice. "You're all right?"

"I'm fine. Did you get the tools?" he repeated. Her hand disappeared as she withdrew it. A few seconds later, they saw the gray canvas wallet beginning to appear as she pushed it through two bars.

"Got it," she said. "Here it comes."

Jesper gave a quick nod of appreciation. "Excellent!" he said, positioning himself under the spot. "Let it come."

The wallet, some twenty centimeters long by nine wide, slid through the bars, teetered for a moment on the edge of the sill, then dropped with a soft metallic clink into Jesper's waiting hands. Jesper quickly untied the thong securing it and checked the contents, satisfying himself that everything was in place.

"Yes!" he whispered triumphantly.

"Is that it?" Lydia asked apprehensively. She had a sudden fear that she might have brought the wrong tool kit. After all, she had no idea what lock-picks looked like.

"From the look on Jesper's face, that's it, all right," Hal replied. "Good work, Lydia. Did you have any problems finding it?"

"Not too many. They've moved the *Heron* to a different mooring. Took me a few minutes to find it," she replied. Then she added, "Oh, and it looks as though somebody has searched the ship."

"Doutro had that done. He was trying to find the strongbox."

"Thought it might be that. How long will it take for Jesper to open the door?"

Hal looked at Jesper, who had already moved to the heavy iron gate. He repeated the question. Jesper frowned, studying the lock.

"Give me a few minutes. It's a pretty old lock. Shouldn't take too long."

Hal repeated the information to Lydia. She paused a few seconds, then replied.

"I'm feeling a little obvious lying here on the paving stones with my face against the window. I'll wait for you in the alleyway across from the main entrance."

"We'll see you there," he replied. Again, her hand appeared through the bars, the fingers fluttering briefly in farewell. Then he heard her soft footsteps receding. Hal turned to see how Jesper was managing at the door.

The keyhole, of course, was on the outside of the door and Jesper had to reach out through the bars to work on it. He studied the strangely shaped tools in his kit, then selected two. One was a thin bar with the end twisted down at right angles. The other was much the same thickness, although twice as long. Its end was bent in a shallow arc, about a third of the circumference of a circle. The other end of each pick widened into a flat surface that allowed him to get a good purchase on the tool.

He reached through the bars with the first tool, pursing his lips in concentration as he worked entirely by feel, inserting the pick a few millimeters into the lock, then turning it slightly. There was a very faint click and he nodded in satisfaction.

"Got that part," he said. "Bit tricky. I usually work from the other side. I'm used to breaking in, not out."

He glanced around and saw Stig watching, fascinated—as they all were. He jerked his head at the tall boy.

"Here, Stig, come and hold this steady while I work the other one," he said. Stig stepped forward to stand beside him. He reached through the bars, on the side opposite to where Jesper was working, and gingerly took hold of the flattened end of the pick as Jesper relinquished it.

"Hold it still," Jesper told him. "That one turns the whole lock just a little and frees up the other tumblers." He reached through the bars with the curved pick. "Then I should be able to run this one along them and release them."

He frowned in concentration as he attempted to do this. The watching crew held their breath. Jesper muttered angrily as his first attempt failed and the crew released a concerted sigh of frustration. He turned and grinned at them.

"Early days yet. It's stiffer than I expected. Let me have that one back, Stig."

He placed the curved pick between his teeth and took the right-angle one back from Stig's grasp. He jiggled it slightly. Once more they heard the faint clicking sound, and he nodded for Stig to take hold again. Then he went back to work with the curved pick, easing it into the lock and feeling with sensitive fingers for the slight resistance on each of the successive three tumblers that held the lock in place.

There was another click. Then another in swift succession. Jesper's brow knitted in concentration as he slid the pick farther into the keyhole, feeling the inner workings of the lock. His wrist was bent back at a ninety-degree angle so that the farther he inserted the pick, the weaker his leverage became.

Finally, the watching crew heard a third click and Jesper expelled his breath in a satisfied hiss. He slid the curved pick free and grinned at Stig.

"All right," he said. "Turn yours. Gently, but firmly."

Stig hesitated. He had no idea what Jesper had been doing and he didn't want to mess up the whole procedure. "Which way?"

"Left," said Jesper, then hurriedly corrected himself before Stig could obey. "No! Right!"

Stig glared at him. "Which is it?"

Jesper grinned. "Right. Sorry. I forgot we were working backward here."

Shaking his head, Stig began to turn the pick he was holding. For a moment nothing happened and he increased the pressure.

"Gently," Jesper cautioned him.

Stig gritted his teeth. "I just tried gently. It didn't work." He twisted the flattened metal, gradually building up the pressure. Suddenly, there was a loud, metallic *clank*, and the lock opened.

A low chorus of approval came from the crew. Jesper patted Stig's muscular shoulder.

"Just as I said, gently but firmly," he said.

Stig wiped his hand across his forehead. He hadn't realized that he had been sweating. Then he pushed the gate open a few centimeters, worried that it might somehow relock itself, and removed the pick from the lock, handing it back to Jesper.

"One day," he said, "I'll get you to tell me how that worked."

"It's simple, really," the thief began. "The lock has three—" He stopped as Stig held up a hand.

"I said 'one day.' I'm sure it's fascinating. But right now, we have to get out of here."

"Any ideas, Thorn?" Hal asked. He was the captain, but Thorn was their battle commander, and Hal had the feeling there might be a bit of fighting in the near future.

"Let's be subtle," Thorn said. "We'll go up the stairs to the guardroom as quietly as possible. Then we'll bash anyone who's there and head for the main door. Anyone else gets in our way, we give them the same treatment."

"That's subtle?" Stefan asked.

Thorn looked at him and shrugged. "It's as subtle as I get. The bit about going up the stairs quietly is subtle," he said. "Perhaps I should have said 'uncomplicated.'" He turned toward the now-open gate, but a voice from farther back in the cellar stopped him.

"What about me?" It was Pedr, his hands held out, palms upward, in a gesture of supplication.

"What about you?" Hal asked. "You're free to come with us."

"But I don't *want* to come with you," Pedr objected, his voice high-pitched. "Once my wife pays Doutro my bribe, I'll be free. But if I escape with you, he'll come looking for me and I'll have to leave Bayrath."

"Then stay here," Hal told him.

But again, Pedr objected. "If I stay here and don't raise the alarm that you've gone, he'll take it out on me," he said. "Couldn't you tie me up or something?"

Hal glanced around the cellar and shook his head. "There's nothing to tie you up with," he pointed out. But Stig placed a hand on his arm.

"I think I have an idea," he said. He crossed the cellar to where Pedr stood. He smiled at the gambler, who smiled nervously back, not sure what Stig had in mind. Then Stig hit him with a blinding right cross that sent him sprawling. Luckily, there was a pile of dirty straw to break his fall. He lay spread-eagled on it, out cold.

"I was growing a little tired of his whining," Stig explained to the others.

Thorn grinned at him. "Nice work, Stig," he said. "Very subtle."

"About as subtle as a bull walrus," Stefan commented, and Thorn eyed him innocently.

"Bull walruses can be very subtle . . . when they choose."

"Shall we leave?" Hal suggested mildly. "Lydia will be wondering what's happened to us."

They went through the guardroom like a hurricane.
Thorn, Stig, Ulf and Wulf led the way, and the jailer
and the three guards had no chance. In seconds, they
were sprawled unconscious on the floor.

At least here, there were materials available to make sure the
guards didn't raise the alarm when they regained consciousness.
There were at least a dozen sets of manacles hanging from pegs
along the wall. Hal and Stefan took two each and passed them to
Stig and Thorn. They chained one man's wrist to the next man's
ankles so that they were contained in a tangled mass. Then Ingvar
took a cloak hanging inside the door and tore it into long strips,
which they used to gag the unfortunate men.

Edvin studied the sprawling heap of bodies.

"Aren't we making it a bit obvious that we've gone?" he asked.

Hal tilted his head thoughtfully. "The unlocked cell makes it obvious," he said. "This just makes it unanimous."

They encountered nobody else on their way to the main entrance on the ground floor. This was an administrative office, after all, not a garrison post, and most of the daytime staff had gone home.

As they emerged onto the street, looking around cautiously, a low voice called to them from the entrance of an alley opposite. It was Lydia, concealed in the shadows, and they hurried to join her.

"This way," Lydia said, pointing down the alley in the direction that led to the riverfront.

Thorn hesitated, peering back at the Gatmeister's office building, and at the lighted window showing on the third floor.

"He's up there, isn't he?" he said.

Lydia followed the direction of his gaze and nodded. "Probably. That's about where his office should be. What about it?"

Thorn shrugged. "I don't know. I'd like to pay him a visit—after what he did to Hal."

"Me too," Ingvar said, looming out of the shadows to stand at the alleyway entrance with Thorn.

"Forget it," Hal said crisply. There was an unmistakable note of command in his voice and they turned toward him. "We're free and nobody's looking for us. If you go back there now, you're taking the risk that we'll be discovered."

"I'm willing to take the risk," Thorn said, and Ingvar nodded agreement. But Hal was adamant.

"You're not just risking it for yourself. You're risking all of us, just for the sake of a few minutes' revenge. I'm the one with the bruises and I say we forget it. We can deal with Doutro another time."

For a few seconds, Thorn looked as if he were going to rebel. But then he relented, grinning at his young friend.

"You're right," he said. "I guess that's why you're the skirl."

"I guess so," Hal replied. "Now let's go and get our ship back."

With Lydia leading the way, they moved in pairs through the darkened alleys and narrow streets. As she had done earlier, they occasionally encountered other figures moving stealthily through the shadows. But one look at the large party of determined young Skandians was enough to send them skulking back into the shadows.

Now that she was sure of the way, it took Lydia only a few minutes to lead them to the waterfront, and to the dock where *Heron* was impounded. They stood in the shadows of a ship's chandlery building opposite the jetty, studying the situation.

"There's one guard," Lydia told them. "There he is now."

The sentry was making his slow journey back down the jetty toward the street.

"How do we deal with him?" Hal asked.

Stig grinned. "I suggest we try the subtle approach again. Wait here."

As he went to step out into the well-lit street, Hal caught his arm. "What do you think you're doing?"

Stig jerked a contemptuous thumb at the sentry, who had stopped to scratch himself.

"Look at him! He's bored to tears. He's not expecting any trouble. My guess is he'll be grateful for a little light conversation."

Hal considered his friend's reply. He decided that he was probably correct. The jetty wasn't any sort of high-security area, after all. The entrance from the street was open and unsecured. The guard was probably posted there as an afterthought. He nodded.

"All right. But be careful," he said. He saw the flash of Stig's teeth as his friend grinned at him.

"I'll be subtle. That's pretty much the same thing."

He stepped out into the street and crossed to the far side, thumbs thrust through his belt. He whistled a rather tuneless air as he went, peering at the ships in the basin, making no attempt at concealment. The sentry, noticing him, looked up curiously. As Stig had suggested, he was glad for any break in his boring routine.

Stig sauntered along the road to the end of the jetty, then seemed to take notice of the ship moored beyond *Heron*. He stopped and looked more closely at her, then started down the jetty. The guard stepped out to bar his path, the spear held casually across his body.

"Where do you think you're going?" he challenged. Stig took one hand out of his belt and pointed at the larger ship.

"Just wanted a look at that ship. She's a neat craft, isn't she?" The ship was trimmed with polished timber and brass fittings that caught the uncertain lantern light in the basin. She was freshly painted and in excellent condition. From her well-kept appearance, she was obviously not a working boat.

"She should be." The sentry relaxed. It wasn't the first time someone had admired that particular ship. He spoke with a certain proprietorial air. "She's the Gatmeister's personal yacht."

Stig whistled in admiration. "Doutro has a yacht?" he asked. He sounded impressed. "What does he use her for?"

The sentry, hearing the newcomer refer to the Gatmeister by name, relaxed even more. People who knew the Gatmeister by name tended to be further up the food chain than a mere sentry. He grounded the spear and leaned lightly on it as he answered.

"Oh, he takes business associates out when he wants to entertain them. Takes them on cruises down the river. Lots of girls, lots of ale, lots of good food. I've seen some pretty wild parties on that craft, let me tell you."

He hadn't but he liked to imply that he knew what was going on in the town. Stig nodded admiringly.

"I'll bet you have. Any idea how much he wants for her?"

The sentry looked puzzled. "Wants for her? What do you mean?"

Stig pointed. "That sign says she's for sale," he said. The sentry turned to follow his pointing finger and Stig almost sighed. It was really too easy, he thought. The sentry's jaw was nicely exposed as he turned to look at the ship and he never saw the crashing left hook coming.

His knees gave way under him and he sagged to the jetty deck. Stig managed to catch the spear as he released it, to prevent it making any noise as it fell. Then he wrinkled his nose. He might as well have saved himself the effort. The sound of the sentry's body, clad in his mail shirt, hitting the planks was louder than the clatter of the spear would have been.

He bent down and grabbed the prone figure under the shoulders, quickly dragging him behind the fish traps Lydia had used for cover earlier in the night. Then he stepped out into the light and picked up the spear again, holding it in the at ease position, in case any passerby might wonder what had become of the sentry. He checked to see if anyone was watching, satisfied himself that nobody was and beckoned to the others.

A few seconds later, a line of dark figures ran furtively across the street and onto the jetty, concealing themselves in the shadows as they arrived.

Hal moved to stand beside Stig. "No trouble?"

Stig shook his head. "He didn't suspect a thing. But guess what? That rather pretty ship moored behind us is Doutro's personal yacht."

Hal studied the ship for several seconds. "Is that so?" he said thoughtfully. Then, checking to make sure that nobody on the riverfront was paying them any undue attention, he signaled to his crew.

"All right, everyone. Get on board and take your stations." He wet a finger and held it up, checking that the wind was coming off the shore. "Sailing stations," he added. "We'll sail her out once we fend off."

As the crew clambered aboard the *Heron,* he beckoned to Thorn.

"Make me a torch and light it, will you?" he said. "I think we'll create a little diversion."

Thorn nodded and moved to the pile of equipment and boxes by the confiscated fish traps. There was plenty of tarry rope and dried canvas there. He wrapped bundles of both round the end of a piece of scrap timber. He looked around. On the jetty, beneath the nearest light, there was a jar of oil used to replenish the lantern. He retrieved it and opened it, pouring the oil over the dried canvas until it was soaked.

Hal was at the tiller, removing the restraining loop that kept it from banging against the hull with the movement of the water. Out of the corner of his eye, he saw the brilliant flash of Thorn's saxe against his flint. It came again, then there was a pause, followed by a dull glow that quickly grew into a yellow flame as the oil-soaked cloth and tarred rope caught fire. Thorn rose from his crouched position, crossed the jetty and dropped onto the deck of the *Heron.* Stig was already standing by the bow rope. They were moored facing out toward the river, which made things a lot easier.

"Cast off!" Hal called softly. He heard the soft thump of the rope on deck as Stig tossed it aboard, then his friend ran to the stern and cast off the stern rope as well. The ship rocked as he jumped aboard.

"Starboard sail," Hal called, and Stefan and Jesper sent it soaring up the mast. Forward, Ingvar and Lydia used an oar to fend off from the jetty, swinging the ship's bow toward open water. The rattle and squeal of ropes running through the blocks told Hal that the twins were already sheeting the sail home. *Heron* began to slip through the dark water, gathering speed with each second. Hal smiled at Thorn, standing close by with the flaring torch in his left hand.

"Would you like to get rid of that now?" he asked, gesturing toward the immaculate ship they were passing, now only a few meters away from their stern. Thorn nodded and tossed the torch underarm onto her decks, onto a coil of rope. There was a momentary lull, then the heavily tarred rope caught fire. Flames leapt into the sky, and within seconds, the standing rigging was ablaze. Fire on a ship, with its dried timbers and tarred rigging and ropes, was a terrible hazard.

Forward, Hal heard a voice call a challenge. He peered under the sail and saw a guard boat rowing toward them, on the port side. Then he heard Lydia's quick-witted reply.

"Fire!" she shouted, and that in itself was sufficient reason for them to be on the move. No sane captain would keep his ship moored close to a burning vessel. But Lydia had more to add.

"The Gatmeister's ship is on fire! Get help at once!" she shouted, pointing to the ship by the jetty, now outlined starkly against a mass of flames.

That was enough to distract the guard boat. The news that a ship belonging to the most powerful official in Bayrath was on fire dismissed any other consideration from their minds. Hal heard the helmsman on the guard boat issue a string of orders, then the long, low craft swept down their port side, heading to try to quell the fire consuming Doutro's ship. At the last moment, as a cascade of sparks showered down onto the guard boat, her helmsman hauled on the tiller and swung clear, deciding discretion was the better part of valor. In any event, the Gatmeister was no friend of his.

The *Heron* was clear of the basin now. On her port side, the boom and its attendant vessels stretched across the dark river. Hal checked to starboard, making sure he was clear of any other shipping.

Hal swung *Heron's* bow to starboard. The bow wave began its steady hiss as they gathered speed.

Thorn looked back at the fire, which had now engulfed the entire ship at the jetty. He had a wide grin on his face.

"Did I hear right?" he said. "Does that ship belong to Doutro?"

"It did," Hal said succinctly, and Thorn shook his head in delight.

"Beautiful," he said softly. "Just beautiful."

There was no pursuit.

Any troops who might have mounted one were totally occupied fighting the fire that had engulfed Doutro's ship. After some minutes, the mast collapsed across the jetty, spreading the flames to the piles of spare lumber and confiscated equipment stored there. As the *Heron* rounded the first bend, the glow of the fire was vivid in the night sky behind them.

Lydia walked aft and stood by the steering platform, gazing at the orange light in the sky, visible above the headland they had just rounded.

"Well, that certainly caught their attention," she said. Hal smiled at her. But Stig was rubbing his chin thoughtfully.

"You know, I've been thinking . . . ," he began slowly. Hal called to Edvin, who was seated amidships.

"Edvin. Note the time and the date, please. A unique event has just occurred."

"Very funny," Stig said. Edvin glanced up briefly from his knitting and shook his head.

"If I might continue?" Stig persisted, and Hal made a gracious, sweeping gesture with his free hand.

"Pray do."

"Well then, I was th—" Stig realized he was about to say *thinking* again and leave himself open to further sarcastic comment. He changed his choice of words. "Wondering . . . yes, wondering. Why don't we try something similar, instead of running this Wildwater Rift?"

"Similar to what?" Hal asked.

Stig gestured toward the glow in the sky behind them. "Why don't we start another fire and, while everyone's distracted, open the boom and sail on through?"

"What, now?" Thorn asked.

Stig shook his head impatiently. "No. They're all alert now. We could come back tomorrow night. Sneak into the town and start a fire, then head for the boom."

Hal considered the idea for a moment or two, then shook his head.

"Too risky," he said. "It's one thing to head out of the harbor and sail away while they're all distracted by the fire. But if we want to break through the boom, we'll have to board one of the boom vessels, overcome the crew, then figure out how the opening mechanism works. It'll take time and we're bound to be spotted."

Stig pursed his lips as he thought about Hal's words. "I suppose so," he said. But he sounded only half convinced.

"On top of that," Hal continued, "it'll cost us another day while we lay up somewhere waiting for tomorrow night. And we can't afford that."

"Fair point," said Stig. "But maybe we should keep the idea in mind."

Hal nodded. He wanted all the crew willing to suggest ideas and new plans if they thought of them, and rejecting Stig's idea out of hand would discourage the others from coming forward in the future.

"We'll keep it in mind," he agreed, smiling at his friend. "Let's keep our options open until we've seen this Wildwater Rift."

"It sounded pretty bad," Stig said.

Hal shrugged. "Remember," he said, "Pedr wasn't a sailor and he knew nothing about boats. Besides, he's never actually seen the rift. Often these things get blown out of all proportion. It's probably a whole lot better than it sounded."

"That's a whole lot worse than it sounded," Stig said. Hal had to agree. He felt his heart sinking as he studied the Wildwater Rift below them.

They had found the tributary stream just after first light and turned into it. The farther they went, the narrower the stream had become, and the faster the water flowed, until it was rushing by the banks on either side, its surface made smooth and slick as oil by the speed of its passage.

The banks had also become progressively higher and they were conscious of the fact that the stream was now rushing downhill. With the water moving so quickly, it was difficult for Hal to maintain steerage. They had lowered the sail and continued under oars.

The stream had twisted continually so that Hal had been unable to see more than fifty meters ahead at any time. But he'd become aware of a deep, roaring sound somewhere up ahead. It was constant and unvarying and the farther they fled down the stream, the louder it became. Finally, he had seen a small indentation in the left bank of the stream, where a jutting outcrop of the bank formed a calm eddy, with a small level stretch of bank.

"Back water!" he shouted, somewhat louder than he had intended to. All six oars were manned. The rowers heaved on them in reverse to slow the onrushing ship. She shuddered and lost speed, slewing slightly as the current swung her. Then they were in the slower water of the eddy and she grated her bow ashore.

Moving with a little more urgency than he was accustomed to, Stefan leapt over the bow and ran ashore with a rope, passing it round a stout tree, then bringing the end back to the *Heron* to make fast.

"Let's go and take a look at this Wildwater Rift," Hal said.

Hal, Stig and Thorn went ashore and began to make their way up the steep sides of the bank. It was hard work. The ground was soft and muddy, and the rocks, soaked with ever-present spray from the river, were wet and slippery. Eventually, they reached the top of the bank and looked down on the stream, a narrow cut running between the banks below them. The *Heron* looked like a toy, moored in the shelter of the rock outcrop.

Hal pointed downstream, where a fine mist of spray stood high above the river, catching the rays of the early sun.

"Looks like we're heading that way," he said.

Thorn shook his head doubtfully. "Looks ominous," he replied.

It took them another half hour to work their way along the precipitous edge of the bank to a spot above the rift. They gazed down at the water, smooth and dark and fast running, as it raced over the downhill slope and poured down into a narrow gulf between the banks. The banks themselves couldn't have been more than five meters apart in some places, and as they grew closer together, the river rushed with increasing velocity between them. They were steep, with no possible landing places in sight. Once the *Heron* was committed to running the rift, there could be no stopping.

The rift shot downstream in a straight line for approximately three hundred meters. The water was black and its surface was silky smooth—except where wet, glistening rocks broke through. There, the water piled up against them, smashing itself into fantastic clouds of white spray, flinging a fine mist high in the air. As it leapt up out of the gorge, the sun refracting through it, the mist formed dozens of rainbows.

"If we can stay in the middle, we should be all right," said Stig, trying to convince himself as much as the others. "Those rocks are mainly on the side of the stream, not in the middle where the water is deeper."

"Except for that one," Thorn said, pointing with his wooden hook toward the bottom of the gorge.

At that point, the river hurled itself headlong against a massive black rock that was a third of the stream's width away from the left bank. Spray erupted from the collision and drifted high in the air. Stig whistled softly as he saw it.

"Now that is quite ugly," he said. And he was right. Even worse was the fact that at that point, the river, which had so far run in a relatively straight line downhill, made a thirty-degree turn to the right. The huge rock was on the outside of the turn.

"If we hit that, we're done for," Thorn observed. Hal looked at him for a second or two, then knelt to study the water flow around the rock, his chin resting on his hand.

"It looks worse than it really is," he said finally. The others regarded him as if he had lost his mind.

"How bad would you like it?" Stig asked, but Hal shook his head and pointed.

"There'll be a lot of back pressure there where the current hits that rock," he said. "The water builds up against the rock and has nowhere to go. Then it sort of . . . rebounds, I suppose. If we get it right, it'll actually throw us back away from the rock."

"And if we get it wrong?" Stig asked him.

He shrugged. "I prefer not to think of that."

He was silent for a few moments, assessing the speed of the river and the force of the current.

"We'll need to keep two oars out," he said.

Stig frowned. "Why waste energy rowing? The river will keep us moving."

"That's the point," Hal told him. "If we're not moving a little faster than the water, I can't steer. We'll put Ulf and Wulf on the oars. The rest of you can stand by in the bow and stern to fend off from any rocks that come too close."

He paused, chewing his lip as he thought further into the problem. "I'll need a longer tiller—something that will give me greater purchase. I'll have to be able to heave the stern around against the current."

"Use an oar," Thorn said.

Hal nodded. "That should do it." Abruptly, he rose, brushing the damp dirt off the knee of his trousers. "All right, take one last look and try to memorize where the rocks are. Then we'll get back to the *Heron* and get under way."

"You're going to run it now . . . today?" Stig asked, his voice very quiet against the background roar of rushing water.

"We don't have time to waste. And it's not going to get easier if we wait," he said.

Stig looked morosely at the thundering river below them.

"Are you sure?" he said.

They made their way back to the ship, slipping and sliding on the treacherous muddy surface of the riverbank. Seven pairs of eyes watched them as they appeared out of the trees.

Jesper voiced the thought that was on all their minds. "What's it like?" he asked.

Hal, Stig and Thorn exchanged a quick look, and Jesper's shoulders slumped.

"I think you just told us," he said. But Hal hurried to reassure him.

"No! It's not that bad. No, really." He turned to his first mate for confirmation. "Is it, Stig?" But Stig hesitated just a little too long before he replied.

"No. It's . . . a bit wild. But we'll make it all right." The words

I hope hung in the air, unspoken, but heard by everyone. Hal looked around the half circle of despondent faces.

"We'll be fine. We just need to work together," he said.

Jesper looked doubtful. "Maybe we should try Stig's idea," he said. When Hal looked at him, not understanding, he elaborated. "Maybe we should try to break through the boom."

Stefan muttered cautious agreement. The twins looked doubtful. Edvin was similarly undecided. Only Lydia remained neutral. She was no sailor, so she had no real understanding of the problem or whether they could overcome it.

Ingvar stepped forward, peering directly at Hal. "Hal, do you really think we can do it?"

Hal hesitated a moment, then nodded. "Yes, Ingvar. I do," he said firmly. He realized that half the problem was that the rest of the crew hadn't actually seen the rift. As frightening as it might be in reality, their imaginations were building it up to be far worse than it really was.

Ingvar nodded ponderously. "Then, if Hal says we can make it, I'm prepared to give it a go," he said. The others exchanged embarrassed glances. Jesper shuffled his feet awkwardly.

"It comes down to this," Thorn said. "How much confidence do you have in Hal as a helmsman? How much do you trust his judgment?" Usually, the old sea wolf tried to stay out of the decision-making process, unless it concerned a combat situation. But, like Hal, he could see that it was the unknown factor here that was affecting their judgment and he wanted to give them something positive to focus on.

And the point he made was a crucial one. They had all witnessed Hal's skill on the tiller, time and time again, and seen his uncanny ability to judge speed and angles and distances. There was a long moment of silence, then Jesper nodded assent.

"All right," he said. "Let's try it."

The collective mood changed within an instant as the others agreed. Hal seized the opportunity to brief them on their roles during the descent of the rift.

"Ulf and Wulf, you'll row. You need to keep us moving slightly faster than the current or I'll lose steerageway. If we can keep the ship in the middle of the stream, we'll be fine."

"Except for that last turn," Stig said, without thinking. Hal could have cheerfully kicked him. The crew turned to him, the concern back on their faces.

"What about the last turn?" Edvin asked.

Stig shrugged in apology at Hal.

"The rift runs straight until the end, then it swings to the right," Hal said. "There's a big rock in the stream there and we're going to have to fend off. Stig, I want you in the bow to shove us clear with an oar."

"I could help with that," Ingvar said, then added reluctantly, "of course, I don't see too well."

"I'll work with you," Lydia chipped in. "I'll position the oar. Then you can do the pushing." Ingvar beamed at her. He hated feeling useless because of his eyesight.

"That should do it," Hal said. He liked the idea of having Ingvar's massive strength in the bow to help fend them off from that black hulking rock. He glanced at Thorn, who shook his head apologetically.

"I think this might be beyond me," the old sea wolf said. "My hook is good, but it doesn't have the sort of dexterity I'd need to be swinging an oar over the side and fending us off."

Hal nodded. He'd been thinking the same thing but hadn't wanted to put the thought into words. There had been a time when Thorn would never have admitted such a shortcoming, he thought. But he had another task ready for him.

"Stay for'ard, by the mast, and keep an eye out for rocks and snags. Edvin, Jesper and Stefan, you position yourself astern and fend off from there. When Stig and Ingvar swing the bow clear of the big rock, make sure the stern doesn't swing into it. All right?"

They all nodded. Now that they had definite tasks to attend to, the nervousness about facing the unknown dangers of the rift was receding a little. Hal unshipped the tiller, then bound a spare oar to the tiller bracket. He heaved on it experimentally, feeling the drag of the blade in the water. *Heron*, tethered by the bow, swung her stern back and forth. The others watched with interest as he did so.

"It'll give me more purchase for heaving the bow around," he explained. Then he caught Edvin's eye. "Edvin, be ready to drop what you're doing if I call you and help me. I might need an extra pair of hands." He took a deep breath. "All right, everyone. Positions."

There was a patter of feet on the deck as the crew moved to the positions he had assigned. Ulf and Wulf moved to the rowing benches. As Ulf dropped into the port-side well, Wulf looked at him, hands on hips.

"What are you doing?" he asked.

Ulf glanced up. "I'm rowing port side today."

Wulf gritted his teeth. "I row on the port side. I always have."

"Well, a change is as good as a holiday," Ulf replied airily. Wulf started to step down into the rowing well but Hal stopped him.

"Are you two starting up again?" he said. "Remember the rule."

"We're not at sea," Wulf said. "The rule only applies when we're at sea."

"A river is an extension of the sea," Hal said. "After all, it flows into the sea."

"I suppose that could be said to be true," Wulf agreed, and Ulf nodded thoughtfully.

"It's definitely a point worth considering."

"Whether it is or not, remember Ingvar's promise." Hal looked forward and beckoned. "Ingvar?" he called. The huge boy turned and began to thread his way aft. As he came level with the twins, he stopped, eyeing them from close range. Ingvar at close range could be an unnerving sight.

"Ingvar, do you consider that a river is part of the sea?" Hal asked.

Ingvar nodded. "Oh, definitely."

Ulf and Wulf exchanged worried looks. Hal smiled frostily at them. He inclined his head toward the black, racing river a few meters away.

"Would you like to be thrown overboard into that?" he asked, and they hastened to shake their heads and say that, no, they certainly didn't think that would be pleasant, not at all. Hal looked meaningfully at the rowing benches and the two meekly took their places, Ulf to port and Wulf to starboard.

"Thank you, Ingvar," Hal said.

"Anytime, Hal." Ingvar began to make his way back to the bow, stepping carefully over ropes and stowed equipment. Hal noticed a few of the others hiding their smiles and he suddenly looked at the twins with a certain amount of suspicion. Their performance had taken everyone's minds off the dangers that lay ahead and he wondered if they had done so on purpose. He shrugged the thought away. Even if they had, there was a devious side to the twins' natures that meant they would probably never admit it.

"Cast off, Stefan," he ordered. Stefan unfastened the rope from the deck bollard, then hauled the loose end in hand over hand. The ship began to move like a nervous horse, even in the calm waters of the inshore eddy.

"Back water," Hal called, and Ulf and Wulf rowed the ship backward to gain a little room. "Give way together," Hal ordered, and they began rowing forward. He heaved on the steering oar and was gratified by the ship's instant response. The long shaft of the oar gave him much greater purchase and the bow swung rapidly.

They nosed out into the main stream and the racing current gripped them immediately.

"Keep rowing!" Hal shouted as they shot downstream. If the *Heron* lost steerageway, they'd broach sideways and begin to spin in the current, helpless as a piece of driftwood. He felt the stern begin to swing to port and checked it with back pressure on the oar, keeping the ship centered in the current. The roar of the water echoed back from the steep walls of the canyon. There were no trees here, no potential landing places—only stone walls that rose vertically out of the water for ten meters or more.

Heron shot down a slope. The water had looked smooth from above, but it was actually following the contours of the river bottom, first dropping away, then rearing up again in smooth mounds, and the ship tossed and bounced as she went. The prow dug in as they reached the bottom of the slope, and spray and solid water sheeted back on either side. Hal had the feel of her now and worked the steering oar to keep her from yawing or spinning.

"Rocks!" Thorn yelled, pointing to starboard. Stig responded instantly, moving to the starboard bow and setting his oar against the black, glistening object that reared out of the water. Hal felt the bow move to port, which set the stern swinging to starboard, toward the rock. He rowed frantically to heave the stern away and the black fang shot past them, barely two meters away.

Heron plunged again, sliding down a chute, then smashing into the mound of disturbed water at the bottom. Out of the corner of his eye, Hal saw Stefan lose his balance and fall, hurriedly regaining his feet. The roiling water as they passed the chute set the stern swinging again, and this time Hal couldn't check it sufficiently.

"Ulf! Back water!" he yelled. "Wulf, row like hell!"

The two oars working in opposition, aided by the pressure of the steering oar, dragged the bow back to a straight course.

"Ahead together!" he yelled.

Hal's heart was pounding and his throat was dry. The moment when he had felt himself unable to control the ship had been terrifying.

They raced on, the cliffs either side flying past at a frightening rate. Thorn called and pointed, and Stig moved once more to fend off the bow from an exposed rock. This time, Lydia joined him, with Ingvar ready to add his weight to the oar as she placed it.

Hal felt the extra thrust of Ingvar's strength and the bow seemed to bounce clear of the rock. That augured well for the right-hand turn at the end of the chute, he thought. Instinctively, he checked the movement of the stern, swinging it out away from the danger. Again the rock flew by, only meters away. But now he saw that as a comfortable margin.

The deck heaved under him as *Heron* rode up a swelling curve in the river. Obviously, there was a large underwater obstruction deep below them. He rode the movement with his knees flexed, ready this time for the sudden yawing effect as the water raced down again. For a few seconds, *Heron* was sliding downstream at an angle to the current, but he heaved on the oar, setting his right foot against the bulwark for extra purchase, and she came straight again. Almost immediately, she dived into an unseen trough and water drenched him as it broke over the bow and gunwales, along the length of the ship.

Another one like that and they'd have to start bailing, he thought. He could feel the extra weight of water in the hull. Strangely enough, it seemed to help, keeping the ship a little more stable as the river tried to wrench her this way and that.

He glanced to port and saw Edvin, Stefan and Jesper fending them away from a rock that only just broke the surface. He gulped in fear. He hadn't seen that one. Then Stig, Ingvar and Lydia were at work again as Thorn yelled and pointed to another potential danger in their path. The river roared at them, the sound bouncing back from the cliffs, battering at their senses. It seemed like a living, malevolent thing, trying to lull them, then suddenly springing a surprise in the form of a piled-up wall of water or a sudden trough to one side that they would lurch down, slamming heavily into the water at the bottom, sheeting spray up higher than the stumpy mast.

The speed they were moving at was terrifying. He had never before felt a ship moving so fast. And he sensed now that the downhill course of the river was steepening, and the speed was increasing with each meter. Ulf and Wulf kept stroking desperately. Hal heaved and shoved on the steering oar. He had a sudden, terrifying thought that he mustn't work it too hard in case he snapped it. If that happened, they would spin out of control and be tossed downriver at the whim of the rapids. But he had no choice as the river fought him, trying to wrest control of his beloved *Heron* out of his hands. He began screaming insults at the river, defying it, challenging it. His words were lost in the roaring, thundering sound of the water rushing between the rocks.

He could hear Thorn yelling and looked to see him pointing downstream. Amazing, he thought, that the old sea wolf's voice could conquer the thundering river around them.

He stopped to peer ahead. There was the final turn, and the huge, black rock that barred their way. From above, it had seemed normal enough. From here, it looked like a cliff in their path—a solid wall.

The angle of their descent steepened suddenly and the ship accelerated down the smooth slope of water. He heaved on the steering oar as the rock grew closer, trying to drag the bow away from it. But the current had them and it was rushing them straight at the rock.

For'ard, he could see Stig was yelling, shouting instructions to Lydia and Ingvar, but his words were lost in the thundering roar of the river. *Heron* plunged on.

"Edvin!" Hal yelled. "Help me!"

Edvin scrambled across the heaving, plunging deck and threw his weight on the steering oar with Hal. Slowly, she began to crab across the current, so that her bow was no longer pointing at the black mass rising from the river. But they were still being swept toward it. Then Stig leaned far over the port bow and set his oar against the rock. Lydia was half a second behind him, yelling at Ingvar as the three of them threw their weight and their strength against the inexorable force of the river. Again, Hal felt Ingvar's power make the difference as the bow shifted away from the rock. But he could tell it wasn't going to be enough. They were going to be smashed against that black, evil piece of granite. He felt, more than heard, an ugly grating sound as *Heron*'s planks made contact with the rock and despair swept over him.

Then the backwash that he'd predicted hit them and shoved the ship clear.

"Reverse it! Reverse it!" he yelled to Edvin and together they pushed against the oar to shove the swinging stern clear of the rock as *Heron* tried to pivot.

The black mass hung there for an instant in his vision, seeming to be close enough to touch. Then it whirled away in their wake as *Heron* plunged down one more smooth slope of water, splitting it high into spray on either side of her bow. In the bow, Ingvar stumbled and Lydia tried to help him. The two of them fell to the deck. Stig looked down at them, laughing.

Then the banks seemed to fall away on either side as the river suddenly widened, and the *Heron* shot clear of the rift into calm water.

chapter twenty - seven

Gradually, the stream widened and the current slowed. They drifted with the flow, Ulf and Wulf taking an occasional stroke with the oars to give Hal steerage-way. But he could see that his crew was exhausted, mentally as well as physically. And he felt the same way himself—wrung out by the terrifying experience of running the Wildwater Rift. He waited until he saw a piece of open land on the bank and steered toward it, letting the prow ground with its customary gentle grating sound.

Stefan dropped over the side with a rope, fastening it round a tree, then returning it to the ship, where Jesper tied it off around a bollard. But they both moved without the usual spring in their step.

The rest of the crew were watching him, dull eyed. They felt strangely let down. The excitement and fear that had built up during that wild ride down the rift was suddenly gone, leaving a sense of deep fatigue as the adrenaline that had been racing through their bloodstreams slowly dispersed.

"We'll rest here for an hour," Hal announced. He looked at Edvin. "Edvin, can you get a meal together, please?"

They hadn't eaten since they'd left Bayrath. Slowly, the crew climbed over the railing and dropped ashore. Moving like sleepwalkers, they began to collect firewood under Edvin's direction, then got a fire going. Thorn filled a kettle from the stream. As he placed it over the fire, he announced:

"None of that wishy-washy herbal tea today. Let's have coffee."

Edvin checked in his supplies. "We're almost out," he warned, but Thorn shook his head dismissively.

"Then let's use what's left. No sense in hoarding it. We need a good, strong drink and we need it now."

Stig and the twins chorused their agreement and Edvin nodded. After all, he thought, sooner or later they would have to have that one final pot. And the strong, bracing taste of coffee was far more restorative than the thin, earthy-tasting herbal teas he had in his supplies.

Hal, meanwhile, was inspecting the bow of the *Heron*. He remembered the grating sensation he had felt through the timbers of the ship as they brushed against the final rock in the Wildwater Rift and he wanted to make sure there had been no major damage done.

He was reassured by the sight that met his eyes. One plank had been gouged and splintered. Obviously, they had struck a glancing blow against the rock. There was a scar of fresh wood some thirty centimeters long, and they'd lost some of the caulking material that sealed the plank against its neighbor. A nail had been torn loose where the plank was attached to a frame. But the timber hadn't fractured and the damage could be easily repaired.

Although right now, Hal wasn't inclined to leap to the task. "I'll do it tonight," he said to himself.

The aroma of sizzling beef raised all their spirits, and their appetites. They crowded eagerly around the fire as Edvin doled out generous helpings of hot beef and toasted flat bread. Best of all, Hal thought, they began to talk as the food loosened their tongues, chattering excitedly as they recalled the more hair-raising moments of their ride down the rapids.

He stood back, watching them, gauging their mood and feeling pleased by what he saw. Of course, it was Ingvar who brought him a plate of bread and beef and a cup of hot coffee.

"Thanks, Ingvar," he said. "You did well today. I could feel the difference you made."

Ingvar nodded solemnly. "Thank Lydia," he said. "I couldn't have done it without her. She's quite a girl, Hal."

Hal sensed an underlying message in Ingvar's words. The big boy was regarding him steadily, and nodding meaningfully, as if to underscore his statement. Matchmaking, Ingvar? Hal thought. But he nodded in return.

"I know, Ingvar." Then something caught his eye and he pointed to Ingvar's shirt, just below his belt. "What's that?"

There was a dull red stain on the shirt, and on the trousers beneath it, near Ingvar's hip. Ingvar glanced down and touched it delicately, wincing as he did so.

"Oh, I think I might have reopened my wound when we pushed off that last rock," he said. "It's all right. I re-bandaged it as soon as I noticed." Hal regarded him with some concern.

"Have Edvin check it out as soon as you can," he ordered. "We can't take chances, Ingvar. I'm going to need you when we catch up with the *Raven*."

"I'll be fine, Hal. I just did a little too much, a little too early, that's all."

"Have it checked," Hal repeated, in a tone that brooked no argument. Ingvar spread his hands in submission.

"I will," he promised. Hal tossed the dregs of his coffee onto the grass and walked to the fire, washing his plate and cup in a basin of hot water that Edvin kept ready. He dried them both and stacked them away into the canvas pack where Edvin kept the utensils. He glanced around the faces of his friends. They were relaxed now and that gaunt, haunted look that had followed the sudden letdown after the terror of the rift was gone.

"We'd better get under way," he said crisply. "Every moment we sit here, Zavac is moving closer to Raguza." He glanced at his first mate.

"Get them ready to move, Stig," he said. Sometimes, he thought, as he listened with half a mind to Stig bellowing commands for the fire to be put out and the cooking and eating utensils to be stowed back aboard, it was good to be the skirl.

While the stream had widened considerably since they left the rift behind, it was still much narrower than the main river, so they continued under oars. But the water was calm and the current was with them, so the effort was minimal. After a further hour, they emerged once more onto the broad surface of the South Dan, and Hal ordered the oars to be stowed and the sail to be run up. The wind was slightly off their port bow and he held the ship on a long, smooth tack, enjoying, as he always did, the sense that he was guiding a living object as the ship sent its subtle messages through its timbers and into the soles of his feet.

Lydia and Stig joined him at the steering platform. Nobody spoke, but all three of them enjoyed the feeling of companionship. Thorn placed his back to the keel box and went to sleep, his new watch cap pulled down over his eyes. The rest of the crew relaxed on the rowing benches. Edvin checked Ingvar's wound, as Hal had ordered. There was a small amount of blood seeping from it.

"Nothing to worry about," he reassured the young giant as he re-bandaged it. "Just don't do anything strenuous for a few days."

"Like what?" Ingvar asked.

Edvin considered for a few seconds, then said, straight-faced, "Well, for example, I wouldn't go throwing Ulf and Wulf overboard for a day or so."

Ulf brightened at the words. "That's encouraging," he said.

Instantly, Wulf picked up his ears. "That's a poor way to describe it."

Ulf sat up a little straighter. "Oh, do you think so . . ."

But Edvin cut off any further comment. "On second thoughts, a bit of light throwing exercise might be good for it. Just don't extend too far on the follow-through," he said to Ingvar, while ostensibly ignoring the twins.

Ingvar nodded solemnly. "I'll bear that in mind," he said. He looked meaningfully at Ulf and Wulf, who had fallen into a wary silence. Satisfied, Edvin sat back on the rowing benches and began to knit once more.

"Who's that for?" Wulf asked, eyeing the half-finished watch cap.

"You . . . if you don't annoy me," Edvin said, without looking up. His fingers flew and the needles set up a staccato rhythm as the cap grew, row by row. Wulf said nothing. He really wanted one of the new caps and he felt silence was the safest course.

Further conversation was curtailed as Hal called them to their sail-changing stations. They had come to the end of their current leg. He judged that they had enough room to clear the next headland if they went to the opposite tack now. For a few minutes, the ship was the scene of the usual well-ordered turmoil as one sail came flapping down and another soared up in its place and was sheeted home. Then she settled on her new course, her bow butting rhythmically into the small waves that rippled the river's surface.

As they rounded the bend, the next stretch of river was laid out before them.

"Hullo," Stig said. "Who can they be?"

He was the first to speak, but everybody had seen the ships at the same time—except, of course, for Ingvar.

There were five of them, four maintaining a ragged formation on this long, broad stretch of the river. They were wide-hipped, deep-hulled ships. They sat low in the water, bustling valiantly downriver under relatively small sails. To Hal, they resembled a group of elderly ladies, huffing and puffing on their way to market, eager to get the best bargains before their neighbors did, but not managing to move very quickly.

The fifth was a different matter altogether. She was lean and fast, with a tall mast and a large square sail that was currently filled in a tight curve as she chivvied the slower ships like a sheepdog herding a group of fat, lazy sheep, keeping them moving as quickly as possible. There were ten shields mounted on either side and the hull was pierced for eight oars a side as well. She was obviously a fighting ship.

"Twenty men in the crew, maybe more," Thorn said. Hal looked round in surprise. Nobody had noticed the old sea wolf rising from his snoozing spot by the keel box. Yet he must have moved before Stig had spoken. Maybe he sensed the presence of these ships, Hal thought.

As they watched, the warship caught sight of them and she turned toward them, the square sail swinging round the mast so that she was sailing on a broad reach. She heeled over and a white bow wave formed at her prow.

"Checking us out," Hal said thoughtfully. "Keep your weapons handy, everyone, just in case."

There was little need for the order. The crew always had their axes and swords within easy reach. He simply wanted everyone to be on the alert. He noticed that the crew of the other ship hadn't taken their shields down from the bulwarks yet. Had they done so, it would have been clear that they were seeking a confrontation.

He nudged the tiller. He had refitted the normal rudder after they had passed the rift. The long oar he had used in the rapids gave greater purchase, but it was unwieldy. *Heron*'s bow fell off a few degrees as he angled her away from the approaching ship.

His eyes narrowed as the ship matched his change of course, keeping her bow pointed straight at them.

He saw the helmsman on the approaching ship hand the tiller over to one of his crew and walk quickly forward to the bow. He was wearing chain mail and a helmet, Hal noticed. And a long sword was belted round his waist.

The man stood in the bow of the ship and made a palms-down waving gesture with both hands. The meaning was obvious. Heave to. Then he held up his right hand, palm outward—the international signal for peace. Hal thought for a moment. The other crew outnumbered the Herons, and he was reluctant to give away their sole advantage, which was his ship's superior speed and maneuverability. But he sensed that the approaching ship wasn't looking for a fight.

"Let the sheets go!" he called. As Ulf and Wulf spilled the wind from the sail, he brought the *Heron* to port, head to the wind. A few seconds later, he saw the other ship swing head to wind as well, and as the way came off her, the two ships drifted, five meters apart. They bobbed gently on the waves. The other ship had a carved hawk as a figurehead on her bow post, Hal noticed. The hawk and the heron seemed to bow to each other with the motion of the two ships.

"So let's hear what he has to say," Hal said.

The skipper of the other ship cupped his hands to form a speaking trumpet and called across the intervening water.

"Can I come aboard to talk?"

Hal hesitated for a second. He looked around the faces of his friends. Stig shrugged. Lydia was impassive. But he noticed she was fingering one of the long darts in her quiver—probably without realizing it. Thorn returned his gaze and gave a brief nod. Hal was pleased to see it. His own reaction had been to agree to the request. Somehow, he didn't think the other ship offered a threat to them.

"Tell them one person only," he said to Stig. As the skirl, he didn't need to be bellowing across the river to other ships. Stig relayed the message and the man on the other boat nodded.

"Just me," he agreed. "Stand by for a line."

He had a coiled rope in his hand and he swung it now, hurling it toward *Heron*. Stig caught it as it sailed over his head and began to draw the other ship toward them. He grunted with the effort and Ulf and Wulf moved quickly to help him.

As they hauled on the rope, the other ship turned bow on to them. They walked forward as they continued to haul in, and as their point of purchase changed, *Heron* swung as well, so that the two ships came together, bow to bow.

Stig was standing in the bow of the *Heron* as the stranger went to board. He held up a hand.

"Leave the sword," he said. The man glanced down, grinned and unbuckled his sword belt, letting the sheathed weapon fall to the deck of his ship.

"Forgot I was wearing it," he said, then stepped lightly across the gap between the two ships, ignoring the hand Stig stretched out to steady him. He's a sailor, Stig thought. The carved heron and hawk now seemed to be sizing each other up at close quarters, bobbing up and down on the small waves as Wulf made the line fast.

The stranger gestured aft, his eyebrows raised in a question, and Stig motioned for him to precede him. He looked with interest around the ship as he walked toward the steering platform, paying particular attention to the twin yardarms and sails. Reaching the stern, he looked around, and addressed Thorn.

"What ship is this?" he asked. Thorn shook his head and pointed to Hal.

"Ask the skirl," he said. Then realizing that people this far south might not know the Skandian term, he explained, "The skipper."

The newcomer reacted with surprise as he saw how young the skipper of this ship was. But he recovered, and held out his hand in greeting. They clasped forearms briefly.

"My apologies. My name is Mannoc, skipper of the *Seahawk* there." He indicated the craft behind him with a slight movement of his head. "I'm escorting that fleet of traders downriver to Drogha. May I ask what ship this is, and where you're from?"

And what you're doing here? Hal heard the unspoken question as he studied the stranger. He was a well-built man in his late twenties. He was a few centimeters shorter than Stig, but equally muscular and athletic in appearance. His blond, shoulder-length hair was tied back in a queue. Hal noticed now that his helmet was surmounted by a small silver hawk, identical to his ship's figurehead. He was clean shaven and had a guileless face and frank blue eyes that returned Hal's gaze directly. *He looks honest*, Hal thought.

Not that looks mean anything, he realized. If pirates and thieves looked like pirates and thieves, they'd never catch anyone by surprise. But . . . he felt an affinity for this man.

"This is the *Heron,* and we're the Heron brotherband." He indicated his crew with a sweeping gesture. Mannoc frowned at the term. He wasn't familiar with it. "We're from Skandia originally, but more recently we've been in Limmat on the east shore of the Stormwhite."

Mannoc nodded. He knew the name.

Hal took a breath, then continued. "We're heading downriver toward Raguza," he said.

He saw the blue eyes narrow with suspicion and a frown furrowed Mannoc's brow. He took an involuntary half pace back and his hand instinctively felt for his missing sword. Hal waited, then continued.

"We're hunting a pirate named Zavac. He's skipper of a black ship called the *Raven*."

There was another flash of recognition from Mannoc at the two names. Before he could speak, Stig chipped in.

"And when we catch her, we're going to sink her."

There was an angry growl of agreement from the Herons. Lydia stepped forward.

"And kill Zavac," she said bluntly. This time, the growl of assent from the crew was louder, almost feral. Mannoc relaxed visibly. The suspicion in his eyes died away.

"So I take it you have no love for pirates," he said. It was Lydia who answered.

"They invaded my town and killed my grandfather," she said. The hatred in her voice was all too apparent.

"And they stole something very precious from us before that, and shamed our entire brotherband," Hal said.

Mannoc nodded slowly, his gaze traveling from one face to another. He saw a mixture of determination and anger there. He knew of Zavac. Over the years, he had encountered the black ship on more than one occasion. And the encounters usually turned out to Zavac's advantage. Now this crew of youngsters were planning to hunt him down and sink him.

A thought sprang into Mannoc's mind: The enemy of my enemy is my friend. But he couldn't be certain.

"All right," he said. "Your story sounds logical. But those ships are in my care and I don't plan to lose any of them." He gestured toward the small fleet of traders.

"You have nothing to fear from us," Hal said.

Mannoc regarded him steadily. "That's as may be," he replied. "I doubt that you're pirates, but I have to be sure." He looked around the river, gesturing to the thickly wooded banks. "This is a dangerous part of the river," he said. "We're only two days from Raguza and pirates come up to this stretch to look for prey. Usually, they come in fleets of longboats, big rowing boats with a dozen or fifteen men in each. They dash out from cover along the banks and attack traders passing by. Their boats are fast and maneuverable, and there are usually a lot of them. My job is to fight them off."

"And this concerns us . . . how?" Hal asked. But he thought he knew. Mannoc looked at him, assessing him.

"I don't know you. I think you're what you say you are, but I can't be sure. So I don't want you or your ship anywhere near those trading craft."

Hal shrugged. "Problem solved. We're in a hurry, so we'll go by you and keep sailing downriver."

But Mannoc was shaking his head.

"I don't want you getting in front of me. Too easy for you to hide, then dart out and take one of the traders. I need you to stay here behind me. Stay back where I can't see you, and where you can't see me."

"And if we don't?" Stig said pugnaciously. Hal shot him a warning look—there was no point in antagonizing the stranger—but Mannoc answered calmly enough.

"If you don't, I'll be forced to sink you." He looked quickly at Thorn as the sea wolf snorted with laughter.

"That might not be quite as easy as you think," Thorn said. "These boys are young, but they're highly trained."

"I'm sure they are. But I have twenty-five men on *Seahawk*, and they're all seasoned fighting men."

He switched his gaze back to Hal and for a few seconds there was an impasse. Then he said, in a reasonable tone:

"Look, I'm giving you the benefit of the doubt. I'm nine-tenths convinced you aren't a threat. But I have to be ten-tenths. I don't want to fight you and I'm sure you don't want to fight me. But I can't continue downriver looking back over my shoulder to see what you're up to."

"I told you, we're in a hurry. We don't have time to waste," Hal said.

Mannoc shrugged. "I can't help that. But if we end up fighting each other, that's going to cost you more than time. I'll get those fat old trading ships moving as fast as they can. But I have to insist that you stay back, out of sight, while I get them to Drogha. It's only four hours away."

Hal glanced quickly at his friends. He could see that Stig would prefer to ignore Mannoc's demand, but Stig had always been impulsive. Thorn raised his eyebrows and pouted his lips. Hal took that to mean that the old warrior thought Mannoc's point was a reasonable one. Lydia, as ever, was impassive. He hesitated, then realized that he was the skirl and the decision was his.

"All right," he agreed. "We'll let you get clear. But keep them moving as fast as you can."

Mannoc smiled gratefully. He held out his hand to Hal once more and Hal took it.

"I'll get them rowing as well as having their sails set," he promised. He looked around the others and nodded to them all. "Thanks. If you ever need a favor from me, just ask."

"Well, we might need one if the *Raven* makes it to Raguza before we can catch her," Stig said belligerently.

"Let it go, Stig," Hal told him. Stig flushed, then shrugged.

Mannoc nodded to them all again, then turned back toward the bow. He was already calling orders to his men as he went for'ard. As he reached the *Heron*'s bow post, he untied the rope lashing the ships together and leapt lightly across to the bow of *Seahawk*. His crew had run out several oars and they wasted no time backing the ship away from *Heron*. Hal heard the creaking of ropes as the sail went up the mast, before they'd completed their turn. Then it filled on the port tack and *Seahawk* pulled away from them, accelerating to catch up with the four traders, now a third of a kilometer downriver.

"We should have told him to mind his own business," Stig said truculently.

Thorn couldn't help smiling at the incongruity of his words. "Actually, that's exactly what he was doing," he pointed out.

"We should have called his bluff. He wouldn't have fought us," Stig said, but Lydia disagreed.

"He wasn't bluffing. Didn't you see his eyes? I think he's a man who doesn't make idle threats."

"Put yourself in his position, Stig," Hal said. "He's responsible for those ships getting to Drogha safely. The river is infested with pirates and he doesn't know us from a piece of beef jerky. And if we had fought him, we would have taken casualties. We could hardly go after Zavac if we lost two or three of the crew."

Stig went to answer, then thought better of it. Hal had a point, he thought. Sometimes, it was better not to fight—particularly when a fight wasn't really necessary.

"I suppose you're right," he said reluctantly. Then he paused, and smiled ruefully. "No. I *know* you're right. Sometimes, I just don't think things through."

"Only sometimes?" Hal said.

Stig scratched his head, thinking. "Well, I remember one time when I thought something through. I was ten at the time."

Hal grinned at him, glad that good feeling had been reestablished among them. He glanced around, taking stock of their situation. *Heron* was drifting gently with the current, but she had swung broadside on to it.

"Well, we may as well make some distance at least," he said. "There's no need to just drift." He was about to call on Ulf and Wulf again, then realized that they'd been doing the bulk of the rowing in the past hours.

"Stefan, Jesper," he called. "Take the oars and keep us moving slowly. We'll spell you in an hour. For now, we might as well relax and enjoy the sunshine."

They continued, moving just ahead of the current. When they rounded the next bend, the little convoy was out of sight. Obviously, Mannoc had been true to his word and had convinced the trading ships that they needed to muster their maximum speed. The *Heron* half drifted, half rowed down this stretch of river, then rounded the next bend, this time to port.

Ahead of them lay a short stretch, a quarter of a kilometer in length. The next turn would be to starboard and the headland on that bank was a high, wooded bluff.

As he looked at it, Hal realized that there was a thick column of smoke rising from somewhere beyond it.

"Get the sail up!" he ordered. "I think our friend Mannoc might be in trouble."

With the sail raised and a good stiff breeze from abeam, *Heron* leapt forward like a wolfhound off the leash. The hull resonated to the rapid *thump-thump-thump* of the small waves on the river, with the occasional larger wave being sliced apart so that white spray reached up past the gunwales.

"Shields and weapons," Thorn called, and there was a flurry of activity on board as the crew unhitched their shields from the bulwarks and placed them ready. Hal looked forward to where the Mangler was covered by its canvas wrapping.

"Ingvar," he called. "Clear away the Mangler."

"Yes, Hal. Do you want me to load her?"

Strange, thought Hal, that the dreadful, destructive weapon

had taken on a feminine identity. He was about to agree to Ingvar's suggestion when he remembered that stain of blood on his side.

"No. Ulf and Wulf can do it." He thought for a moment. Once they were in a fight, Ulf and Wulf would be busy on the sail trimming sheets. That meant he'd have only one shot with the Mangler. They could hardly leave the trim and come forward to reload for him. He gestured for Stig to take the tiller for a few minutes, while he fetched his crossbow and sword belt from his own weapon rack, at the rear of the rowing well.

The next bend in the river was coming closer. The column of smoke beyond it was thicker and darker now. A ship was burning, he thought. The upcoming bend was to starboard, so there would be no need to change sails. All these thoughts flashed through his mind as he took stock of the situation, then they were skimming past the wooded headland and the river opened up before them.

His eyes were drawn first to the burning ship. As he had supposed, it was one of the traders and it was heeled over and low in the water. As he watched, a long, lean rowing boat slipped away from it and headed after the other traders.

They were farther downriver, fleeing like clumsy cattle ahead of a group of three more longboats, snapping at their heels. As the Herons watched, they saw *Seahawk* speeding back upriver to intercept the leading pirate. The longboat hesitated as her helmsman ordered his rowers to row back one side and forward on the other, spinning the boat in its own length to dodge *Seahawk.*

But Mannoc had anticipated the move. He put his helm over, and as the pirate turned sharply to port, *Seahawk* was already swinging to meet her. The crew of the *Heron* heard the shouts of terror from the longboat as the sailing ship bore down on them. Then there was an ugly cracking sound as *Seahawk*'s bow smashed into the longboat's exposed side. For a moment, *Seahawk* rode up on the other craft, then, as the timbers shattered and splintered, the sailing ship's prow came down like an ax, gouging a huge gap in the longboat's side.

The pirate was already sinking, her crew pouring out of her into the river, grasping oars and any piece of loose equipment they could find to keep them afloat. But the attack had cost *Seahawk* her position of advantage between the pirates and the trading fleet. The remaining longboats veered away to slip past her, rowing furiously, their oars splashing white foam with every beat.

Seahawk had lost most of her speed when she rammed the pirate. Now she turned slowly to pursue the others. But one of them had swung in a wide arc and was turning back to intercept her, while its companion continued after the traders.

Thorn summed the situation up in a second. He pointed to the boat that had been pulling away from the burning trader when they first saw her.

"That one!" he yelled. "Stig and I will board her over the stern while you go after the other one!" He bent down, pulling at the fastenings of his hook and replacing it with the huge war club Hal had made for him.

Hal nodded. He saw nothing incongruous in Thorn's plan—for two warriors to board a ship with a crew of twenty. The boat was narrow and if Thorn and Stig boarded her over the stern, the crew could only face them two at a time. And Hal would back Thorn and Stig over any two pirates in the world.

Still, he thought, it wouldn't hurt to reduce the odds somewhat. He beckoned to Edvin, pointing to the tiller.

"Take over!" he ordered, and as Edvin seized the smooth oak handle, Hal grabbed his crossbow and quiver and ran forward, motioning for Lydia to join him. He realized now how right Thorn had been to suggest that he train Edvin as a replacement helmsman.

The longboat was forty meters away when they reached the bow. As Hal stooped to cock the crossbow, he heard the whipping sound of Lydia's atlatl, and the faint whimpering sound of the dart as it sped away. He glanced up to see one of the longboat's crew rise to his feet in agony as the dart transfixed him. Then the pirate crashed over, falling on the rower in front of him and causing him to lose his grip on his oar. The two loose oars trailed in the water, and the boat yawed to starboard while the helmsman struggled to keep her straight.

Hal raised the loaded crossbow, sighted and shot. He was aiming at the helmsman but he missed by the smallest margin. The bolt slashed past the man and buried itself in the upper arm of the crewman in front of him. In the same space of time, Lydia had hurled another two darts. One buried itself in the timber of the boat. The other struck an oarsman who had turned to look at them, half rising from his seat. The impact of the heavy projectile threw him backward so that he trailed over the bulwark. A red ribbon of blood stained the water behind him.

Hal shot again. The range was closer this time and he didn't miss. The helmsman collapsed over the steering oar and the longboat swung wildly. But Edvin matched the movement and brought the *Heron* up astern of the pirate, riding in her wake. Hal was bending down to reload, his foot in the stirrup of the crossbow, when he felt a hand on his arm.

"Move aside," Thorn said gruffly. Hal realized that it hadn't been a hand that he'd felt, but the head of the war club. He and Lydia stood down as Thorn and Stig moved forward, stepping up to balance on the bulwarks as the *Heron* moved closer and closer, until there was only a meter of open water between her bow and the pirate's stern.

"Let's get 'em!" Thorn yelled the time-honored Skandian battle cry, and propelled himself across the gap and onto the longboat. Stig followed a fraction of a second later. The boat rocked wildly as they landed, but they were experienced sailors and they kept their balance easily. Not so the pirate crew, who were caught unprepared for the sudden lurching, and tumbled over thwarts and the butts of oars as their boat plunged and rocked.

Before they could recover, Thorn and Stig moved forward like a two-man battering ram. The huge club and Stig's whirling ax swept away any who tried to oppose them—and as Hal had foreseen, the pirates could only do this two at a time. In fact, their superior numbers were a disadvantage, as they got in one another's way, trying to avoid the terrifying pair who confronted them. Some solved the problem by simply hurling themselves overboard and swimming frantically for the shore. Unlike the seagoing Skandians, these men were river bred and swimming was part of their life. Others chose to stand and face the crushing blows of the club and the humming battleax as it flashed in a terrible circle of light. Their attempts were unsuccessful and they quickly joined their crewmates in the water—but they weren't swimming.

Thorn took a second to glance back at Hal, still in the bow of the *Heron.*

"Go after the other one!" he bellowed. "Come back for us!"

It was obvious that they had the situation well under control. Hal turned and yelled to Edvin.

"Bear away! Go after the other boat!"

Hal took time now to take stock of the situation. The boat rammed by *Seahawk* was showing only a meter or so of her stern above water. The river around it was dotted with the heads of swimming men. To starboard, *Seahawk* was battling the longboat that had swung out in a wide arc, moving into the shallow water by the bank, then sliding out to approach *Seahawk* from astern. The lean rowing boat was grappled to *Seahawk* like an evil parasite. Her men had managed to storm aboard the sailing craft and a savage battle was being waged on her decks.

The fourth longboat, taking advantage of *Seahawk*'s situation, was rapidly overtaking the slow trading ships. Hal could see that she carried extra crew in addition to her oarsmen. They were standing, brandishing weapons and screaming abuse at the helpless traders. Hal estimated the relative positions, thinking rapidly. They would need to tack twice to run down on the longboat. But they should reach it just in time.

With nearly thirty men on board the longboat, there was no question of boarding her—particularly with Thorn and Stig busy on her companion. He'd have to do the job with the Mangler.

And he had only one shot.

"Stand by to come about!" he yelled back to Edvin. For a moment, he considered going back to take the helm, but every second counted now.

"Down starboard! Helm to port! Up port!"

Jesper and Stefan had sprung to the halyards. The starboard sail clattered and flapped down and the port sail shot up in its place. The twins hauled in. At the same time, Edvin brought the ship's head round to port and the ship turned neatly through the tack.

The pirates, seeing the small ship astern of them turning away, thought *Heron* was retreating and that they had already won. They redoubled their yelling and jeering.

Hal slipped into the seat behind the Mangler, his face grim.

"Enjoy it while you can," he said. He looked up to where Lydia was standing beside him. "Keep them busy," he said, and she nodded.

"Range is a bit long at the moment. When we get closer," she said. She already had a dart clipped to the atlatl and she held it by her side, swaying gently with the movement of the ship. Hal smiled. Her sea legs had improved in the past few weeks, he thought. He felt the Mangler move slightly and turned. Ingvar was in position with the training lever. He grinned at Hal.

"I can handle this all right," he said. "You concentrate on shooting." Hal nodded acknowledgment. He glanced at the pirate longboat, now heading on a diverging course from *Heron*. He measured angles and speeds and distances in his mind, waiting for the right moment, when their next tack would put them on an interception course. He had to gauge where the longboat would be at the end of that tack, mentally projecting a point out ahead of it. But it was second nature to him. He turned and called to the crew.

"Stand by to tack!"

Edvin waved acknowledgment. Stefan and Jesper met his eye and nodded. The twins were crouched by the sheets, ready to release one sail and harness the other. Hal checked the longboat's position once more. It was getting awfully close to the traders, he thought. He'd better get this right the first time. He pushed the worm of doubt aside.

"Tack!" he yelled. He'd seen how Edvin had performed on the previous tack and realized there was no need to issue a sequence of specific orders. The crew executed the smooth sequence of actions perfectly. *Heron's* bow swung back to starboard, heading toward a point where she would intercept the pirate. As they gathered speed, Hal saw that he had judged the movement perfectly. Best of all, the crew of the longboat, convinced that *Heron* was running away, were paying her no attention. Their eyes were fastened on the nearest of the trading ships, fat and slow and wallowing, like a hen being pursued by a fox.

"Don't shoot yet," he cautioned Lydia. "They haven't seen us."

She nodded. The *Heron* plunged on, slicing through the water, overhauling the longboat hand over fist.

"Left a little," he said to Ingvar, and felt the big crossbow swivel beneath him. There would be no need for the sight. He'd be shooting at point-blank range. He wound the elevating wheel, angling the Mangler down. He was planning to get close and shoot down into the longboat, so that the bolt smashed out through her bottom.

"They've seen us," Lydia said, and in the same moment, Hal

heard the whip of the atlatl again. He didn't see the dart hit, but he heard a cry of agony. The longboat was drifting to their left once more as the *Heron* came in on an angle.

"Left a little, Ingvar," he said. "That's it. Keep it there."

Another dart flashed away toward the longboat. Another cry of pain. They were getting closer now. Barely ten meters separated the two craft. The helmsman on the longboat watched them bearing down and swung his boat to starboard, attempting to escape. It was a mistake. Had he gone to port, *Heron* would have had to tack to follow him. As it was, Edvin saw the move and matched it, Ulf and Wulf trimming the sail to compensate for the change in angle.

Hal held his breath. *Heron's* bow rose slightly on one of the small waves. As he felt it reach the crest, he angled the Mangler down as far as possible and pulled the trigger.

There was the usual *SLAM!* as the limbs released and the cradle leapt upward in recoil, then crashed back as the leather thongs checked its movement. The heavy bolt flashed away, plowed through the crowded men in the longboat, then smashed into the bottom.

It struck the join between two planks, smashing them apart. It split one and tore the other completely loose from its fastenings, opening a gap over a meter long and thirty centimeters wide in the bottom of the hull.

Water poured in and the crew tried desperately to stem it. In their haste, they tried to plug the gap with shirts and jackets. But as they pushed the clothes into the gap, they put pressure on the second, weakened plank and forced its shattered ends aside, doubling the size of the hole in the boat's bottom. What had been a serious wound became a fatal one and the boat was already beginning to settle. Some of her crew saw the inevitable end coming and dived overboard. More and more followed, swimming desperately for the shore. Half a dozen, presumably non-swimmers, stayed aboard the drifting hulk.

"Bear away," Hal called to Edvin. As they swung away from the wreck, he saw that Mannoc and his men had overwhelmed their opponent. The pirate longboat was barely afloat, sinking by the bow.

He looked toward the third pirate boat. Thorn and Stig were sitting in the stern, waving cheerfully to him. There was nobody else in the longboat, although at least a dozen men were in the water beside it, clinging to the gunwales.

"Looks like a bad day all round for pirates," he said. "Let's go fetch Stig and Thorn."

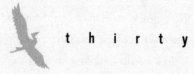

It was late in the day and it would be dark in two hours. Hal decided to spend the night in Drogha, the town where the trading fleet were headed, and make for Raguza the following day. With all the delays they had experienced, he had virtually given up hope of catching the *Raven* before it reached the pirate citadel.

"We'll have to figure something else out," he told Thorn, and the shaggy-haired old sea wolf agreed.

"It was never a good chance that we'd catch up with her on the river anyway," he said. "We may as well have a comfortable night while we figure out what to do next."

At Mannoc's invitation, they sailed in company with *Seahawk* and the three remaining traders. They pulled alongside the *Seahawk* for a quick council of war. Mannoc expressed his gratitude to them for their prompt action in coming to his aid.

"I would have lost another two of those ships without you," he said. "And the skippers know it. Don't be surprised if they want to feast you tonight."

Hal pointed to the drifting remains of two of the longboats, still with members of their crew clinging to the wreckage.

"What will we do about them?" he asked.

Mannoc shrugged. "Leave them. Most of them got away ashore and we'd never catch them if we went after them. As for those"—he indicated the forlorn figures drifting with the wrecked boats—"the river can have them. The crews are scattered now and they've lost their boats. They won't be a threat for months to come. And I have no wish to rescue them."

Aside from that, Hal realized, there would be an inherent danger in taking so many of the pirates on board. There were at least fifteen of them on the two wrecks.

"There's another point," Mannoc added. "There's nothing to say that they're the last pirates we'll encounter today. There could be another band waiting round any bend in the river. And I don't want to have to spare men to guard prisoners if I have to fight another action."

Hal nodded. Six of Mannoc's crew had been badly injured in the fight with the longboat. He was short-handed—probably the reason why he had invited them to sail in company with his little fleet.

In the end, the trip to Drogha was uneventful and they reached the town just before dusk.

It was a pretty port, well maintained and with a harbor filled with ships. On Mannoc's order, *Heron* and *Seahawk* hove to and let their three charges precede them into the basin. Mannoc pointed to a mooring to one side and Hal steered to follow him, tying up alongside the larger ship.

Now that they were safely moored and there was no further chance of another pirate attack, Thorn removed the war club from his right arm and replaced it with his grasping hook.

"That's better," he said, flexing his elbow and flourishing the polished wood hook. "That club gets a little weighty after a few hours."

The crews of both ships were kept busy for some time, stowing gear, furling sails and checking weapons. Lydia took stock of her supply of darts for the atlatl. She'd been using them at a rapid rate over the past few days and had barely a dozen left.

"I'll need to make some more," she muttered. As she was doing this, Stig was inspecting the blade of his ax, where a chance blow against the iron rim of a pirate's shield had left a large nick. Sighing, he sat down and took out his whetstone, working away to grind it out and restore the razor-sharp edge. Thorn nodded approvingly. Taking care of weapons, and not leaving the task till later, was the sign of a good warrior. His club-hand was scarred and scratched in several places, but that didn't reduce its effectiveness.

It was half an hour after they moored when Mannoc made his way to the waist of *Seahawk*, calling across the narrow gap to Hal.

"Mind if I come aboard?"

Hal smiled and motioned for him to step across. He saw with some surprise that Mannoc was accompanied by three other men.

They were all somewhat older than Mannoc. The average age of the three of them would have been around forty, he decided. Their clothes were tar stained and their long hair was gathered in pigtails and queues. Their hands were calloused and obviously well used to hard work. Sailors, he thought. Then he noticed an air of authority about them that marked them as separate from common sailors. Their clothes, although stained with tar, were more expensive in cut and fabric than the traditional rough wool that deckhands would wear, and two of them had gold earrings.

Before Mannoc could introduce them, he realized who they were. They were the skippers of the trading ships *Heron* had helped rescue that afternoon. They stepped aboard, moving easily with the ship as she swayed under their weight. As Mannoc had done earlier that afternoon, they reacted with surprise when they saw how young the skipper of this ship and her crew were.

"They're boys," one of them said before he could stop himself. His face reddened instantly with embarrassment, but Mannoc stepped in to soothe any possible ruffled feelings.

"They may look like boys," he said, "but they fight like men. Especially that one there." He pointed to Stig, who flushed with pleasure. Behind him, Thorn caught Mannoc's eye and nodded almost imperceptibly. Good move, the look said.

"Hal," Mannoc continued, putting a hand on the young skirl's shoulder and drawing him forward. "These men are the skippers of the ships you saved this afternoon. Algon, Freyth and Crenna."

Each of the men nodded as his name was mentioned, then stepped forward, offering his hand to Hal. Hal shook with them in turn, reflecting on the roughness of the calluses that hardened their palms.

"Delighted to meet you," he said, feeling a little foolish. He wasn't quite sure what was the correct thing to say under such circumstances. Perhaps he should have said something seamanlike, like *avast there and belay, shipmates all, let's splice the mainbrace,* but he would have felt even more foolish saying that. The captains didn't seem to mind.

"That was well done this afternoon, young Hal," said Crenna, who appeared to be the oldest. He hesitated, then added, "You don't mind me calling you 'young Hal,' do you?"

"Not at all," Hal replied, grinning. "That's what I am, after all."

"It was well done indeed," Algon put in. "No matter what your age." And the other two mumbled their agreement. They stood nodding their heads and smiling at Hal and the rest of the crew. Finally, Mannoc prompted.

"Algon, was there something else you wanted to say?"

Algon gave a start of surprise, and reached inside his jerkin to produce a soft leather bag that chinked in a most attractive way.

"Aaah, yes. Well, we reckoned that you lads saved our bacon today."

"And a good more besides," Freyth put in. "Reckon you saved our cargoes as well."

"'At's right," Algon continued, holding out the leather sack to Hal. "So we reckon we owe you the going rate for escorts—same as we pay Mannoc here."

"And that's five percent of the value of our cargoes," Crenna said. "So we collected it up and there you are."

Algon thrust the purse out to Hal once more, and the young skirl, somewhat taken aback, accepted it awkwardly.

"Well, we're very grateful," he said, "but it hardly seems fair to pay us the same as Mannoc. After all, he protected you all the way downriver. We only took a hand—"

"When we were in trouble," Freyth completed the sentence. "Take the money, Hal. It doesn't reduce Mannoc's payment one penny piece. But you boys earned it, well and truly."

Hal glanced quickly at Mannoc, who was standing slightly behind the three men. He gave Hal a small nod of confirmation.

"Freyth's right," he said. "You've earned the money. Matter of fact, I'd like to talk to you about joining us in our convoy escort business. You could make a lot of money escorting traders on this river. Particularly with that giant crossbow you've mounted in your bow. I've never seen the like of it."

Hal put the money sack down by the steering platform and made a deprecatory gesture to Mannoc.

"I appreciate the offer," he said. "I'm sure we all do. But we've got other business to take care of first."

"Ah yes. Zavac and his crew," Mannoc said. "Well, I wish you well with that. I'd be glad to see this river rid of that cursed black ship of his. But if you won't join us on a more permanent basis, how about joining us tonight, for a feast? I'm paying."

Hal looked around the crew and saw nothing but grins of anticipation. "Well, since you put it that way, we'd love to," he said.

• • • • •

They gathered later that night in one of the more pleasant taverns, a little removed from the rough-and-ready venues that were to be found close the waterfront. Mannoc had secured them a large, low-ceilinged private room, with a log fire blazing at one end. The Herons, the three trading captains, Mannoc and his first mate gathered round the giant table, eyeing a row of glistening ducklings that were roasting on a spit in the fire. The fat hissed and spluttered as it hit the coals. While they were watching, with stomachs rumbling, the innkeeper entered with two huge game pies, covered with golden brown flaky pastry. As Mannoc cut into one, steam erupted from inside, along with an even more delectable smell than the ducks. The diners fell to eagerly, and within minutes, there was little left of the pies but a few crumbs and a stain or two of gravy.

There were bowls of steamed green vegetables, the ducks and a leg of pork roasted so that the skin was crisp and crackling. Potatoes were served. They had been baked in their jackets in the coals of a fire. They were black on the outside, but the charred outer skin peeled away to reveal that they were beautifully crumbly and moist inside. Stig heaped a couple onto his plate, cut them open and slathered them with butter.

"This is the life!" he exclaimed. The rest of the crew agreed noisily.

"I hate to say it, Edvin," Stefan proclaimed, "but I prefer this to your cooking."

Edvin regarded him for a moment. Then, with a completely straight face, he replied, "I hate to say it, Stefan, but so do I."

As the meal continued, the sound of talking died away as the diners concentrated their attention on the food. Hal looked around the sumptuous spread and turned to Mannoc, who was seated next to him.

"Are you sure you can afford this? It looks pretty expensive." Hal was speaking from experience. His mother ran an eating house in Hallasholm.

Mannoc grinned. "I can afford it, all right. An escort ship is paid for results. If the pirates had taken those ships today, I would have ended up with nothing. So this is well worth the price." He paused, looking at Hal, his head tilted slightly to one side. "I wish you'd reconsider joining us," he said. "Good fighting crews are hard to find and I think we'd make a great team."

Hal nodded at the compliment. "I wish we could," he said. "But we need to settle with Zavac. Maybe after that."

"Ah yes, Zavac. That reminds me." Mannoc beckoned to the waiter and, when he approached, spoke quickly to him. "See if Doric has come in yet, will you? If he has, ask him to join us."

"Doric?" Hal asked. "Who's he?"

"He's skipper of another escort ship. He's due in tonight. He was bringing a convoy upriver, past Raguza. He may have sighted the *Raven*."

A few minutes passed and the door reopened to admit the waiter. A few paces behind him was a broad-shouldered, dark-haired man. He had a long scar across his face and wore a mail shirt and war belt, from which hung a long sword and a heavy dagger. As the food had disappeared, the babble of talk had swelled up again. He

looked round the noisy room and saw Mannoc. He smiled and
headed toward him.

"This is Doric now," Mannoc told Hal. "Let's see if he has
news of the *Raven.*"

After introducing Hal to the newcomer, Mannoc asked how
his trip had been. Doric shrugged.

"No trouble," he said. "We had four fighting ships with the
convoy, so those scum from Raguza weren't going to try anything
with us."

Mannoc turned to Hal and explained. "The northbound con-
voys come up past Raguza. We always provide a strong escort for
them. That's why I was on my own today." He turned back to
Doric. "Hal helped me out of a nasty spot this afternoon. We were
hit by a fleet of longboats. He and his men sank two of them."

Doric looked at Hal with new interest. Previously, he had paid
little attention to the young man.

"Good work," he said, sizing him up. Young, he thought, but
he's got an air of confidence about him. Looks as if he knows what
he's about.

"Thing is," Mannoc went on, "Hal and his crew are hunting
the *Raven.* Did you see any sign of her today?"

"Zavac's ship?" Doric said, scowling. "Yes, I saw her all right.
She was heading downriver and came sniffing around the convoy.
But once Zavac saw that I had four fighting ships to back me up, he
took off quick smart. Headed into Raguza with his cowardly tail
between his legs."

Hal's face fell. "He's already in Raguza?"

Doric nodded. "He is. And you'll have a tough time winkling him out of there." He looked around the table, counting the crew of the *Heron.* "There are dozens of ships in port, most of them pirates. You'll be a little outnumbered if you try to barge in there and fight them."

But an idea was beginning to form in Hal's mind. He realized it had been flitting around the edges of his consciousness most of the afternoon, when he had realized that Zavac would probably make it to Raguza before the Herons could catch up with him. Now it began to crystallize.

"Maybe we shouldn't fight them," he said thoughtfully. "Maybe we should join them."

"Join them?" Doric said, and Mannoc frowned at his young companion, equally puzzled. Hal smiled at them.

"That's right. My crew and I are going to become pirates."

al said no more about his plan that night. It was a rough idea only and he wanted to flesh it out before he discussed it with the others. He spent the rest of the evening quizzing Mannoc about Raguza: who ran the port, how ships gained entry and protection, what were the rules of the city, and any other details he could think of. He wanted to gain as full a picture of the pirate haven as possible. Later, after he and the crew returned to the *Heron*, he sat for long hours in the bow, his back resting comfortably against the shrouded mass of the Mangler. He watched the moon traverse the sky, and the stars slowly wheel around the dark night in their stately procession, as he thought the idea through. Finally, yawning, he pulled his sheepskin up around his ears, tugged his watch cap down and slept.

He woke stiff and cold to the delicious smell of fresh coffee. He opened one bleary eye. Edvin was crouching over him, a cup held enticingly under his nose.

"Where did that come from?" he asked, his voice thick with sleep. Edvin grinned as Hal took the cup and sipped it, closing his eyes with pleasure.

"Freyth's ship was carrying a cargo of it," he said. "He insisted on giving us several pounds. Naturally, I objected—for approximately two seconds. Then I graciously accepted."

"Lorgan's ears but it's good," Hal said. The coffee they had brought with them from Limmat had been mediocre, to say the best. This was rich and powerful. Best of all, it was freshly ground. He sipped again and felt the hot drink draining through his entire body, sweeping away the stiffness of his muscles.

Around him, the ship was slowly coming to life as the crew woke, rose and stretched. When they were safely moored like this, Edvin could light a cook fire on board—the charcoal grill resting in a tray of wet sand. The smell of the coffee, and sizzling bacon and eggs in his large cook pan, wafted to the boys' nostrils and brought them out of their sleep.

"Nothing wakes a boy like the smell of food," Thorn observed to nobody in particular. He eyed Hal curiously. "Spend the night there, did you? Something on your mind?"

"You could say that. I was thinking about our problem with the *Raven*. I think I've come up with a way to get us into Raguza without having the locals attack us."

Lydia had approached while Hal had been speaking. She caught the last few words.

"Is that what you were talking about last night?" she said. "When you said we should become pirates?"

"Well . . . yes," said Hal, a little stiffly. He had been hoping to state that part of his plan as a dramatic denouement. Now Lydia had jumped in and preempted him. Girls have no sense of drama, he thought, frowning. No wonder none of them were saga-tellers.

Thorn, however, looked interested in the idea, drama or no drama. "How do you propose we do that?" he asked. In answer, Hal pointed to *Seahawk* bobbing gently on the wavelets beside them.

"I was thinking about the way Zavac tricked his way into Limmat harbor," he said. "I thought we might take a leaf out of his book. If we turn up outside Raguza, with *Seahawk* in hot pursuit, chances are they'll take us for another pirate."

Lydia frowned. "Zavac will hardly fall for his own trick," she said. "In any event, he knows the *Heron*. He's seen her."

"That's the point," Hal replied. "We don't have to convince Zavac. We have to convince the man who is in charge at Raguza—Mannoc told me he has some strange title, the Kropajo or something like that. We'll say Zavac recruited us for the raid on Limmat, then left us in the lurch—along with the *Stingray*. That'll give us the high ground if Zavac tries to discredit us. Of course he'd turn on us if he'd betrayed us and left us to die. He'd have to."

Thorn stroked his chin with his forefinger and thumb as he thought over what Hal had said.

"It's not a bad idea," he said. "Of course, it'll depend on us reaching this head man and putting our case before Zavac does."

Hal shrugged. "It'll be better if we can, but it's not essential. In any event, once we're in Raguza, we'll have a chance to get on board *Raven* and find the Andomal."

"How do you propose to do that?" Lydia asked.

Hal shrugged. "I haven't quite figured that part out yet," he admitted. He paused, thinking for a few seconds. Then his mind went off on a tangent. "It's a pity we don't have any of the emeralds from Limmat," he said.

Thorn cocked his head in question. "Why's that?"

"I was talking to Mannoc about it last night. The system in Raguza is that each ship pays ten percent of her plunder to a central council. That's what buys them the protection of the port. That means Zavac will have handed over a share of the emeralds he stole. If we could produce more of them, it'd strengthen our story that we were at Limmat with him. They're pretty distinctive, after all."

Lydia cleared her throat noisily and they turned to look at her. A slow smile was spreading over her features.

"What is it?" Hal asked. She paused, trying to fight past the smile, then spoke.

"Remember that parcel I gave you when we left Limmat? You put it in the strongbox."

Hal nodded. "Yes. What about it? I assume it's some particular valuable of yours."

"Actually, it contains eight Limmatan emeralds," Lydia told them. She enjoyed the way both of her listeners' jaws dropped.

"And . . . where did you get them, may I ask?" Hal finally managed to say.

She shrugged airily. "I took them. They were in the counting house. They were part of the last batch delivered from the mines. But Zavac missed them. After all, he was in a hurry to leave. Nobody had noticed them. They were left in a linen sack on a table in the counting house anteroom. I looked in the sack and saw them, and I figured you all deserved some reward for saving the town. I also figured Barat would never pay you anything. So I . . . took them."

"You stole them?" Hal asked, and she scuffed her shoe on the deck, not meeting his eyes.

"I . . . liberated them. In the name of a deserving cause."

Thorn emitted a low rumble of laughter. "Ah, girl," he said, "you definitely are a keeper."

Lydia flushed with anger. "I've told you not to call me that, old man," she said, a warning glint in her eyes. Thorn continued to smile at her, totally unabashed, and she finally had to look away, shaking her head. He was incorrigible, she thought, not for the first time.

"The thing is," she said to Hal, "if we show them, and hand over one of them in payment, it'll be pretty obvious that they're from the same source as the ones Zavac paid over." She spread her hands out to either side, palms upward.

"So it will appear that we were working with him," Hal said slowly. "That's excellent! That'd be worth handing over all of the emeralds!"

"Let's not be hasty," Thorn told him. "Whoever's running Raguza will expect us to try and hold back as much as possible. Pirates aren't known for their generosity, after all."

"That's why they're pirates, in fact," Lydia said, smiling.

Hal finished his coffee and rose to his feet, yawning and stretching. He returned the empty cup to Edvin's cooking area, then glanced across to the decks of the *Seahawk*. There was a small guard left on board, but the majority of the crew had gone to their homes. He could see no sign of Mannoc yet, but the skipper had said he'd come down to the ship during the morning.

He and Stig spent the next two hours going over the ship, checking sails, masts, halyards and standing rigging for any sign of wear and tear. It had been some weeks since they had enough free time to attend to such matters and soon the entire crew were hard at work making minor repairs—splicing ropes, greasing blocks and pulleys and re-tarring the stays where there was any sign of fraying.

When Hal had shot the massive bolt into the bottom of the pirate longboat, he'd noticed a slight extra movement in the massive recoil of the giant crossbow. It had seemed to lurch a little to one side. He removed the canvas covering and crouched to examine the two leather restraining straps that absorbed the recoil. He hadn't checked them since the battle at Limmat and he found that the starboard-side strap had frayed slightly where it passed over a timber piece of the crossbow's frame. The timber was hard edged and the constant rubbing back and forth as Hal had shot had caused wear on the strap. As the strap thinned, it had stretched a little, leaving the Mangler slightly unbalanced.

He fetched his tool kit and took out a hand plane, working it on the wood until the sharp edge was rounded off. Then he rubbed it with a smoothing stone to make it even less abrasive. As soon as he began to examine the weapon, Ingvar had joined him, crouching beside him to see if there was anything he could do to help. Hal smiled to himself. Ingvar had a proprietorial interest in the Mangler. He alone was strong enough to cock it and load it single-handed. After a lifetime of being made to feel superfluous, Ingvar was delighted to find a vital task that only he could accomplish.

"How's the side?" Hal asked as he worked away with the plane. Ingvar touched the spot where he had been wounded, and pressed experimentally.

"Feeling a lot better. I should be fine in a day or two."

"Good. Because I may need you in a day or two." Hal bent closer to study the strap. He chewed his lip thoughtfully. It seemed strong enough. He pointed it out to Ingvar.

"Give that a good yank, will you?"

Ingvar complied and they both examined the strap again. "Felt solid enough," Ingvar said, and Hal grunted.

"I'll grease it to stop it from fraying any further."

That done, he tightened both straps until they were evenly balanced, collected his tools and stood, looking once more across to the *Seahawk*. This time, he was pleased to see Mannoc standing in the bow, checking the forestay and discussing a repair with his first mate. In addition to the damaged rope, there were several raw patches on the hull and bulwarks, where ax strokes or spear thrusts from the pirate longboat had scarred the timber. They didn't make the ship any less efficient, but Hal knew a proud skipper like Mannoc wouldn't tolerate having his ship scarred and marked in that way. Before too long, he'd set men to work, sanding and patching the marks of battle.

He looked up and saw Hal watching. He smiled and waved a greeting, then Hal moved to the port rail, stepping up onto it and balancing with a light hold on a stay. It was freshly tarred and he felt the sticky substance, still slightly warm, adhering to his fingers. Absentmindedly, he wiped his hand on the seat of his pants, smiling as he thought of what his mother would have to say about such behavior. He gestured to the *Seahawk*'s deck.

"Come aboard?" he asked. That was simply good manners. Mannoc nodded and beckoned him forward, moving to the rail to greet him as he stepped lightly across the gap between the two ships.

"What's on your mind?" Mannoc said cheerfully as they shook hands.

"Zavac and Raguza," Hal replied.

Mannoc's smile faded a little. "Ah yes. And what exactly did you want to know about them?"

"You've run across Zavac before, haven't you?" Hal asked.

Mannoc nodded. "Several times. I could never catch him, unfortunately. His ship was too fast for me and he always ran back into the safety of Raguza harbor."

"So the *Seahawk* is well-known in Raguza? I mean, they'd recognize her if they saw her?"

Mannoc smiled grimly. "Oh, they'd recognize her, all right. Zavac aside, we've caused a lot of problems for the citizens of Raguza over the years." He paused and studied the younger man shrewdly. "I assume this has something to do with all the questions you were asking last night?"

Hal nodded. "From what you said, I take it that the most important person in the town is the Kopple . . ." He hesitated over the word and Mannoc supplied it.

"The Korpaljo. Yes. The ruling council is called the Korpal, which means 'Circle.' They're called that because they meet in a circular tower room, sitting at a circular table. The circle theme reflects the fact that all members are equal, except for the Korpaljo, or Circle leader. He's elected by the others for a term of four years and his word is law."

He frowned, thinking, then added, "The current Korpaljo is called Mihaly. He was elected two years ago. He's a former pirate captain himself and he can be a very bad enemy to anyone who crosses him. He's a cruel, merciless man and he rules the Circle with an iron fist—doesn't tolerate any disagreement with his decisions." He smiled ironically. "His name, incidentally, means 'close to the gods.' I think he believes it's true. He thinks he has godlike powers."

Hal was frowning as Mannoc described the organization of Raguza's ruling body.

"If the Korpaljo has absolute power, what's the point of being on the Circle?" he asked.

Mannoc nodded. "Good question. The members of the Korpal carry out his orders. And they have no authority of their own. But of course Circle members wield a lot of influence in the city. And the only way to be elected Korpaljo is to be a member of the Circle in the first place."

"Aha. That makes sense," Hal said. "So if I can convince Mihaly that we're pirates, nobody else can gainsay his decision—least of all Zavac?"

"I should say that's true. After all, Zavac's not a member of the Korpal. But how do you propose to convince Mihaly?"

"I thought I'd get you and the *Seahawk* to chase us into Raguza harbor," Hal said. Mannoc considered the idea for a few seconds, weighing it. Then he nodded.

"Yes. That might work. It's a good idea."

"It's not mine," Hal admitted. "I stole it from Zavac. I'm going to say that he recruited us for the raid on Limmat, then deserted us, along with *Stingray* and her crew."

Mannoc was familiar with the details of the invasion of Limmat. Hal had described it to him the previous evening.

"Mentioning *Stingray* will add to your credibility. She was well-known in Raguza. Mind you, if Mihaly doesn't believe your story, you'll be in a real fix. And there'll be nothing I can do to help you."

"We have something to help sway him," Hal said, and when Mannoc looked questioningly at him, he added, "We've got a stash of Limmatan emeralds we plan to bribe him with."

Mannoc thrust out his bottom lip and nodded slowly. "Yes. I should think that would do it."

"Something else I was wondering about," Hal said. "Do you think your trader friends would object if I returned the money they gave me and took their payment in cargo instead?"

Mannoc considered the idea, then shook his head. "I think they'd be delighted," he said. "They calculated your payment on the basis of their cargoes' market price. If they pay you in goods, they'll be saving money. But why do it that way?"

"If we're carrying some cargo, we can spin a story that we took it from a trading ship on the river—one that you were escorting. Then you turned up and chased us off. It all adds to our credibility as a pirate."

Mannoc regarded the young man with increased respect. This one is a thinker, all right, he thought. He covers every angle. Then another thought struck him. There was a further small detail they could add, and he was beginning to realize that small details could make a big difference.

"You'll need a black flag. All pirates fly them—a black flag with your own individual device on it."

Hal smiled. "I'll get Edvin onto it. If all else fails, he can knit us one."

PART 2

THE DUEL

M ihaly, Korpaljo of the pirate haven of Raguza, strode resolutely along the waterfront, as he did most days. His secretary, Hugo, hurried behind him, struggling to keep up with the Korpaljo's fast pace.

Mihaly's dark eyes scanned the jetties and moorings, looking for new arrivals, checking for ships that had been in port too long. The one-tenth tribute paid to the Korpal bought a ship haven for a month. At the end of that time, the ship could either leave harbor or pay an additional tribute—although at the lesser rate of one-twentieth.

His eyes fastened on a ship moored along the stone-edged waterfront. She had a distinctive blue paint job, and two large eyes were painted on her bow. Her captain, noticing the Korpaljo passing by, called a cheerful greeting.

"Good morning, Mihaly! A beautiful day!"

He smiled and waved back at the man. "It is indeed, Drakis!" he agreed. Then he swung round to his assistant, the smile fading as he turned away from the ship.

"How long has he been in port?" he demanded.

Hugo fumbled through the ledger that he always carried with him, checking ships' names and arrival dates.

"Let's see . . . *Bluefire* . . . *Bluefire* . . . ," he said, turning the pages as quickly as he could. Mihaly glared at him and snapped his fingers.

"Get a move on, curse you."

Hugo finally found the page he was looking for. "Yes, Korpaljo. Ah! Here it is. They came in four weeks and two days ago. They're overdue," he added.

Mihaly glared at him. "I could work that out myself. Do you think I'm a dullard? Send the guard later to collect another tribute."

"Yes, Korpaljo," Hugo replied, making a mark against *Bluefire*'s name.

Mihaly stopped, hands on hips, surveying the wide harbor, crowded with ships and surrounded by elegant, white-painted buildings built on the hills that rose on all sides round the harbor.

"Any new arrivals?" he asked, and Hugo shook his head.

"None since *Raven*," he said, watching his master carefully.

A scowl came over Mihaly's swarthy features at the name. "Ah yes, our friend Zavac. Where's he moored?"

This time, Hugo didn't need to check his ledger. He pointed down harbor, toward one of the inner bays.

"You put him in Goathead Bay," he said. Mihaly snorted.

"Good place for him." He shaded his eyes and followed the direction Hugo had indicated. But from this point, a headland obscured the view into Goathead Bay. "I don't trust that man," he said softly. "He's a liar and a cheat."

Hugo shrugged. "He's a pirate, after all," he said, without thinking, then went pale as he realized his mistake. Mihaly turned those dark eyes on him so they seemed to bore into Hugo's brain.

"So was I," he reminded him. Hugo backed away a few paces, stammering.

"Well, yes, Korpaljo . . . I didn't mean to . . . I mean, I didn't intend . . ."

Mihaly made a disgusted gesture. "Oh, shut up your bleating!" he ordered. "What I mean is, Zavac has a bad habit of cheating his own kind. There should be a sense of trust between us, after all. If we don't stick together, if we can't trust one another, then we'll become easy prey for the rest of the world. That's why Raguza is such a powerful and impregnable haven. We stick together and provide mutual support."

And in addition, you're paid large bribes by every ship that enters the port, Hugo thought. But he was wise enough not to voice the sentiment. He stood silent, nodding agreement.

Mihaly stood, feet braced wide apart in the unconscious stance of an experienced sailor. He was a dark, swarthy man, with close-cropped black hair and heavy eyebrows above his dark brown, almost black, eyes. His face was weathered by years of sun, wind and salt water. He was stocky and a little below average height, although to compensate, he wore knee-high boots with high heels. His career as a pirate had taken him through the eastern reaches of the Constant Sea, into the Sea of Rostov and out through the Assaranyan Channel to the Blood Sea. His wide war belt held a long, curved saber and two heavy daggers.

It had been many years since his last raiding cruise, and his waist had begun to thicken. Still, Hugo knew, he was incredibly fast with the sword or either of the daggers—and with either hand. He was not a man to trifle with.

The Korpaljo grunted. The thought of Zavac and his ship had put him in a bad mood. He sensed that the Magyaran was hiding something from him, that he had underpaid the amount of tribute owed to the Korpal. But he couldn't prove it. He swung on his heel and turned abruptly back toward the town. Mihaly tended to move abruptly, Hugo thought.

"Right! Let's get back to—"

"Sail! Two ships approaching!"

The shout came from a wooden lookout platform set at the end of the harbor mole. Mihaly spun on his heel again to face it. The lookout on duty was pointing out to sea and Mihaly hurried along the cobbled surface of the harbor front, where it curved out in a long sweep to the narrow harbor entrance.

As he went, with Hugo skipping hurriedly in his wake, they heard the rattle of a drum as the harbor guard turned out on either side of the entrance. Armed men lined the stone harbor walls on either side. On each headland, a dozen archers took up shooting positions.

Mihaly and Hugo reached the end of the mole. The guard captain, recognizing the Korpaljo, saluted briskly.

"Two ships, sir," he said, before Mihaly could ask. "Heading for the harbor. They're coming fast."

The lookout was crouched on his platform above them, staring through a viewing tube set on a swiveling mount, designed to cut side glare and focus his vision.

"Second ship is the *Seahawk*!" he called.

Mihaly's head jerked up at the name. He hated the *Seahawk*, and her commander, Mannoc. The escort ship commander had cost him a great deal of money over the years. While Mihaly no longer went to sea, he held shares in many of the ships operating out of Raguza. Mannoc had burned and sunk far too many of them.

"Are you sure?" he called. The lookout stood away from the viewing tube and looked down to the stocky figure on the ground below him.

"I'm sure," he replied. "That Droghan swine chased us in the old *Naska* for three days before he caught us and burned her. I only just got away. I'd know her anywhere."

"What's the other ship?" Mihaly asked.

"She's smaller. Looks like *Seahawk* is after her, but she's holding her own. Strange rig, like one of those Blood Sea craft. Triangular sail, set fore and aft."

Mihaly climbed the first few rungs of the ladder leading to the platform until the two ships came into sight. The lookout was right, he thought. The second ship was definitely the *Seahawk* and she was obviously in pursuit of the smaller ship.

"She's flying a black flag," the lookout added. No need to say which ship he was talking about. *Seahawk* would never fly a black flag. It was the universal sign of a corsair—a term that Mihaly generally preferred to the word *pirate.*

As they watched, the leading ship changed course, turning toward the wind—and the harbor entrance. The fore-and-aft rig let her lie closer to the stiff breeze than *Seahawk*'s square mainsail would allow.

If I were starting out again, I'd have a ship with that sort of rig, Mihaly thought.

Gradually, the two ships began to diverge, the distance between them widening. Mihaly sensed an air of frustration about the *Seahawk*, although he realized he was probably being fanciful. He could see a small knot of men in the bow of the *Seahawk*, armed with bows and launching arrows after their escaping quarry. But the leading ship was already out of effective range and he saw several quick splashes in her wake as the arrows fell short. Some of her crew gathered in the stern to wave and yell abuse at the Droghan ship pursuing them.

A few hundred meters from the harbor, Mannoc admitted defeat and the *Seahawk* sheered away, not wanting to come within range of the waiting archers on either side of the harbor entrance. Bitter experience had taught Mannoc that there was nothing to be gained from coming too close to Raguza.

"Orders, sir?" the guard captain asked.

Mihaly thought for a moment, then replied, "Send out the long-boats to escort her in."

The captain saluted and turned away, bellowing orders.

"And keep an eye on *Seahawk*. Mannoc may try one last throw of the dice."

It was just possible that when her quarry lowered her sails to row into the harbor, Mannoc might try a desperate, last-minute dash to run down and seize her. That was why Mihaly had ordered the two longboats to bring the newcomer in. They were guard boats kept in constant readiness for an event such as this. With twenty armed men in each, they would ensure that Mannoc kept his distance.

Now that the smaller ship was closer, Mihaly could see that she was festooned with arrows and there were several long rips in her sail. Obviously, it had been a long chase and Mannoc had come close to catching her. The black flag at her stern was discernible now. It was decorated with a white device—the skeletal head of a sharp-beaked bird. As he watched, the helmsman on the newcomer acknowledged the longboats heading out to escort him into harbor. The punctured sail slid down and was gathered in and oars were run out either side.

Mihaly cast one more look at the *Seahawk*, but she was far out on the broad river now. At this point, where the river ran into the Constant Sea, it was five kilometers or more across. At high tide, the water was noticeably salty. *Seahawk* was little more than a faint flutter of white sail against the blue of the water. There was no further risk from her.

He jerked a thumb at the small ship as it rowed toward the harbor, flanked by the lean, predatory longboats.

"Assign them a mooring, then send them to me," he ordered.

"Aye, sir," the captain replied. "Alongside? Or out in the bay?" he added.

Mihaly turned a baleful gaze on him. "Do I look as if I give a water rat's behind?" he snarled, and the captain hastily apologized.

"No, sir. Sorry, sir. I'll attend to it, sir." He remembered, too late, that it was unwise to ask the Korpaljo to bother with details—unless they involved a payment due to him. Then he was a real stickler, the captain thought.

"Bring their captain to me within the hour," Mihaly said, turning away. "And bring him under guard until we know who they are."

"Yes, sir," the captain said briskly. He was already thinking. That meant he'd need to put the new ship on a mooring alongside the harbor front. It'd take too long to moor them out in the bay, then find a small boat to bring the captain ashore. And he knew that he'd better get the captain of the ship to Mihaly's office without delay.

His sergeant watched the Korpaljo's thickset figure as he stalked off down the wharf, walking with a sailor's rolling gait. As ever, Hugo skipped awkwardly behind him, trying to keep up.

"Whew!" the sergeant breathed. "Always a pleasure seeing him, isn't it?"

The captain made a sharp cutting gesture with his right hand. "Shut up!" he snapped. "He has ears like a hawk. Hears everything you say."

He didn't know if a hawk had good ears or not. But at the moment, he couldn't think of a better simile to use.

chapter thirty-three

This is getting to be a habit," Stig said as he, Thorn and Hal strode down the pier, accompanied by a sergeant of the guard and two armed troops. Thorn turned to look quizzically at him.

"What is?" he asked, although he had a shrewd idea that he knew what Stig was talking about. The tall boy shook his head in annoyance.

"It seems every harbor we put into, we're frog-marched off to see some jumped-up local nonentity whose main interest lies in separating us from our money. It's starting to get tedious."

"It's the way of the world," Thorn told him. "On a river like this, everyone has his hand out. Besides, if a foreign ship moors in Hallasholm, it pays a harbor tax to Erak."

"And I'd go easy with the 'jumped-up local nonentity' talk,"

Hal advised in a lowered tone. "From what I've heard, the Korpaljo can be very dangerous if you make him mad."

Stig sniffed disdainfully. But he resolved not to make any more disparaging comments about local authorities.

The land around Raguza harbor rose in steep hills, with the gleaming white buildings of the town built in a series of rising terraces. They followed their escort up a narrow, winding street that ran up from the harbor. As they went higher, Hal took a moment to glance back. The harbor lay below them, the masts of the ships moored there looking like a leafless, branchless forest. In addition to the thirty or so pirate ships in harbor, there were scores of smaller craft—fishing boats, barges and longboats, similar to the pair that had escorted *Heron* into harbor. The buildings below his vantage point were predominantly white, with orange terra-cotta-tiled roofs.

The sergeant escorting them called impatiently and Hal turned and resumed toiling up the winding street.

At the very top, they came to a large building that took up one side of a small plaza. The building was colonnaded along the front, providing a deep shade area. It was painted white, of course, and it rose for three floors above the square. Rows of arched windows ran along the upper floors. At the left-hand end was a massive round tower, which soared up to twice the height of the rest of the building. Their escort pointed to the tower, then led the way.

"The Korpal," Hal muttered, and the others looked at him curiously. "The ruling council here is called the Korpal," he explained. "*Korpal* means 'Circle.' They meet in a circular room and I'm guessing that's where it's situated."

The sergeant led them into the tower and up a staircase running round one of the walls, following the curve of the building. They went up two floors. On the first, the entire central floor consisted of a vast open space, with a circular table set in the middle and fifteen chairs placed around it. Hal guessed this was the meeting room for the Korpal, where official business was carried out. The next floor was divided into several spaces. A semicircular anteroom took up half the floor space. It was sparsely furnished with wooden chairs and benches, presumably for those who were waiting to be summoned through one of the several doors that led off it. The sergeant didn't hesitate, but led them to a door set on the harbor side of the tower, knocked once and waited.

There was a pause of a few seconds, then a harsh voice from within called for them to enter. The sergeant opened the door and ushered the three Skandians in ahead of him. He and his three men followed, ranging themselves along the wall.

If the outer room was sparsely furnished, Mihaly's office was a different matter altogether. His large desk dominated the room and he sat behind it on a high-backed chair marked with intricate carvings. There were several other chairs, matching in design but not as large as the Korpaljo's, ranged around the room, upholstered with thick, brightly colored cushions. The wood was dark and lustrous and bore the mark of constant polishing. Several large, dark wooden chests were ranged along the walls. The curved outer wall of the tower was behind Mihaly's desk. It was undecorated, but a large curved window looked down over the terra-cotta roofs of the houses and the sparkling blue of the harbor.

The other walls were hung with rich tapestries, and a painting of a two-masted ship was in a prominent position. Hal eyed it with professional interest but he decided that it had been painted by an artist with no concept of good ship design. The masts were badly spaced, so that the rear sail would mask the breeze reaching the forward one.

Above the Korpaljo's desk, a large embroidered rectangle of tasseled fabric hung from a narrow, polished wooden beam. As they watched, it swayed slowly back and forth, providing a pleasant breeze through the room. Stig wondered what kept it moving. Then he noticed a thin draw cord leading away from it and through a small hole in the upper part of the wall. Presumably, somewhere outside the room, a servant sat, pulling the cord, then releasing it, so the square of heavy fabric maintained its steady back-and-forth motion.

It was the room of a rich and powerful man. By comparison, Doutro's office in Bayrath had been small, shabby and unimpressive.

"Sit down," Mihaly said. He waved a hand at three chairs that had been placed in front of his desk. It was not an invitation, Hal thought. It was an order. He guessed that most of the Korpaljo's conversation would be phrased the same way. The three Herons took their seats, Thorn in the middle, Hal on his right and Stig on his left. It had been agreed that, as before, Thorn would act as the ship's captain.

"So, who are you? Where are you from? What do you want?" Mihaly shot the questions out in rapid succession. Thorn replied calmly.

"We're Skandians. We're from Hallasholm on the Stormwhite originally, but we've been raiding down the east and south coasts, then down the Dan. We're looking for refuge here in Raguza. We've been told it's friendly to raiders."

"Pirates, you mean?" Mihaly might prefer to apply the term *corsair* to himself. But these newcomers hadn't earned the distinction.

Thorn shrugged. "If you prefer."

Mihaly's eyes bored into his for a few seconds, then switched to the two young men beside him. He noted that all three of the Skandians wore identical woolen watch caps.

"Who are these two?" he snapped.

"My helmsman and my bosun," Thorn said, indicating Hal and Stig in turn. Mihaly's eyes flicked back to the shabby old sea wolf.

"Bit on the young side, aren't they?" he sneered.

Thorn took no offense. He replied evenly.

"They're the best I could do. Not many experienced sailors want to serve with a one-armed man." He held up the carved hook on his right arm. "But these lads have done well by me. I've trained them and they know how to fight."

"So you say," Mihaly said, a sneer in his voice.

"So I say," Thorn replied, still keeping his voice even. But his eyes met the Korpaljo's in an unwavering stare. Eventually, Mihaly nodded and glanced away. This wasn't a man he could browbeat or intimidate too easily, he thought. He felt a small flicker of respect for the one-armed man opposite him. Mihaly preferred to deal with men who were straightforward and plain speaking—unlike Zavac, he thought sourly.

He gathered his thoughts, glancing down at some papers on his desk, then looked up again after a few seconds.

"So, you want the protection of the Korpal," he said.

Thorn frowned slightly, as if not understanding. "The Korpal?"

Mihaly gestured impatiently. "The Circle Council. The ruling body here in Raguza. Perhaps you should have found out a few basic things about us before you blundered in here."

"We were in a bit of a rush when we arrived," Thorn said, and Mihaly smiled scornfully.

"I saw," he said.

Thorn shook his head angrily. "We'd taken a trader about ten kilometers upriver. We were transferring her cargo to our ship when that blasted Droghan cruiser came round a bend and nearly caught us."

"The *Seahawk*," Mihaly commented.

Thorn shrugged, anger still evident on his face. "Is that what she's called? I don't know. We were outnumbered, so we took as much as we could from the trader and ran for it. I'd heard talk about this place, so that's why we came here."

Mihaly sat back in the tall chair, thinking over Thorn's words. "You know the rules here?" he asked finally.

Thorn nodded. "We pay a levy of ten percent of our plunder and that buys us protection."

"That's right. For a month," Mihaly said.

"Well, we're carrying leather goods, some high-quality olive oil and a dozen bales of fine silk we took out of the trader. I'll happily hand over ten percent of that."

He waited while Mihaly made notes on a sheet of paper in front of him, using a long, ornate peacock feather quill pen to do so. Then Thorn leaned forward in his chair.

"There's another thing," he said. "I heard a rumor that a captain called Zavac might be heading this way. I'd like to talk to him if he's here."

Now Mihaly's interest was piqued. "Zavac?" he said casually. "He might be here. What did you want to talk to him about?"

He sensed there was no love lost between these tough Skandians and the oily, smooth-talking Zavac. He was interested by a possible conflict between the two. There might be a way to turn it to his advantage. He could usually find one in such cases.

Thorn looked him steadily in the eye as he answered.

"I'd like to talk to him about how I plan to kill him," he said.

Mihaly made an imperious gesture in the air between them.

"Fighting between crews is banned in Raguza," he said automatically. "Otherwise the system would fall into anarchy within a few weeks. If you have a grudge, you settle it somewhere else."

Thorn nodded. "That's fair."

But Mihaly wanted to know more. "Why are you intent on killing him?" he asked.

Thorn sat back, feigned a scowl, then answered.

"He betrayed us. He recruited us to help him attack a town called Limmat. You know it?"

Mihaly shrugged. "I've heard of it," he said, and Thorn continued, the anger apparent in his words.

"We sailed in company with Zavac and another ship, the *Stingray*." As he said the name, Mihaly's interest was all too obvious.

"Nagy's ship?" he said. "We were wondering what had become of her."

"Well, she's gone. Turns out Limmat was a tougher nut to

crack than Zavac told us. And the townspeople were reinforced by a Skandian wolfship that had come after us. We probably could have won. We were getting the upper hand, then Zavac decided to cut and run. Just up and deserted us.

"That's when we lost *Stingray,* and most of her crew. Her first mate, Rikard, was the only survivor. We took him on board."

Mihaly frowned. "He's with you now?" he said quickly. "He can vouch for your story?"

Thorn shook his head sadly. "He could have. But he was murdered up north, in a town called Krall. Went into a tavern one night and never made it back to the ship."

Thorn and Hal had worked on this story over the past day. They decided that mixing elements of true events into it would make it more convincing—particularly if rumors of events in Krall had happened to reach Raguza. And even if Mihaly hadn't heard of Rikard's violent end, the odds were good that he would know the man's name, and that would add credibility to the story.

Watching now, Hal decided that it was time for them to play their winning card.

"Mind you," he put in, "there is something that can definitely vouch for it."

The Korpaljo looked quickly at him. "And what might that be?" he asked slowly.

In answer, Thorn reached into his jerkin and produced a small sack of untanned leather, placing it on the desk and opening it. Mihaly leaned forward, his eyes glittering, as the eight perfect emeralds rolled out onto the polished wooden surface.

"I told you about our cargo," Thorn continued. "But this is our share of the plunder from Limmat. You're entitled to your ten percent, of course."

Mihaly reached across the table and picked up one of the emeralds, holding it to the light from the window to appraise it.

"This is beautiful. Very distinctive color," he said softly. "I've never seen one quite like it before."

Hal and Thorn exchanged a quick glance. Then Thorn said, with a note of surprise in his voice, "But you must have." And when Mihaly looked at him, frowning, he explained, "Didn't Zavac pay you ten percent of his share? He's got four times as many as these."

Mihaly set the emerald down on the polished surface of the table with a soft click. Now it all fell into place. He'd had a suspicion that Zavac had been holding out on him, trying to cheat him. Now these northmen had confirmed it.

"No," he said softly. "He never mentioned anything like this." He looked up at the sergeant, standing to attention against the wall. "Sergeant," he said, "go and fetch your captain for me, would you? I think I'd like to have words with our friend Zavac."

Zavac was relaxing on the stern deck of the *Raven*, sitting in a canvas-and-wood chair and enjoying the mild sunshine.

Accommodation was expensive in Raguza and the local property owners were all too ready to gouge the purses of captains and crews who stopped there. As a result, most crews chose to stay aboard their ships. Zavac's men had rigged a tent-shaped awning that ran two-thirds of the length of the *Raven*, providing shelter from the weather. Most ships in the harbor were rigged in a similar fashion. The crew spread their bedding on the sheltered deck space inside the tent. Zavac, of course, had his small enclosed personal space below the central decking in the ship's stern.

He heard the sound of running footsteps and looked up with mild interest.

Vargas was running along the jetty, his face red from the effort. Sweat stained his shirt. Obviously, he had been running for some distance. But then, Zavac thought sourly, Goathead Bay was some distance from just about everywhere in the harbor.

Vargas clambered down onto *Raven*'s deck and hurried aft to where Zavac sat. The Magyaran skipper leaned forward in his chair, interested to hear what had Vargas so hot under the collar—literally.

"They're here!" Vargas said, wasting no time in getting to the point. Zavac nodded with exaggerated interest.

"They are?" he said sarcastically. "How amazing."

Vargas glared at him. Your tune will change in the next few seconds, he thought. He was angry with himself for blurting out the statement, angrier at Zavac for his sneering rejoinder.

"The Skandians," he said. "They're here in Raguza."

The superior look was wiped from Zavac's face in the space of a heartbeat. His brows contracted and his face darkened with anger.

"Here? Where? What are they doing?" he demanded.

Vargas shrugged. "I've no idea what they're doing," he said. "But I saw their ship moored alongside the quay in the main harbor."

"You mean they're prisoners? Their ship was captured?" Zavac said, clinging to hope while he could. But Vargas was shaking his head.

"Didn't look like it to me. They were moored alongside, as I said, near Winder Street. I didn't see anyone standing guard. Their crew was going about their business normally enough."

Zavac slumped back in his chair, his hand to his chin, thinking furiously. How could they have gotten here? How could they have gained entry to the harbor? How had they broken free from Bayrath? He cursed silently. He had paid the Gatmeister a lot of money to throw that crew in prison and hang them. Now here they were. He took a vow that he would kill Doutro for this betrayal. They could only have made it past Bayrath if he'd let them through the boom.

His frantic thoughts were interrupted by the regular *tramp* of multiple heavy-shod feet approaching. He looked up and saw a captain of the Korpal guard, with a squad of half a dozen armed men, marching at double time down the wooden jetty.

It wasn't hard to tell where they were heading. The captain's eyes were fixed on the *Raven*. Slowly, Zavac rose from his seat. This didn't bode well, he thought. As they came level with the *Raven*, the squad ranged themselves along the jetty, facing the ship. The captain climbed down the access ladder fixed to the jetty and stepped aboard. This was a distinct breach of etiquette. Normally, any visitor would ask permission before coming aboard a ship— unless they had unpleasant official business to transact. The captain glanced around, saw Zavac and Vargas in the stern and walked toward them. Zavac rose from his chair and stepped forward to meet the soldier, forcing a smile on his lips.

"Good morning, Captain," he said smoothly. "Can I help you in some way?"

The captain ignored the smile. He answered brusquely with his own question. "Are you Zavac?"

Zavac nodded, still smiling, although it was the last thing he felt like doing. The captain's manner was unnerving.

"I'm Zavac," he said, "captain of this ship." He added this last pointedly. A ship's captain was entitled to a certain amount of deference, after all. But the soldier was unimpressed. He jerked a thumb toward the jetty behind him.

"You're to come with me," he said. "The Korpaljo wants to talk to you."

Zavac raised his eyebrows. "He does? What does he want to talk about?"

"No idea. Let's get going. Now." He half turned, jerking his thumb toward the ladder once more. Obviously, the Korpaljo's summons wasn't for a friendly chat, Zavac thought. The captain mightn't know what Mihaly wanted to talk about, but he knew it wasn't anything favorable to Zavac. Zavac shrugged, showing what a good-natured person he really was. He turned to Vargas.

"Well, Vargas, apparently the Korpaljo wants to see us . . . ," he began. But the captain cut across him.

"Just you. Nobody else."

Zavac cursed under his breath. He'd wanted to have a witness to the discussion. You never knew when a witness would come in handy—particularly when dealing with the Korpaljo, who tended to be high-handed and autocratic. But he hid his anger and walked submissively to the ladder. He paused and called back to his crewman.

"Tell Andras I'll be back in . . ." He paused and turned to the captain. "How long will this take?" he asked.

The captain shrugged indifferently. "How would I know?" he replied.

His unfriendly, uncooperative manner continued to worry Zavac. Mihaly definitely had something against him. He racked his brains, trying to think what it could be. He had a sinking feeling that it might concern the emeralds he had kept hidden. That might have been a mistake, he realized.

He wondered briefly if the summons had anything to do with the appearance of the Skandian ship in Raguza, but he dismissed the thought. He could see no way they could be associated with this predicament. Most likely one of his crew had talked about the emeralds in a tavern—and had been overheard.

He strode quickly through the narrow streets, keeping pace with the captain. The rest of the guard were formed closely around him, hemming him in and forestalling any chance of escape. Passersby glanced curiously at the party as they marched through the streets, heavy boots ringing on the cobbles.

It took them twenty minutes to reach the tower building. Zavac was ushered up the stairs and into the Korpaljo's office. Mihaly looked up as he entered. His gaze was stony and unfriendly. He said nothing, and an uncomfortable silence developed in the room.

"You wanted to see me, Korpaljo?" Zavac said finally. It was a disingenuous statement, he knew. Obviously the Korpaljo wanted to see him. He'd had him dragged here through the streets under guard. Mihaly disdained to answer the question.

"You're a liar, Zavac," he said bluntly. "A liar and a cheat."

Zavac thought it best to say nothing until he knew more. He had no idea what Mihaly was talking about and blustering about his innocence would do more harm than good.

To his surprise, Mihaly didn't pursue the matter but made a sign to one of the guards in the room.

"Let them back in," he said. The guard moved to one of the doors leading to side rooms and opened it.

Zavac recoiled in shock as the guard stood aside to admit the three Skandians. They were the last people he was expecting to see here. Obviously, they didn't share his surprise. One of the younger ones, the tall, broad-shouldered warrior, lunged forward toward Zavac.

"You coward!" he cried. "I'll kill you!"

Two of the guards intervened, blocking his path and restraining him. Mihaly's voice cut like a whip.

"That's enough!" he roared. "There'll be no brawling in here!"

Stig subsided reluctantly and the guards released him— although they remained close by him in case he erupted again.

Zavac pointed an accusing finger at the trio.

"Arrest these men! Lock them up!" he demanded, his voice cracking. "They're enemies!"

"Your enemies, you mean," the older Skandian said, sarcasm thick in his voice. "You abandoned us, you traitor. You betrayed us and left us to die—like the crew of the *Stingray*."

"*Stingray*?" Zavac said, not prepared for that line of attack. "What about her?"

He had mentioned nothing to the Korpaljo about the raid on Limmat. Now, at the mention of the *Stingray*, his guilt was plain on his face. He recovered quickly, but it was too late. The Korpaljo had noticed the sudden wariness that came into his eyes. Zavac appealed to him.

"These men fought against me!" he said. "I raided the Skandian capital of Hallasholm and they came after me. They're enemies!" he repeated.

Mihaly assessed him coolly. "You raided Hallasholm? Then where is the plunder from that raid?"

Zavac made a desperate, dismissive gesture in the air.

"I sold most of it on the way here!" he said. "We had to buy supplies. There was little enough to start with. These northmen have no sense of value. They think wool and mutton and salted fish are valuables," he added scornfully.

Mihaly eyed him shrewdly. He was an expert dissembler and he prided himself that he could tell when anyone was lying to him. There was a desperate note in Zavac's tone that indicated all too clearly that he wasn't telling the truth.

"And what about this raid where they claim you deserted them?" he asked, his tone deceptively uninterested.

"I know nothing about it!" Zavac answered immediately. He was beginning to recover from the initial shock of seeing the Skandians here in the Korpaljo's office. He threw an indignant look at them now. "I was never anywhere near Limmat," he said firmly.

Mihaly went silent. He looked at the three Skandians, then back at Zavac.

"Who mentioned Limmat?" he said mildly.

Zavac felt the blood draining from his face as he realized he had gone one step too far in his denial. He tried to recover.

"You did!" he said desperately. But the Korpaljo shook his head slowly.

"No. I didn't," he said. "And neither did they. I told them not to mention the town. So I can't help wondering why you brought it up."

Zavac said nothing. There was nothing he could say. He realized that he had been at a major disadvantage from the beginning. The Skandians had gotten to Mihaly first, with their version of the story, and had cleverly mixed facts with their own lies to make it convincing. Maybe, he thought, he could still ride this out. Given time, he might be able to prove that the Skandians were enemies— not just to him, but to Raguza and its inhabitants as a whole.

But Mihaly had another shock in store for him. He reached into his pocket and dropped something onto the desktop. It clattered and rolled a few centimeters before coming to rest. Zavac's eyes were glued to it.

Its distinctive deep green coloration marked it as a Limmatan emerald. He had never seen emeralds that rich shade of green anywhere else.

He opened his mouth to speak, but no words came. Where had Mihaly gotten hold of the fabulous stone? It had to be one of the fifty such gems that were secreted on board the *Raven*. But how had it fallen into the Korpaljo's possession? Mihaly's next words told him.

"The Skandians paid part of their one-tenth levy with this stone. It's a remarkable color. I've never seen anything like it before." He paused and those dark, almost black, eyes rose from the jewel on the table and bored into Zavac's like twin augers.

"Have you?" Mihaly demanded. "They tell me it was part of their plunder from Limmat. And they tell me you have a lot more stones like this one in your possession."

"No! I . . . I've never seen anything like this before. I . . ." He turned his gaze on the three Skandians. The two younger men's faces were set and grim. He could read the hatred and contempt in them. The older one, the raffish, one-armed old seafarer, was smiling at him. It was a cruel smile, devoid of humor, devoid of pity. Too late, Zavac realized that by hiding the existence of his emeralds, by trying to cheat Mihaly, he had alienated the Korpaljo and seemingly validated the Skandians' story.

Mihaly studied him for several seconds, then turned to the guard captain, standing at ease against the wall with his men.

"Captain," he said, "take your men back to the *Raven*. Give them axes and crowbars and tear the ship apart until you find where Zavac has hidden his share of the emeralds. They'll be there somewhere, probably in a very clever hiding place. If you have to destroy the ship to find them, then do it. Then tow it out of the harbor and burn what's left of it."

"Yes, sir!" the captain replied. He turned to his men, who came to attention as he looked at them.

"Men—," he began, but Zavac's desperate cry stopped him.

"No! No need for that! I'll tell you where they are." Better to lose the emeralds, he thought, than to lose his ship.

Mihaly held up a hand to stop the captain. He regarded Zavac with interest.

"In the stern, under the decking, I have a sleeping cabin. On the inboard bulkhead is a plank with an oval knot in it. Push on the knot and the plank will come loose. The emeralds are behind it."

"How many?" Mihaly demanded. Zavac's shoulder slumped.

"Fifty-two of them," he admitted. The Korpaljo leaned back in his seat, a grim smile playing around his lips.

"Then I'll take half," he said. "If you'd told me about them in the first place, I would have taken five as your fee. Now you'll pay five times that much for lying and for holding out on me." He gestured for the captain to leave the room. "Go and fetch them," he said. "Bring them here."

The captain saluted and led his squad from the room. Zavac turned and spat his venom at the Skandians.

"Be careful where you walk at night, you swine!" he said. "I'll kill you for this. I swear it."

Surprisingly, it was the slightly built youth who responded. He took a step toward Zavac, who couldn't help falling back as he read the cold hatred in his eyes.

"Feel free to try anytime, you gutless piece of garbage," he said. "If you have the courage to do it yourself. I'll be happy to put my sword through you."

"Enough!" Mihaly snapped, slamming his open hand down on his desk with an echoing crack. "There is no fighting in Raguza. I keep the peace here. If any of you try to break that peace, I'll have you crucified. Is that clear?"

Zavac and the three Skandians said nothing. He was obviously furious, Zavac thought. The normal punishment for fighting within the city limits was instant expulsion, not death.

"IS THAT CLEAR?" Mihaly repeated, his words echoing off the white-painted walls of the semicircular room. Raguza, packed full of pirates, thieves and murderers, was a potential tinderbox. If he ever allowed the residents to begin fighting among themselves, he could lose control and the resultant chaos could destroy the haven. This time, they all mumbled an acknowledgment. He took a deep breath and sat back. "It had better be," he said.

The captain returned within the hour. He had a large sack that he handed to Mihaly. The Korpaljo opened it and spilled the lustrous emeralds out onto the desk. He sighed with pleasure.

"Was there anything else?" he asked idly, flicking through the beautiful stones with his forefinger. The captain shrugged.

"There was a large yellow ball in a leather sack," he said. "Looked like glass of some kind. But it had no value. I left it there."

Mihaly, Zavac and the guard captain were intent on the pile of lustrous green gems on the table. None of them noticed the quick look that passed between the three Skandians.

R aguza was a remarkably pleasant town to spend time in, Hal thought. The streets were clean; the buildings were attractive and well kept. The harbor itself was a focal point of interest and activity.

There were excellent eating houses, offering cuisine from half a dozen different countries, and comfortable well-run taverns. Of course, close to the harbor, there were the usual dives and noisy, dirty saloons that would be found in any port. But once you moved away from the waterfront area, the class of establishment improved markedly. There was a good selection of pleasant, comfortable inns as well, although the prices were such that crews could only afford the occasional overnight stay.

Amazing what money could do, Hal thought. And there was plenty of money available in Raguza—although it was depressing when one considered the source of such funds.

Hal, Stig, Lydia and Jesper were seated at a table in one of the better eating houses. They had just finished a delicious meal—cuttlefish coated with crumbs, salt and pepper, and shallow fried until it was tender and delicious. It was an expensive dish, mainly because of the liberal use of pepper—one of the most expensive spices in that part of the world. But it was worth the price. There had been a green salad to accompany the cuttlefish, with an astringent dressing that awakened the mouth and complemented the spiciness of the fish.

Thorn had elected not to join them. "I'll get some sleep on board," he declared. The rest of the crew were sampling the delights of Raguza as well. In the light of Zavac's threat, Hal had warned them to stay together—he doubted anyone would be willing to attack a group that included the massive Ingvar. There was a general rule in Raguza that people went about the town unarmed, although that didn't apply to the Skandians' saxes, or the massive oak staff that Ingvar carried.

But Hal and his companions weren't out simply for a night on the town. Once it was dark, they had made their way to Goathead Bay, where they had learned the *Raven* was moored. Finding a vantage point on the next jetty, they had crouched in hiding behind a pile of lumber and used rope and studied the ship intently.

Or rather, Jesper had.

Now they sat, waiting for his opinion. Stig, as usual, decided they had waited long enough.

"Well, what about it? Can you do it? Can you get aboard and steal the Andomal?"

Hal glanced around apprehensively and gestured for Stig to

keep his voice down. His friend shrugged an impatient apology. Jesper hesitated. He had been thinking over the problem all the way back from Goathead Bay. He looked at Hal when he answered.

"I don't know. It'll be tough. You're sure they've got the Andomal on board?"

"Would we have wasted an hour spying on the *Raven* if we weren't?" Stig asked. Lydia laid a hand on his left arm.

"Keep it down, Stig," she said quietly. "You never know who might be listening. Best not to mention any names, all right?"

He flushed, realizing his mistake. He made an uncertain gesture with his right hand. He took care not to move his left. He liked the feel of Lydia's hand on his arm.

"Yeah. Yeah. Sorry," he said. "It's just so galling to know that the . . . you-know-what is so close to hand."

"So we are sure?" Jesper repeated.

Hal answered him. "We're as sure as we can be. The guard captain said he found a ball of yellow glass. What else could it be?"

Jesper shrugged. "I don't know. Maybe a ball of yellow glass?" He saw the pained look on Hal's face and added quickly, "Sorry. I guess you're right."

"And we know where he keeps it. Zavac said himself, there's a concealed hiding place in his sleeping berth at the stern of the ship. It should be child's play to sneak on board and find it."

Jesper raised an eyebrow at the words. "You must know some very badly brought-up children if you think so," he said.

Hal made an apologetic gesture. "All right, I might be simplifying things a little. But——"

"A little? You're asking me to sneak on board their ship without being seen, make my way to Zavac's sleeping cabin without being seen, get into it without being seen, steal the Andomal and get out again without being seen."

Hal shifted uncomfortably in his seat as Jesper described the sequence of events. He thought the former thief was making it sound more difficult than it really was.

"I thought you were good at that sort of thing," he said.

Jesper snorted derisively. "Nobody's good at that sort of thing," he said. "The ship is halfway along a jetty. The jetty is well lit and there's very little cover on it. That said, I might be able to reach the ship without being seen."

"Well, that's good, isn't it?" Lydia asked, and Jesper gave her a withering look.

"Problem is, I then have to get from the jetty to the deck of the ship. Have you noticed, Lydia, what happens when someone steps on board a ship?"

She shook her head, gesturing for him to explain. He did so, enunciating his words with exaggerated care.

"The ship moves," he said. "Particularly if it's tied up alongside in calm water. It rocks."

Lydia shrugged. "Yeah, but . . . not very much, surely?"

"It doesn't have to rock very much. These men are sailors, experienced sailors. They know what it feels like if somebody steps aboard."

"Well," said Lydia, frowning, "couldn't you step aboard so that it doesn't rock?"

Jesper leaned back in his seat, looking at her for several seconds. Finally, he turned to Hal. "Do you want to take that one?" he asked.

Hal held up his hands in a gesture for peace. He could see that Jesper's reaction had annoyed Lydia, just as her question had annoyed him.

"It's not possible, Lydia. They'll be on the alert now that they know we're in Raguza. Just as we'll be. If we felt the *Heron* move in the middle of the night, we'd all notice it and we'd know what was happening." He looked thoughtful, then turned to Jesper. "What if you got on board over the bow or the stern? If you were in the middle of the ship, it wouldn't rock, would it?"

"Maybe not," Jesper agreed reluctantly. "But how do you propose that I get on board over the stern? I'd have to jump from the jetty to reach it and that'd be sure to set the ship moving."

"I was thinking you could approach from the harborside, not the jetty side. If you swam out . . ."

He got no further before Jesper stopped him. "Hold it right there! I don't swim, remember?"

"No, but we could organize a way for you to float out . . ."

"We did that before, at the beach gate in Limmat, didn't we? You nearly drowned me."

"But I'd come with you this time—"

"You came with me that time! You nearly drowned both of us. Sorry, Hal, but I'm not going drifting round the harbor in the middle of the night." He studied Hal's face and could see that his skirl was close to abandoning the idea. He added the final argument. "Besides, let's say we managed it and I hauled myself up over the stern without rocking the boat. Can you imagine the noise I'd make with the water dripping off me back into the harbor?"

"Yes. I suppose you're right," Hal said heavily. But Jesper was only just warming to his theme.

"And even if I did manage to make it on board undetected, *Raven* has—what, fifty men in her crew? Even if half of them were ashore, I'd have to sneak past twenty or thirty men on an open deck, then find the access hatch to Zavac's sleeping cabin. Then get in and hope he wasn't snoozing away in there. And *then*, finally, I'd have to do it all again on the way out. Sorry, Hal. I don't think it can be done."

For a few moments, the four of them sat, disconsolately staring at the table and the remnants of the meal in front of them. A waiter came and cleared it away and still they sat in silence, thinking over Jesper's words. The waiter looked at them curiously, then returned with the reckoning.

Hal paid it. He had sold a second emerald to a gem trader in the city, to provide funds for the crew. Surprisingly for someone in a pirate haven, the trader had given him a very fair price.

Then again, he thought, maybe it wasn't so surprising. Cheating people who made their living killing and robbing others was probably not a good career move.

They left the eating house, emerging onto a broad, well-lit street that wound back down to the harbor. For a moment, they stood uncertainly. Then Hal broke the downcast silence that had settled over them.

"I guess we'll have to find another way."

Jesper hunched his shoulders, shoving his hands through his belt. "Sorry, Hal. I just don't think I could pull it off."

Hal slapped him on the back. "Not your fault, Jesper. We'll come up with something else."

They started down the street toward the harbor. They had gone fifty meters when they passed the dark mouth of a narrow alley running off to the left. As they did, Lydia stopped, her head cocked to one side.

"What was that?" she said. The three boys all looked at her, puzzled.

"What?" Stig asked. But she held up her hand for silence and this time they all heard it. A faint voice from the alley, weak and high-pitched.

"Hal! Help m—" The voice was cut off suddenly, as if a hand had been suddenly clamped over the speaker's mouth.

"Was that Edvin?" Jesper asked. The voice was distorted and weak. But whoever it was had called Hal by name. It had to be one of their crew. They all reached the same decision at the same moment.

"Come on!" said Hal, and he led them in a rush into the narrow alley. It was pitch-black after the brightly lit main street, but in a minute or two their eyes became accustomed to the darkness. They ran deeper into the alley but there was no further sound. Edvin, if it had been Edvin, had been silenced. Hal's mouth went dry as he wondered what had happened to his crewman.

Stig, who had taken the lead from Hal, suddenly called out angrily and they heard him collide with something and stagger back. Peering closely, Hal saw that the alley ended in a blank wall. Stig had run headlong into it and was nursing a cut on his forehead, cursing quietly. Hal's hand dropped to the hilt of his saxe.

"I don't like the look of this," he said. He realized now that they had been tricked. They should never have run pell-mell into the darkness of this alley, not knowing who or what might be waiting for them.

"Stay close, everyone," he said, and the small group instinctively moved closer together. Stig had stopped his swearing now. He mopped a trickle of blood away from his eyes and quietly drew his saxe. The muted sound of steel sliding against leather and wool was strangely comforting.

They faced back the way they had come. The entrance to the alley was no longer visible. It had taken a sharp curve halfway in. But now they saw a shaft of light suddenly illuminate the dark, narrow space twenty meters away. A door in one of the buildings lining the alley had opened, emitting bright lamplight from inside.

It emitted something else as well. Dark figures emerged from the doorway and moved toward them—armed men, silhouetted by the yellow light behind them.

"I guess it wasn't Edvin," Hal said.

"Backs to the wall, everyone." Stig's voice was calm and steady. He was always at his best when violent action was imminent, Hal thought. Hal and Jesper drew their saxes. Lydia already had her long, razor-sharp dirk ready. The four of them shuffled carefully backward, until they felt the rough brickwork behind them. At least now, Hal thought, they were safe from attack from the rear.

Although *safe* might not be the best word for this situation.

He could see now that the shadowy figures of the men advancing down the alley were armed with a selection of swords, clubs and axes. Armed only with saxes and a dirk, the Herons were at a big disadvantage.

"So much for the no-weapons-in-the-town rule," Jesper muttered bitterly. "I always knew that obeying the law would get me into trouble someday."

chapter thirty-seven

S tig watched through slitted eyes as the men slowly advanced on the small group of Herons. Without thinking about it, he had assumed command. This was his area of expertise, after all. He was the warrior among them and he was bigger, stronger and faster than Hal or Jesper. It was up to him to lead the defense.

The gang paused uncertainly. They were only a few meters away now and Stig realized what was going through their minds. Like any rabble, they were all waiting for someone else to take the lead, to make a decision. He recalled something Thorn had told him during one of their private training sessions.

Take the attack to the enemy. Take the initiative. If you wait for them to come to you, you're giving them control of the situation.

The eight men couldn't seem to decide who would launch the first attack. So Stig decided for them. With a loud cry that rang off the stone walls enclosing them, he leapt forward at the nearest swordsman, swinging his saxe in a backhanded stroke.

The saxe was heavy bladed and razor-sharp, almost a short sword rather than a knife. The thug saw Stig coming at him, his shape blurry in the dim light, and instinctively raised his sword to parry the blow. The two blades rang together and shrieked against each other as Stig's saxe slid down to the sword's crosspiece. Instinctively, the other seven attackers had faltered and stepped back in the face of Stig's unexpected advance. Nobody expected one man to attack eight.

Stig had been counting on that element of surprise and shock. With his blade locked against the sword, he grabbed the swordsman's right hand with his left, twisting it down and around, bending the wrist back. The man howled in pain and inadvertently leaned forward to try to lessen the twisting pressure on his wrist. As he did so, Stig head-butted him in the face and jerked his wrist one more time.

The sword clattered to the ground. Stig put his shoulder into the man's chest and sent him reeling back into two of his companions, then bent and scooped up the fallen sword.

The entire sequence of actions took less than two seconds.

Stig retreated now, the sword weaving and darting in front of him like the head of a snake. The gang, their number reduced by one, stood uncertainly. The game had changed. They had set out to attack four virtually unarmed teenagers. Now one of them had a sword and looked as if he knew how to use it. And while they knew that one man could never hope to match seven, they also knew that if they did attack, there was a good chance that some of them would be injured, or even killed. None of them wanted to be in that number.

Then Vargas, who was among them, took control. His harsh voice lashed them like a whip.

"Come on! He's one man! Not even that, he's a boy! If we come at him from three sides, we can finish him!"

Stig sensed a stirring in the gang as a sense of resolution passed through them. Then Vargas, sensing it as well, yelled the command.

"Get him!"

The seven men, with Vargas safely in the rear, surged forward in a semicircle, attempting to envelop Stig. The first man to move had taken two paces when Stig's sword darted out and back. The thug clutched at his chest, a surprised look on his face, then crumpled to his knees. But Stig wasn't watching him anymore. He knew he'd struck a fatal blow. Now he whirled the sword in a flashing circle and cut at a man on his left. The man parried the blow but was staggered by the power behind it.

Knowing he posed no more threat for a few seconds, Stig reversed his cut and sliced the arm of another with the flashing sword. The man's hand opened and his club clattered to the cobblestones. Yet another attacker had gone wide to Stig's right, and he slid in now, a short spear ready to lunge under the Skandian's guard. As he drew it back, he felt an intense flame of agony in his leg as Lydia's dirk stabbed deep into his thigh.

Jesper and Hal had noticed that the attackers were getting in their own way, hampering one another and leaving Stig free to slash and lunge at any of them who came close. The two of them stayed back, ready to guard Stig's rear, as Lydia had just done, but leaving the brunt of the fighting to Stig. Hal watched carefully. He knew Stig would eventually tire. He couldn't keep up this whirlwind pace indefinitely. He watched for any sign of Stig's slowing down, ready to take the sword from his friend and carry on the fight whenever it might be necessary.

But it never was.

Suddenly the dark alley rang and reverberated with a terrible sound—a roaring sound that combined rage and bloodlust and uncontrolled fury. A huge figure emerged from the shadows behind the remaining five men. There was a sickening, crunching thud as Vargas, in the rear, turned to see what was happening and was struck by a massive studded club. He fell to the filthy cobbles, stunned.

Thorn kept coming, his massive club-hand rising and falling, then sweeping from side to side, smashing ribs and skulls and arms as he scattered the gang, spilling them like ninepins before him.

And all the time, he kept up that dreadful, wordless war cry.

Stig stepped back, grinning, and grounded his sword, leaning both hands on the hilt. He could tell he wasn't needed anymore as Thorn went through the remaining members of the gang like a battering ram. One of the gang managed to evade him and ran from the alley as if a fiend from the netherworld was after him. Thorn sent another reeling with a casual backhanded sweep of the club. The remaining attacker, trapped between Thorn and his four friends, faced the terrible, berserking Skandian, holding his heavy war mace protectively in front of him.

Later, recalling the moment, Hal would swear that he saw Thorn's eyes flash with red fire. The shabby old sea wolf, transformed into a terrible and terrifying instrument of violence, simply lunged the club-hand in a straight-armed punch at the terrified thug. It hit him in the chest and hurled him backward. Hal and Lydia stepped smartly to one side as the man flew between them, smashing into the brick wall with a sickening sound, then sliding to the ground as his knees gave away.

"Well, Thorn," said Stig in the sudden silence. "How very nice to see you." He dropped the sword and it rang briefly on the cobbles.

Thorn was breathing deeply as the berserker rage slowly subsided. He realized he was still half crouched in readiness for an attack and slowly stood upright.

"Good work, Stig," he said quietly.

But Hal had stepped forward. "Where did you spring from, Thorn? Have you been keeping an eye on us?"

Thorn nodded. "Yes. Thought that swine Zavac might try something like this. It's right up his alley." He paused, realizing what he'd said. Lydia allowed herself a faint smile.

"That's a really terrible pun," she said, and Thorn nodded apologetically.

"Not one of my best," he admitted. "In any event, I've been keeping an eye on you since you left *Heron* earlier tonight. Trouble was, I had to hang back in the main street so you wouldn't notice me. I didn't see you turn off into this alley. When I realized that's where you'd gotten to, I had to double back."

"Well, Stig held them off until you got here," Hal said. He slapped his friend on the shoulder. "Nicely done, Stig."

"I'll second that," Lydia said. "That was a brilliant move when you took that sword off the first man."

Stig flushed with pleasure, conscious that Thorn had turned an approving eye on him. He shrugged.

"Ah, someone had to do something," he said. "As Thorn says, make the first move, and make it fast. I . . ."

He stopped as they heard a clatter of boots on the cobbles, and saw lights wavering and reflecting off the alley walls. Then a squad of the town guard, five men under a corporal, rounded the corner and stopped, staring, at the tableau that faced them.

"What's going on here? We had a report there was fighting," the corporal said warily. Two of his men were carrying torches and their light revealed a scene of carnage in the alley. The cobbles were strewn with unconscious men and scattered weapons. "And it looks as if there has been. Don't you know that the Korpaljo forbids fighting within the boundaries of the city?"

Hal stepped forward. "These men attacked us. There were eight of them but one got away. We were simply defending ourselves—as you can see, we're unarmed and they outnumbered us."

Unobtrusively, Thorn had allowed his club-hand to fall to his side. In the dim light of the torches, it was virtually unnoticeable. Looking round, the corporal could see that the four young people were armed only with knives, which most seamen carried as a matter of course, while the seven men sprawled on the cobbles had obviously been carrying an assortment of clubs, swords and spears. He frowned.

"How did you . . . ?" he began, but Hal cut across him, indicating Stig.

"My friend here disarmed one of them and took his sword. Then, when they attacked us, Thorn heard the noise and came at them from behind." He shook his head dismissively. "They weren't very good fighters."

"Obviously not," said the corporal, shaking his head as he surveyed the unconscious bodies littering the alley.

"Why did they attack you?" the sergeant asked.

"We're from the Skandian ship *Heron*," Hal explained. "We had a falling-out today with Zavac, skipper of the *Raven*. It was in the Korpaljo's office. He'll confirm it. I'll wager these men are from the *Raven* and Zavac sent them to kill us."

"Can you prove that? Do you recognize any of them?"

One of the soldiers with a torch had been examining the dead and unconscious gang members. As he reached Vargas, he held the torch down to illuminate the man's face.

"This one's alive, corporal," he said.

Thorn stepped forward as the soldier went to move the torch away. He stopped him and studied Vargas's face. The man was familiar. Then he remembered where he'd seen him before.

"I know this one. He was in the tavern in Krall," he said, looking up at Hal. "I'll wager he's one of Zavac's crew."

The corporal chewed on the ends of his mustache, considering the situation. On the whole, he tended to believe Hal's story. It was highly unlikely that one older man and four teenagers, one of them a girl, would attack seven or eight heavily armed men—all of whom looked to be warriors. And he'd heard talk that Zavac had been in trouble with the Korpaljo earlier in the day. He came a decision.

"Very well. Get back to your ship. And present yourselves at the Korpal building tomorrow at ten. The Korpaljo will want to hold an inquiry into this. If he decides that Zavac's crew started the fight, they'll be punished."

He turned to one of his soldiers. "Get extra men from headquarters and clean up around here. The dead ones can go to the mortuary. Any still alive, take them to the infirmary. But keep them under guard."

He stepped back and pushed his helmet off his brow, still wondering about what had happened here. How had these five managed to cause such havoc among their attackers? He looked at the young Skandians again. The tall one looked pretty capable, he thought. But the other two were smaller and not as heavily built. Any one of the pirates would have been bigger and stronger. And of course, the fourth member of the group was a girl. She'd hardly count for anything in a fight, he thought, having no idea how very wrong he was in that assumption.

As for the older man, he noticed now that he had some kind of false arm. He couldn't see any details, but he noticed the dull gleam of the polished wood where the flickering torchlight reflected from it. The northman was holding it close by his side, partially concealing it from view. Probably embarrassed him if people took too much notice of it. A one-armed man and four kids, he thought. Would wonders never cease?

It was beyond him. But he wasn't paid to solve problems like this. He decided he'd leave it to the Korpaljo to get to the bottom of things.

"Are you finished with us?" Hal asked.

The corporal nodded distractedly. "Yes. Yes. You can go. But be at the Korpal building tomorrow and don't try to leave Raguza in the meantime. I'll set a guard over your ship to make sure of it."

"There's no need for that," Hal said. The corporal eyed him cynically.

"Of course not," he said. "But I'm going to do it anyway. And remember, the harbor is patrolled by guard boats night and day."

Hal nodded. He had no intention of trying to leave Raguza. He gestured to his friends and the five of them trooped out of the alley and down the hill toward the harbor.

"What if it turns out they're not from Zavac's crew?" Jesper asked. Hal glanced at him.

"They are," he said grimly.

chapter thirty-eight

The evidence against Zavac was overwhelming.

Naturally, he swore on the gods of several different religions, none of which counted him as a devoted follower, that he knew nothing about the fight in the alley. But two town guardsmen who were stationed in Goathead Bay recognized Vargas and some of the other men as coming from *Raven*'s crew.

Even then, Zavac might still have claimed innocence. The evidence against him was all circumstantial. But the crucial moment came when one of the survivors of the fight in the alley, offered immunity from punishment if he testified, swore to the Korpaljo that Zavac had sent him and seven others to ambush the Skandians and kill them.

After hearing the evidence, Mihaly eyed Zavac and the five

Skandians with distaste. It was obvious that the Magyaran captain was to blame for the ambush. But if the cursed Skandians had stayed away from Raguza, and not brought their private feud with them, none of this would have happened.

Still, he thought, Zavac was the guilty party in this affair and he had to be punished. It did nothing to help his case that he had deceived the Korpaljo over the matter of the emeralds and tried to cheat him out of his fee. On top of all that, Mihaly simply disliked the man. Zavac was devious and untrustworthy, and Mihaly had no doubt that he had done exactly as the Skandians said—deserting his comrades in Limmat and leaving the *Stingray* to her fate.

"You've got forty-eight hours," he said, glaring coldly at Zavac.

The Magyaran recoiled in his seat, knowing what Mihaly was talking about, but feigning ignorance on the faint chance that he could change his mind.

"Forty-eight hours? For what?" he asked.

"To get out of Raguza. You're expelled. You, your ship and your crew. You know the rules, Zavac. That's it."

Zavac, his jaw hanging open, pointed to Hal and the others. Like him, they were sitting before Mihaly's massive desk. But there was a noticeable separation of space between them and Zavac.

"What about them?" he demanded.

The Korpaljo glared at them as he replied. "They stay here. You're the guilty party. But if I have any more trouble from them, or any more incidents involving them, they'll be thrown out as well."

A crafty look came into Zavac's eyes. "Then I'll be expecting you to refund my haven fee," he said. "I paid for a month's refuge and I've been here less than a week. In fact," he added, "I paid way beyond the going rate. I demand you return my emeralds to me."

"Demand away," Mihaly told him, with a hollow laugh. "You lied to me. You tried to cheat me. And then you violated the most basic rule of this city. You planned an attack on another crew. There are no refunds for rule breakers and you know it."

Zavac turned his furious gaze on Hal and his friends. "This is your fault," he snarled. "I'll kill you for this. Every one of you!"

Hal said nothing, but Lydia leaned forward so that she could see past the others and met Zavac's poisonous glare.

"I think that's the sort of attitude that got you into all this trouble in the first place," she said mildly. "Are you really so slow on the uptake?"

Thorn emitted a short bark of laughter. Even Mihaly's lips twisted slightly in a smile.

Zavac stabbed a forefinger at Lydia. "You'll be the first to die, girl," he spat.

She raised one eyebrow. "How terrifying," she said calmly. "Will you send another gang after me, or will you try to do it yourself?" Her eyes went cold as she remembered her grandfather, killed without mercy in Limmat by Zavac and his marauders. "Because I'd love you to try. I'd really love that."

Zavac knew little about this girl. He studied her uncertainly. Now he saw her fingers playing round the hilt of the long dirk she wore on her belt and he felt a twinge of doubt. Something told him that she would be a good person to steer clear of. He looked away, but Mihaly had been watching the exchange with keen eyes.

"Just as I thought, Zavac," he said, shaking his head with disdain. "Faced down by a girl. You're a coward as well as a cheat and a liar. I'll be glad to be rid of you."

"Don't be too hard on him," Thorn said with a grin. "She's quite a girl. I keep telling the boys here, she's a real keeper."

"Shut up, old man," Lydia snapped. It was a reflex reaction by now and Thorn grinned.

Mihaly was less amused. "Very well," he said. "It's decided. Zavac, you and—"

"Just a minute," Hal interrupted. He shook his head doggedly. "It's not enough."

Mihaly looked at him, one eyebrow raised sardonically. "It's not enough?" he repeated. "What, exactly, is not enough?"

"Simply expelling him. He tried to kill us. And he deserted us in Limmat—"

"Are you still trying to peddle that lie?" Zavac sneered.

Hal faced him directly now. "You caused the deaths of our friends. You tried to kill us when you left Limmat. And you tried again last night." He turned back to the Korpaljo, his face flushed with anger. "Expelling him is not enough. He deserves much more. He owes us."

But he realized now that he had misread Mihaly's motives. The Korpaljo disliked and distrusted Zavac. But that didn't mean he was on the Herons' side. Mihaly wasn't interested in justice, he was interested in expediency. He had a chance to get rid of Zavac, a disruptive element who had tried to cheat him, and he had possession of the emeralds he had confiscated from the Magyaran. Beyond that, he had no interest in what Hal and his crew wanted. He leaned forward now.

"That's between you and him," he said. "As far as I'm concerned, there's nothing more to say. He and his ship are expelled. You can stay here or go—as you choose."

But that was the problem Hal had been considering. They had finally run Zavac to ground here in Raguza. If he left now, there was always the chance that he would slip away from them again. He had forty-eight hours to leave port. Since he had been in Raguza, Hal had noticed that the wind tended to die away around midnight, blowing up again around dawn. If Zavac left in the hours of darkness, they could lose him.

The *Raven* was faster under oars than *Heron*, and without a good breeze, they could never keep up. He could slip away to the south, into the Constant Sea or the Sea of Rostov. Presumably, Zavac would know of a dozen places there where he could hide from pursuit, and the *Heron* would be sailing in unknown waters. After all this, Hal couldn't let that happen. He could see the Andomal slipping out of his grasp, when he had come so close to retrieving it. He thought desperately. Mihaly was interested in getting rid of Zavac, not providing justice for Hal and his crew. But before he could speak, Mihaly turned to Thorn with an exasperated gesture.

"Just one minute. Who's in charge here? Are you the skipper or is the boy?"

Thorn smiled. "In point of fact, he is the skipper," he said. "I just go along with him to carry the heavy baggage."

Mihaly's brows drew together in anger. "But you told me you were—"

Thorn held up a hand to stop him. "No. I didn't. You simply

assumed that I was the skipper and you addressed all your questions to me."

Mihaly sat back, trying to remember their earlier encounter, trying to remember what had been said. He realized that the shabby northman was right. He had just assumed that, as the oldest member of the party, Thorn was the ship's captain. But while Thorn had never claimed to be the skipper, he had allowed the Korpaljo to assume that he was. Mihaly threw an angry look at him.

"We'll discuss this further," he said. "I don't like being misled."

While this exchange had taken place, Hal had been thinking furiously. Mihaly, he decided, was a controller. He liked to manipulate people to his own ends and then watch them as they reacted. He would enjoy sitting back and observing a dispute between others, so long as it didn't interfere with his wishes in any way. Hal thought he saw a way to exploit that tendency and he rolled the dice now, hoping he was right.

"I want a duel," he said.

Mihaly looked at him in surprise. "A duel?"

"With Zavac. I challenge him to a duel."

"You what?" Zavac replied. "You're still wet behind the ears! I'd finish you in two minutes!"

"Then go ahead and try," Hal shot back.

Thorn leaned forward, blocking Hal's view of Zavac.

"Hal, just a minute. Think about this . . . ," he began. Hal was good with a sword—very good, Thorn knew. After all, he had taught him. He was young and fast. But Zavac was a killer. He had killed before and he would do so again without hesitation—

and in a one-on-one duel, that gave him a huge advantage. If they met in the heat of battle, Hal would have a more than even chance. But in the cold-blooded, organized atmosphere of a duel, the pendulum would swing Zavac's way.

"He's challenged me! Let him fight!" Zavac said quickly. This young Skandian had thwarted Zavac at every turn. Now there was a chance for revenge. He glared at Hal. "I'll be more than happy to accommodate you, boy!"

"No!" Thorn began desperately. "He—"

"Quiet!" Mihaly slapped his open hand on the table for silence. They all turned to him as he rubbed his chin between his forefinger and thumb, thinking. His gaze swept quickly back and forth between the two antagonists, measuring them. One young and angry, the other sneering and calculating.

A duel, he thought. That might be an amusing diversion. And it might be a good opportunity to turn a profit. Not that Mihaly would wager on the outcome, but he would take control of any wagering that was done, and take a healthy commission. In fact, handled properly, a duel like this could become a major event in Raguza. He snorted with laughter as he realized that if he took control, he could charge admission. Plenty of the sailors in port would pay good money to see two of their peers fight to the death.

Brawling and murdering in back alleys was one thing. But an organized, properly sanctioned duel was a different matter. On the whole, he liked the idea. A thought struck him. This boy had let the older Skandian act for him before and that still rankled with the Korpaljo. He decided that wasn't going to be an option this time.

"One thing," he said, holding up a forefinger. "If I decide to allow this, you do your own fighting." He fixed a basilisk stare on Hal. "We're not some fancy royal court here. We don't allow challengers to appoint champions. If you challenge, you fight."

"He's not challeng—," Thorn tried to interrupt, but Hal was too quick for him.

"Yes, I am! I'm challenging and I'll fight," he snapped.

Zavac looked at him. Young, inexperienced, flushed with anger. The boy had *victim* written all over him, he thought.

"And I accept," he said, a cruel smile on his face.

Thorn sank back in his seat. They were committed now. There was nothing he could do to change it. He knew that Mihaly would never allow Hal to back down, even if Thorn could persuade him to. The Korpaljo wanted to teach them a lesson for the subterfuge they had pulled, letting him think Thorn was the captain of the *Heron*. He heard Stig whisper a curse, saw Lydia regarding Hal with wide-eyed concern. Hal stared straight ahead, his chin set, his shoulders back.

"Then it's agreed," Mihaly said in a silky voice. The more he thought about this duel, the better he liked the idea. The young Skandian would almost certainly be killed. Zavac was an experienced and wily fighter, he knew. That would teach the Skandians a lesson for lying to him. And he could still expel Zavac from Raguza, as he had already decided. All around, a good result, he thought.

"You're the injured party, Skandian," Mihaly continued. "That means you have the choice of weapons. What will it be? Swords? Axes? Knives?"

Knives, Mihaly hoped. Without realizing it, he was rubbing his hands in anticipation. With axes or swords, one quick lucky stroke could finish it all in seconds. A knife fight was likely to be a more prolonged affair, and it appealed to the Raguzan temperament.

Swords, Thorn was thinking. Hal's good with a sword, and I can work with him and make him better, so he's ready to face this snake in the grass.

Then Hal sprang his second surprise of the morning.

"Ships," he said.

Ships?" both Thorn and Zavac exclaimed at the same moment. Thorn frowned and turned to his young friend.

"What are you talking about, Hal?"

Hal met his gaze evenly. "Ships," he repeated calmly. "I'll back my ship against that black barge of his any day. And my crew against his band of cowards." He hesitated as a thought struck him for the first time, and he looked at Stig. "That's if you and the others are willing," he said.

A wide smile spread slowly over Stig's face.

"Count me in," he said. "And I'll speak for the others. Count us all in."

"And me," Lydia said promptly. Hal nodded gratefully to the two of them.

Thorn shook his head angrily. "Well, me too, of course. I'm with you!"

Hal smiled at him. "I always knew you would be."

"But have you thought about this?" Thorn went on.

Hal nodded. "I have. I usually think this sort of thing through."

"You haven't missed out on any little details?" Stig asked mischievously.

Hal eyed him seriously. "No. For once I haven't." He took a deep breath, assailed by the sudden doubt that perhaps he *had* forgotten something. He couldn't think of anything, but then, he thought, if there were some detail he'd forgotten, he wouldn't be able to think of it.

Mihaly rolled his eyes. This was all becoming tiresome, he thought.

"If we're finished playing All Friends Together, can we get on with it?" he said. He looked at Zavac. "Are you happy with this idea? To fight ship to ship?"

Zavac smiled. "I'm more than happy with it," he said. The *Raven* was nearly twice the size of *Heron* and his crew was nearly four times as large. As far as he was concerned, Hal had just put his own neck, and that of all his friends, into a noose. And Zavac held the end of the rope. "In fact, I can't wait to send his skiff to the bottom of the sea."

Already, in his imagination, he could feel the shuddering, grinding impact as the *Raven*'s ram smashed its way through the little ship's planks, opening her hull to an unstoppable inrush of water.

"Then all that remains is to set a time," Mihaly said. Hal answered promptly.

"Mid-morning. The day after tomorrow." By the middle of the morning, the breeze was usually blowing briskly. Later in the day, he knew, the growing heat meant that it tapered off and became fluky.

Zavac shrugged. He had no real idea of *Heron*'s sailing qualities. "I've got no objection."

Mihaly made a note and rubbed his hands. A duel between ships, he thought. This was going to be fascinating. He'd seen the *Heron* and knew she was much smaller than Zavac's ship. But the young Skandian seemed very confident. Perhaps he had some trick up his sleeve. He knew that a fight between the two ships would arouse a lot of interest among the people of Raguza and the pirate crews who were currently in harbor. The timing would give him plenty of opportunity to publicize the event and set up wagering booths around the town.

"The duel must take place in sight of the harbor," he said. "No more than two or three kilometers offshore."

Both Zavac and Hal nodded.

"I'll have buoys set up marking the battleground. A square area with sides . . . three kilometers long. You'll fight inside that space," he added, and both skippers indicated their assent.

Set up what you like, Hal was thinking, I'll go anywhere I please if I have the chance to sink the *Raven.* He glanced at Zavac and had the sudden insight that the Magyaran was thinking the same thing about the *Heron.*

"Very well then," Mihaly said, a satisfied smile on his face. The morning had turned out much better than he had expected. "We'll see one another again the day after tomorrow."

"One thing," Zavac said. "When I win, will you revoke the expulsion order? After all, there'll be no further conflict between me and the Skandians, so there'll be no potential for trouble in the town."

The Korpaljo pushed out his bottom lip as he considered the point. Thorn let out a short bark of laughter and Mihaly turned his gaze on him.

"Something amusing?" he said.

Thorn shrugged. "It just reminds me of the classic recipe for bear stew," he said, and as Mihaly frowned, not understanding, he continued. "The recipe begins: *First, kill a large bear.*" He looked at Zavac, his eyes narrowing. "First, you have to sink the *Heron*," he said. "And that might be a little harder than you expect."

Stig and Lydia both laughed in their turn. Zavac swept his gaze across them. The girl and the tall boy were looking confident, he thought. He noted that Hal's face was pale and set in determined lines.

"I'll take my chances on that," he sneered.

"So, what's the plan?" Stig asked. They were back on board the *Heron*. The rest of the crew were gathered around, sitting in a circle in the stern of the ship.

When they had arrived back from the Korpal tower, the others were eager to hear what had happened. As Hal had opened his mouth to tell them, Stig held up a hand to stop him.

"Let me," he said. He quickly outlined the events that had taken place, ending with the news of Hal's challenge to Zavac.

"Lydia and I are both with him," he said finally. "What about the rest of you?"

There was no hesitation. The crew responded with a roar of assent. Hal shook his head gratefully. It was Ingvar who put into words what everyone was thinking.

"After all," he said, "in spite of what Erak might think or say, we're the Heron brotherband, aren't we? And together, we can do anything we set our minds to."

When the Andomal had been stolen, Erak, the Skandian Oberjarl, had ordered all mention of the Heron brotherband expunged from the records at Hallasholm's Great Hall. That shame still rankled with the crew. There was a low growl of agreement from the others as he finished speaking.

Now, in answer to Stig's question, Hal gathered his thoughts. The crew leaned forward expectantly. As always, Thorn stood aside from the group, leaning casually against the stern post. He was a highly respected senior warrior, and it would be all too easy for the young crew to turn to him for advice. But Hal was the skirl of this ship and Thorn knew he must do nothing to undermine the young man's authority. Besides, he admitted to himself, Hal was a much better thinker and planner than he was. He'd undoubtedly come up with much better ideas than Thorn could muster. Thorn's planning tended to center round one concept—finding the nearest enemy to hit, then hitting him as hard as possible.

"Let's remember," Hal said, after a short pause, "our main aim here is to recover the Andomal—"

"Yours may be," Lydia interrupted grimly. "Mine is to put a dart through Zavac's heart."

Jesper grinned. "Might be hard to find," he said. But Hal bowed in acquiescence to Lydia's statement.

"And we'll certainly do nothing to prevent you from attaining that goal," he said. "In fact, if you do it, we will be eternally grateful—and the sooner you do it, the better. Naturally, we'll be using the Mangler." He indicated the massive crossbow set in the bow, concealed under its canvas cover. "So far as I know, Zavac will have little idea about it. After all, he never actually saw it in use."

"Won't some of his men have told him?" Lydia asked, frowning. But Hal shook his head.

"Most of the men from the towers were killed or captured," he pointed out. "They were the ones who really saw what it could do."

"And the men at the beach gate," Stig reminded him. The beach gate had been the point where the Herons had assaulted the town of Limmat. But again, Hal shook his head.

"They were scattered through the town. And even if any of them made it back to the *Raven*, they didn't really see the full force of the Mangler." Stig nodded, thinking about it, and Hal continued.

"So I'll try to use the Mangler to disable the *Raven*." He saw the others frowning as they tried to understand how he might do this, so he explained further. "I'll aim for vital points like the tiller or the bulwarks, where the main stays are set. If I can smash them, the support for the mast will be weakened and we may just bring it down."

"That would be a big help," Stefan said.

Hal nodded at him. "And of course, I'll also be using the Mangler to try to reduce the numbers against us." He looked at Lydia. "I hope you'll be doing the same thing."

"Count on it."

"Ingvar, how's your side?" Hal asked. The big boy, with his massive strength, was essential to the employment of the Mangler. Ingvar felt his side, then nodded.

"It's fine. A little sore still, but I can put up with that."

"Good. Because I have another task for you. Once we've damaged the *Raven*, and hopefully dismasted her, we're going to have to board her."

"Is that wise?" Ulf asked.

Hal smiled at him. "Not at all."

It was an indication of how seriously they were all taking this matter that Wulf made no disparaging comment about his brother's question.

Hal went on. "But if we're going to get the Andomal back, we have to board her."

"Zavac has fifty men," Stig pointed out mildly. "You don't think we're biting off more than we can chew, do you?"

Hal shook his head. "We've always known they outnumber us. But think about it. We're all in the habit of saying Zavac has fifty men. But he lost some of them at Limmat—maybe ten or a dozen, who knows? And after the other night, he's short another eight. The men who attacked us are either dead, in the hospital or in Mihaly's jail. So his numbers are dropping."

"Still more than us, of course." That was Stefan.

Hal acknowledged the comment. "True. And that will work for us. They won't expect us to board them."

He paused, looking round the faces of his crew, and saw that they appreciated his point. A ship with a crew of forty or so would never expect a crew of eight or nine to attempt to board them. And the boarding party would be led by Thorn and Stig, a terrifying combination.

"I'll bring us in from astern. We'll grapple them and board over their stern quarter. Thorn, you and Stig will lead the way, with Ulf and Wulf backing you."

"Make that Wulf and Ulf," said one of the twins, presumably Wulf.

Hal smiled at him. "Since none of us can tell one of you from the other," he said, "you can make it any way you like."

"Ulf and Wulf then," said Ulf. Or perhaps it was Wulf. Hal wouldn't put it past them to swap identities at a time like this, just for the sake of confusing their shipmates.

"Whatever," he said firmly, closing the discussion as he saw Wulf, or Ulf, gathering breath to reply.

"All right. The rest of you will follow behind. Form a wedge and drive the pirates back." He glanced at Thorn. In matters relating to battle, he was happy to defer to the old sea wolf. "How does that sound to you?" he asked.

Thorn nodded slowly. "No problem there," he said. "It's always easier when you're in confined quarters, like a ship's deck. Their numbers can become a disadvantage. They tend to get in one another's way."

"What about me, Hal?" Lydia asked quietly.

"You know your greatest value is to fight from a distance," Hal told her. "If you stay back, you can pick off any of the Magyarans who start to look dangerous. You'll be more use to us that way than trying to join in the general melee on the *Raven*'s deck."

She nodded, appreciating the fact. Her uncanny accuracy with the atlatl could be a crucial factor in their victory. Besides, with Thorn and Stig swinging axes, supported by the twins, there would be little chance for her to use her dirk against the pirates.

"Am I in the boarding party, Hal?" Ingvar asked. He sounded a little wistful. He knew that his poor eyesight usually dictated against his taking part in a fight like this. He was liable to hit the wrong person at the wrong time. Hal surprised him by nodding.

"You are indeed, Ingvar. Once the others have the pirates engaged, I want you to sink their ship."

A few heads snapped up at that. But Ingvar was beginning to grin.

"Get hold of the heaviest ax or hammer you can find," Hal continued, "and once you're aboard the *Raven*, start bashing holes in her. Smash the planks. Smash the central watertight compartment. Smash anything you can see."

"I don't see too well, remember," Ingvar pointed out, and Hal acknowledged the point.

"Smash anything you can reach, then. Smash bulwarks, rowing benches, the ship's bottom. Smash it all. Destroy it."

"And while all this is going on, I assume you'll be going after the Andomal," Thorn said.

Hal nodded. "We know where it is. That's why I want to board her from the stern. If you can drive them forward and keep them off me, I'll make for Zavac's sleeping berth and get hold of it. Lydia, I'll rely on you to take care of any pirates who slip past Stig and Thorn."

Lydia nodded, while Stig looked affronted and Thorn snorted disdainfully.

"That won't keep you very busy," Thorn said.

Hal sat back, looking at the ring of determined faces that surrounded him. This was what they had come all this way for, he thought. This was why they had pursued Zavac for the entire length of the Stormwhite Sea. This was why they had destroyed the watchtowers and stormed the beach gate at Limmat. This was why they had faced the terror of the Wildwater Rift. This was their chance to regain their former lives. Their dignity. Their pride.

He felt he should make some resounding statement along those lines—something that would spur them on and lift their spirits so that they were ready for this final challenge.

But for the life of him, he couldn't think of anything.

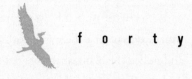

The night before the battle, sleep eluded Hal for hours. He tossed and turned in his blankets, listening to the stray sounds of the harbor around him—the lapping of water against the hull, the squeak of the fenders as the small waves pushed the *Heron* against them, the occasional splash of a fish jumping and the cheerful, often drunken voices of sailors heading back to their ships after an evening in the taverns close to the waterfront.

In the small hours of the morning, most of the noises died away. Then, a few hours before daylight, he felt the ship stir and the halyards and the rigging mutter softly, and he sensed that the breeze was slowly building. He sighed with a sense of relief. He had worried that on this day, of all days, there might be no wind. At least that concern was out of the way.

Now all he had to do was work out how to fight forty pirates with a crew of nine. He went over his tactics for the hundredth time. Content that there was nothing he had missed, he rolled over and pulled the blankets up against the damp chill of early morning. At least now it was all coming to a head, he thought. One way or another, it would be over. They would either recover the Andomal or they would be dead.

And with the strange sense of comfort that thought gave him, he finally managed to sleep.

He woke at about the seventh hour, roused by the bustle on board *Heron*. Edvin was awake and lighting his small cook fire. He had dispatched the twins to a bakery a few streets away to bring back fresh bread. His pride didn't allow him to serve the crew hard stale bread on such an important day.

But Edvin had another surprise for the crew when they began to gather around his cook fire, sniffing the sizzling sausages and listening to the eggs sputtering in his huge cast-iron pan. The previous afternoon, he had collected all the watch caps he had knitted for the crew. Now he handed them out once again. But each cap now had a small cloth badge sewn to its front—a figure of a heron with its wings spread in flight. It was the same design that was on their sail and the boys studied them with pleasure.

"This makes us look like a real crew!" Jesper said, delighted.

Ingvar eyed him curiously. "We *are* a real crew," he pointed out.

Jesper made a dismissive gesture with his hand.

"Yeah. But this makes it sort of . . . official." He donned his cap and the others did the same. Hal grinned at them. It was good to have a kind of uniform, he thought. Edvin produced a final cap and handed it to Lydia.

"I figure you're part of the crew now too," he said simply. A wide smile lit up her normally grave face, and she took the cap and donned it, looking round at the others for approval.

"How do I look?" she asked. It was Thorn who answered.

"You look as if it fits," he said quietly, and the boys murmured their agreement.

Lydia flushed with pleasure at Thorn's statement. She shook her head. He could be so annoying at times, she thought. Then, just when you least expected it, he'd come out with something like that.

Ulf and Wulf arrived back with several fresh, warm loaves of bread and Edvin busied himself serving breakfast. As they sat on the deck and ate, the twins announced a welcome piece of news.

"By the way, we heard that Zavac's lost ten more men," Wulf said.

"Well, I heard it," Ulf said. "I repeated it to you."

"Which means I heard it, when you repeated it, doesn't it?" Wulf said. Before the usual wordy battle could begin, however, Hal intervened.

"What do you mean, he's lost ten more men? Lost them where?"

Ulf shrugged. "Everyone was talking about it in the bakery," he said. Then Wulf interrupted, seeing that Hal and the others wanted to know what had happened, not where they were when they heard about it.

"Seems that ten of his men said they weren't going to fight us. They said they hadn't signed on to fight warriors." He paused, smiling at his friends. "How about that? They think we're warriors."

"We are warriors," Ulf said, and his brother glared at him.

"I know that. But it's pleasing to see that others agree with—"

"GET ON WITH IT!" Hal shouted at them. "What happened when they told him they weren't fighting?"

The twins looked at each other, not sure who was going to answer. Finally one of them took the plunge, although Hal wasn't sure which one it was. They had been moving about while they spoke and had changed positions several times.

"Zavac told them they could get off his ship if they wouldn't fight. So they did," Ulf or Wulf replied. Hal shook his head in wonder, then smiled at Thorn.

"So the odds are improving all the time," he said.

Thorn nodded. "Yes. Now we're only outnumbered by three to one."

Stig grinned widely. "That's nearly a fair fight."

"Speaking of which," Hal said, "I've been thinking about how we should approach this battle."

The crew gathered more closely around him, their faces serious now.

"My guess is, Zavac will want to fight the way he always does. His tactics will be to ram, or to grapple us and board us. He'll want to fight at close quarters." He glanced up at Thorn. "Is that how you see it, Thorn?" Thorn was their battle leader and Hal would welcome his contribution.

The old sea wolf nodded. "I can't see why they'd plan to change. That's the way ships have always fought. Up until now, the ship has been no more than a method for bringing the warriors into combat. You're the first one I know who's thought of having a weapon as an integral part of the ship," he said.

Hal was glad that the experienced warrior agreed with him. "That means our best bet is to stand off at a distance and batter him with the Mangler. And with Lydia's darts," he added, glancing at the girl.

"It's a new style of fighting," Hal continued. "And I doubt that Zavac will be ready for it, so it should come as a surprise to him."

"An unpleasant one," Jesper said, grinning. Some of the others chuckled quietly in response, but Hal remained serious.

"Let's hope so," he told Jesper. "But our best bet will be to use *Heron's* speed and mobility. Zavac hasn't seen them so far either. We had that one encounter off Limmat harbor when he got away. But that will hardly have told him anything."

He looked now at the twins, and at Stefan and Jesper. "That means that sail handling and trimming are going to be vital. We can't afford mistakes. We'll have to get in close—although not as close as Zavac will want us—and then get out again. So you four have to be on your toes."

They all nodded, serious now, and he turned his gaze on Ulf and Wulf.

"And that means no arguing. Is that clear?"

Ulf and Wulf exchanged a quick glance. Then they both said in unison, "You can count on us, Hal."

Hal felt a momentary surprise that they had come up with exactly the same words at exactly the same time. He noted it away. Twins, he thought. There was a lot more to them than people ever realized.

"Will we be using fire bolts?" Ingvar asked. In the attack on

Limmat, they had used fire bolts—bolts from the Mangler with their heads wrapped in oil-soaked rags and set on fire—to great effect.

But Hal shook his head. "I thought about that. But we'll be twisting and turning and heeling all the time. The decks will be unsteady and I don't want an open fire on board. Besides, if we make a mistake and Zavac gets alongside us, we could be in big trouble. At Limmat there was no other ship near us. But here, it's just too big a risk."

"I'm relieved to hear it," Thorn said. Like most experienced sailors, the idea of a source of fire on board ship was a terrifying prospect.

"We've got visitors," Stig said, looking down the jetty.

The others followed his gaze. There were three soldiers approaching, wearing the purple-and-green livery of the Korpal. One marched ahead of the others. His armor and equipment marked him as an officer. He paused as he came level with the *Heron*, looking down on her decks from the jetty.

"Are you the Skandian crew?" he asked, although it was obvious that they were. Hal stood and walked to the rail. The jetty was a meter or so higher than the ship's bulwarks, so he had to look up at the officer.

"We are," he said. "Do you want to come on board?"

The officer shook his head. He looked distastefully at the little ship. He didn't like walking on anything that seemed to move of its own accord and he could see the decks slowly rising and falling with the small waves of the harbor.

"No need for that. I'm here to tell you the conditions for this duel of yours. Then I'll be on my way."

Hal made a gesture indicating that the man should continue. "Let's hear it then," he said. The captain reached inside his tunic and produced a sheet of paper. He consulted it for several seconds, then spoke.

"The wind is from the northeast," he said. "Korpaljo Mihaly has had a square fighting area marked with buoys outside the harbor, in the bay. Both ships will begin with the wind on their beams." He frowned. He was a landsman and he had no idea what that meant. But he noticed that the young Skandian was nodding, so he assumed he had gotten it right.

"The Korpaljo drew straws for positions. Your ship will start from the western side of the square. The Magyarans will begin from the east. You'll be escorted out of the harbor by one of our longboats, and another will be anchored at the spot where you'll begin. All told, four longboats will monitor the battle."

And what do they plan to do? Thorn thought sarcastically. The longboats could indicate the starting positions for the two ships. But once the battle began, they could have little effect. However, if it gave Mihaly a false sense of being in control, that was no problem to him.

"The longboat will arrive to escort you out of harbor at the ninth hour," the officer said. There was a final note to his voice that indicated he had said everything he had to say. "Any questions?"

Hal shrugged. "It all sounds clear to me." He turned to Thorn. "Thorn? How about you?"

Thorn grimaced. "No. It's all pretty straightforward."

Hal turned back to the officer. "No questions," he said, and the man folded the sheet and replaced it inside his tunic. He called a curt order to his two escorts, who came to attention. But he was stopped by Jesper.

"I've got a question," he said. "Aren't you going to wish us good luck?"

The man stiffened at the mocking tone in Jesper's voice. "I've got ten crowns wagered on the Magyarans. They're favored three to one to win," he said. Then he turned and marched away, followed by his men.

Jesper turned to his friends and pouted. "Well, that's hardly encouraging."

little before the ninth hour, the longboat that was to be their escort arrived, pulling smoothly round the end of the jetty.

She was nearly as long as *Heron* and packed with men. Without the need for rigging or a mast, she could fit six oars down each side. In addition to the twelve men rowing, Hal could count another eight men aboard her, all armed and wearing chain mail and helmets. As she came level with *Heron*, she pivoted neatly and allowed the wind to drift her in closer, until she was four or five meters away. Her helmsman cupped his hands around his mouth and called to them.

"Aboard the *Heron*! Are you ready?"

They had been ready for well over half an hour, with all surplus gear stowed away and just a bow and stern line holding the ship alongside. Stig looked interrogatively at Hal, who was standing by the tiller. The skirl nodded and Stig bellowed in reply:

"Ready!"

"Then follow us! Keep station ten meters astern." He spoke in a lower tone, giving an order to his rowers, and the oars went forward, lowered, then began a slow stroke. The longboat moved smoothly away.

While this was happening, Stig leapt up to the jetty and cast off the bow and stern ropes, jumping lightly down to the deck once he had done so.

"Oars," Hal called quietly, and the crew ran out their oars. The two for'ard rowers on the port side fended off from the jetty so that *Heron*'s bow swung to face clear water. Stig scrambled down to his rowing bench and ran his oar out. He and Hal made eye contact and Stig called to the others.

"Give way all! Stroke . . . stroke . . . stroke . . ."

He set a slow pace for the rowers and *Heron* glided away from the jetty, down the narrow fairway to the main channel. As ever, Hal felt a thrill of excitement as the tiller came alive and the water began to chuckle down the length of the hull. At the same time, his stomach was balled in a tight knot—as it always was before they went into action.

He glanced along the twin lines of rowers. Their faces were set and pale, and he realized they were feeling the same pre-combat nerves that he was. Only Thorn, standing in his usual position by the keel box, and wearing his massive horned helmet, seemed unconcerned. Hal realized they were overhauling the longboat, moving faster than she was. He waited until they were just over ten meters astern of her and called to Stig.

"Slow it a little."

His voice was tight and his throat felt dry. It sounded more high-pitched than he had intended and he hoped the others hadn't noticed. Stig didn't seem to. He began to call the stroke again, more slowly this time, and the ship settled into her position astern of the longboat.

"Good," Hal said. He didn't trust his voice for more than one word. He licked his dry lips and swallowed nervously.

They turned into the main channel leading to the sea. They passed ships on either side, all of them with their crews lining the sides and watching. Interest in the coming duel was high among the people of Raguza. Several men on ships they passed called out greetings and good wishes. He guessed they were men who had wagered on the *Heron*, taking advantage of the three-to-one odds offered. Depressingly, they were a minority. Most of the sailors watched them in silence as they passed by. Hal had elected to row out of the harbor, as it was crowded with so many ships at anchor and the channel was relatively narrow. Once they reached the harbor mouth, he'd set the sail and let the crew relax a little.

They glided on. He heard a bell in a tower ashore chiming the ninth hour. He glanced up at the wind telltale. It was streaming out steadily in the northeasterly breeze. That was to the good, he thought. The wind was brisk enough so that they could use their speed under sail, without being so strong that it would cause them problems. The sky was clear and blue, with a few scattered clouds sliding across it.

A beautiful day for a duel, he thought. He met Thorn's eyes and the old sea wolf nodded reassuringly. But something was amiss, Hal thought. He looked more closely and realized with surprise that Thorn was wearing his grasping hook, not the massive club that Hal had made for him. He pointed to it and cocked his head in a question. Thorn glanced down, then walked slowly aft to stand beside him.

"The shaft of the club has a rather nasty crack in it," he explained. "Only noticed it this morning when I was getting ready. Must have done it the other night in that alley."

"You should have told me. I could have repaired it," Hal said, but Thorn shook his head.

"There wasn't time. It's no problem. I'll use a sword and fight left-handed. I can hold a shield in this hook of yours."

"If you say so," Hal said doubtfully. He hoped this wasn't some kind of omen. Thorn seemed to read his thoughts and smiled grimly.

"I do. I have done this before, you know," he said, with a faint smile.

Hal forced a smile in reply. "So I've heard."

Thorn nodded, the horns on his helmet bobbing as he did, then returned to his station by the keel box. The fin was still raised. They'd lower it when they hauled the sail up.

"Hullo," called Stig. "Look who's joined us."

Hal turned and looked astern. Two hundred meters behind them, following its own escort, was the sinister black shape of the *Raven*. Looking carefully, he could see the disturbance of white water at her bow where her ram protruded, just below the surface.

The knot in his stomach wound itself a little tighter. He faced forward. Jesper, intent on getting a look at their enemy, miscued his stroke, the oar blade splashing awkwardly. The ship faltered and Hal had to make a small adjustment to the tiller to compensate for the error. He glared at Jesper, but before he could say anything, Stig was on the job.

"Pay attention to what you're doing!" he rasped. Jesper flushed, muttered an apology and bent over his oar, avoiding the gaze of his skirl and the first mate. Hal felt a small glow of warmth toward his best friend. Stig was the ideal first mate, he thought. He was always ready to catch any small lapse of discipline or seamanship, freeing Hal up for the larger decisions that needed to be made. And he could step in and take over the tiller at any time. Hal looked down at Stig to signal his thanks, but Stig wasn't looking at him. Then he realized there was no need for thanks. Stig was simply doing his job. He'd expect no thanks for that.

They were coming up to the harbor mouth now, a twenty-meter opening between two stone moles. On the left-hand side, a wooden watchtower stood. He noticed that it was currently flying a huge blue-and-red flag. He'd never noticed that before.

He glanced at it with idle curiosity, then turned his attention to negotiating the entrance. There was plenty of room but he had a sudden, horrifying vision of misjudging it and scraping the *Heron*'s sleek flanks along the rough stone of the harbor walls.

They slid smoothly out into open water and he felt the breeze pick up as they did. The telltale now streamed out in a straight line as Hal surveyed what lay ahead of them.

Raguza was situated at the very end of the Dan River, on a

huge gulf that opened out, in turn, to the Constant Sea. There was a slight swell running and he felt *Heron* lift to it, momentarily pressing more firmly against the soles of his feet, then sinking away into the low trough. He loved feeling her move beneath him. For perhaps the thousandth time, he thought it made her feel like a living being.

The longboat was swinging out in an arc to head back toward them.

"Easy all," he said. Stig repeated the order so the crew could hear it clearly, and they rested on their oars, the shafts parallel to the surface, the blades clear of the water. The longboat came alongside, facing back toward the harbor. The two craft were separated by the length of their respective oars. The helmsman cupped his hands once more.

"Aboard the *Heron*! D'you see the longboat to the east, flying the blue flag?"

He pointed and Hal stepped lightly up onto the bulwark to follow the line he was indicating. About two kilometers offshore, he could make out a dark, low-lying shape, and see a flicker of blue above her.

"I see it," he replied.

"That's your start position. *Raven* will start here, by the boat with the red flag."

He indicated another longboat, a hundred meters away. Hal nodded. There was no need to reply. The helmsman of the longboat continued.

"The signal to start is when the red-and-blue flag on the watchtower comes down. Understood?"

"Understood!" Hal shouted. Once again, he was annoyed at the high-pitched tone of his own voice. Get over it, he told himself. Now he realized the significance of that red-and-blue flag on the tower. The helmsman pointed to the distant longboat under the blue flag.

"The duel starts in half an hour," he called. "You'd best get to your starting position."

He spoke to his oarsmen and their oars dipped and pulled. The longboat slipped smoothly away from them, heading back to the harbor. Hal reached over to the thirty-minute sandglass mounted near the tiller and tipped it. The grains began to trickle through from top to bottom.

"Nice of him to wish us good luck," Hal said.

Stig grinned at him. "He's probably got his money on *Raven* too."

"Then he'll lose!" Lydia's voice called from the bow. Ingvar rumbled agreement.

Hal took a deep breath. The wind was coming from the starboard side.

"In oars," he called. There was the usual sliding rattle of wood on wood as the oars came in and were stowed. Then the crew moved to their positions for sailing.

"Jesper, Stefan, raise the port sail!"

There followed the squeak and rattle of halyards through the blocks and the port yardarm and sail slid quickly to the top of the mast, clunking into place in the cradle that held it steady. There was no need to order Ulf and Wulf to the sheets. They were already in place.

The ship seemed to hesitate for a second or two, then the twins hauled in on the trimming sheets and the sail flapped momentarily, then filled with a dull *whoomp* sound. The *Heron* accelerated as smoothly as her namesake, swooping smoothly across the low swell toward their starting position.

"Keel please, Thorn," Hal called, and Thorn shoved the fin down through the keel box. Instantly, Hal felt the steadying pressure as the ship's downwind drift was reduced to almost nothing. He glanced astern. They were carving a pure white wake through the brilliant blue of the sea. As he looked, he saw *Raven*'s black prow emerging through the breakwater.

"Ease the sheets a little, boys!" he called. "No sense in showing him how fast we can travel."

Ulf and Wulf eased the sail out and the *Heron*'s speed fell away. But even at this reduced speed, they reached the blue-flagged longboat in a matter of minutes. Hal glanced at the timer. Less than half the sand had run through. He passed the longboat, then tacked and came round level with her, facing back toward Raguza.

Then he ordered the sail down and they drifted.

Waiting was the worst part of it, he thought. The ball in his stomach was tighter than ever. He studied his crew's faces. They were grim and tight set for the most part. Stig tried to appear unconcerned, but Hal could see his fingers drumming on the handle of his battleax, where it lay ready beside him. He wanted to say something that would raise their spirits and ease their nerves. That's what a good skirl would do, he thought. But he couldn't think of anything to say and besides, he knew that if he tried to speak, his dry mouth and tight throat would betray him and his voice would break into a squeak.

Not an inspiring sound, he thought.

The silence dragged on. He looked at the sandglass again. The grains seemed to be falling one at a time. He peered at the red-and-blue flag. Had it moved? He thought it had, then realized it had simply flapped in a momentary lull in the breeze and now was standing out from the staff once more. The two harbor breakwaters were black with small figures. Spectators, he realized—most of them betting against him and the *Heron.*

Come on, he thought, his fingers clasping and unclasping on the smooth oak of the tiller. Let's get it over with.

"See this helmet?"

Thorn's booming question took him by surprise. The old sea wolf had moved away from the keel box to a position in the very center of the ship. He was pointing at the massive horned helmet he wore—the treasured headgear of all Skandian warriors.

"I've had this helmet for nigh on thirty years. I've worn it on raids. I've worn it in battles. It's seen more action in its time than most warriors you'll ever meet. It's saved my life on a dozen occasions. And I've been proud to wear it. It's the symbol of a Skandian warrior."

He had the attention of everyone on board now. Then he stepped to the port rail and removed the helmet.

"But I don't want it anymore."

There was an audible intake of breath from the entire crew as he drew back his left arm and tossed the helmet high into the air, so that it arced, then tumbled, spinning slowly, end over end, into the sea. All eyes followed its trajectory and someone let out a low cry of amazement as the helmet threw up a white splash, surprisingly smaller than they expected, then disappeared. When they looked back to Thorn, he was wearing a new piece of headgear. He had pulled on his black watch cap, with the white outline of a heron on it.

"This is the symbol I choose to wear now. The Heron brotherband symbol. No beat-up old helmet could make me as proud as this."

There was a moment of stunned silence. Then the entire crew began cheering as he grinned at them, nodding his head and pointing proudly to the black watch cap, identical to the ones they all wore. He strode up and down the center of the deck as they continued to cheer. And Hal cheered with the rest of them. The tight ball in his stomach had gone. He felt relaxed, confident and ready to face whatever was to come. He looked at the cheering, laughing faces of his friends and knew they all felt the same way.

Thorn, you're a genius, he thought. Then the old sea wolf drew his attention to the harbor mouth.

"I think the party's starting," he said cheerfully.

The red-and-blue flag was sliding down the flagstaff as Hal looked. The duel had begun.

A stir of excitement ran through the crew. Jesper and Stefan moved toward the halyards, ready to raise the sail. Hal held up a hand.

"Wait," he said. He wanted to see what Zavac's tactics were going to be.

Heron rocked gently on the swell and he saw the rectangle of *Raven*'s sail suddenly appear as her crew unfurled it and let it drop. Then the shape narrowed as they braced it round to port and the black ship began to surge forward, heading straight for them.

Hal nodded to himself. As he expected, Zavac wasn't wasting time with subtleties or fancy maneuvering. He was charging head-long at them, intent on getting to close quarters as soon as possible, then ramming and boarding them. He was conscious that his own crew had their attention fixed on him. He realized, with a remote part of his mind, now that the waiting was over, he was calm and steady. He cleared his throat, making sure he didn't squeak his first order.

"Starboard sail," he called. He was pleased to find that his voice was normal.

The yardarm went up smoothly. The sail filled and *Heron* came alive again, accelerating smoothly away, leaving the longboat behind in her wake. As she gathered speed, the initial *thump-thump-thump* of small waves against her hull blended into one constant—a hissing, sluicing sound as she sliced through the water before her.

Hal crouched to look below the sail so he could see *Raven*. She had her bow pointed at the *Heron* but, with her shallow keel, she was drifting downwind. Her real course would take her well to their right. Zavac should have pointed her higher if he wanted to intercept them. But, as Hal had suspected since he saw Zavac run his ship aground during his escape from Limmat harbor, the Magyaran wasn't a very accomplished helmsman. He didn't have Hal's instinctive feel for speeds and angles.

Heron, with the additional steadying effect of her fin, was going downwind at a much slower rate. That didn't suit Hal's purpose. He twitched the tiller and brought the bow around to starboard, so that she was heading closer to the black ship, aiming to pass down her starboard side, on a parallel course.

"Ingvar! Load the Mangler!" he called. He didn't like to leave the massive weapon under strain for too long, but now was the time to get it ready. Ingvar waved and stepped forward to the giant crossbow, seizing the twin levers and hauling them back to set the cord. Then he placed one of the massive bolts in the loading trough and signaled that he was ready.

"Stig!" Hal called, and the tall young warrior moved from the rowing bench to stand beside him, ready to take the tiller.

"We'll head down his starboard side. He'll try to turn into us to ram. I'll swing away at the last minute, then we'll circle back in at him from astern. Point me at his starboard side," Hal said. The Mangler was restricted to shooting in a forty-five-degree arc on either side of the bow. To engage the *Raven*, they'd have to be pointing toward her.

Stig nodded, frowning in concentration. He'd leave it to Hal to judge that initial turn away from their enemy. It had to be timed perfectly and Hal's judgment was better than his.

The crew were tensed at their positions. Hal noticed that Thorn had equipped himself with a large circular shield from the racks on either side of the ship. The old warrior was standing ready, just astern of the mast. Lydia was crouched in the bow, her atlatl in her hand, a dart already fitted to it. He became aware of a new sound, realized it was the crew of the fast-approaching *Raven*, shouting threats and curses at them. He studied them closely. He could see that two of them had short bows. The others were armed with an assortment of spears, swords and clubs.

"Lydia!" he called. "There are two bowmen."

He saw her nod, although she didn't look back at him. Her gaze was fixed on the onrushing *Raven*.

"They'll be first to go," she said. Thorn chuckled. This time she did take her eyes off the enemy. She glared at the bearded old sea wolf. Then she returned her attention to the *Raven*.

"Wait!" Hal called. "We're going to swing away, then back in."

She didn't reply, but raised a hand in acknowledgment.

One of the bowmen on the other ship took a shot at them. But either he was too excited or he misjudged the roll of the ship. Or maybe he was just a bad shot. His arrow soared well ahead of them. The other man shot a few seconds later. His arrow rattled against the hull, forward of the mast.

"He's getting close," Stig said. His voice was tight and his eyes were fixed on the whitewater foaming away from the vicious ram in *Raven*'s bow. Hal said nothing. If he turned too soon, Zavac could slip away and they'd start all over again. He wanted the other skipper to try to follow his turn, before he became too accustomed to *Heron*'s superior maneuverability.

On the other hand, he thought, if he turned too late, the ram would smash into *Heron*'s timbers and it would be all over.

"Ready, Ulf and Wulf!" he shouted. As he turned, they'd have to adjust the sails. Ulf waved a hand. Or maybe it was Wulf, he thought, grinning in spite of the seriousness of the situation.

Now!

He swung the ship away to port, heard the sheets squealing through the pulleys as the twins adjusted the sail, keeping it taut to the wind. *Heron* responded instantly, pivoting away from the larger ship. As he'd hoped, Zavac tried to match their turn, to keep the ram pointed at them. But the bigger ship had a wider turning circle than *Heron*. The *Heron* was turning inside her, cutting across *Raven*'s course so that the bow, and the Mangler, were pointing at her.

"Take over!" he yelled to Stig, and as his friend took the tiller, he ran fleet-footed down the deck to the bow, dropping onto the seat behind the Mangler. Ingvar was ready on the training lever as Hal peered down the sights. The *Raven* was barely forty meters away. He aimed at the crowded group of men in her bow, now turning back to stare at the small ship swooping toward them. He'd hoped for a shot at Zavac, but the sharply up-curving stern concealed him so that only his head was visible. That was too small a mark to hope to hit.

"Left . . . ," he ordered Ingvar. "Steady now . . . steady . . ."

SLAM!

The Mangler bucked wildly as he released. The bolt streaked away and plowed through the packed men in the bow of the ship. Ingvar was already reloading. Hal heard a thud as Thorn stepped forward to intercept an arrow with the huge shield.

Then he heard a vicious *flick-hiss!* as Lydia released a dart. One of the bowmen fell.

Now Hal had a new target. He figured that first bolt had killed or wounded at least four men. But now he was training the Mangler on the side of the *Raven*, where the rigging was attached.

There were three main shrouds—thick ropes, fastened to the bulwark—that supported the mast. He called directions to Ingvar, and lowered his aiming point until it was lined up where the center rope was attached. Then, as the target filled his sights, he released.

SLAM!

Too high. The bolt skimmed over his aiming point, glanced off the upper part of the bulwark and soared high into the sky, causing no damage. Ingvar reloaded. They were very close now. Some of the pirates had run to the stern of the ship and were hurling spears at the *Heron*. So far, they had no effect.

Flick-hiss! Flick-hiss!

Two more darts from Lydia. Two more Magyarans down. And suddenly some of their companions lost their enthusiasm and retreated to the far side of the deck, seeking cover on the rowing benches.

Hal centered his sights on that heavy, tarred rope once more, at the point where it was attached to the hull.

"Right . . . right a little . . . steady there . . ." He wound the elevating wheel down so that his sights were set just below the block that secured the rope. He felt the ship begin to lift on a wave and pulled the trigger lanyard. There was a fraction of a second delay, then . . .

SLAM!

They were barely twenty meters apart and he saw the bolt smash into the timbers of the other ship at the exact point he'd aimed for. Splinters flew as a large section of the bulwark disintegrated under the impact. The center shroud snapped loose, recoiling high into the air in an S shape as the tension on it was suddenly released, and flailing a large piece of shattered timber still attached to it.

The crew of the *Heron* cheered. But Hal was already screaming orders to Stig. They were almost on board the other ship.

"Bear away! Bear away!"

He felt a surge of relief as the *Heron* began to swing clear and the gap between the ships widened. There were cries of alarm from the black ship, then Jesper was standing, pointing and shouting excitedly.

"She's gone! The mast has gone!"

With the full thrust of the wind still in its sail, the sudden loss of one-third of its support was too much for the *Raven*'s mast. It lurched to one side, and a second shroud parted with a loud, deep twanging sound. Then the barely supported, unbalanced mast snapped clean off, a meter above the deck, and crashed overboard to port, dragging rigging, yardarm and sail with it.

Raven heeled to port under the drag of the wreckage lying over her side. The Magyarans rushed to cut away the tangle of ropes and mast and sail. But for the moment, they were helpless. And, more importantly, heeled under the weight of the wreckage as she was, an expanse of her starboard side, normally below the waterline, was exposed.

Hal stood clear of the Mangler and yelled orders back to Stig, his voice cracking into a shriek in the excitement of the moment.

"Circle!" he yelled, describing a circle in the air with his hand. "Bring us back to bear on her!"

Stig nodded his understanding and heaved on the tiller, continuing the tight curve they had already begun. The Herons were cheering and pointing at the crippled black ship. Hal yelled at them now.

"Shut up! Shut up and get back to your posts! We've got to finish her before she gets the wreckage cleared."

Hurriedly, and a little shamefaced, they returned to their stations. Stig tacked the ship and brought her round the full circle so that she was heading for the *Raven* once more.

Hal climbed back into the seat behind the Mangler. Ingvar had already reloaded. They grinned at each other and Ingvar stroked one hand on the wood of the huge crossbow.

"Good old Mangler," he muttered.

On board the *Raven*, Zavac had seen the little ship circling back to attack them again. He screamed orders at his men as they cut and hacked at the tangled cordage, chopped the shattered timber and heaved armloads of the massive canvas sail over the side. The *Heron* was still a hundred meters distant when he saw another bolt streak away from the terrible weapon she carried in her bow. He felt the shattering impact against *Raven*'s starboard side as it struck, punching a hole below her waterline. Then the ship lurched upright as the last of the wreckage was cleared and heaved overboard.

"Oars!" he screamed. "Run out the oars!" And the crew scrambled to the rowing benches. *Heron* was fifty meters away and he could see her skipper in the bow, crouched over that massive crossbow.

Hal had seen the *Raven* come upright as her crew cleared the wreckage. He estimated he had time for one more shot before Zavac got her under way again. Already, the long oars were appearing, sliding out from the hull.

Heron was coming in on a steeper angle this time, and Zavac was exposed at the tiller.

"Left! Left! Right a little! Steady!" he yelled at Ingvar as he brought the sights to bear on the Magyaran captain. Zavac was staring back at him now, looking straight at the dreadful weapon that was training on him, singling him out. He looked around desperately but there was nowhere to hide.

Flick-hiss!

Obviously, Lydia had the same idea. But her dart missed Zavac by centimeters. His first mate, standing beside him, staggered and fell. Hal grinned mirthlessly. Lydia didn't often miss, he thought. But this time it didn't matter. This time, he had Zavac dead in his sights, barely thirty meters away. He pulled smoothly at the trigger lanyard.

Disaster struck.

SLAM-CRACK!

The Mangler leapt back in recoil, and at that instant, one of the leather restraining straps parted, hurling the giant weapon to one side so that it lurched clear of its cradle and crashed to the deck. The bolt soared wildly into the air and Hal was thrown off his seat, under the heavy weapon as it toppled, falling sideways to the deck. As the Mangler fell, the left-hand limb of the bow took the initial impact as it struck the deck. The bow limb flexed and that momentary resistance saved Hal from being crushed and seriously injured.

But then the limb snapped and the full weight bore down on him, trapping him between the Mangler and the deck.

chapter forty-three

I t's said that catastrophe is the result of a random series of smaller mistakes or disasters coming one after the other.

As Hal lay trapped under the Mangler, Stig stooped to peer under the sail, trying to see what had happened. Ingvar was already heaving at the huge weapon to lift it clear and free Hal, shouting to his friend to make sure he wasn't seriously injured. Thorn and Lydia had Hal by the arms, ready to drag him clear as soon as his lower body and legs were free.

Distracted by the struggle going on in the bow, Stig allowed his grip on the tiller to loosen. And he failed to see the disturbed surface of the sea that heralded a stronger-than-usual gust of wind coming across the water toward them.

The gust hit them and drove the *Heron* sideways, closer to the damaged Magyaran ship. As it did, one of the pirate's crew saw a sudden advantage.

"Hook her! Hook her!" he yelled to his companions as they swarmed back into the rowing benches.

The *Raven*'s oars were fitted with an unusual device—one of Zavac's making. At the end of the shaft, before the wood flattened into the shaped oar blade, each oar was fitted with an iron hook, for use in situations like this one. Four of the rowers instantly ran their oars out toward *Heron*, setting the hooks into her bulwarks and dragging her closer. Then the rowers set their weight on the oars to hold them steady, forming a precarious but useable walkway between the two ships. Within an instant, four of their crewmates leapt onto the makeshift boarding bridge. It was an action they had practiced many times. They moved sideways, each man balancing on two of the oars and shuffling quickly across the gap.

The twins were first to realize what was happening. They let go the sheets and grabbed for their weapons, rising to meet the first of the boarders as he stepped onto *Heron*'s port bulwark. The first man, however, was caught by the suddenly released sail flapping loose. It hit him in the face and he tumbled off the narrow walkway and fell, screaming, into the seething water trapped between the two hulls.

But there were three more close behind him and they ducked the heavy flying canvas, then came on. They drove Ulf and Wulf back and leapt aboard. Others were poised on the *Raven* to follow them.

Stig yelled at Edvin to take the helm, although there was no steering to be done at the moment. He grabbed his ax and shield and, with an ear-shattering roar of rage, launched himself at the nearest of the three men pressing Ulf and Wulf back against the mast. Even as he cut him down, more of the *Raven*'s crew were making their way across the oar-bridge.

But now Hal was free of the Mangler. He scrambled to his feet, drawing his sword. Then he and Thorn launched themselves at the boarders from the other side.

Hal twisted aside from a spear thrust. The man who had aimed it at him was momentarily off balance, teetering awkwardly on the oars, which flexed beneath his weight. Hal thrust quickly, hitting him in the thigh. The Magyaran dropped his spear, reached to clutch the wound in his leg and toppled off the oars into the sea.

Now Thorn and Stig, in a concerted pincer movement, crashed into the other Magyarans who had made it aboard. Thorn's sword swung in a deadly arc, then darted out like a serpent and another pirate was down. A third tried in vain to block Stig's overhead ax cut with a small metal hand-shield.

But Lydia saw three more men edging carefully across the oars toward the *Heron*. She grabbed an oar and shoved it into Ingvar's hands.

"Come with me!" she yelled, seizing his arm and dragging him to the side of the ship.

The would-be boarders hesitated. Thorn and Stig had left the last of the boarders to the twins and now moved to stand ready at the end of the improvised boarding bridge. Hal stepped back to give them room. The Magyarans stopped, sizing up the situation, just out of reach of the Skandians' deadly weapons.

But not out of reach of Ingvar's oar. Lydia pointed to the three men and shouted to Ingvar.

"There, Ingvar! There they are!"

The huge boy squinted at them for a second. They were blurred shapes, and he couldn't see any detail. But Lydia had told him they were the enemy and that was good enough for him. With a mighty roar, he swung the oar at full length, smashing it into them, sweeping them from their unsteady foothold. One fell back aboard the *Raven*, three of his ribs fractured by the oar. The others went into the sea. One momentarily surfaced, gasping and clawing at the water's surface. Then, burdened by the weight of his chain mail and shield, he disappeared.

Ingvar turned to Lydia. "Any more?" he asked.

She smiled and shook her head. "I think you've frightened the others off."

Even as she spoke, Stig was busy with his ax. Four blows in rapid succession sheared through the oars holding the two ships together. As she saw him do this, Lydia took the oar, placed it against the *Raven*'s hull, then put the butt end into Ingvar's hands.

"Push us clear!" she shouted, and she helped as Ingvar leaned his massive strength against the oar, shoving the two hulls apart, so that *Heron*'s bow swung away from the black ship.

"Get on the sail!" Hal yelled as the gap between the ships widened. Ulf and Wulf tossed their weapons to the deck and scrambled back to the trimming sheets. They heaved in on the ropes and the flapping sail hardened to the wind, driving the ship away from *Raven*. Edvin watched anxiously, easing the tiller so that *Heron*'s stern didn't swing too far and come into contact with the black ship. A Magyaran crewman was poised on the *Raven*'s stern rail, his arm drawing back to cast a spear at Edvin. Before he could bring it forward, one of Lydia's darts thudded into his side and he fell, with a small groan, back onto the deck.

Then they were clear and accelerating away. Hal sheathed his sword and looked astern. *Raven*'s oars were running out on either side, although there were four fewer of them than there had been. Zavac had transferred two from the port side to even them out. As he watched, they began their steady beat, like a bird's wings, and the black ship surged after them.

Ingvar and Lydia went to work clearing the wrecked Mangler, tying it down so that it wouldn't lurch around the deck and cause damage. Ingvar peered disconsolately at the ruined weapon.

"How bad is it?" he asked.

Lydia patted his arm. "Hal can fix it," she said.

Ingvar shook his head. "But not today."

And that was the problem Hal, Thorn and Stig were discussing in the stern, where Hal had taken the tiller once more. Edvin, relieved of the responsibility of steering, was tending to Wulf, who had sustained a cut on his calf.

"The Mangler's wrecked," Hal said. "We can't stand off and do any more damage from long range. We're going to have to fight them close in."

Stig smiled grimly. "We've done plenty of damage to them already," he said. "One way or another, we've probably gotten rid of half Zavac's crew."

"We're still outnumbered," Thorn said. "Without the Mangler to keep their heads down, how will we get close to them?"

Hal looked steadily at him, then looked astern to where *Raven* was accelerating after them, cutting across the arc they were describing, just as they had done before. Under oars, the black ship was much more maneuverable and, in the short term, nearly as fast as *Heron*. He could make out Zavac's tall shape at the tiller.

"We'll make him think it's his idea," he said. He checked *Raven's* position again. She had turned inside them and was heading to intercept them and ram. At the moment, she was gaining slowly. But as her rowers tired, that might not continue.

"Ulf! Wulf!" Hal called. "Gradually ease the sheets, a little at a time. I want to slow down. But I don't want Zavac to realize we've done it on purpose."

The twins both waved that they understood. Gradually, they began to ease the sheets, letting the wind spill from the sail. Hal felt the ship slowing.

"That's enough!" he called. "Keep it there!"

He looked at *Raven* again. She was closer now. Zavac had learned his earlier lesson and was pointing his ship ahead of the *Heron's* course, at a spot where he would intercept her.

Hal had a plan in mind to further disable the pirate craft. As the *Raven* came closer, it would call for split-second timing and coordination between Hal, Stefan, Jesper and the twins. But they had trained and practiced as a crew for months. Hal was confident they'd pull it off.

There were several factors in their favor. Zavac had spent most of his career attacking slow trading ships. Aside from their one encounter outside Limmat, he hadn't seen how fast and agile *Heron* could be. Their battle so far today had depended more on the devastating power of the Mangler, rather than *Heron*'s superior handling qualities.

Their other advantage lay in the fact that Zavac, like most skippers of square-rigged ships, preferred to change direction by wearing, keeping the wind astern, rather than tacking, or turning head into the wind. Wearing ship was a slower process. Tacking was faster, but much riskier. Chances were he would not expect them to take such a course.

And that could lead to his undoing.

forty-four

The *Raven* was slowly gaining on them. Hal watched her through narrowed eyes, counting the oar beats as they thrashed at the sea's surface.

"No foxing this time," he said. "He's coming at us as fast as he can."

It was a common tactic for ships that were intending to ram to approach at less than full speed, putting on a sudden spurt in the last thirty or forty meters. But Zavac wasn't trying any such subterfuge. He was bearing down as fast as he could, his men straining at the oars to keep the *Raven* skimming toward them. Hal looked closely now. Two of the oars Stig had smashed seemed to have been replaced. Zavac must have been carrying spares.

"What's the plan?" Thorn asked. Hal licked his lips, studying the *Raven* once more, judging her speed and the time he had left before she reached them. He checked the telltale. The wind was still coming from their right, or starboard, side.

"I'm going to fake a turn to the left," he said, "and make him think we're wearing the ship round."

"Why should he think that?" Thorn asked, frowning.

"Because it's what he'd do. It's what he's used to. It's what everybody does. With any luck, he'll turn after us."

Wearing the ship meant turning with the stern of the ship to the wind, so that the wind blew from behind throughout the turn and powered the ship through it. It was the preferred method for turning a square-rigged ship. No right-minded skipper would turn a square sail up into the wind. The pressure on the sail, rigging and mast would be enormous. At best, the ship would be brought to a stop in the water. At worst, she could be dismasted.

But the *Heron*, with her fore-and-aft sail and its rigid leading edge, could turn easily into and across the wind. Hal was banking on the fact that Zavac wouldn't realize that.

"He's never seen us tack up into the wind," he said. "He won't be expecting it."

I hope, he added grimly to himself.

"Get your weapons ready," he said. He saw Lydia, crouched ready in the bow, steadying herself with one hand on the forestay. He called to her and she turned, a question on her face.

"We'll be passing close to him on the starboard side," he told her. "Do whatever damage you can."

She nodded and checked the darts in her quiver. She still had nine left. Hal was going to call to Jesper and Stefan and the twins, to tell them to stand ready for fast sail handling. Then he shrugged the idea away. They were ready, he knew. He could see all of them, tensed at their stations, eyes on the black ship coming up fast astern.

She was getting close. Foam was flying from the water as her oars beat at it. The evil-looking ram loomed closer and closer to his ship.

He edged the tiller over and *Heron* began to swing to port. Looking over his shoulder, he saw the *Raven* hesitate for a second, then she began to swing as well, aiming to cut inside *Heron*'s turn.

Now, he thought.

"Going about to starboard!" he yelled, and heaved the tiller hard over. *Heron* swung smoothly back in the opposite direction. Jesper and Stefan released the port sail and yardarm, letting them slide down the mast. They had linked the sails via a pulley, so as the port sail came down, it helped the starboard sail swoop up the mast.

Heron turned sweetly across the wind, swinging through the turn so that she was now on the opposite tack and heading back toward *Raven*.

It all happened so quickly that Zavac was caught by surprise. He might have matched the *Heron*'s turn if he had ordered one bank of oars to reverse and the other to go forward, but that would have cost him speed, stopping the *Raven* almost dead in the water. In the event, he didn't have time to issue the necessary chain of orders, and he reacted instinctively, simply heaving on the tiller so that the *Raven* began swinging to the right, following the smaller ship.

Now they were heading for each other on parallel courses. He tried to swing his bow up toward the *Heron* to ram her, but she easily moved away and stayed on a parallel course. A dart from Lydia's atlatl sent one of the men in the bow of the *Raven* staggering back. The others crouched below the bulwark. The two ships were going to pass each other with about ten meters separating them.

Until, at the very last moment, Hal twitched the tiller, turning the *Heron*'s bow in toward the pirate ship, angling in at the hull a few meters behind the bow.

"Hang on!" he yelled to his own crew. Then he straightened her out so that the *Heron* was running alongside the other ship, parallel once more, but now with only a few meters' separation. It was so unexpected that the *Raven*'s oarsmen had no time to react. *Heron*'s sharp prow sliced like a giant blade along the starboard bank of oars, smashing and splintering them as she went, hurling the oarsmen off their benches as the butt ends of the oars jerked forward and smashed into them.

The air was filled with the shouts of injured men and the grinding, smashing sound of the oars as they flew into splinters.

Then the *Heron* was clear, turning away from the Magyaran ship and swinging up into the wind once more.

Raven was in a shambles. With most of her starboard-side oars smashed and useless, she drifted helplessly. Gradually, her men picked themselves up, although four of them remained where they had fallen, two nursing broken limbs caused by the flailing butt ends of the oars as *Heron* smashed into them. The other two lay unconscious.

A crewman, regaining his feet groggily and shaking his head to clear it, glanced up and stared in horror. The enemy ship had tacked in a circle once more and was bearing down on them, this time from astern. He could see, poised in her bow, the two warriors who had led her defense a few minutes earlier—a burly, shaggy-haired older man and a broad-shouldered young fighter, armed with a battleax.

"Look out! They're coming back!" he yelled, a fraction of a second before the *Heron*'s bow, the strongest section of her hull, smashed into the corresponding weakest point of her enemy, the planks of the *Raven*'s side.

There was another grinding crash as the two ships came together and three of the *Raven*'s planks were stove in. The impact threw her still-recovering crew from their feet again.

Then Stig and Thorn were upon them, yelling and screaming war cries, cutting down any who tried to resist them, smashing their way into the confused and disoriented pirate crew. Behind them, Ulf and Wulf added their battle cries to the general noise, and the air hummed with the deadly whir of their axes as they swung them in giant, horizontal arcs, smashing through shields and hurling enemies aside like rag dolls.

Stefan, Edvin and Jesper paused briefly to lash the two ships together, then they leapt across the bulwarks and onto the *Raven*'s deck, adding their numbers to the sudden assault. Lydia watched for a few seconds, seeing the boarding party driving the *Raven*'s crew across the deck and forward. Then she gestured to Ingvar, standing ready with a huge ax.

"Come on, Ingvar!" she said. She took his hand and steadied him as he stepped clumsily onto the other ship. He took a quick look around, gathered himself and began smashing the ax into the hull. Seawater poured in around his feet and he switched his attention to the watertight central section of the deck that served to keep the ship afloat if she was swamped. A few solid blows of the ax smashed it wide-open. If the *Raven* filled now, she would sink. Satisfied that he had his task well in hand, Lydia stepped back onto the *Heron*'s upward curving bow and searched for a target among the enemy. The deadly *flick-hiss!* of the atlatl began once more, and Magyarans began to fall.

A Magyaran deflected Ulf's ax with his shield, then scored a cut across the Skandian's forearm with his sword. Ulf recoiled, looking at the shallow wound angrily. Before he could counterattack, Wulf hurled himself at the swordsman in fury, ax swinging. Again, the Magyaran deflected the blow and his sword flickered out, catching Wulf in the same spot. Blood welled out and the twins glared at the man in rage. Then he went down as Thorn swung a back-handed stroke across his head, shearing through the helmet.

"Will you two stop playing around?" he demanded roughly, and the twins returned to the fight, blood streaming from their wounds.

Astern on the *Heron*, Hal waited till the boarding party had driven the Magyaran crew back. Then he stepped up onto the rail and leapt across to the other ship, narrowly avoiding the rampaging Ingvar, who was now going about his task with a vengeance.

"Watch out, Ingvar!" he shouted, ducking as the huge ax whistled past him on its backswing.

"Sorry, Hal," Ingvar mumbled. He'd discovered that the black watch caps worn by the Herons were a useful recognition aid. He could make them out relatively easily and that stopped him from attacking his own side. But that didn't help if someone was behind him, as Hal was.

Hal shook his head and ran toward the stern, crossing the deck and searching for the hatch that led to Zavac's private quarters. He slid it open and slipped inside. There wasn't enough headroom to stand erect here. The space was barely a meter and a half high. He noted that water was already ankle deep in the confined space, and the level was rising by the minute. Ingvar's handiwork, he thought.

He crawled aft, scrambling over Zavac's bedroll, trying to re-member what Mihaly's officer had said about the sleeping space. The emeralds had been hidden behind a concealed sliding hatch and he had no time to look for that now. But the Andomal—the big yellow glass ball that the officer had described—had been in plain view. A bulwark ran down the center of the space, and as his eyes became accustomed to the dimness, he could see that it was lined with square recessed shelves, angled so that the contents wouldn't spill out when the ship rolled. He saw a small jewel box and several items of clothing tucked into the first few. Then he peered into the third and his heart lurched. The angled recess held a large leather sack. He reached for it and withdrew it, undoing the drawstrings with trembling fingers.

The rich, warm glow of the Andomal shone back at him, catch-ing the meager light belowdecks, seeming to have an inner glow of its own. He refastened the drawstring and looped it around his wrist. The water was several inches higher, and he noticed that the ship was now listing heavily to starboard. Time to go, he thought, turning to retrace his steps out of the sleeping cabin.

Then a figure slid through the low hatchway and into the compartment, a long dagger held between his teeth.

Zavac.

Zavac, staying well back behind his crew as the Skandians drove them inexorably toward the bow, had seen a flash of movement astern as Hal crossed the deck and dropped into the well where the rowing benches were situated.

Instantly, he knew what the young Skandian was after. The Skandians had been present when Mihaly's man described the spot where he'd found the emeralds. And he'd mentioned the "large yellow ball" of glass as well.

Zavac was seized with a sudden rage. The cursed young Skandian, and his shabby old one-armed friend, had checked him and foiled him at every turn. They had been instrumental in his defeat at Limmat. They had rescued the wolfship he had rammed outside

Limmat harbor. They had caused him the loss of half of the emeralds he had stolen.

And now they were destroying his ship. He had no doubts about that. The decks were heeling sharply as the giant member of the *Heron*'s crew went on a berserking rage, smashing through the hull and the watertight compartment with a massive ax. *Raven* would never recover from that.

And now that cursed boy—he searched for the name, then found it—*Hal*, would recover the great treasure of the Skandians and return home in triumph.

Zavac snarled in fury. He glanced around. The battle was going badly for his men. Some had even taken oars and spare pieces of timber, hurled them into the sea and dived after them, hoping to be picked up by the Raguzan longboats standing by. Dead and wounded men littered the decks—all of them from his crew. It was only a matter of minutes before the rest of them surrendered.

A red rage flashed before his eyes. Looking around, he could see that the Skandians were fully occupied by the battle. He crept to the port side and dropped into the recess where the rowing benches were situated. Keeping low and out of sight, he slipped like a snake toward the stern. As he came level with the open hatch to his sleeping berth, he took a long dagger from his belt, placed it between his teeth, then crawled forward. With the dagger between his teeth, his mouth appeared to be set in an insane, enraged grin.

"You!" Hal cried as he recognized the Magyaran. Zavac reached up and took the dagger from his teeth. He smiled cruelly at the young man as Hal tried desperately to scrabble for his saxe. But the weapon was beneath him and he couldn't reach it.

Then Zavac hurled himself forward, the dagger plunging down at Hal's throat as he landed full length on the younger man.

Cramped and confined in the low, narrow space, Hal was trapped by Zavac's weight on top of him. He clawed desperately for the other man's knife hand and managed to catch his wrist. But the Andomal, tethered around his own wrist by the drawstring to its bag, swung awkwardly and hit him across the forehead. He was momentarily dazed and he felt the dagger skip closer to his throat as Zavac brought all his weight to bear behind it.

He locked his free hand around the Magyaran's wrist and managed to heave the knife a few centimeters away from his throat. But then Zavac placed his own left hand on the knife handle as well and began to bear down.

Slowly, slowly, the knifepoint came closer. Hal struggled and heaved desperately. But Zavac was heavier and bigger than he was, and in this cramped space, weight and strength would tell. Hal realized that the water was deeper in the hull now and he could hear a dull rush from farther forward—the sea pouring into the massive rents that Ingvar had smashed in the hull.

If I don't get out of here, I'll drown, he thought. Then he giggled insanely as he realized that he'd be dead long before that could happen.

Zavac's face was only centimeters from his own. The man's breath was hot on his cheeks. "Think it's funny, do you?" Zavac snarled. "You young swine. You're dead!"

And he suddenly thrust down with a convulsive heave, putting all his weight behind the knife. Hal just managed to twist his body to the side. The dagger scored a shallow cut across his neck and he felt the hot blood flowing from the cut.

Strangely, he felt no pain. The dagger point buried itself in the planking and Zavac had to struggle to release it.

Dimly, Hal heard voices shouting, heard Stig calling on the *Heron*'s crew to disengage and fall back. The ship beneath him lurched and the angle of the deck increased even farther. It actually threw Zavac slightly clear of him and he wriggled away. But then Hal had to grab for Zavac's knife hand again as the pirate wrenched the knife clear of the deck and attacked once more. Using both hands, Hal tried to twist the blade away from his throat—but with little success.

Zavac heaved himself back on top of Hal and once more the deadly contest of strength began—Zavac putting all his weight behind the knife as he forced it down, Hal trying with all his strength to stop it.

But this time, he realized dully, he wouldn't manage it. This time, Zavac would force the dagger slowly through his throat. He summoned all his strength into one last, supreme effort to force it back. He heaved upward desperately. But it was useless. The dagger didn't budge. Then it began to descend. He could hear Zavac snarling with the effort, feel his breath, and he knew that this was the end. He had nothing more to give.

I don't want to die here in the dark, he thought. Somehow, it might be more bearable if he could see the sun.

Then something peculiar filled his vision. A piece of polished wood shaped like a double-sided hook came into sight. It looked familiar somehow. The two halves opened like a claw, then closed again over Zavac's knife hand. The Magyaran looked up in surprise, his weight momentarily coming off the knife and giving Hal a brief respite. Then Thorn's bearded face appeared over Zavac's shoulder and he seized the adjusting thong on his false hand and jerked it tight around the Magyaran's wrist.

"How lovely to see you again," Thorn said.

Then he pulled the hook tighter. Then tighter. Then tighter still.

Zavac screamed in agony as the two-piece clasping hook clamped down on his forearm like a vice. Hal actually heard several small bones cracking as Thorn increased the pressure. Then the dagger fell from Zavac's hand and splashed into the water filling the compartment. The Magyaran threw his head back and screamed in pain.

As he did so, Thorn jerked him sideways, freeing Hal from his constricting weight.

"Get out of here, Hal," he said, and Hal scrabbled awkwardly on his back past the two of them, forcing his way through the narrow space, backing out of the hatch into the rowing well. He was startled to see that a good two-thirds of the *Raven* was now below the surface, with only the stern still afloat—and that listing heavily to starboard.

He staggered to his feet. The decks were empty. Zavac's men had either abandoned the ship or were dead or wounded. His own crew were back aboard the *Heron*, shouting for him to join them. He leaned against the butt of an oar, trying to get his breath. Then he saw Stig leap back aboard and sprint toward him. His friend grabbed him under his arms and hoisted him up onto the main deck. Hal tried to turn back.

"Thorn's in there!" he said.

"He'll be fine," Stig replied, and half carried, half dragged him to where the *Heron* was still lashed alongside, and willing hands were ready to lift him aboard. The Andomal, in its leather sack, bumped awkwardly against his side.

"Thorn!" he shouted desperately, feeling the *Raven* give one more lurch.

Belowdecks, Thorn smiled into Zavac's contorted, furious face. His hand was busy with the strap that held his false arm in place.

"Try to knife my boy, would you?" he said in a conversational tone. He slipped his right arm free of the socket that held the false hand in place. The wooden hook was still clamped firmly at right angles across Zavac's wrist and the Magyaran writhed in agony. Thorn looked around, saw a V-shaped frame on the inside of the hull. He seized Zavac's wrist with his left hand, twisting it so that he could pass Zavac's forearm, and the attached hook, through the narrow V. Then he twisted it back again so that the wooden hand was firmly jammed between the frames, trapping Zavac by the arm.

"A good captain always goes down with his ship. It's time for you to start being a good captain," Thorn told him. Then he backed out of the cabin on his hands and knees and ran across the sloping deck to the *Heron*.

"Cut her loose!" he shouted as he leapt aboard. Ulf brought his ax down on the ropes lashing the ships together, and *Heron* seemed to bounce back and up as she was suddenly freed of the weight of the sinking black ship.

They drifted clear, and for a minute or two, *Raven*'s stern remained above the surface, buoyed up by a pocket of trapped air.

Then a huge bubble burst on the water and she began to slide under. They heard one last, lingering scream, rising in pitch, then suddenly cut off.

And then she was gone.

"Good riddance," said Lydia, her face grim.

chapter forty-six

E rak, Oberjarl of the Skandians, had taken to walking down to the harbor front each morning and staring out to sea. Then, after fifteen minutes or so, he would walk back to the Great Hall. People noticed this change in his routine, of course, but nobody commented. Nobody but Svengal, his old friend, that is.

"Why the morning walk, chief?" he asked one day, grinning widely.

Erak pretended not to notice the ridiculous grin on Svengal's homely face. He replied gruffly. "Need the exercise," he said. "I'm putting on weight and the walking does me good."

"Well," said Svengal expansively, "if that's the case, why not walk up the mountain? There's a lot more exercise involved there.

Get the blood pumping. Get the legs working. That'll bring your belt in a few notches in no time."

The Oberjarl regarded his friend stonily. "I prefer the view at the harbor," he said, and Svengal nodded wisely. He knew very well what Erak was looking for every day.

On this particular day, he had elected to join the Oberjarl on his walk. They passed Anders's shipyard, where *Wolfwind* had been relaunched the day before. After Zavac had rammed the wolfship during his escape from Limmat, Svengal had patched her up, then sailed her home, where permanent repairs could be undertaken by Hallasholm's master shipwright.

"*Wolfwind*'s looking good," Svengal ventured. "You can hardly see any sign of where Zavac hit her."

Erak sniffed. "There's a plank dented badly on her starboard bow," he said. "It's just been painted over."

Svengal raised an eyebrow. "Um. I don't like to mention it, but that happened two years ago when you rammed the wharf coming alongside."

Erak turned to look at him. "I don't ram wharves," he said, and Svengal shrugged philosophically.

"Of course not. My mistake. The wharf rammed you. I remember now, it fairly leapt off its pilings and banged into the ship. Terrible things, wharves. You can never trust them."

"Do you ever shut up?" Erak asked.

Svengal appeared to consider the question. "Rarely." He grinned.

Erak grunted. "Didn't think so."

They walked along the mole to the harbor entrance. Erak leaned on a waist-high bollard there and stared out to sea, his eyes moving from left to right as he quartered the horizon. There were half a dozen small fishing boats, probably on their way to Loki's Bank, and a deep-laden trader was heading for the harbor. But nothing more.

Erak sighed, not realizing that he did so. Svengal laid a hand on his shoulder.

"They'll turn up one day," he said. There was no sign of his previous jocularity. Erak pretended to look puzzled.

"Just who are you talking about?" he asked.

Svengal nodded as if he'd made a mistake. "I've no idea," he said.

They scanned the ocean for another ten minutes, then Erak turned and headed back to the Great Hall, his friend keeping pace with him. They had reached the landward end of the mole when a shout came from the watchtower behind them.

"Sail to the southeast!"

Erak stopped, his back to the ocean, listening as the watch commander called back up to the young sailor in the tower.

"Report properly. What is she?" There was a pause, then the youngster replied, a note of puzzlement in his voice.

"I'm . . . not sure. She looks sort of . . . weird. The sail is . . . kind of . . . triangular."

Slowly, the two old friends turned and began to retrace their steps down the mole, moving faster and faster as they went. By the time they reached the seaward end, the ship was in sight from ground level.

Small, with a jaunty triangular sail that looked like a bird's wing. Moving fast, seeming to fly low across the sea, dashing the waves apart in regular showers of white spray from her bow. As she came closer, they could see the white heron insignia on her sail and there could be no mistake. Erak grabbed one of the young members of the harbor watch by the shoulder.

"Run as fast as you can and tell Karina Mikkelswife her son has come home. Then spread the word through the town. The *Heron* has flown back to Hallasholm."

The young man ran off on his errand, his boots slapping on the stones of the mole. Erak and Svengal watched, shading their eyes, as the little ship tacked neatly, one sail disappearing as another took its place, and arrowed toward the harbor entrance.

"He's good," Erak murmured.

Svengal looked at him. "He's better than good."

Erak didn't reply immediately, watching the ship heading like a homing pigeon for the harbor. But he nodded. Then, after a few seconds, he commented.

"I'm glad *Wolfwind* is in the shipyard. He'd be heading right at her again."

Word had begun to spread through the town, and people were streaming onto the harbor mole now. Erak glanced round and saw Karina, Hal's mother, trying to force her way through the jostling crowd and make her way to the front. He glared at the people who were unintentionally blocking the small woman's way.

"Let Karina through or I'll send for my ax," he warned them. The crowd parted miraculously and she came forward, breathless after running all the way from her eating house.

"Is it really them?" she asked, and Erak pointed to the fast-approaching ship.

"D'you know anyone else who could handle a ship like that?"

Tears sprang to Karina's eyes. She wiped them with her apron and Erak tactfully turned away. Then somebody started cheering, and the rest of the watchers followed suit. Their cheers rang over the harbor, startling the gulls, who wheeled high into the air in fright, then chattered back angrily.

The parents of the other boys began to arrive. Stig's mother was first, then the others followed. By now, the people on the mole knew well enough to let them through. They stood in the front row of the assembled crowd, grinning at one another, then watching the ship as she approached.

The *Heron* shot through the harbor entrance under sail, disdaining to row in. The cheering was replaced by a sudden, concerted intake of breath from the crowd as it seemed she must smash against the stone wall of the mole. Then Hal rounded her up, and she spun in a neat circle into the wind. The sail slid down her mast and she came to a stop in a matter of a few meters, rocking in the waves generated by her own passage.

The crowd exhaled as one, in relief.

The breeze drifted her in to the mole, alongside the mooring permanently reserved for Erak's ship, *Wolfwind*.

"Cheeky beggar," the Oberjarl muttered as bow and stern lines were tossed up and made fast.

Then he strode to the edge of the mole and looked down at the decks of the little ship. The disreputable Thorn was the first person he saw. He looked as shabby as ever, and his false hand was missing. He grinned at Erak and Erak pretended to ignore him. Thorn had no sense of occasion.

Then Hal lashed the tiller in place and stepped toward the shoreward rail, a leather sack in his hand. He held it up.

"Oberjarl!" he called in a loud, clear voice. "We've brought back the Andomal."

Erak looked at the sky for a few seconds, then back at the serious young faces on the ship a few meters below him. He tugged at his beard, then hitched his belt up.

"Well then," he said, "you'd better come ashore."

e p i l o g u e

Even for Hallasholm, a town with a longstanding record for sensational festivities, the celebration of the *Heron*'s return was one that would be remembered for decades to come.

Lydia had come to Hallasholm with the crew. Hal had offered to take her back to Limmat, but she smiled wryly and shook her head.

"I don't think Barat would be pleased to see me after I ran off and left him," she said. Then she colored slightly. "And besides, I *did* steal a small fortune in emeralds from them."

"Then come back to Hallasholm with us," Hal said. "You're one of the crew now, after all." The crew reacted enthusiastically to this idea, assuring her that she'd be welcome in their hometown.

"Do you think I'll like Hallasholm?" she asked.

Hal smiled at her. "I think so. And I'm sure Hallasholm will love you."

And so it had proved. Hal's mother, knowing how difficult life could be for a foreigner in a foreign land, took the slim, olive-skinned girl under her wing immediately. When Erak announced that there would be a massive celebration to mark the Herons' return, Lydia had reacted in a most uncharacteristic way.

"A party? But I've got nothing to wear!" she said. The Herons stared in amazement. This was a side of Lydia they had never seen. But Karina patted her hand reassuringly and hustled her away.

"Don't worry. I've got just the thing. It'll be perfect for you."

Karina wasn't exaggerating. When Lydia arrived at the Great Hall that night, she was wearing a green dress of soft, fine wool. Its simple lines and elegant style made the most of her slim figure. Her long glossy hair, tied back by a green ribbon, had been brushed until it shone under the torchlight. Hal took a step back in mock surprise as he saw her.

"Why, Lyd!" he exclaimed, with a beaming smile. "You're positively beautiful!"

"Hadn't you noticed that before?" Stig asked, his eyes fixed on her.

Lydia flushed lightly, not sure what she should say. Ingvar solved the problem for her.

"Even I can see that!" he said. "And I claim the first dance with you!"

Ingvar might seem big and ponderous at times, but he was no

slow thinker. She smiled at him, then was surrounded by the rest of the crew, each one clamoring for the promise of a dance.

"First things first!" Hal shouted, holding up his hand for silence. "We have to introduce our new crew member to the Oberjarl."

He took her hand and, accompanied by the rest of the Heron brotherband, led her through the crowded hall to the raised podium where Erak sat in his large carved pine armchair. The Oberjarl looked with interest at the beautiful girl standing between Hal and the ever-present Stig. He rose and stepped forward.

"And who might this vision be?" he asked.

"Oberjarl," Hal said in a ringing voice that carried to every corner of the hall, "this is our new crew member. Her name is Lydia and she's been a brave and faithful member of the crew. She rescued us from prison in the town of Bayrath."

"And," Stig put in, not to be outdone, "she's also a formidable warrior. She can hit the eye of a gnat with a dart from her atlatl. She took care of at least half a dozen of Zavac's men when we regained the Andomal."

The hall buzzed with interest as the two boys extolled Lydia's qualities. People jostled to get a closer look at her. Many of the men, after a first look, shoved to get even closer for a second look.

Lydia had never learned to curtsy, so she bowed her head slightly, which was fine by Erak. Skandians were an egalitarian lot who didn't go in for a lot of bowing and scraping. He stepped forward, took her hand and bent over it, pressing it lightly to his lips. Then he straightened, still holding her hand, and eyed the two boys.

"And she's also remarkably easy on the eyes. This one is definitely a keeper!"

Lydia smiled warmly and inclined her head. "Why, thank you, Oberjarl. How sweet of you to say so," she said.

Thorn was instantly scandalized. "'Thank you, Oberjarl'?" he shrieked incredulously, his voice rising several tones. "'*Thank you, Oberjarl*'? What am I, chopped whale blubber? When I say that, all she can say is, *Shut up, old man.* 'Thank you, Oberjarl'? Words fail me!" And they did.

Erak eyed him with a superior expression on his face. "It's a matter of charm, Thorn. Some got it. Some don't got it."

"Some don't got good grammar either," said Edvin, grinning, in an aside to Stefan.

The Oberjarl continued. "And you, apparently, are numbered among the *Don't-got-its.*"

Lydia's smile grew wider. She turned to Thorn, who was red faced and muttering, and slowly lowered one eyelid in a wink.

Then the dancing and feasting began, with Ingvar shouldering his shipmates aside to claim his promised first dance with Lydia. From then on, she was besieged by dance partners. Hal and Stig managed one dance each before she was whirled away by others. She noted with amusement, and perhaps a slight twinge of jealousy, that two local girls, a blonde and a brunette, were paying a lot of attention to the two boys.

There were sheep and pigs roasting on spits, the fat sizzling and spitting on the coals beneath them, as the attendants carved thick slices of succulent meat from them. There were platters of roast vegetables and barrels of ale and wine for those who wished it. The town of Hallasholm went out of its way to welcome the heroes home.

Erak made a short speech, welcoming them back as returning heroes. Their actions in restoring the Andomal to its rightful owners more than made up for any sins of the past, he said. The name of the Heron brotherband would be restored to the records of Hallasholm, and they would be credited as winners of the contest for their year. The crowd cheered enthusiastically.

Erak even offered to return the horned helmets they had been awarded, but Hal smiled and gracefully refused. He pointed to the watch caps they all wore.

"We have our own headgear now," he said.

Erak peered more closely. "They are rather smart," he said. "I wonder if I could get hold of one?"

Hal smiled. "I'll speak to Edvin about it."

After Erak had spoken, Jesper and Stefan clambered up onto a table in the middle of the hall. As the noise swept around them like a tide, Jesper nodded to Ingvar, who filled his lungs and bellowed.

"QUIET!"

Instantly, the hall fell silent. All eyes turned to the two Herons, perched on the table, crouching slightly beneath the low roof beams.

"People have been asking us for the full story of our amazing voyage," Stefan said, and cries of agreement and encouragement rang around the room. He held his hands up for silence once more. When he had it, Jesper spoke.

"So we've written a saga," he said. *"The Saga of Hal and the Heron Brotherband."*

"Oh Gorlog help us," Hal muttered.

"Let's hear it!" bellowed one enthusiastic listener. Jesper turned a pitying eye on him.

"Um . . . that's why we're standing here on this table, in case you hadn't realized it."

Shouts came from all corners of the hall for the two to perform their saga. Skandians loved a good party. They loved good food and drink. They loved a fight from time to time. And they dearly loved a saga—and the more full of exaggeration, self-praise and utterly shameless boasting it was, the better they loved it.

"All right!" Stefan shouted, and the crowd quieted a little. "We'll sing you the chorus. Then you can join it. Someone hand me a lute or a harp or something."

A small harp was passed up to him, and he struck a random chord on it, then he and Jesper began to sing, in a key that had absolutely no relationship to the one he had just sounded:

> *The Herons! The Herons!*
> *The mighty, fighting Herons!*
> *No other brotherband you'll see*
> *is even half as darin'!*

Hal shook his head sadly. "*Herons* and *darin'*?" he said. "Orlog's toenails!"

Erak was standing close by him. He frowned at Hal's obvious lack of cultural appreciation.

"What's wrong with you?" he said. "This is good!" He began to beat time with his tankard, slopping ale over people within a two-meter radius. Jesper and Stefan continued.

Now, Erak told the members of the Heron brotherband,
"Your name will be reviled by everybody in this land."

The crowd turned to Erak and shook their fists.

"Boooo!" they shouted. He shook his own fist back, drenching a few more bystanders in the process.

"They deserved it!" he roared. But he was laughing. People love being mentioned in a saga, and he was no exception. He turned back as the boys continued.

"So turn in all your weapons and then give your ship to me."
But Hal, the Herons' skipper, said, "That isn't going to be."

"Hooray!" bellowed the crowd. Hal hid his face in his hands.

"I know this is going to get worse," he said, to nobody in particular. "I just know it."

When mighty Thorn had joined with them to help them fight their foes,
they sailed away from Hallasholm, right under Erak's nose.

This time, Erak frowned. His nose was a trifle on the large side and he never liked anyone referring to it.

Svengal cackled with laughter. "They got that right!"

And then the room joined in on the chorus, shaking the walls and setting plates rattling on the tables.

The Herons! The Herons!
The mighty, fighting Herons!

No other brotherband you'll see
is even half as darin'!

Jesper and Stefan began the next verse.

Hal spied a lovely warrior girl. She said, "My name is Lydia."
He said to her, "Please come aboard. Have a drink and
then we'll feed ya."

"What?" Hal looked at Erak, shaking his head. "*Lydia* and *feed ya*? What sort of rhyme is that?"

"Shut up!" Erak told him. "You don't know good poetry when you hear it." Now that they were past the reference to his nose, he was enjoying the song again.

She said, "A bunch of pirates have invaded my hometown."
Hal shot his mighty Mangler and the walls came tumbling down.

Again, the hall resounded to the chorus, booming tunelessly from hundreds of lips, then Jesper and Stefan launched into the next verse.

They chased the Raven *'cross the sea and down the River Dan.*
When Zavac tried to stop them, Lydia foiled his evil plan.

"Hooray!" shouted the crowd, all of them beaming and raising their tankards to the girl in the green dress. Skandians loved a heroine—particularly one as beautiful as this.

> *They sailed right down a waterfall a hundred meters high*
> *then sank a dozen pirate ships as they were passing by.*

"It was two! Two! That's all. And they were boats, not ships!" Hal said, shaking his head at the dreadful exaggerations flowing from Stefan's and Jesper's lips. The crowd sang another chorus with them and Erak looked at him in pity.

"You probably had to be there to appreciate it," he said knowingly. Hal threw his arms wide in frustration.

"I *was* there!" he protested. "It was nothing like this!" But Erak was listening to the next verse.

> *They sailed into Raguza and Hal said, as bold as brass,*
> *"We've come to challenge Zavac and we plan to kick his—"*

"Language!" bellowed Svengal, interrupting them just in time. There was a rather attractive lady present who had been teaching him love poems and he didn't want her tender ears sullied by such bawdiness. Stefan and Jesper paused, conferred quickly, then sang an amended version:

> *"We've come to challenge Zavac, and he's going to breathe his last."*

They glanced interrogatively at Svengal. He nodded his approval, and they continued.

> *They fought a mighty combat on the sea outside Raguza.*
> *The* Heron *was triumphant and the* Raven *was the loser.*

More cheers from the audience. Hal had by now given up trying to bring any sense of accuracy to the story being recounted.

Erak was entranced. His tankard was now empty. Those standing near him were thoroughly drenched.

> *They fought their way aboard her to retrieve the Andomal*
> *and sailed back home to give it to the mighty Oberjarl.*

More cheering, led enthusiastically by the mighty Oberjarl himself. Then one last chorus. Hal shook his head and joined in.

"Might as well," he said. "Nobody will ever believe the true version."

> *The Herons! The Herons!*
> *The mighty, fighting Herons!*
> *No other brotherband you'll see*
> *is even half as darin'!*

As Stefan and Jesper clambered down, the crowd mobbed them, slapping their backs, praising their brilliant saga. Erak shook his head happily.

"Now that's real poetry!" he exclaimed. Then he looked into his tankard and frowned. "Who drank my ale?" he demanded, and stalked off to get a refill.

There was one more event that night that was remembered for years to come. As the Herons sat happily at a table together, receiving the good wishes and praise of passersby, one person watched with a baleful eye.

Tursgud had hated the Herons since they had beaten him and his crew in the brotherband contest. And he bitterly resented that when Erak punished them he hadn't proclaimed Tursgud's team winners by default. Now he scowled and watched as people slapped them on the back and wished them well. Finally, he could bear it no longer. He rose and shoved his way through the thronging crowd to stand before Hal, swaying belligerently.

"So you're back," he said. The ill humor was obvious in his voice.

Hal eyed him carefully, not wishing to spoil the night and the mood of celebration.

"Good evening, Tursgud," he said evenly. Around him, the Herons tensed, half expecting Tursgud to launch a sudden attack. He glared around their faces, sneering.

"You're back with your crew of cheats and liars," he said. Then, seeing an unfamiliar face, he added, unwisely, "And you brought a scullery maid back to work in your mam's slophouse."

Both Hal and Stig began to shove their chairs back to rise. But they were prevented from doing so by a pair of heavy hands that descended on their shoulders. Hal looked up in surprise and saw Ingvar standing behind him, peering shortsightedly at Tursgud.

"I think I'd like to take care of this," Ingvar said. He stepped closer to Tursgud, leaning forward slightly, his eyes squinting half closed to see him more clearly. Tursgud stood his ground angrily, which turned out to be a mistake.

"What are you staring at, squint eyes?" he said, his voice a snarl.

But Ingvar said nothing. He studied the unpleasant former

leader of the Sharks brotherband for several seconds. Then he took a deep breath and, remembering Thorn's instructions, closed his eyes. In his mind's eye, he could see Tursgud clearly. He could sense that the other boy hadn't moved.

"Fallen asleep, have you?" Tursgud sneered. "Well, if I were you . . ."

He never got to finish. Ingvar's massive hand, balled into a fist, flashed up in a thundering, devastating uppercut. It caught Tursgud on the point of the jaw, picking him up and hurling him backward for several meters. He slid across a table, collapsing it, then crashed to the ground amid the broken platters and spilled food.

"Oh, well done, Ingvar," Thorn muttered as the big boy calmly resumed his seat.

As has been said, Skandians liked good food, good ale, good sagas and a good fight. And if the good fight only lasted for one perfectly thrown punch, it left more time for the good food and good ale.

And that was so much the better.

Much later, Karina showed Lydia to a spare bedroom in her home. Hal and the rest of the crew were still enjoying themselves at the feast, but Lydia had wanted to slip away. She was used to being by herself in the forest, and too much attention could become daunting.

Karina fussed around her, turning down the bed and trimming the lamp. Lydia had already donned a soft linen nightgown. She watched the older woman as she plumped a pillow for her.

She's really quite beautiful, Lydia thought.

Karina looked up. "You look very serious," she said, smiling.

Lydia hesitated, then said, "I don't want to offend you, Karina, but I don't think I should stay with you permanently. You and Hal, I mean."

Karina continued to smile. She sat on the edge of the bed and took the younger girl's hands in both of hers.

"I understand," she said. "There's a rather nice widow who has a place in town. Her daughter has just married and moved out. She could use the company and I think you'd like her. Would you like me to ask her?"

Lydia nodded, looking down at her hands. "I would." She felt compelled to explain further. "It's just that Hal . . . and Stig . . . you know, they're both . . ." She paused, not sure how to continue. Karina squeezed her hands gently.

"It's hard when there are two very attractive men in your life, isn't it?" she said. Then she added softly, "I know how that can be."

Her voice had become wistful and Lydia looked up quickly. There was a long-ago look in Karina's eyes. Then she shook herself slightly, brought herself back to the present and smiled at the girl.

"May I give you a little advice?" she said.

Lydia nodded. "Please."

"Don't be in any hurry to choose between them. You're only sixteen and there's plenty of time for that. Besides, you never know who might come along one day."

It hurt her to say it. She instinctively liked this girl and would have loved to think of her as a prospective daughter-in-law. But Lydia had to make up her own mind, without pressure. She was among strangers, newly arrived in a strange town, and Karina didn't want to see her gravitate to either Hal or Stig too quickly, out of the need to reach out for something familiar.

"You don't have to choose tomorrow—or the next day. Wait till you're ready. Wait till you know," she said.

Lydia looked into her eyes and saw the honesty and the affection there.

"Thank you," she said. Then Karina smiled.

"Besides, a little uncertainty will do them both good."

Turn the page to read an excerpt from

BROTHERBAND
CHRONICLES

BOOK 4: SLAVES OF SOCORRO

"I think we should reset the mast about a meter farther aft," Hal said.

He peered down into the stripped-out hull of the wolf-ship, rubbing his chin. *Wolftail*'s innards were bare to the world. Her oars, mast, yard, sails, shrouds, stays, halyards, rowing benches, floorboards and ballast stones had been removed, leaving just the bare hull. She rested on her keel, high and dry on the grass beside Anders's shipyard, supported by timber props that kept her level.

A plank gantry ran along either side of the denuded hull, at the height of her gunwales. Hal knelt on the starboard-side gantry, accompanied by Anders, the shipwright, and Bjarni Bentfinger, *Wolftail*'s skirl and owner. Hal and Anders wore thoughtful, reflective expressions. Bjarni's was more anxious. No ship's captain likes to see the bones of his craft laid bare for the world to view. Bjarni was beginning to wonder whether this had been such a good idea. It wasn't too late, he thought. He could always pay Anders for his work so far and ask him to return *Wolftail* to her former state.

Then he thought of the extra speed and maneuverability the new sail plan would give his ship. He shrugged and looked anxiously at Hal. The young skirl was so . . . young, he thought. And here Bjarni was, entrusting his precious *Wolftail* to Hal's hands for a major refit. Of course, Anders was a highly experienced shipbuilder. He ought to know what he was doing. And Bjarni had seen proof of the effectiveness of the fore-and-aft-sail plan that Hal had designed for his own ship, the *Heron*.

Bjarni took a deep breath, closed his eyes and bit back the request that was trembling on his lips. Between them, these two knew what was best, he thought.

"The mast goes where the mast support is," Anders said doubtfully. "How do you plan to move that?"

The mast support was a squared piece of timber, a meter long, that stood vertically at right angles to the keel. It was used to hold the mast firmly in place, and was an integral, immovable part of the keel itself. When the original shipbuilders had shaped a tree to form the keel for *Wolftail*, they had trimmed off all the projecting branches, save one. They left that one in place, shortening it and trimming it so that it formed a square section that projected up to support the mast. Its innate strength came from the fact that it hadn't been fastened in place. It had *grown* there.

Hal shrugged. "It's not a problem." He climbed down into the hull and knelt beside the keel, indicating the existing support. "We leave this in place, so that the strength is retained, and we shape a meter-long piece to match it, and attach it behind the existing support."

Anders chewed his lip. "Yes. I suppose that'd work."

"But why set the mast farther astern?" Bjarni asked.

"The new fore and aft yards will reach right to the bow," Hal explained, "and that will put more downward pressure on the bow when you're under sail. This way, we'll compensate for that pressure." He indicated with his hand, describing an angle behind the mast support. "We could even slope the edge of the new piece back a little toward the stern. That'd let us rake the mast back and give us even better purchase."

"Hmmm," said Anders.

The worried look was back on Bjarni's face. He hadn't understood the technical details Hal had spouted so confidently. But he understood "hmmm." "Hmmm" meant Anders wasn't convinced.

"Never mind raking it back," Bjarni said quickly. "I want my mast to stand square. Masts are supposed to stand square. That's what masts do. They stand . . . square. Always have."

After all, he thought, a raked mast would be a little too exotic.

Hal grinned at him. He'd overseen the conversion of four square-rigged wolfships to the *Heron* sail plan in the past months. He was used to the older skirls' conservative views.

"Whatever you say," he replied agreeably. He stood and clambered up the sloping inside of the hull toward the gantry. Anders reached down a hand to help him.

"Now, have you made up your mind about the fin keel?" Hal

asked. He knew what the answer was going to be, even before Bjarni's head began to shake from side to side.

"I don't want you cutting any holes in the bottom of my ship," he said. "She might sink."

Hal smiled reassuringly at him. "I did the same to the *Heron*," he pointed out. "And she hasn't sunk so far."

Bjarni continued his head-shaking. "That's as may be," he said. "But I don't see any good coming from cutting a hole in the bottom of a ship. It goes against nature." He noticed Hal's tolerant smile and frowned. He didn't enjoy being patronized by a boy, even if he suspected that the boy might be right.

"I don't care that you did it in your ship," he said. "It might just be luck that she hasn't sunk . . ." He paused, and added in a meaningful tone, "So far."

Hal shrugged. He hadn't expected Bjarni to agree to a fin keel. None of the wolfship skirls had done so thus far.

"Suit yourself," he said. He turned to Anders. "So, can you get your men started on an extension for the mast support? I can send you over a design sketch if you'd like."

Anders nodded slowly. Anders did most things slowly. He was a deliberate man who didn't leap to decisions without pondering them. That was one of the things that made him an excellent shipbuilder.

"No need for a sketch," he said. "I can work out how to manage it."

Hal nodded. Anders was right, of course. The design work involved would be a simple matter for an experienced craftsman. He had really only offered out of politeness.

"Well then . . . ," he began. But he was interrupted by a booming voice.

"Hullo the ship!" They all turned to see Erak, the Oberjarl of Skandia, on the path that led from the town. Anders's shipyard was set outside Hallasholm, so the constant noise of hammering and sawing—and the attendant curses as fingers were mashed by incautiously wielded mallets—wouldn't disturb the townfolk.

"What's he doing here?" Bjarni said idly.

Anders sniffed, and wiped his nose with the back of his hand. "He's on his morning constitutional," he said. Noticing Bjarni's puzzled glance, he added, "His walk. He walks along here most days. Says the exercise keeps him slim." A ghost of a smile touched the corners of his mouth as he said the last few words.

Hal raised an eyebrow. "How can it keep him something he's never been?"

Erak was an immense bear of a man. *Slim* was not a word that sprang readily to mind when describing him. The Oberjarl was striding across the grass toward them now, flanked by Svengal, his constant companion and former first mate.

"What's that he's got?" Bjarni asked. Erak was wielding a long, polished wood staff in his right hand, using it to mark his strides. The staff was about a meter and a half tall, shod with a silver ferrule at the bottom and adorned with a small silver knob at the top. At every third or fourth pace, he would twirl it between his powerful fingers, setting the sunlight flashing off the silver fittings.

"It's his new walking staff," Anders explained. "There was a delegation in from Gallica two weeks ago and they presented it to him."

"But what does it do?" Hal asked. In his eyes, everything should have a practical use.

Anders shrugged. "He says it makes him look sophisticated," he replied.

Hal's eyebrows went up in surprise. Like *slim, sophisticated* was not a word that sprang readily to mind when thinking about the Oberjarl.

Erak and Svengal paused at the foot of the ladder leading to the gantry.

"All right if we come up?" he called.

Anders made a welcoming gesture with his right hand. "Be our guest," he said.

They felt the timbers of the gantry vibrate gently as the two men climbed to join them. Erak was huge and Svengal was built on the lines of the normal Skandian wolfship crewman—he wasn't as big as Erak, but he was tall and heavyset.

Perhaps, thought Hal, it had been wise of Erak to ask permission before mounting the ladder.

The two men approached down the gantry, peering with professional interest into the bared hull below them.

"Getting one of Hal's newfangled sail plans, are you, Bjarni?" Erak boomed. "Old ways not good enough for you anymore?"

"We've done four other ships before this one," Anders said. "Been no complaints so far."

Erak studied the shipwright for a moment, then switched his gaze to the young man beside him. Secretly, he was proud of Hal, proud of his ingenuity and original thinking. On top of that, Hal had shown leadership and determination in pursuing the pirate

Zavac halfway across the known world. Erak admired those qualities, although he considered himself to be too set in his own ways to adapt to the sort of change that Hal represented. Deep down, he knew that the sail plan the young man had designed was superior to the old square rig of traditional wolfships. He had seen it demonstrated on more than one occasion. But he loved his *Wolfwind* as she was and he couldn't bring himself to change her.

"Time for a change, chief," Bjarni said, as if reading that last thought.

Erak thought it was time to change the subject. "They've really ripped the guts out of her, haven't they?" he commented cheerfully.

Bjarni looked as if he might argue the toss, but then he subsided. In fact, they *had* ripped the guts out of her. It was strange, he thought, how when craftsmen set about making improvements to anything—be it a ship, a house or an ox cart—their first step almost always involved practically destroying it.

Erak paced along the gantry, his walking staff clacking noisily on the timber walkway.

"There's a plank or two could use replacing," he said, peering keenly to where several of the planks were showing wear between the joins.

"We've noted those," Anders replied. Still, he was impressed that Erak had spotted the problem from a distance.

Clack, clack, clack went Erak's staff as he paced farther. Hal caught Svengal's eye and winked.

"Decided it's time for a walking cane, have you, Oberjarl?" the young man asked, his face a mask of innocence. Svengal turned away to hide a grin as Erak turned slowly to face Hal.

"It's a staff of office, young man," he said haughtily. "They're all the rage in Gallica among the gentry."

"The gentry, you say?" Hal asked. He knew the Oberjarl had a soft spot for him and he knew how far to push things. Or at least, he considered ruefully, he *thought* he knew. Sometimes he overstepped the mark—and then a hasty retreat was advisable. "Well, I can see why you'd have one—you being as gentrified as you are."

Erak twirled the staff, the sunlight catching the silverwork again.

"It makes me look sophisticated," he said. There was a note of challenge in his voice.

"I've definitely noticed that, chief," Svengal put in cheerfully. "I was only telling the lads the other night, 'Have you noticed how sophisticated the chief is looking these days?'"

"And what did they say?" Erak asked, with just a hint of suspicion.

"Well, they had to agree, didn't they? All of them. Of course, then they spoiled it by asking what 'sophisticated' meant. But they did agree—wholeheartedly."

Bjarni let out a short bark of laughter, and Anders's shoulders appeared to be shaking. Hal had found something fascinating on the handrail of the gantry and was studying it closely.

Erak snorted. "People never appreciate sophistication," he said. He *clack-clacked* his way along the gantry once more toward the ladder, his old friend following a few paces behind. At the head of the ladder, Erak turned back and called to Hal.

"Drop by and see me tomorrow morning, young Hal. Might have a project for you and that band of misfits of yours."

Hal's interest was aroused. Life had been a little on the slow side lately, with nothing but routine sea patrols to fill in the time.

"What do you have in mind, Oberjarl?" he asked. But Erak only smiled sweetly and tapped the side of his nose.

"I never discuss business in public, Hal," he said. "It's so un-sophisticated."

BROTHERBAND
CHRONICLES

Join the Herons
on all their adventures!

BROTHERBAND CHRONICLES BOOK 1: THE OUTCASTS

Hal never knew his father, a Skandian warrior. But unlike his esteemed father, Hal is an outcast. In a country that values physical strength over intellect, Hal's ingenuity only serves to set him apart from other boys his age. The one thing he has in common with his peers? Brotherband training. Forced to compete in tests of endurance and strength, Hal discovers that he's not the only outcast in this land of seafaring marauders.

BROTHERBAND CHRONICLES BOOK 2: THE INVADERS

As champions of the Brotherband competition, Hal and the rest of the Herons are given one simple assignment: safeguard the Skandians' most sacred artifact, the Andomal. When the Andomal is stolen, however, the Herons must track down the thief to recover the precious relic. But that means traversing stormy seas, surviving a bitter winter, and battling a group of deadly bandits willing to protect their prize at all costs.

BROTHERBAND CHRONICLES

Journey onward
with the Herons!

BROTHERBAND CHRONICLES BOOK 3: THE HUNTERS

Hal and his fellow Herons have tracked Zavac across the ocean, intent on recovering the stolen Andomal, Skandia's most prized treasure. And though a fierce battle left Zavac and his fellow pirates counting their dead, the rogue captain managed to escape right through the Skandians' fingers. Now, the Herons must take to the seas if they hope to bring Zavac to justice and reclaim the Andomal.

BROTHERBAND CHRONICLES BOOK 4: SLAVES OF SOCORRO

Hal and his fellow Herons have returned home to Skandia with their honor restored, turning to a new mission: tracking down an old rival turned bitter enemy. Tursgud—leader of the Shark Brotherband and Hal's constant opponent—has turned from a bullying youth into a pirate and slave trader. After Tursgud captures twelve Araluen villagers to sell as slaves, the Heron crew sails into action . . . with the help of one of Araluen's finest Rangers!

BOOK ONE: THE RUINS OF GORLAN

The Rangers, with their shadowy ways, are the protectors of the kingdom who will fight battles before the battles reach the people. Fifteen-year-old Will has been chosen as a Ranger's apprentice. And there is a large battle brewing. The exiled Morgarath, Lord of the Mountains of Rain and Night, is gathering his forces for an attack on the kingdom. This time he will not be denied.

BOOK TWO: THE BURNING BRIDGE

On a special mission for the Rangers, Will discovers all the people in the neighboring villages have been either slain or captured. But why? Could it be that Morgarath has finally devised a plan to bring his legions over the supposedly insurmountable pass? If so, the king's army is in imminent danger of being crushed in a fierce ambush. And Will is the only one who can save them.

BOOK THREE: THE ICEBOUND LAND

Kidnapped and taken to a frozen land after the fierce battle with Lord Morgarath, Will and Evanlyn are bound for Skandia as captives. Halt has sworn to rescue his young apprentice, and he will do anything to keep his promise—even defy his king. Expelled from the Rangers he has served so loyally, Halt is joined by Will's friend Horace as he travels toward Skandia. But will he and Halt be in time to rescue Will from a horrific life of slavery?

BOOK FOUR: THE BATTLE FOR SKANDIA

Still far from home after escaping slavery in the icebound land of Skandia, young Will and Evanlyn's plans to return to Araluen are spoiled when Evanlyn is taken captive, and Will discovers that Skandia and Araluen are in grave danger. Only an unlikely union can save the two kingdoms, but can it hold long enough to vanquish a ruthless new enemy?

BOOK FIVE: THE SORCERER OF THE NORTH

Will is finally a full-fledged Ranger with his own fief to look after. But when Lord Syron, master of a castle far in the north, is struck down by a mysterious illness, Will is suddenly thrown headfirst into an extraordinary adventure, investigating fears of sorcery and trying to determine who is loyal to Lord Syron.

BOOK SIX: THE SIEGE OF MACINDAW

The kingdom is in danger. Renegade knight Sir Keren has succeeded in overtaking Castle Macindaw. The fate of Araluen rests in the hands of two young adventurers: the Ranger Will and his warrior friend, Horace.

RANGER'S APPRENTICE

BOOK SEVEN: ERAK'S RANSOM

In the wake of Araluen's uneasy truce with the raiding Skandians comes word that the Skandian leader has been captured by a dangerous desert tribe. The Rangers—and Will—are sent to free him. Strangers in a strange land, they are brutalized by sandstorms, beaten by the unrelenting heat; nothing is as it seems. Yet one thing is constant: the bravery of the Rangers.

BOOK EIGHT: THE KINGS OF CLONMEL

When a cult springs up in neighboring Clonmel, people flock from all over to offer gold in exchange for protection. But Halt is all too familiar with this group, and he knows they have a less than charitable agenda. Secrets will be unveiled and battles fought to the death as Will and Horace help Halt in ridding the land of a dangerous enemy.

BOOK NINE: HALT'S PERIL

The renegade outlaw group known as the Outsiders may have been chased from Clonmel, but now the Rangers Halt and Will, along with the young warrior Horace, are in pursuit. The Outsiders have done an effective job of dividing the kingdom into factions and are looking to overtake Araluen. It will take every bit of skill and cunning for the Rangers to survive. Some may not be so lucky.

BOOK TEN: THE EMPEROR OF NIHON-JA

Months have passed since Horace departed for the eastern nation of Nihon-Ja on a vital mission. Having received no communication from him, his friends fear the worst. Unwilling to wait a second longer, Alyss, Evanlyn, and Will leave and venture into an exotic land in search of their missing friend.

BOOK ELEVEN: THE LOST STORIES

Some claim they were merely the stuff of legend: the Rangers as defenders of the kingdom. Reports of their brave battles vary; but we all know of at least ten accounts, most of which feature Will and his mentor, Halt. There are reports of others who fought alongside the Rangers: the warrior Horace, a courageous princess named Evanlyn, and a cunning diplomat named Alyss. Yet this crew left very little behind, and their existence has never been proven. Until now, that is . . . behold the Lost Stories.

BOOK TWELVE: THE ROYAL RANGER

Will Treaty has come a long way from the small boy with dreams of knighthood. He's grown into a legend, the finest Ranger the kingdom has even known. In this series finale, Will takes on an apprentice of his own, and it's the last person he ever would have expected.